GODS OF ROME

RISE OF EMPERORS

The Rise of Emperors Series

Sons of Rome
Masters of Rome
Gods of Rome

ALSO BY GORDON DOHERTY

The Legionary Series

Legionary
Viper of the North
Land of the Sacred Fire
The Scourge of Thracia
Gods and Emperors
Empire of Shades
The Blood Road
Dark Eagle

The Strategos Trilogy

Born in the Borderlands
Rise of the Golden Heart
Island in the Storm

The Empires of Bronze Series

Son of Ishtar
Dawn of War
Thunder at Kadesh
The Crimson Throne
The Shadow of Troy

ALSO BY SIMON TURNEY

The Damned Emperors Series

Caligula
Commodus

The Marius' Mules Series

The Invasion of Gaul
The Belgae
Gallia Invicta
Conspiracy of Eagles
Hades' Gate
Caesar's Vow
Prelude to War
The Great Revolt
Sons of Taranis
Pax Gallica
Fields of Mars
Tides of War
Sands of Egypt

Civil War

The Praetorian Series

The Great Game
The Price of Treason
Eagles of Dacia
Lions of Rome
The Cleansing Fire
Blades of Antioch

Roman Adventures

Crocodile Legion
Pirate Legion

Collaborations

A Year of Ravens
A Song of War
Rubicon

GODS OF ROME

RISE OF EMPERORS: BOOK THREE

DOHERTY & TURNEY

HEAD of ZEUS

An Aries Book

9 7 5 3 1 2 4 6 8

A catalogue record for this book is available from
the British Library.

ISBN (HB): 9781800242067
ISBN (XTPB): 9781800242074
ISBN (E): 9781800242111

Typeset by Divaddict Publishing Solutions Ltd.

Printed and bound in Great Britain by
CPI Group (UK) Ltd, Croydon CR0 4YY

FSC
www.fsc.org
MIX
Paper from
responsible sources
FSC® C020471

Head of Zeus Ltd
First Floor East
5–8 Hardwick Street
London EC1R 4RG

WWW.HEADOFZEUS.COM

GODS OF
ROME
RISE OF EMPERORS

EBORACUM

COLONIA AGRIPPE

TREVERORUM

MEDIOLANUM

POLA

MASSILIA

ROME

TERRITORY OF CONSTANTINE

CARTHAGE

TERRITORY OF MAXENTIUS

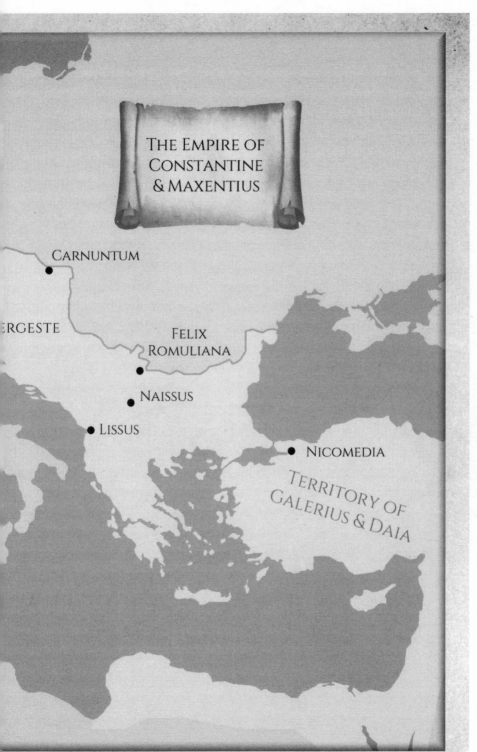

THE EMPIRE OF
CONSTANTINE
& MAXENTIUS

CARNUNTUM

ERGESTE

FELIX
ROMULIANA

NAISSUS

LISSUS

NICOMEDIA

TERRITORY OF
GALERIUS & DAIA

ROME
306AD

SEPTEM BALNEA

VIA FLAMINIA

VIA SALARIA

MILVIAN BRIDGE

R. TIBER

R. ANIO

ROME

VIA FLAMINIA

VIA SALARIA

VIA LATA

PRAETORIAN FORTRESS

NEW BATHS OF DIOCLETIAN

CAMPUS MARTIUS

QUIRINAL HILL & BATH HOUSE

THEATRE OF POMPEY

SUBURA

CAPITOLINE HILL

OPPIAN HILL

GARDENS OF TORQUATAS

FORUM

VIA PRAENESTINA

FLAVIAN AMPHITHEATRE

LUDUS MAGNUS

VIA CAELEMONTANA

DISUSED IMPERIAL PALACE

VIA LABICANA

PALATINE

TIBER

CIRCUS MAXIMUS

CASTRA PEREGRINA

IMPERIAL HORSEGUARD BARRACKS

VILLA OF MAXENTIUS

RIVER PORT

AVENTINE HILL

HORREA GALBAE

VIA APPIA

TO VILLA OF HERODES ATTICUS

PART 1

Fortuna belli semper ancipiti in loco est
(The fortunes of war are always doubtful)
– *Seneca the Younger*

1

CONSTANTINE

The Cottian Alpes, 27th January 312 AD

We moved through the mountains like winter wolves. The ferocious blizzard sped southwards with us, carried on the famous bora winds, singing a dire song. For days we marched through that driving snow, seeing nothing but great white-clad peaks either side of us; rugged, inhospitable highlands which in these frozen months soldiers were not meant to cross. All around me the gale screamed, boots crunched endlessly through the successively deeper drifts of white, men's teeth chattered violently, mules brayed, exhausted. It felt at times as if we were wandering, snow-blind, to our deaths, but I knew what lay ahead... so close now.

I called upon my chosen men and a handful of their best soldiers – a group of thirty – and we roved ahead of the army like advance scouts. The blizzard raked through my bear cloak, the snow rattling like slingshot against my gemmed ridge helm and bronze scales as I scoured the valley route. Yet I refused to blink. When the speeding hail of white slowed and the murky grey ahead thinned a little, I saw them: a pair of stone and timber watchtowers, northern faces plastered in snow. Gateposts watching this passage between two realms.

I dropped to my haunches behind the brow of a snowdrift and my chosen men hunkered down with me. I gazed over the drift's brow, regarding the narrow gap between the towers and the valley route beyond, on through the winter-veined mountains. Thinking of the land that lay beyond these heights, my frozen lips moved soundlessly.

Italia…

Land of Roman forefathers. Home of the man I had once considered my friend… but that territory was rightfully mine. *Mine!* My surging anger scattered when I spotted movement atop one of the two towers: a freezing Maxentian scout blowing into his hands, oblivious to our presence. Then the blizzard fell treacherously slack, and the speeding veil of white cleared for a trice. I saw his ice-crusted eyebrows rise as he leaned forward, peering into the momentary clarity, right at us. His eyes bulged, mouth agog.

'He is here!' he screamed to be heard over the sudden return of the storm's wrath. 'Constantine is h—'

With a wet punch, an arrow whacked into the man's chest and shuddered there. He spasmed then folded over the edge of the timber parapet and fell like a sack of gravel, crunching into a pillowy snowdrift at the turret's foot. I glanced to my right, seeing my archer nock and draw again, shifting his bow to the heights of the other tower, his eyes narrowing within the shadow of his helm brow. He loosed, but the dark-skinned sentry up there ducked behind the parapet, screaming and tolling a warning bell. At once, three more Maxentians spilled from the door at the base of that rightmost tower, rushing south towards a simple, snow-topped stable twenty paces away, in the lee of a rocky overhang. This was one of the few gateways through the mountains – albeit the least favoured and most treacherous – and it was guarded by just five men?

Instantly, suspicion and elation clashed like swords in my mind. We had no time to rake over the facts. These watchmen could not be allowed to ride south and warn the legions of Italia. They had to die.

The armoured figures by my side rose with me and surged ahead, each eager to show their valour. They spilled around the rightmost of the two watchtowers. With a crunch, one of my feather-helmed Cornuti legionaries booted open the timber door and rammed his spear into the chest of the dark-skinned scout hurrying down the stairs to join his fleeing comrades. My soldier screamed in time with the dark-skinned one's death cry, driving him back inside and slamming him against the tower-room's far wall. Of the three scouts fleeing towards the stables, a hurled javelin took one in the back of the neck. The second turned to attack us, running my Cornuti man through then swinging his blade at me. I blocked his vicious strike then cut deep into his shoulder with a swift downward swipe. He crumpled into the snow in a blossom of red, thrashing in pain, before I put an end to his suffering with a clean thrust to his neck. Yet the man had delayed us just enough: the last of the fleeing trio was now upon his mare. He geed her into a panicked turn, kicking one of my approaching soldiers in the face then breaking into a gallop. South… to his master's side.

I twisted to my archer, who was taking aim already. 'Don't let him escape,' I growled. The arrow spat forth and my small party halted, panting, watching it fly. It fishtailed and shivered then slashed down, only scoring the man's thigh before plunging into the snow. The man sped on, chased by the driving blizzard, hugging the steed's neck, droplets of blood falling in his wake to taint the snow.

'Bastard!' Tribunus Batius rumbled nearby, his bull-like

form unmistakable in the driving blizzard. He had been by my side since I was a boy – though now he was showing his years, the stubble on his head and broad chin silver like his armour and his brutish features lined with age. The big man twisted to shout back whence we had come. '*Equites! Cataphracti!*'

'No,' I shouted as the bora winds keened and the blizzard softened for a moment, revealing that the rider was already gone from sight. 'Our hidden approach was never going to see us all the way through this range. We have reached deep into the mountains unseen – done well to get this far. It would be folly to send our precious cavalry charging ahead – what if this weak watch was but a ruse? What if there is a trap further along this valley? Let us advance as one, carefully, while still making the most of our advantage before news reaches our enemy.'

'Aye. Advance as one – out of this valley and upon Segusium,' said another voice with a confidence I envied. Krocus, the shaggy-haired leader of the Regii, chin-tied beard encrusted with frost and snow. He and his men had served my father before me and he wore a mesh of battle-scars on his arms and face like marks of honour.

'The first city that must be taken,' Batius agreed with a sideways glance at Krocus – once his nemesis but now more of a comrade and a drinking rival. These two, my most trusted generals and leaders of my strongest regiments, did not salt their words with doubt.

A soldier brought me my horse, Celeritas. The dappled-grey stallion was old for a war horse, but still strong, as loyal a companion to me as my trusted generals – and just as stubborn. 'Signal back to the army,' I said to the soldier as I took the reins. 'Bring them forward. We will advance with caution.' I climbed onto the saddle and patted my horse's war-scarred neck. I continued gazing south as an iron thunder rose behind me. Forty thousand legionaries and riders cannot move without such a din, you see. I turned my head to watch their approach. I saw standards ancient and proud, bearing hawks, capricorns, leaping hounds and howling wolves. These were the legions of old: the Second Augusta, Father's Sixth Victrix from Britannia, the Gemina, the Martia, the Primigenia. In days past, each of these regiments counted over five thousand men in their ranks. Now they were smaller but hardier too, with two or three thousand veterans in each. There was my inner core of newer legions too, my *comitatus*, raised from the tribes – once enemies of the empire but now undyingly loyal to me: Batius' Cornuti, Krocus' Regii, the Petulantes, the Ubii and the Bructeri – led by Hisarnis, once a rugged chieftain yet now shaved and shorn and as Roman-looking as a man from the provinces of Italia. Each of these units sported one thousand crack soldiers. The cavalry, a small but hardy component of my army, cantered on the flanks, led by a fearless whoreson of a *praepositus* by the name of Ingenuus. His standard bearer, *Draconarius* Vitalianus – a man who also bore the esteemed title of *Protector*, one of my trusted guards – held the cavalry standard high: the dragon head swallowed the wintry gale and emitted an eerie howl from its tail – a thrashing mass of coloured ribbons.

When this war machine came to a halt behind me like great silver wings outstretched, the ranks raised their spears in the air and bawled in unison, 'Augustus!' and I felt every bit the saviour they had proclaimed me to be. Gods, if only I had known then how many of those men would fall in the months that lay ahead...

A silence passed, all eyes on me, waiting for my signal to continue through the valley.

I regarded the snowy route ahead and let a thousand futures race through my mind. 'Are we underestimating him?' I said quietly. *Him*, I thought. Once I had called him my brother. Now, I could not even bring myself to utter his name.

'Maxentius is underestimating *us*, I would say,' Batius replied, gesturing somewhere into the sea of white-veined peaks. 'This flimsy outpost is the first of his we have encountered. Word has it that he houses strong forces near Verona. He's more concerned about the passes from the east. He fears Licinius more than us!'

Licinius, I almost laughed. I had defeated and cowed that eastern mutt, forcing him to agree with me a non-aggression pact. At the time it was merely to remove him from this rapidly building game of power. Now, I realised, it had played perfectly into my hands – for he was a perfect distraction, hovering just beyond Italia's north-eastern limits, turning all Maxentian eyes from these more treacherous westerly passes. *Not all eyes*, I mused, thinking of the scouting report I had received a few days ago – of Maxentian soldiers in these mountains about one hundred miles east of our position. 'He *did* send a small reinforcement garrison to Eporedia to block the most direct route through the mountains.'

Batius scratched his anvil jaw, frost spraying from his bristles as he nodded in agreement. 'True. And he sent a flotilla to watch the coastal mountain routes. But nothing here in this cursed pass… nothing apart from five men.'

'These were no ordinary watchmen, *Domine*,' Krocus reasoned, kneeling by one of the scouts' corpses. Then he pointed to the trio of still-tethered horses. 'Those mares are from the imperial stables. The finest. The fastest.'

'The first of my spoils,' I said, hot with anger as Maxentius' litany of aggressions flickered across my thoughts: he had claimed Rome and Italia as his own when they were rightly mine; seized Africa – that great bread basket of the West – as his too; dangled threats of a grain embargo upon me. He had even sent a vile cutthroat to kill me. Worst of all was not the trade threats, the theft or the hired blades. It was the acid words he had spread: *Constantine is nought but the son of a whore!* He – more than any other – must have known how deep those rumours would burn. For he was there the day my father estranged Mother and me. *He* was the one in whom I sought counsel. And he had kept that private weakness of mine all these years only to sharpen it into a blade and turn it upon me. *Me*, the man who had rescued his son from a blazing grain house.

I had tried to resist the clamour to act, the urgent warnings from my advisors... the bare and brutal truth. Then more rumours had spread on top of this, that Maxentius had ordered the massacre of thousands of Rome's people in a bloody frenzy – an act fitting of Galerius or Diocletian, the emperors of old we once both detested. The boy Maxentius, the friend, the brother, was gone. The cur and his wretched, civilian-massacring Praetorians had given me no choice in the end. Steeling myself, I turned my head to meet the eyes of the *buccinators* and *aquilifers* lining the front of my army. 'Onward,' I said, my low growl echoing through the valley.

Brass horns blared, many bright standards rose and caught the gale, and we marched on. The bora screamed in our ears as we went, snow flicking up from every stride, cloaks rapping. I organised a legion on each flank to watch the mountains and screen us from attack, and despatched a small knot of scout equites ahead as a vanguard. We funnelled into the tightest section of the pass, the winds blowing settled snow down flanking slopes, tumbling down towards the valley floor in clouds like an ambush of wraiths. When we reached the banks of the frozen River Duria, the blizzard intensified to a point where my men were striving to make any headway at all, and we halted and made camp here.

I drew Celeritas to the edge of the campsite and watched in the fading light as men dug and erected ramparts of snow – for the rocky earth below was frozen solid and impenetrable by pick or spade. As they worked, I saw her.

So far I have spoken only of men, of warriors and officers. Yet here was the woman who should have been closer to me than any of them. Fausta, my young wife and the sister of the man with whom I was marching to make war. She watched me from a wagon, swaddled in a woollen winter stola while soldiers erected a tent for her. Aye, *her* tent, for she and I were like strangers these days. We had not shared a bed, nor even a meal, in over a year. After six months of that I had known we would never again be the same.

Once, we had been in love. It was a golden time... even if she could never live up to my dear, sweet and departed Minervina. Perhaps that fondness I still held for my first wife had been the start of our undoing. Maybe it was my almost constant absence on campaigns and duties of state that had begun to fray the twines even further. There was no doubt over what had snapped the bond between us.

I had ordered her father's death because I had no choice. After being chased from Rome following a failed coup on his own son's throne, old Maximian had arrived at my court a sorry sight. I knew he was a sly one, but I offered him the shelter he needed. I took him in for Fausta's sake, because I loved her and I knew better than most that everyone needs a father. Yet at the first opportunity, the old bastard had tried to usurp me! And when I crushed his uprising, he knew – damn it, he knew! – that I would have no choice but to execute him. The snake used this fact to manipulate his own daughter, persuading her from his jail cell that the only way to save him was for her to kill me. Thus came the stormy night when she held a blade to my neck when I was at my most vulnerable. I have never once blamed Fausta for holding steel to my throat, for it was precisely her father's gambit to make her choose between him or me. That he would throw his daughter onto the sharp horns of such a dilemma is a measure of him and not her. More, she could not go through with it, could not kill me... yet neither from that moment on could she love me anymore, for she knew what it meant. Duly, her father was despatched, and the bond she and I had once shared was broken.

Now my path and hers only crossed when we were both with Crispus, my boy. Fausta was an attentive and caring stepmother, and Crispus adored her, but slaves told me she had a habit of blackening my name when I was not around, telling the boy stories of things I had done. I suppose the sad truth of it was most of the stories were true. Given the wall of estrangement between us, it had surprised me – nay, astonished me – when she had pleaded her case to travel like this with the campaign party. I had warned her of these bitter winter passes, of the months of tent-life and tasteless rations. 'I know what you are, Constantine,' she had replied quietly. 'A creature bred in battle, reared on a diet of blood. You had my father put to death, alone in a cold cell. Now you march to war against my brother. This time, I want to be there when the moment comes, when you hold a sword at his neck... or when he has his blade at yours. This time, I want you to look me in the eye, before the blade falls.'

So, while Crispus remained back in Treverorum in the care of my mother, here Fausta was; a constant, silent presence, watching my every move like a judge.

I shook my head of the matter and turned my attentions to the nearly complete camp. The mountains and the low snow rampart offered little lee from the incessant storm and the billowing clouds of drifting snow. The men struggled to erect their tents let alone light fires by which to warm their frozen hands and thaw out their ice-veined rations of salted meat. Gone now were the silver wings, the sense of invincibility. Just a huddle of men in a strange land, their hopes invested in me. Even the iron-core of my comitatus legions, setting their tents up in a square around mine like the walls of a fort, stood in shivering packs, eyes nervously peering out into the wintry squall.

Maxentius has three men for every one of yours, my inner doubts mocked me, *and his forces right now rest in comfortable billets. Soon they will hear of your approach, and will begin honing weapons, planning where and when they will stamp out your march.*

'My men are calloused, mule-stubborn and wise to the ways of war,' I argued with myself. It was true: they were lean, strong, laced with scars and stigmas – some Roman and some tribal. Seasoned in battle thanks to their endless clashes on the Rhenus frontier and during the uprisings in Britannia. My army was small but hardy. I conjured in my mind's eye the vision of a *testudo*, iron-walled, marching through a storm of battle-hail, unbreakable, all the way to our prize... *Roma!* The thought brought great comfort to me. However, something wasn't right – something didn't match up with the sight of the army before me in the winter camp. Groups and packs of men. Cliques. Some setting tents facing away from comrades in the same regiments. Some legions deliberately spacing their tents as far from others as they could. It had been this way ever since I had summoned them together for the campaign – the first time I had amassed my legions like this. They loved me, it seemed, but not one another.

I heard the drawl of one man casting sour words at another. My eyes searched through the scudding snow until I saw the source: an *optio* of the Second Italica Divitensis – a legion formed from my garrison at the Rhenus fort of Divitia. Pushed by an Ubii legionary, he flailed backwards, dropping his gathered kindling into the snow. Hot words flew back and forth as others gathered round. It would not do for an emperor to break up a scuffle between soldiers, but I watched on, seeing the Ubii soldier belittle the Second Italica optio, pointing at the fallen man's sword hilt, scoffing at the Christian fish emblem engraved there. Now men of the Sixth Victrix crowded round, most of them Christian too these days, supporting the offended optio, pointing skywards, throwing words of scripture like missiles. The Ubii legionary made to swipe a boot at the fallen Italica man, but one of the Christians grabbed his outstretched leg and flipped him off-balance and onto his back. No sooner did he try to rise than a fist hammered into his cheek. A moment later and punches were flying, noses smashed, jaws cracking, more men piling in, tents collapsing under grappling fighters. I closed my eyes slowly, the image of my small but invincible army crumbling. A testudo collapsing from within.

I heard Batius bawling at them, wading among them like a bull. Even his legendary presence was not enough to quell the fray. When at last the din of the scuffle faded, it was to the tune of a wavering old voice.

'God watches!' cried Lactantius, my boyhood tutor. 'And

He weeps.' The fighting men broke apart, swinging to the sound of the old man's cries. 'Yes! Your God, your God.' He stabbed his walking cane at the ringleaders in turn like an admonishing finger as he shuffled through the snow, his long, white hair and beard flailing in the winds. 'Do you not see? There is a reason we have all been brought together like this. In this icy waste, think not of your differences, but your bonds. Think of one another not as fellow soldiers but as brothers.' The men parted, brushing snow from their shoulders, nursing sore jaws and cupping kicked and tender testicles, muttering but acquiescing to Lactantius' pleas.

The root of their animosity was a problem that had infected the whole of the empire in recent decades. The search for the one true god among the many had ripped Emperor Diocletian's Tetrarchy apart and set light to the tatters, and still the ashes refused to settle. The panoply of gods to which my army looked was bewildering. Within the Bructeri, factions clung to their old forest deities, the Christian converts among their number more like rivals than kinsmen. Amidst the ancient imperial legions, it had almost been the reverse, with cliques of Christians, suspicious and wary of overtly showing their faith – thanks to the Great Persecution – loathed the men of their own units who honoured Jove, Mars and Sol Invictus. Some – particularly those who had served along my borders – had taken to renouncing their old faiths in favour of the shadowy cult of Mithras: the Primigenia Prefect had complained that half of his men spent their nights on the Rhenus frontier in caves or cellars, tight-lipped about the mysterious eastern creed. My men were loyal to me and to my cause, but all too often at odds with one another. Not enemies, but not the way comrades should be either. I knew well that a man could only march into battle confidently when he knew he had brothers by his side. My forces, just as Lactantius had proclaimed, were not yet brothers.

I watched as Lactantius – despite the brutal cold – stayed with the Ubii and Italica men as they kindled a fire, talking to them as he strolled in loops around their fires, regaling them with ancient stories. They were rapt. He knew what he was doing, for those tales were embellished with Christian teachings, not that the soldiers of the old gods realised. Nor even did some of the Christians. The old man spent long hours alone in his tent writing his scripts, 'master works' as he put it 'designed to persuade the world that the Christ God was the one *true* God'. That said, he was wise enough to understand that, were he to preach his writings verbatim, he would merely fan the flames of division. Thus was his way: to guide these divided men with the gentlest of steering words.

I knew they would be at peace only as long as the old goat was nearby. I could rouse my men to march into fire with me, but I could not pacify them like the old man. 'You have solved many of the riddles in my life, old goat, and blessed me with so much wisdom,' I whispered, as if he could hear from this distance. 'Why can't you impart upon me this gift of yours?'

He had tried. In the days after that strange moment at the Shrine of Apollo in southern Gaul, when the sun had cast a bright a wreath of light upon me while my armies watched, he had implored me: *Find the one true god for all your people... Walk the road to unity! Concordia!*

I looked south-east, regarding the bends in the valley that would take us deeper into Maxentius' territory. This was the only road for me. My mind flashed with images of battles past, knowing that far worse loomed. What sort of god might one find on such a bleak path? I smiled sadly, thinking of my childhood and that night of the ruinous storm that drove the sentries from the city walls to seek shelter. One legionary had remained at his post, clutching a Chi-Rho amulet in his hand. It had fascinated me – at a time when I was only just learning about the many gods – that a man should have so firmly decided that one alone was for him, and that his choice gave him such strength.

'*What brings a man to war?*' I had asked Mother that night. '*What brings a man to choose his god?*'

'*That is for each of us to find out, Constantine,*' she replied. '*Our choices in this life define us. That is the journey we each must make.*'

'The journey,' I whispered, gazing ahead into the blizzard.

'Domine, the camp is complete,' a voice called.

Blinking as my thoughts evaporated, I looked up to see a sentry on the newly completed snow gate on the huge camp's western side, waving a hand to beckon me inside. I walked my stallion in, dismounting to lead the beast through the serried rows of tents, taking salutes and acclaim from the soldiers who were huddled around fires, blowing into their hands, pinching their fingers for heat and thankfully distracted from their differences.

I came to my tent and ducked inside the flap to be blessedly free of that scourging blizzard. I stepped over to the small table with a map and an oil lamp upon it, nodding to the semi-circle of men who stood around it, awaiting me. This was my *consilium* – my generals and advisors. They saluted as one… apart from a cadre of four in non-martial garb. These Christian bishops instead beheld me as if it were I who should salute them.

Ossius, Bishop of Colonia Patricia, had been lurking near me for these last few years, constantly seeking chances to interfere. He sighed through his slack, rubbery lips. 'You look tired, Domine,' he said, pouring wine from a vase into a deep cup, then offering it to me along with a plate of warm bread. 'Perhaps you should have some refreshment. Let us talk and you can listen. We have fine ideas for you.'

I scowled at him and his three cronies. 'If I feel need for refreshment then I shall walk in the snow,' I said flatly.

The four bishops shared chilly looks.

'As for the bread,' said another voice from somewhere behind, 'perhaps you four should plug your mouths with it.' Old Lactantius' cane poked between them, then he barged through the cluster to take his place by the table.

'A man like you, with no formal station in the emperor's court, or in the eyes of God, should choose his words more carefully,' said the reed-thin Bishop Maternus, his gaunt face uplit with the lustre of the golden pectoral he wore.

'Lactantius is part of my *familia*,' I said, offering Maternus a copper-rod stare. Silence reigned within the gloomy pavilion, the wind groaning on outside, tirelessly sparring with the goatskin sides.

Batius broke the icy silence, tapping the tabletop. 'Segusium is but two days march ahead,' he said, moving counters across the map to mark the position of our camp and the Maxentian city. 'We have seventeen legions, plus the Lancearii and the five regiments of your comitatus – that's just over thirty-seven thousand foot in all – though some nine hundred have been stricken with the infernal winter-marching-fever.' He looked around the tent seeking out a *medicus*.

'I already have my staff tending to them, sir, to ensure the fever is contained,' the man said quickly.

'And what about the fever of faith?' Krocus added dryly. Outside the sound of raised voices spiked again – legions devoted to the old gods hectoring the Christian ones, drowning out their low, sombre chants. 'How will you cure that?'

The medicus' mouth flapped a few times as he tried to answer the impossible question.

'Anyway.' Batius shot Krocus an exasperated look then turned back to the assembly of generals: 'As for cavalry, we have fifteen hundred *equites promoti* and five hundred cataphracti. He placed the tips of two fingers near the counter representing the camp, then slid them westwards as if to encircle the Segusium counter. 'The city is garrisoned only by auxiliaries, and barely a cohort's worth.'

'I have never seen the place, but I understand it is high-walled,' remarked Baudio, the short, bare-headed Prefect of the Second Italica Divitensis.

'Aye,' agreed Batius, 'that's the curse of winter in these mountains: no good tracks to draw heavy wagons or siege towers. We have ladders, but we would incur heavy losses with ladders alone, and I would not be confident of success.'

'Equally, we do not have the luxury of time to build heavier devices from the woods near Segusium,' Scaurus of the Petulantes added, tapping the patch of map marking out a forest a few miles south of the city. 'Segusium must be hit and hit hard, before Maxentius hears of our presence and sends reinforcements.'

'Domine,' said Vindex, the hawk-faced Prefect of the First Martia. He took off his helm and cradled it like a cat in one arm, stroking the gold fin in thought. 'I have heard that Segusium's walls are high indeed, and that the gates are strapped with metal on the outside. Some say the city is... impregnable,' he muttered, finishing with a gulp.

I glowered at him for a time. I detested officers who did nothing but throw obstacles into the conversation without ever offering solutions. Vindex was usually better than this. 'Heavily fortified,' I agreed at last. 'Walls like these cursed mountains,' I continued, casting my hands up as I walked around the circle of men. 'Gates plated in metal so they will not crumble to ram nor flame.'

Krocus cocked one eyebrow as if to question the wisdom of my words. I gave him a look that told him all he needed to know, then said to the rest: 'Sometimes, breaking in to a castle is easier for a mouse than for a lion.' Their faces changed, intrigued, perplexed. 'This will require us to wait here for a time... but it may also hand us this first of our enemy's cities.'

Long into the night we discussed how Segusium would be broken. I had their trust, their hopes in my hands... I could only pray to any gods who might be listening that my plan might work before Maxentius' armies rode to Segusium's aid.

2

MAXENTIUS

Rome, 2nd February 312 AD

'Constantine is coming. Make no mistake.'

'This again?' I rounded on Volusianus with an exasperated tone. 'We have no word of any such move. No beacon fires in the high mountains. There is nothing to suggest that anything has changed.'

'What of the courier? The one at Centum Cellae?'

I sighed. 'We have only the word of a drunken Gaulish trader that the man was even a courier.'

'He boarded at Savona,' Volusianus persisted. 'Half delirious, filthy and suffering from an infected thigh wound and some illness. He wore an official uniform and carried the satchel that marked him out, demanding fast passage to Rome.'

'And yet he passed away on the journey from either illness or wounds and is unable to deliver any message or even substantiate whether he is actually a messenger at all. His clothes have been changed, his satchel lost.'

'The satchel was probably lost in winter storms, his clothes riddled with infection and disposed of as any sensible ship captain would. Disease on a ship can kill a whole crew.'

I railed angrily. 'So you would have me plot a campaign, move thousands of troops around and leave the east open to potential invaders purely because of the second-hand tale of a drunken Gaul and the stinking corpse of a man who may, *or may not*, be one of our couriers from the northern border? Volusianus, it will take a damn sight more than this to persuade me to such dire decisions.'

'Yet he came from *somewhere*, and was desperate to reach Rome, and over the winter we saw a growing concentration of Constantine's forces in the south of his domain. Licinius closes upon the east, though not yet pressing the border. Only a blind man or a fool would see all of this as anything other than the first move in the final game, Domine.'

'And which are you suggesting applies to me?' I snapped angrily. The others in my consilium, I noticed, had fallen silent and backed away a little, as was often the case when my Praetorian Prefect and I locked horns, which was almost every time we spoke these days.

'I would not dare insult the imperial person,' Volusianus replied smoothly. 'But you must see, Domine. We have a vast army, far larger than that of Constantine or Licinius, but they need to be used. We cannot support a force of this size indefinitely unless you wish to bleed Rome dry of every last *sestertius* and see a repeat of what happened in the forum.'

I shuddered at the memory of the bloodshed I had witnessed. My own people killing my own people. But then how different was war with Constantine? Were they not also my own people? I claimed – as did he – to be Augustus of the West, and yet we talked of taking the West to war against itself. It seemed that no matter what I did these days I was fated to force Roman to kill Roman.

What had happened to those glorious days when we had

laughed in the sunlight and the worst battle I watched was Anullinus and Volusianus arguing? The days when my glorious Romulus still lived. The days before unfortunate words and even more unfortunate actions. Before Constantine had pushed me to the edge of ire and I had insulted his mother. Before I had allowed his statues to be smashed and defaced all across the city. Before I had stood in the cold funereal hall of Galerius and spat unretractable ire at his face. I shivered, remembering every unfortunate and unintentional step that had brought us to this place, yet my heart hardened as I remembered that I was not the only offender. That the flat-faced opponent I had once called a friend had garrotted my father in a cellar. That he had denigrated me every bit as much as I had done him, that in Galerius' living tomb he had met my ire, shot for shot.

And yet was any friendship ever irreparable?

I had not been aware of the passage of time as I followed a trail of old images in the privacy of my head, right back past this grand disaster to the birth of my precious boy. It was only when Ruricius cleared his throat with a touch of embarrassment that I pulled myself back to the present, trying to ignore the tears that had formed at the corner of my eyes.

'Far be it from me to press matters, Domine,' Ruricius said with a glass-smooth, conciliatory tone, 'but the prefect has the right of it. Send men north. If the ship-corpse turns out to be some provincial chancer seeking a free ride to the capital then so be it, but if he is what he said he is, then this is a warning we cannot ignore. Better to buy the whole wine shipment for the party than to risk waiting until the last minute and having a dry night.'

I narrowed my eyes at Ruricius. He was not a man given to flights of fancy, nor to exaggeration, and somehow coming from his mouth it sounded so much more rational and imperative than it had from Volusianus. I felt my conviction beginning to falter. Perhaps they were right?

'Very well. We shall move north, but this is not war. I am not invading the lands of Constantine. Or Licinius, for that matter. What cavalry do we have that is not committed to any post?'

Ruricius drummed his fingers on the arms of his chair. 'Somewhere in the region of four thousand light horse and three thousand heavy, including units of *clibanarii* and cataphracti, Domine. More could be gathered in time, but they are presently stationed to the north of here in several locations and could be grouped and moved at speed.'

'They present a highly mobile and very effective force. They could be committed to the north-west and would be able to respond swiftly to any trouble. Volusianus, you can take command of them, as well as the Praetorian horse. Rearrange the north-west as you see fit. Guard the passes before the snow melts and they become viable, and garrison the towns in preparation for your purported war, but do *not* move past our outposts. I will not have you start a war that could be avoided. Do you understand me?'

Volusianus simply sat silent, his face contorted into lemon-sucking distaste. I turned away from him – a deliberate slight. 'I am sick of this place, anyway. I also shall move to the north. This city seethes like a cauldron of discontent that cannot be calmed no matter what we do. And the villa...'

No one commented, but sympathy exuded from all the faces before me. Probably not from Volusianus, but I had my back to him now. The grand villa on the Via Appia was for me haunted by the constant presence of my son's tomb. For a time I had needed to be near it, found it impossible to tear myself away, but as I had been reluctantly drawn back into worldly affairs, I had realised that such proximity was gradually tarnishing my soul. Moreover, Valeria would not stay there. Now she urged me to leave Rome entirely. She also urged me to war, but in a calmer, more reasoned manner than my prefect.

'While Volusianus takes the cavalry north-west to Taurinorum and joins up with the forces there, I will concentrate the rest of the forces at Verona.'

'Constantine may not pass Verona, Domine. He will come from the north-west,' Ancharius Pansa, once the master of the *Frumentarii* and now commander of my new personal bodyguard, murmured.

'Constantine will not come at all,' I stated flatly. Fraternity had turned to conflict between us, but surely it could not go that far? I could feel Volusianus behind me opening his mouth to argue, and pressed on to drown him out. 'But Licinius remains a threat, and his forces, if they come, will come past Verona. A good spymaster you might be, Pansa, but a general you are not. Whether war comes from north-east or north-west, the three great bastions of the north would have to be taken before any sensible general considered moving on south. Like Taurinorum in the west or Mediolanum in the centre, Verona is one of the three hinges upon which the defence of the north swings. I will gather the eastern forces there. Volusianus,' I said, finally turning back to him, 'you are my *Dux Militum*. Before we depart, I want you to draw any forces we can spare in the south or in Africa or the islands and send them north, dividing them between the gathered armies at Taurinorum and Verona. The south is under no current threat.'

'At least there we agree, Domine,' Volusianus spat. 'But

to weigh the forces equally between east and west is poor strategy.'

I glared at him, but even an emperor's ire couldn't silence the man.

'Licinius is no real threat, and he has shown a marked lack of command ability in recent months during his clashes with Constantine. He is no great worry. Our traditional north-eastern garrison could stop him. Constantine, on the other hand, is like a wolf with steel fangs. He commands both iron-hard veteran legionaries and tough barbarians who have kept us fighting on our borders for centuries, and he *is* coming, whether or not Licinius plans to.'

The man was like a dog with a bone. He just would not give in. I sent up a silent curse and answered through clenched teeth.

'Constantine knows me of old, and he appreciates the need to keep the West strong when we face animals like Licinius and Daia in the east. No matter what has happened, he will not come south in war. I have allowed you to carry out preparations in order to keep you content, nothing more. I see the value of prudence, so I will allow you to continue to strengthen those defences, but mark my words: Constantine will not come.'

'You are deluded.'

I stared in disbelief. Not even my title or any hint of deference now. The man was overstepping his bounds by a clear mile, and cared not.

'Be very careful, Prefect.'

'You are deluded,' he repeated. 'Everyone else here can see the truth in my words, but you cling to some rosy-tinted past where the pretender emperor in the north was your friend. He is not. He is now your staunchest, vilest enemy. Licinius may be an abominable hog, but Constantine is worse and far more dangerous. To ignore him and live in your happy world of fantasy is to endanger everything we have built. To risk Rome itself.' His eyes narrowed. 'Is this why you go to Verona? You fear confrontation with Constantine, so you will cower behind high walls in the east, where you think he will not attack.'

I was shaking with indignation and disbelief now, but my prefect had not finished.

'Constantine is focused. He knows what he needs to do and he does not fear it. It may leave a sour taste in his mouth to ram a sword through your neck, Domine, but he will do it nonetheless in order to achieve his victory. Yet you dither and dissemble, and worry and plot. If you wish to continue to wear a purple cloak and not a white shroud, you need that same focus. That same will to succeed at any cost. All the years we have struggled to build your domain and then to maintain it have come down to this one year. When the campaigning season starts, Constantine's men will pour through those passes like the pack of wolves they are and will fall upon the north. If you cannot bring yourself to face him and you will not allow me the authority to do so properly, then we have already lost.'

I realised my mouth was flapping open and closed. I was so angry and stunned at this disrespect I could not find the words to reply.

'Time to decide, son of Maximian, whether you are an emperor, willing to defend his domain, or just a love-sick prince, mooning over the loss of a long-dead friendship.'

I think it was the 'dead' part that snapped me. Somehow it brought forth an image of Romulus again, and with the picture came both voice and words.

'You go too far, Volusianus. You always do, and I have always encouraged my consilium to speak their minds, but you have turned to insult and open insubordination. I fear I cannot trust you to carry out my orders. If you are so willing to refuse my plans here and insult me, how can I have faith that you will do as I order and not simply launch the war I deny you? No, Volusianus, you shall not take the cavalry north.'

'You are making a mistake,' he said with an edge of disgust.

'The mistakes are mine to make,' I snapped. 'I am the emperor here. Not you, for all you treat me as though I am merely a façade for your will. No more. You are valuable to me, Volusianus, and be grateful for that. My father would have had your tongue and then your head for such words, but I am compelled to mercy, not because you hold the lofty rank of consul, but because of your ability. You shall remain in Rome and take command of the city's defence. Ruricius? I am making you joint Praetorian Prefect along with Volusianus, who in truth is only still in that role during his consulate because he is too useful to ignore.'

Behind me I could hear Ruricius rumbling in his throat uncomfortably, but I was not to be stopped now.

'You will carry the same authority as your peer. Volusianus will command in Rome. I will command in Verona. Ruricius will take the other army north and west and will command from Taurinorum.'

'Another mistake,' snarled Volusianus.

'What?' This outburst came not from me, but from Ruricius.

Volusianus looked past me to his new co-prefect. 'You are a competent cavalry commander, Ruricius, and a good man. You are a born soldier and brave, but you have little or no experience of grand-scale operations. You are not the man to command the defence of Italia. I mean no disrespect, but the truth should be spoken at these times.'

'And you would be better?' snapped Ruricius. 'A governor from Africa? The man who kills civilians with his Praetorians?'

'That needed to be done. You see? Like the imperator here, you baulk at what the hardiest of us know to be necessary. You cannot hope to succeed if you cannot make the hard choices, either of you.'

'You sanctimonious, arrogant, oiled, pompous prick!' shouted Ruricius, rising from his seat, his balled fists with white knuckles.

'Save that bile for Constantine. You'll need it.'

'*Enough!*' I bellowed, shaking with rage. When had an imperial council become such a childish display? My outburst must have been loud and unexpected, for a shocked silence settled on the room.

'The decision is made. Volusianus, you have Rome. I entrust her to your care. Do not disappoint me. When Constantine makes peace with me, which he must, I want a city to return to, not a field of corpses and bloodsoaked Praetorians. Gather the southern forces to send north. Ruricius, you will take most of the cavalry and a solid infantry contingent to Taurinorum and defend against any feasible incursion. You still have command of the *Equites Singulares*, so take them with you as part of that force.'

Ruricius frowned. 'Domine, they are your guard. They should be with you.'

'They are strong cavalry and loyal to you. Use them well. Ancharius Pansa has my Palatine bodyguard. They will accompany me.'

Ruricius nodded, though he still looked unhappy at the decision.

'Very well. The three cities shall form the solid base of our defence of Italia. The armies will move out immediately, and Volusianus can arrange for the southern units to join us as soon as possible.'

Nodding to them all, I left the room, grateful to breathe the cold air outside that calmed my boiling, raging blood, and to be free of Volusianus and the tension he constantly created. I briefly considered having him exiled to Africa, out of the way, or even executed. That was what my father would have done but Volusianus, for all his troubles, was strong and clever, and I needed strong and clever men. Or, at least, I thought I did at the time.

'You have made a decision.'

A statement, not a question. I turned to see Valeria leaning on the veranda. The sight of her still filled me with confused emotions. We were closer now than we had ever been, and yet there was still an odd barrier there. Perhaps there always would be, because of her father, or our son, or both.

'Your voice carries when you are angry, even beyond the walls of the library, and you were truly angry, from the sound of it. Is it wise to raise Ruricius so and send him in Volusianus' place? The prefect, for all his arrogance, knows command well. He could be useful in the north.'

'He is too divisive, and he drove me to rage. He is lucky he is walking and not hanging from a cross right now. No. Ruricius to Taurinorum and I to Verona. Where will you go?'

Valeria frowned. 'Me? I will come with you, of course.'

'There will be great danger. War is no place...'

'I am the daughter of the great Galerius, and the wife of Marcus Aurelius Valerius Maxentius Augustus, Emperor of Rome. I fear no army, and my place is with you.'

Oddly, I found that more comforting than any cohort of Praetorians or unit of the Palatine Guard.

Licinius might come. Probably not. Constantine would not. I felt it in my heart. Despite everything, he could not. The man I had known would never march on me, as I would not march on him. Somehow I had convinced myself that, before the winter set in once more, we would have peace.

3

CONSTANTINE

The approach to Segusium, 8th February 312 AD

After twelve days in that winter camp, we were ready. Wrapped in thick woollen cloaks, my legions traversed a high pass and rounded the colossal, twin-peaked Mount Geminus, streaks of blown snow stretching across the ice-blue sky from the summits like war pennants. A winter wind skirled like tribal pipes as we spilled around the last of the mountains, and at last I set eyes upon the first act of the tragedy to come.

Segusium. The stony warden of the Cottian passes: a harp-shaped city down on the white-coated lowland of the valley where the River Duria rose as a mere brook, but with its north-eastern corner set against the lower mountain slopes as if it was part of the range. Damn, the city's grey walls deserved every scintilla of their reputation. High as the nearby crags, stout as a cliff face, deep snow drifts clinging to the lower stonework like frozen waves, and the rounded towers rising twice as high as the curtain wall. The chill gale whistled, moaning like the voices of old, forsaken gods. We came to a halt, my consilium looking down upon the city with me. The defenders would not spot us up here, not until I gave the order for my army to descend into the valley.

'Four cohorts,' Batius observed sourly, his nose a shade of blue from the cold, his eyes darting from the unit of men patrolling the battlements to the three other ordered blocks marching in formation around a training area in the north of the city. 'Three more than we anticipated.'

I had sent keen-eyed men to this vantage point to reconnoitre the city, and none had reported more than a single cohort on the city walls. Perhaps it was just poor timing and ill fortune that none of them had watched the city when the other cohorts had been on the drill ground. Some two thousand defenders could hold a city like this for many days. Moons, even. I knew this from bitter, bloody experience. 'This was never going to be about numbers, Batius,' I replied, looking him and the officers nearby in the eye. 'Now we must look to the stratagem I discussed in the snow camp.'

My eyes drifted along the city battlements once again, across the auxiliaries posted there. They and the newly arrived legion would have families, futures, dreams.

Krocus' lips lifted at one edge, reading my thoughts. 'Do not dwell on what must be done, Domine. The herald is ready,' he said, the ice particles in his fiery beard shimmering in the sunlight.

I gave a slow, single nod. 'Send him to the gates.'

The herald walked his horse carefully down the snowy track towards the valley floor, his cloak flapping madly, one hand clasped to his head to keep his felt cap on and the other guiding the steed towards the bronze-strapped gates. Many necks of the legionaries behind me craned and heads shifted, all eager to get a view of the imminent exchange. The herald might secure the city for me without a droplet of shed blood.

I saw the sentries on the lofty gatehouse brace and gesture as they spotted his approach. I watched him slow under the drawn bows and hoisted javelins of the auxiliaries on the walls. Few men can control their limbs and voices when faced with such threats, but my herald did well, sitting tall in the saddle, back straight, as he delivered the terms. I heard nothing other than a muffled echo of his voice, but I knew the words well enough, having crafted them over the previous days.

Citizens of Rome. Liberation has arrived at last. I mouthed as the herald spoke. *The Tyrant Maxentius, the slayer of citizens, is your master no longer. Set down your weapons, open the city gates, and you will be rewarded with the Emperor Constantine's mercy, today and hereafter.* On the herald boomed, ending with open arms: 'What say you, fellow Romans?'

Silence.

I watched as the commander of the Maxentian auxiliary watch appeared atop the gatehouse. He consulted the auxiliaries there about the herald's offer. I felt a pleasant glow in the pit of my stomach. A wise man – taking care to talk, to understand. Then he snapped his fingers overhead. I frowned, then saw a single archer on the gatehouse jerk. The arrow spat down and punched into my herald's belly. Silently, the messenger slid from his horse and into the snow, the mount nickering in confusion and pawing at the drift as if to waken its fallen master. Another arrow took the beast in the neck and it fell with a choking whinny by the herald's side, spots of red staining the pure white.

My eyes slid shut, the warmth in my belly turning to ice. The murmurs and tight gasps of my men rose around me. The other three auxiliary cohorts spilled up from the stairwells of

Segusium's towers and out onto the battlements – forming a thick line of bronze and iron all around the defences. I said nothing, my eyes fixed on the commander upon the gatehouse. A fool, in the end. *You will die today*, I mouthed with absolute certainty.

'Descend onto the plain. Form a ring around the city,' I said, my army exploding into action with a din of iron and clattering shields. 'Remain clear of missile range.' I knew what every man would be thinking: high walls, well defended. Bronze-fronted gates, almost immune to rams – which we did not have in any case – and flame.

'Time for the contingency stratagem?' Batius whispered as the army bristled into marching stance.

I peered across the interior of Segusium – the warren of slums, the mighty baths and theatres and the elegant and ancient archway. This last hope lay within.

'We have heard nothing from the pair since we despatched them four nights ago, Domine,' Krocus warned. 'One was supposed to return, to confirm that all had gone as planned.'

I looked him in the eye. 'You believe the Gods are with me, old friend?'

Krocus replied without hesitation: 'I believe the *true* God is with you, Domine.' His hand clasped his Chi-Rho necklace almost like a salute as he said this. He, like Batius, had turned to the Christian way in recent times. I envied them for their convictions in such muddled times.

'Then have faith that all will be as we hope.' I turned to Prefect Vindex, who already had a lone *sagittarius* readied, bow strung. 'As soon as we reach the low ground, send up the signal.'

* * *

Arrows, slingshot and javelins pelted down from Segusium's parapets and into the snow before my encircling, battle-ready legions, but none coming closer than twelve strides from my men. It was a demonstration of strength – that any who tried to approach the walls would be shot down like pigs. The defenders roared with laughter, pointing at our few dozen rudimentary ladders, the feeblest of siege tools. I squinted up at the gatehouse and saw the auxiliary commander again – I could even see his broad, baleful grin.

So when a flaming arrow streaked up into the air from behind me like a fiery claw, scoring the midday sky, the whites of his teeth vanished, his face falling in confusion. The arrow fell somewhere near the foot of Segusium's southern walls. After a few moments of silence, the witless soldiers up there jeered and mocked it as if the lone missile was our hapless and solitary attempt to shoot back. The smug commander's grin returned and he took to striding to and fro up on the gatehouse, bellowing triumphant messages to his men. Time passed. An hour, then two. I saw cagey looks from my officers, some soldiers watching the sun nervously. There were but a few hours of light left – and no man wanted to spend the night standing like this in the brutal cold, or attempt to lift the siege and withdraw in the confusion of darkness.

I gazed skywards too, towards the sun like them. It was the strangest thing, but I found myself whispering pleas to the blazing orb, seeing in my mind's eye the many gods who stalked my dreams and talked to me in polyglot voices – Mithras, Mars, Sol Invictus, Apollo, Krocus' true God and many more. I beseeched them all that the pair I had despatched from the snow camp were alive, within Segusium's walls, still acting as woodsmen and traders – the mice who might breach the city where a lion could not. I glanced at the dipping sun again; they must have fallen, surely? Else why would neither have returned? Even still, if just one of them had survived... maybe there was still a chance? Yet three hours had now passed since the fiery signal missile had been loosed. I felt my resolve weakening, my mind beginning to reel with the torturous logistics of breaking the siege before nightfall or setting up some form of fortified siege line lest Maxentian reinforcements arrive at our back or the defenders attempt a sally under darkness. Worst of all, I heard my legions' concerned murmurs grow into baleful yammering, the patchwork of faiths strained again, as if great invisible hands were wrenching it apart. The Christians of Britannia's legions began to pray, and this was enough for Hisarnis' Bructeri to pick up the same chant. Next, like a wind combing neatly across a field of wheat stalks only for a sharp gust to come the other way and send it all to ruination, the Seventh Gemina and the First Martia men rose in howls of derision. My army, booing and jeering their own comrades like seditious townsfolk drowning out the words of a disliked governor. The Cornuti and the Petulantes joined in, booming songs to Apollo and Sol Invictus – not at the defenders of Segusium's walls but at their own damned brother-legions! Spittle flew, curses rained and they made swords of threats to one another. Regiments shuffled to maximise the gaps between their ranks and those of neighbouring units. Many later said the strength of my army was its togetherness, its sheer animus; clearly none of them witnessed the sight and sound of the fabric tearing apart like that... and all right in front of my enemy's eyes. At that moment I lamented the absence of old Lactantius, miles distant from the scene, back in the snow camp with Fausta and a guard detachment.

'Enough!' I thundered, thrusting a single hand in the air.

My voice pealed around the mountainous, snow-clad valley like the boom of a war drum, and when the echoes faded… all was silent… just the whistling wind. I knew that just a few short moments of this nothingness would bring them to each other's throats again.

It was then that I heard it: a stark thud from within the city… and the simultaneous outwards jerk of the bronze gates.

Panicked cries rose up from within the city walls. As the enemy commander's confidence faded, my lips rose, lifted with his stolen grin. Then I saw the thin wisp of grey spiralling up from inside the gatehouse like an escaping spirit. My men – officers apart, unaware of my ruse, rumbled in surprise, heads rising as one, entranced. Moments passed before the thin smoke plume blackened and widened. Now orange talons of flame licked between the thin gap in the gates as if a fiery demon was trying to prise them open. Fine gates they were, strapped with bronze and impervious to fire on the outside… but not inside. 'May the gods be with you,' I muttered, thinking of my man inside who had set ablaze his timber-wagon and crashed it into the inside of the gates. The flames soon devoured the gatehouse, and I saw Maxentian auxiliaries on the abutting walls back away from the fierce heat. Some atop the gatehouse itself, realising they were trapped, braved the flames, plunging inside the blazing gatehouse towers, cloaks wrapped around their heads, some emerging from the other side and onto the battlements of the curtain wall. But the fool of a commander lacked such courage and remained atop the gatehouse. He ran this way and that, wailing, until a tongue of fire whooshed up and engulfed him. His screams were shrill as he flailed and thrashed like a living torch, until he tripped and buckled over the parapet, plummeting and landing on a patch of solid road cleared of snow. With a stark crack of vertebrae, he was at last silent.

My heart pulsed like his dying body at that moment, my mind throwing up images of the fires that had engulfed Nicomedia during the Great Persecutions. That day I had fought the flames. Today, I was the burner. As I fought off the guilt, my teeth clenched hard, so hard I thought they might explode in a glassy shower.

Moments later, the mighty gates of Segusium groaned and listed, ruined. One toppled forward and slammed onto the ground, flattening the corpse of the burnt commander. My men roared.

'Domine, it is time,' Batius said, poised, eyes trained on the yawning, fire-edged opening left by the gate and the now bare stretches of battlement near the blaze.

'Advance,' I said in a whisper.

'Ad-vance!' Batius and Krocus bellowed in unison.

'For glory, for the true emperor!' Baudio bellowed as hundreds of *buccinae* keened and the roar of my men rose again, this time like thunder. Like a silvery tide, we rushed the breached defences, cohorts flooding in through the smouldering gatehouse, ladders swinging up to assail the patches of the battlements where defenders had scattered.

The struggle was swift and brutal. My sword arm swung and thrust, and I felt blood and viscera slap onto my bare skin before I realised how many Maxentian soldiers I had cut down. When I looked around me I saw them carpeting the flagstones of the *pomerium*, heaped there at the foot of the walls all along the city's interior. The auxiliary defence was not just beaten, it was destroyed. Only when I saw my soldiers then flood into the city's inner streets did my rage begin to subside. Women stiffened with fright, backing into corners, cradling children. Simple men quailed and fell to their knees, hands raised like hopeless shields.

I saw my legionaries surge in for the slaughter. 'No! No citizen is to be harmed. That was my word!' I roared. 'The garrison rejected my terms, but the people did not.' I saw one legionary caught up in the moment ignoring me, cutting down a screaming girl then slapping the mother to the ground before reaching down to tear at her robe. I loped over to him and smashed the hilt of my sword against his temple, knocking him out cold. 'The citizens are *not* to be harmed, do you hear me?' My voice pealed like a bell, and my officers relayed the command.

I stared at the young girl who had been killed, as the mother knelt over her, weeping uncontrollably. I felt my chest rise and fall more slowly, heard the *drip-drip* of blood from my *spatha*, then sensed the shadows of Segusium's walls and the high mountains draw across me as the sun began to set. Guilt, shame... and a rising sense of triumph. For it was over. Segusium was mine. The key was in the lock. The door to Italia was open.

4

MAXENTIUS

Verona, 22nd February 312 AD

Verona was an ideal place for the imperial court. A city of ancient origin, which had played host to a number of emperors in its time, bedecked with all the grand facilities required of such a place, well defended and at the meeting point of a number of critical roads. And yet the grand *domus* we had been given was, while the most lavish in the city, paltry compared to the imperial palaces to which I was now used.

Still, I was not setting up home here, just camp.

Ruricius had raced north from Rome with his cavalry, leaving the bulk of his army to march on behind, set on pushing all the forces he could muster forward to the border cities. I was less vehement. Unlike my officers, I did not see the urgency. Still, we had come to Verona with a sizeable force and all the entourage of the court, and been greeted with grace and spectacle by the city's *ordo* and its people.

My officers sat around the *tablinum* discussing the disposition of troops here, there and everywhere. I might disagree that Constantine would march into my domain, but we had all agreed that there was a very real possibility of Licinius doing just that. He had an alliance with Constantine now and would not be fettered by the need to guard his north. My officers constantly rose from their seats and crossed to the table in pairs, shoving markers around the map from one city or fortress to another. I had the urge to laugh. It looked so much like a game.

Finally, the board was set and the game was ready. All sat back and looked at me. I perused the table. 'It all appears in good order,' I announced. 'Stretched a little thin, perhaps, but covering the border well, with a second line of solid garrisons and a sizeable force back here in Verona. Very well. To your units. Deploy immediately.'

The officers rose and saluted, making their way from the tablinum out of the imperial presence. I watched them go with an odd feeling. Despite everything, I was missing the presence of Volusianus. The man was insolent, difficult and troublesome, but he was a good commander and strategist.

As the last man left, I examined the table. Yes, it all looked fine. It took me a while to realise the room's doorway still stood open and was now occupied. I looked up sharply to find Valeria standing there, her best disapproving look in place.

'What have I done wrong?'

'You need to take more personal control of matters like these.'

I shrugged. 'They are good men. They know their business.'

She entered the room, the door swinging quietly shut behind her with a click, and studied the table herself. I waited.

'Well?'

'Yes, they've done an acceptable job of setting out your defences.'

'And you would have done something different?'

'Me? No. But if I were you, then yes. Men need to think

of you as their lord and master, and leaving such matters entirely in their hands diminishes your *imperium*. It does not matter that nothing is out of place here. You needed to find something, produce a coherent reason, and impose your will upon them. Men must always remember that you are the emperor.'

I rolled my eyes. 'Make something up?'

'Look,' she said, and reached out. She grasped the markers for the Second Sicilian and the First Mauretanian in the towns of Vicetia and Patavium, and swapped them with a Venetian cohort and an Aemilian one. 'See? Now tell me why I did that?'

'I have no idea,' I shrugged. 'You've just halved the number of men in major frontline installations and doubled them on third-line places.'

'Pay attention, Maxentius,' she said with exaggerated patience, as though trying to teach a difficult child. 'It is not the numbers I focused on, but the origin and nature of the units. Both towns were garrisoned by legions from the south who are unfamiliar with the territory and with little in the way of highly mobile personnel. I have replaced them with mounted units from the general region. They know the land and can respond quickly. It is flat and perfect cavalry land. Ruricius would have spotted that. Volusianus too.'

I stared at the map. She was right. She was absolutely right.

'Of course, Volusianus would have called me a moron while doing it.'

'I nearly did that myself, dear.'

I sighed. 'I cannot bring myself to believe Constantine will come. I know,' I said hurriedly, raising a hand to ward her off. 'I know I've said it a hundred times, but there are good, logical reasons to believe it, Valeria. The simple fact is that

Constantine is more than just a usurper. He and I have shared peril and joy, victory and fear, all together. I would not be the man I am without his influence. I have raged and snarled about the shit he has spread across the empire, blackening my name and attempting to turn my people against me, and, gods, but there are times when I hate him for it. But while he executed my father, even I can acknowledge that he had reason, and he *saved* Romulus in Nicomedia. Together we challenged the bitter might of the tyrants. What has been done cannot be undone, yet perhaps it can be overcome. Walls crack, but they can be plastered and repaired. In some ways, Constantine is still my brother, for all the shit we sling, but Licinius? He is a dog who needs putting down. While I still spit at the thought of what Constantine has done, I will always believe there is a way to repair the rift. Licinius does not hold such a distinction.'

Valeria nodded. 'There is a solution.'

'What?'

She had an odd, faraway look in her eye. 'I think it is a solution. A way to put pressure on Licinius, and therefore to weaken his alliance with Constantine and make your old friend slightly less secure.'

I stared at her desperately. 'Go on...'

'Daia.'

'What?' I snorted. 'Daia is every bit the dog Licinius is, and with just as strong an army.'

'Good intelligence among your court places Daia at Cyzicus, at least as of the last report. He has his armies there. There is rumour that he intends to cross the Hellespont into Licinius' realm.'

'So my enemies in the east might fight among themselves,' I mused. 'That *would* weaken their alliance.'

'No. Do not rely upon them solving your problem for you, Maxentius. Take the reins and guide the *quadriga* of state. Seek an alliance with Daia. He may decide not to come west, but if he were assured of an alliance with the master of Rome, his reasons to falter evaporate. Better still, an official alliance with Daia will make both Licinius and Constantine think twice before waging war in Italia.'

'Valeria, Daia is a pig. What sort of message would it send about me if I ally with him? The man will use me to gain complete control in the East as undisputed master, and then those lands will revert to that awful time years ago when fear and persecution reigned.'

'Maxentius, you are not a Christian. You owe them nothing.'

I thought back over the many times I had had trouble with that difficult sect. I *did* owe them nothing, but then there were men like Zenas and Miltiades, both of whom had served me faithfully, despite their religion.

'I will not tailor my realm to the Christians, Valeria, but they constitute a sizeable sector of my people. I remember the horrors Diocletian and Galerius inflicted upon the world, and I will not be remembered in the same breath as them. Daia, on the other hand, would revel in such infamy.'

'You don't have to *like* Daia. You don't have to *approve* of him. You only have to *ally* with him. One seal on a document and suddenly Licinius is looking over his shoulder in panic. You can then strip half your defences in the north-east and commit them to the west. Hopefully you will not need to, for Constantine will pull back those forces he is said to be amassing at your borders if he suddenly finds half the world arrayed against him and his only ally busy with other worries.'

I stood silent for a while, mulling it over. I hated Daia.

He was, as an emperor and as a human being, everything I aspired to avoid. But to have his eastern army, which was probably the most powerful force in the empire, compelling Licinius to turn his gaze east, it was worth swallowing such bitter seed. Valeria was right.

'Of course, Daia might not accept.'

Valeria gave me an odd smile. 'He cannot afford to refuse. The deal would secure you in the West, but it will also give him the East.'

Breathing heavily, as though I had just made a momentous and dangerous decision, I crossed to the door and opened it. Ancharius Pansa, the commander of my personal guard and former frumentarius, was sprawling on a couch in the outer room. He looked up as the door opened and hurriedly rose to his feet. He would never look truly martial and impressive, but he had other qualities that recommended him to me.

'Domine?'

'Pansa? I am going to produce some extremely important documents in sealed cases. I need them delivering to Zenas in Rome. Detail your best men as an escort.'

As Pansa nodded and turned, Valeria shot a curious look at me. 'Zenas?'

'I need a man I can trust as ambassador to Daia. Zenas is that man. He will take the documents east to Daia and secure the alliance. I am confident.'

'Zenas is a Christian.'

'Yes.'

'Do you not think it inflammatory to send a Christian as an ambassador to a man who persecutes them?'

I pursed my lips. 'I would worry a little over Zenas' safety, but if he returns with Daia's agreement, then I will know the man is serious enough even to treaty with a Christian.'

Valeria nodded. 'Will you inform Volusianus and Ruricius of your intentions?'

I paused. I was not at all sure how Volusianus would take the news. He would almost certainly hear about it from Zenas anyway. Ruricius? Perhaps, but then I had heard nothing from him in more than half a month since he had left for Taurinorum. Perhaps I would receive news from him soon. The silence was beginning to wear on my nerves.

5

CONSTANTINE

Augusta Taurinorum, 6th March 312 AD

We were free of the Alpes at last. Northern Italia, gentle, fecund and drenched in the spring sun, stretched out before us. The petrichor of dew-wet grass sweetened the air. Meltwater brooks chuckled and fizzed into the River Duria in an excited chatter. Larks sped overhead and blue tits and sparrows chirped and whistled in the branches of thin larch stands lining the road. Hills, green and rolling, hugged the way ahead. A paradise, maybe, for another man, in another age. For us, it was the ongoing road to war: to the famed city of Taurinorum – the first of the three hinges of the north.

The Prefect of the Third Herculia, mounted on a white mare, took a scroll from my clerks, saluted, then turned his horse around and rode back down the road whence we had come, back to the mountains, saluting me stiffly as he went. The drum of hooves faded and I felt a certain sense of security, of certainty, about the mountain passes we were leaving behind. The Herculia legion – a regiment of the old style, still counting more than five thousand men in their ranks, but in reality with less than half that number – would now garrison captured Segusium and watch those mountain passes and the approach to Taurinorum. I was loathe to lose the Herculians, but they were one of the most vocal of the religious dissenters, whole centuries of them having spent nights at camp lighting deliberately high pyres and performing overly elaborate sacrifices upwind of the Christian regiments. Now, they could do as they wished in Segusium without stoking trouble. In the interests of balance, I would be sure to detach one of the more zealous Christian units the next time I needed to leave men at my rear. I knew it was not an answer, merely an avoidance, but it allowed me some degree of contentment.

I swept my gaze round and over my right shoulder. Fausta's wagon rumbled a short way behind me. In the penumbra inside the wagon, I could just make out her pale face at the side window. She wasn't looking at me but I knew she had been. I just knew.

A sudden cawing startled me and all nearby. A raven swooped down, making a grab for the white plume on Batius' helm.

'Winged bastards,' Batius yelped, ducking away then shaking a fist as if the bird were an enemy outrider.

I looked askance at the bird as it sped away, and I saw ranks of my legionaries cast wary looks at the feathery fiend too. In an age of a thousand gods, ancient omens like this still made men shiver.

'If I lie down to rest tonight and the worst we have faced is a plucky raven, then I'll sleep well,' Krocus drawled, mercifully breaking the tense silence, his eyes like slits as they combed the spring hinterland.

I understood. We all did. By now Maxentius must surely have heard from that lone scout who sped from the mountain passes. Even if that scout had perished on his journey to Rome, then my enemy would now surely have heard news of the sudden lack of communication from Segusium and the north-western shoulder of his realm.

'Maxentius, even if he was swift to react, would still need time to reach this road and Taurinorum before we do,' Prefect Vindex boomed confidently, aquiline nose flaring slightly as he swished his bright blue cloak over one shoulder, the crossbow cloak pin and gold-finned helm gleaming like his eyes. He didn't stop there. 'Once we have Taurinorum, the Padus valley, the northern roads,' he counted off each prize city, territory and vital feature of the land on his fingers with absurd irreverence, 'I think we should send south messengers of our own, to spread the news. Once his *people* hear, it will be the end for him. He slaughtered the masses once, and they will not have forgotten.'

I said nothing, my mind fixed on the here and now. The way ahead, an ancient highway, the flags worn smooth and shining like tarnished metal, deeply indented with wheel tracks, led into a picturesque, verdant horizon: gentle hills propping up a pastel-blue morning sky marked only with a few thin twists of cloud.

'I was once as optimistic as you,' Batius chuckled in Vindex' direction.

Vindex' head snapped round, his hawk-like features pinched in offence.

'And, damn, I envy you for it,' the big man added quickly to ease the prefect's temper. Batius pointed over his mount's head, dotting the way ahead with a fingertip. 'You think of tomorrow's fruits. I see instead the poisons of today: every hollow, every shadow in the trees, every boot print in the grass.' I almost smiled then, realising it had been Batius who had drilled that thought-pattern into my mind when he trained me as a youth – in sword-fighting, in hunting, in battle tactics. 'See the haze far to the south?' Batius continued. 'Is it low cloud'—his voice fell into a tense whisper for dramatic effect—'or white smoke from an enemy camp fire?'

As Batius and Vindex debated, I let my thoughts wander. Like an unwanted dog returning home, my thoughts went to that most unpleasant of places. I saw *him* again in my mind's eye. How could men who had shared so much, been so close... become so opposed?

'You will have to face him at some point,' Batius said.

I looked up, realising the debate was over, and Vindex and the others had fallen back a little. 'You think I fear him?'

'I think you fear the moment when you will have to stand before each other, face to face, and answer the questions that dance in your mind.'

'We had our moment,' I drawled, thinking of the fire and spite in Galerius' charnel palace. While that fat old shitbag lay dying, Maxentius and I had nearly come to blows. 'The bastard drew a sword on me, said he wished his assassin had been successful. Ever since, he has cut me to my bones with more wicked words.'

'Maybe Vindex has a point: were you and Maxentius to come face to face now in this early part of the year, here in these northern tracts, the war might be settled. We talk of taking Rome, but the road to Rome is long. Many wives and mothers will be praying this campaign does not take us all the way there.'

'Maxentian women will pray we die upon it,' I said sourly.

Batius rumbled with a dry soldier's laugh.

I flashed looks into the trees again, seeing the dull shapes of my screening cavalry. I was taking no risks. An *ala* of equites promoti on each flank, another as a rearguard, and a fourth ala of cataphracti up ahead as a vanguard, the black-caped

Praepositus Ingenuus riding fearlessly at the fore, the draco standard he carried moaning in the gentle spring wind, the bright ribbons on the tails fluttering like flames.

It was then I noticed the draco tail fall limp, motionless. 'Why have they stopped?' I said tightly, my hand already half-raised to slow the column.

Krocus, frowning, rose in his saddle a fraction using a thigh-grip. 'Because, by the old gods and new... we're there. I can see Taurinorum's turrets.'

At that moment so did my army entire, gasping at the colossal city ahead: at first it was but a pale glimmer on the horizon, then we saw more. Walls six storeys high, the parapets lined with stout crenels, the towers topped with vivid red and golden banners snapping in the wind. The men up there were but argentine flashes. Behind the city ran the mighty River Padus – a pale-blue ribbon, dotted with fishing boats and straddled by an ancient stone bridge. As we drew closer, Ingenuus broke from the van, wheeled round and rode back towards me. 'The path to the city is clear, Domine.' Likewise, the screening riders sent their reports, halting where the road wound onto the plain before the city's western approach. 'There are no enemy forces in the countryside,' they said, their eyes flicking to the square city.

'Another siege,' Batius sighed as we came into full view of the place: a mighty square of stone ramparts. 'This place makes mighty Segusium look like a mere timber *castrum*.'

I thought of his words from just moments ago. The road to Rome. Each successive city would be more defiantly walled.

'We should approach with confidence. Have the men send up a *barritus* cry. Let the citizens see the size of our forces,' Baudio of the Italica suggested. I signalled for it to be so. As we stepped onto the plain, the many regiments issued low, droning cries that gradually rose like a keening wind, then whole legions took to beating their spears against their shields. The sound was terrible.

Until an eerie groan of old timbers echoed across the countryside.

The barritus died almost instantly and my men slowed a little in their careful advance.

Taurinorum's western gates had been thrown open. Now the men began to cheer and cry out in victory.

'They have seen sense,' Vindex gasped over the yammering of triumph.

'I have seen gates opened and men invited inside, only to be crushed into paste under the jaws of an iron *lupus*,' I said, steadying his understandable optimism.

'We cannot ignore open gates, Domine,' Tribunus Ruga of the Ubii legion whispered.

'We won't. Nor will we blunder inside, blind.' My eyes searched the corner towers as I said this, imagining men hidden beyond each, or waiting to pour at us through the open gates. 'Halt!' I boomed. The cheering and songs faded away. 'Baudio,' I cried, 'take a century inside to check the streets.'

We waited there on the mid-section of the plain while Baudio led his century towards the city's western gates. There were no sentries along the curtain wall, watching our approach. Just a few robed citizens, huddled and pointing. It made me uneasy. Why had they opened the gates? Even with a minor garrison – and surely there were *some* troops in there – this fortress-city could be defended for a time even against an army like mine.

'Why no trumpets, no troops,' I hissed to my retinue, 'why do they capitulate?'

'Any Maxentians left inside the city no doubt cower, stunned and voiceless at your approach,' one chinless sycophant purred. I shot up a finger to silence the waste of armour.

From behind, I heard a low moan coming from the halted ranks – not the military barritus this time. My head swivelled round. The dread chanting rose and fell, and only after a time did I realise it was the four bishops, trying to rouse the men with their Christian song. A song of victory, when no victory had yet been had. Worst of all this only stoked the angry shouts from the nearby Apollonians in the Cornuti ranks.

'Find Lactantius in the wagon train. Shut them up,' I snapped at Krocus, who heeled his horse away and back towards the wagons. It was only as I was turning my head to face forwards again that I saw something else – something that the sight of the fine city and the inviting, open gates had distracted me and all of us from: a low, wooded hill south of the city, on our right. There was something strange about it anyway, but then a quarrel of sparrows burst into the air from the top of the hill as if my gaze had provoked them.

'Batius, in their reports, our scout riders never mentioned a mound. Tell me they scouted behind that thing.'

If he replied, I never heard it.

A wall of noise rose up from that spot, and the brow of the hill came alive. Cavalry, thousands of them. Maxentian riders – many more than those we had seen fleeing east – came spilling from the trees like ants.

'It's an ambush!' one of my officers wailed.

Panic slashed through me: not just cavalry, but two masses of steel-clad Maxentian infantrymen pouring around each side of the hill too like the spreading wings of an eagle. I wrenched at Celeritas' reins, overcome with dread. Legions! Seven, eight? More? Only a few hundred paces away.

'They're coming for our right flank,' Vindex bellowed, his horse rearing in panic as he tried to pull it round to face the charge.

'Face south!' Batius roared.

'Destroy them!' cried another voice. I twisted my head towards the city: high up on Taurinorum's parapets a general in silver armour had risen into view, his face a shade of plum as he screamed, orchestrating his ambuscade with swishing arms and cries, the trumpeters by his sides blasting signal notes. My eyes narrowed. *Ruricius*, I realised. One of Maxentius' finest generals.

My mind exploded with a thousand different fears, but quickly focused on one: Fausta! Why had I consented to her presence in this enemy land? I had been sure to keep her safe at Segusium, having a regiment of auxiliaries hold back at the snow camp with her and old Lactantius. But here? Here she was in the jaws of death with me! For all the animosity between us the thought of her on this field of imminent battle made me shudder to my core. My old tutor too was here with the column. What hope would he have against sword-wielding brutes? Especially when my army was lumbering round to face the enemy like a drove of pregnant donkeys. 'Turn to the south!' I screamed to reiterate Batius' order, spittle flying.

Buccinae wailed, men cried out and steel rattled as my army scrambled to avoid disaster. As my men swung round to face the Maxentian ambush, the enemy came at us like a storm, the legions speeding like demons, and the cavalry in the centre – no, not mere cavalry, but Equites Singulares – Rome's finest. Worst of all they were led by a screen of *clibinarii*: the lancers coated in steel – impassive, staring masks, steel-plated torsos, iron-banded limbs. Purple plumes rose from their helms like tall flames, writhing and snapping in the wind of their charge; their steeds were masked in iron with bulging gauze eyes, bodies draped in scale.

My mind flashed with fire and memories of vicious clashes past. Of victories won and defeats dodged. Of dusks walking among thousands of corpses. Which would today be?

The charging force was coming at my now south-facing but largely disordered line like a giant wedge – a *cuneus*. 'They're going to try to break our centre,' I rasped. Perhaps few of my men realised how grave this was, but my officers were quick to react.

Then I saw it, like a light in the depths of night. The glint of hope. '*Forfex!*' I croaked.

Batius heard me. 'Forfex!' he boomed. So too my other officers relayed the order. The legions on the flanks of my jumbled south-facing line took a time to understand the order – but by the gods they were well-trained in it.

I turned to Ingenuus and my cataphracti. My well-armoured vanguard riders were right with me in our centre, but on unarmoured and stumbling horses. The speeding Maxentian clibinarii would butcher the animals and ruin our centre – smash us apart for the following enemy legions to fall upon us and finish the job. 'Dismount!' I cried. 'Dismount! Remember the days past when we faced the Persian Savaran…'

My cataphracti riders now slid from their steeds, slapping the mounts' rumps to send them charging away to the north, riderless. I saw the light in Ingenuus' wild eyes. 'Remember the way we broke those eastern chargers?' he roared to reiterate to his men what I wanted – for them to stand in the face of a cavalry charge. But what sane man would? Well, I stepped forward and into the path of the oncoming riders, alone with just a sword and shield. A wish for death, surely.

'With me!' I yelled regardless. Now they believed – in my madness if nothing else – and swarmed to my side. Animus, glowing, hot and feral.

The ground shuddered violently underfoot as the clibinarii tip of the strong Maxentian force plunged right for us. Demonic they looked in their steely, emotionless masks. I imagined the face of Maxentius himself behind every one. Fifty strides, forty...

'Back, back,' I cried.

Back my dismounted centre went – but in a steady backstep, not a retreat! Such courage in the face of these creatures they showed – both my cataphracti and the legions holding the flanks. Back my centre stepped at haste, dipping away from the point of the Maxentian cuneus so my forces formed a V-shape around them. I looked once over my shoulder, where Krocus and Hisarnis and their men buzzed to and from our supply wagons, laying heavy objects in the grass.

'Back...' I trilled one more time, this time glancing over my shoulder again to see the line of planted objects. Now I raised one hand: '... And... *hoooooold!*'

Like palisade stakes being driven into the earth, each of my men dug one foot into the ground as if braced for a storm, then squatted once to lift the spears laid out there by Krocus and Hisarnis. The lances rose like a maw of fangs. The enemy thought they were going to overwhelm my centre – not so. A spear line, the death knell of a frontal horse charge. They hurtled on, only just seeing the snare when it was too late to slow their steeds. With a din of whinnying, their horses ran onto our spears. Soft earth, froth and spittle lashed up over me before they hammered into our lances in a tumult of ripping meat and screaming. My shoulder wrenched violently as one cavalryman's horse took my lance in its neck, a thrashing hoof near breaking my nose and the dead weight of one of my men sliding down behind me, his arterial blood soaking one side of my face. The foremost riders were catapulted over our heads, their poor beasts run through to their guts. The great weight of those charging behind slammed into the carnage and the earth furrowed behind my boots as we were driven back. 'Hold... *hold!*' Batius screamed from the edge of the spear line, his face showered with dirt and blood. Like a storm caught in a steely urn, the enemy charge slowed to nothing, and when the cavalrymen of the Maxentian cuneus looked around, panicked, they saw the sides of the forfex they had ridden into – my legions arrayed around their flanks, me and my centre facing them, pinning them. Then, when Baudio and Vindex brought their legions round to seal the forfex at the southern end, they were done for.

'Release spears,' I bellowed to my cataphracti.

Down went the spears, some left embedded in the snared Maxentian cavalrymen, and each of us picked up the secondary weapons Krocus and Hisarnis had set out. Fire-hardened shafts of wood, crowned with thick, vicious, flanged iron stars. These maces could smash the peaks from a mountain – and they would certainly shatter the iron shell of a clibanarius. 'Break them!' I bellowed.

Now the storm turned. We forged through our snapped and bloodied maw of earth-bound spears and on into the trapped Maxentian riders, where we swung these feral weapons like savages. The winged mace-heads crushed the flat iron, chest plates and the chests within, smashed legs and hands and – when my men leapt up and brought the weapons swinging down – ruined the heads of the Maxentian foes, whose helms and masks crumpled, the emotionless visages now crying runnels of blood from eyes and mouth. Without the momentum of a charge they were far less a threat – their stout armour slowing their attempts to twist and turn in the saddle and fight us off. Each brutal blow took the life of a priceless heavy Maxentian rider as the forfex drew tighter and tighter. Dead men remained, heads lolling, upright on the saddle for there was nowhere for the corpses to fall, so tight was the crush. More, I saw through the bloody frenzy to the rear portion of the enemy cuneus and beyond – the infantry wings and centre, some way yet from reaching the writhing forfex trap, were slowing. They had banked everything on their iron riders smashing my army apart so they could come in and deal the final blows to seal victory. Instead, they had lost – their only hope, their nerve... and the day itself.

'Break off,' I rasped back towards Hisarnis and his Bructeri, to Ruga and his Ubii, jostling near the flanks of my cavalry-turned-clubmen but not yet engaged in the fighting. Their weight had helped reinforce and tighten the forfex, but that battle was won. 'Charge their infantry,' I screamed.

Horns keened, relaying my call, and a dozen other commanders roared too. I heard my two legions bellow some guttural cry that was a mix of their old tribal pride and their new, surging *Romanitas*. I heard the screams and the din of the Maxentian legions, some turning to flight before even a sword had been bloodied. The forfex shifted slowly in one direction then the other, leaving a trail of steaming, torn-open bodies in its wake. After a time, I stepped back from the forfex, and let my club drop into the blood-wet earth. I staggered away through the tangle of the fallen – hundreds of my men but many more of his. *His*. Broken corpses, bent into inhuman angles, limbs snapped in many places, bones, steaming gut ropes hanging from jutting limb shards like creepers from a branch. Horses, broken. The stench, the foul stench.

I watched the rest in a stupor, seeing a contingent of enemy cavalry somehow breaking free of the forfex – perhaps my men were numb with the effort of slaughter – and galloping madly towards Taurinorum's open gates.

I pressed thumb and forefinger together in a visceral moment of treaty with all and any deities that might be listening. *No*, I mouthed, knowing that if they retreated inside those gates then a long and stubborn siege might pin us here for months. Many would die and our campaign would suffer.

Slam! The gates shuddered shut before the fleeing ones could enter.

My jaw fell slack.

The Maxentian horsemen reared up in panic, the horses throwing some men hard against the barred gates. Some of the fleeing and frantic enemy legions joined the chaos, running towards and swarming around the panicked horsemen at the mighty gates, banging on the wood and demanding entry, some hacking at the thick timbers in futility with their swords. I felt the light of the spring sun on me at that moment, cooking the wet blood on my skin. For a moment, I almost believed my plea to the skies had been heard, that a god had closed the gates for me. Then I saw above the gatehouse that Ruricius was gone. In his place was a man – a senatorial type, scrawny, hoary and hunched, perched up there like a vulture. He held aloft in his right hand an olive wreath, his eyes fixed on me. The wisdom – or at least the instinct for self-preservation – of that old man had won the day for me.

Before I could dwell upon the glorious moment, I heard another paean of war horns. The dismounted cataphracti riders of my forfex had mounted their steeds again, and the three equites promoti alae were formed up with them in a cuneus of their own. My legions too made a great arc, facing the city gate under which the panicked enemy were pinned.

If the gods were watching, then they surely judged me at that moment, for I made no attempt to stop my army. They broke into a ferocious charge and hammered into the terrified Maxentian forces. Wet slashes of steel and curt snapping of smashed bones rose in crescendo. The gates became stained red from ground to well beyond head height before, after nearly an hour of butchery, their cries lessened and died away altogether. I noticed something then: many of the dead... they were young men. Not veterans. Even the officers – the ones with purple *clavica* on their now-red tunics – were not veterans. I felt a terrible chill pass over me. I had slaughtered an army of willing but less-than-able recruits. I even saw one of the dead clibinarii, his iron helm having fallen from his severed head... the head of a young man. What had happened here?

I saw then the faces of the non-military men of my consilium, looking on. From the wagons, Lactantius watched the slaughter like a man being shown how meat reaches a plate for the first time, his old face sagging horribly, one hand cupping his mouth. The four bishops stood in a huddle. Their faces were stony, their eyes narrow. Ossius was the only one to show emotion... a tight, brief, smirk.

A sudden whinny, right by my side, nearly knocked me from my feet. It was Praepositus Ingenuus, his face black with blood, having peeled away from the slaughter at the gates. 'Domine!' he said urgently.

I saw the source of his concern: vanishing into the eastern horizon was a spiral of dust and a small force of Maxentian horsemen. They had fled from the gate on the far side of the city. I noticed one gleaming like a silver coin. Ruricius, I realised. There would be no catching him now. But to where did he ride? I stared at the eastern horizon as Ruricius vanished beyond it, knowing the moment was drawing closer. Maxentius was near. I could feel it.

6

MAXENTIUS

Verona, 9th March 312 AD

It was a typical early spring day in the province of Venetia. The temperature was mild, but the clouds refused to grant access to the wide blue above. A fine patina of rain repeatedly coated the stones of Verona's roads and alleys, burning off the moment each shower stopped, only to be replaced an hour or so later. I stood on the balcony of the extravagant domus that looked down across the forum towards the grand basilica and the temple of Divus Augustus – a domus with an impressive, if unlucky history. The unfortunate Emperor Vitellius had been the building's first notable resident shortly before his army broke and fled at Bedriacum. Philip the Arab had made use of the domus in his time here, departing via the knife of a subordinate after a lost battle. Sabinus Julianus had made his bid for the throne here only to fall to Carinus' army. I know that Valeria disapproved, that she thought the building cursed, but that sort of superstition drives a man to question his very existence right down to not wearing unlucky socks on a market day. I never liked to be so beholden to such notions.

Perhaps I should have listened to her...

The forum was as busy as it ever got the day after market day, a few measly sellers with less-sought-after wares desperately trying to make ends meet now the good fare of the rural traders had gone for another eight days. A few drunken ex-soldiers were playing a game of 'brigands' for small coin on a board carved in the basilica steps. A small boy was crying by the fountain while his angry mother shouted for him to hurry from across the square. Pigeons shat on the likenesses of Verona's great and good where they stood on triumphal columns around the edge. It was all so mundane that I quite fell into the scene, leaning on the balcony with my elbows and drifting on the simplicity of it all while Valeria rattled on about some logistical issue at the doorway.

My attention was piqued at the sound of multiple hoof beats and as I straightened, I could see horsemen emerging from the *Cardo Maximus*. My throat went dry as the hairs rose on the back of my neck. Horses were not uncommon in the town, and even vehicles and oxen and the like were allowed before sunset, but rarely did one see a full unit of cavalry in an urban setting, even with the army encamped in the vicinity. My commanders had stood by my orders that none of the units were to be given furlough in the city in number greater than a tent party. The last thing any city needs is a hundred drunken soldiers sniffing around the women and starting fights, after all.

Yet here they were. *More* than a hundred men, riding into the forum of Verona, armed and armoured as though ready for war. The effect on the square's population was immediate and impressive. The traders lurked behind their carts, uncertain whether this presented a new and unexpected sales opportunity or a danger to their livelihood and their life. The drunken soldiers rose and straightened automatically, their game forgotten. The pigeons scattered like blood spilled from a height onto a flagstone. The woman, who had been cursing her child for disobedience, was now running to scoop him up in case the horses simply rode him down.

And me?

I wondered who in Tartarus had given the order to allow a unit of battle-ready cavalry into the town like this, but as I twitched and tried to decide whether to yell at them, something sank into my senses and settled in my brain.

These men were armoured from head to toe in chain or scale, laminated plates along their arms and thighs, helmets that left only slitted eyeholes for the wearer and great purple plumes that cascaded down the rear, heavy lances jutting skywards with purple pennants. Their horses were no less armoured.

Clibanarii. The most feared cavalry I had at my command. A storm of steel and muscle waiting to rage at an enemy, and they were *my* clibanarii, for the purple plume was an affectation arranged by Volusianus in days past for show, demonstrating that they carried the power of a true emperor. The problem was: I didn't have my clibanarii at Verona. In fact there were heavy cavalry of sorts spread across the lines of my northern defences, but the only clibanarii were supposed to be in the north-*west* with Ruricius' force. Not here.

For a heart-stopping moment I feared that somehow an enemy had invaded – Constantine? – and that the north-west had fallen. It was a shock, for certain, but seemingly an erroneous one. These men, I could see from my lofty vantage point, were untried by recent battle. These were no unit of straggling survivors, dragged from a blood-drenched battlefield to bring the worst of tidings. They were clean and shining and untouched. They had not bloodied their lances yet.

But what in the name of all the gods were they doing in the forum of Verona? They should be in Taurinorum or somewhere in that region, but then they were a relatively small unit, I realised. Not the entire clibanarii of Ruricius, but a turma of them, perhaps. My nervous curiosity only increased as they spread out in the square and came to a halt and I realised that at their heart was a small knot of men in senior officer's uniforms. Some were in white tunics and some in red, the complex hem and cuff decoration visible even from my distance. Several had the knotted military belt around their midriff over their shining cuirass. All were impressive and neat. Not one was bloodied.

'Why are they here?'

I looked round at the question to find that Valeria had dropped her droning subject and turned to the rail to view the troops entering the square. Her furrowed brow matched mine.

'I have no idea.'

'Are they not supposed to be in Taurinorum?' she asked as though I had the faintest clue as to what was going on.

'I believe so, and those officers... they're some of the best.'

'You know them?'

I shook my head. 'Not at this distance, but there are legionary prefects, praepositae, senior cavalry and auxiliary tribunes. These are men that were chosen by Volusianus and Ruricius for their abilities and strength. The best men available to command the armies we've gathered.'

'Then why are they not commanding those armies?'

I turned an exasperated look on my wife, unsure how to further put over the fact that I knew nothing more than her.

Down below, a centurion from my personal guard had exited the building and was hurrying across the square towards the riders, six guardsmen at his back.

'Come on,' I beckoned Valeria. 'Let's go and find out.'

She declined, stepping back from the balcony. 'These are senior officers in your army. Whatever has occurred, you need to be powerful and in command. It will put over entirely the wrong impression if I am standing beside you.'

I nodded and left the room, though in my heart I wished she was with me. Long gone now were the days when Valeria was my ice queen, untouchable behind her wall of disapproval. In fact, I had come to rely somewhat upon her strength, her unexpected insight and her support. I needed to appear stronger than I felt.

As I passed through a large room on my way, I found Ancharius Pansa discussing some minor matter with his second officer. I gestured to him to follow, and he did.

Where were my advisors? I fumed. Those men to whom I turned when I needed answers or guidance. Anullinus, gone to the knife of an opponent. Ruricius, assigned to the defence of the north-west. Zenas, bound for the east with letters of brotherly conciliation for one of the men I hated most in the world. Volusianus, so outspoken and contrary I had been forced to leave him in Rome. Pansa was the only one in Verona, and he was a shadowy master of spies and killers more than a strategist and politician. Again, I wished Valeria was with me now. She was worth a dozen spymasters. Pansa had the forethought to grab the purple cloak on the stand and drape it across me before we left the room.

At the doorway, I found two of the centurions of my protectors, who broke off their discussion to stand at attention as I passed. I gestured for them to join me too. An emperor should have an appropriate entourage even when caught off-guard. The two centurions were young and fresh-faced, but impressive and sturdy. Their armour and weapons were meant for war, not show. I wavered for just a moment at the sight of the Chi-Rho pendants hanging around their necks, openly proclaiming their faith in the jealous Christian god, but I quickly brushed aside my doubt. Throughout those early days I had pondered what force a man could harness if he could gather the Christians to his cause. I would never turn my gaze from mighty Jove, but who was I to shun good men because of such a thing. They still served Rome and they still served me. In fact, between Zenas and Miltiades, I was coming to suspect that the Christians were far less troublesome than men like Volusianus. They served with *all* their heart.

'Who are you?' I asked the two men as they fell in at my shoulders. They gave their names as Valerius Florentius and Valerius Herodius. Brothers, I realised. I would remember them. On the ground floor I collected four more of my guard, two courtiers I could not even name, a scribe, a standard bearer carrying a bronze draco with a drooping windsock, and three men in expensive tunics whose role and designation completely escaped me. Oh, and a weird-looking, mule-like fellow with protruding teeth and a rich robe who I vaguely remembered as being Verona's bishop. I seemed to attract Christians as honey attracts flies. Finally, at the main entrance I collected the twelve lictors who would announce my rank. My more recent predecessors had retained twenty-four lictors, but I had opted to drop the number back to twelve, like the first great emperors. If twelve was a good enough number for a consul or a king, then it should be enough for an emperor. Besides, have you ever tried holding court in a small room with twenty-four unoccupied attendants?

So, appropriately garbed and invested with an entourage, I emerged into the square. The cavalry were still ahorse, impressive and aloof, though the senior officers had ridden out front and then dismounted, handing their reins to the guardsmen who had crossed to greet them. They were making for the domus, and perhaps I should have waited for a more private audience, but I felt the need to be rather proactive at that moment, and the need to know what in the name of blessed Minerva was going on was too strong to put aside.

My heart lurched at the sight of the officers. Now I was closer I recognised several of them, and their presence backed up my notion that these were the best veteran officers I had. In particular, the stony face of Quadratus, prefect of the Second Parthica, spoke volumes. He was probably the ablest of the lot, one of those men who had placed the purple cloak upon me all those years ago in Rome. It was he who moved to the front and bowed low, his face still grave.

'What is it, Quadratus? What has happened?'

As he straightened I was somewhat taken aback to see a flash of surprise on his face.

'Domine?' he asked in a perplexed tone.

I swept my arm out, indicating the gathered skill and strength of Rome in the square. 'This? The clibanarii? The senior officers? Here, in Verona? Presumably something astonishing has happened to bring you here untouched by battle?'

Bafflement was still plastered across Quadratus' face and I noted frowns and confusion across the entire group. I felt as though a pit were opening beneath me.

'Domine, we came at your call.'

'My call?' Now it was my turn to wear their expression and throw their bewilderment back in their faces.

'Your call, Domine. The letter.'

I was starting to lose my patience now. 'Stop being so cryptic, Quadratus.'

'Domine, your letter arrived three days ago. We have ridden like the wind to attend.'

'What letter?' I demanded, the ire beginning to build. Ah, Father, but I did owe you my temper.

'Demanding our attendance at Verona, Domine. All senior officers. We came as soon as we could.'

'I sent no such letter.' I almost spat the words. What was going on?

'It bore the imperial seal, Domine. It was genuine. Ruricius refused. A few others, feeling that to abandon the defence of Taurinorum was foolish at best, but in these days of treachery and perfidy, it was decided that to refuse a summons from the emperor himself would be unacceptable.'

'My seal?' I know I was shaking now. 'My fucking *seal*? I sent no such letter. You left Ruricius to defend the north-west without the support of an officer core?'

Quadratus nodded, his brow creased and worried now. 'He was furious, Domine. There was hardly a unit left in the place commanded by a man with more than a year's experience – just hopeful boys and wastrels. Junior tribunes and exarchs, primicerii and the like, most barely old enough for whiskers.'

'*He* was furious?' I managed to stutter. My hand was reaching for the sword that I'd not thought to strap on. Good thing, really, since I might just have used it. Certainly, I was on the edge of ordering some sort of agonising punishment for the entire crowd. It was Ancharius Pansa who calmed me. He knew me of old and could see the warning signs. So, of course, could Quadratus, though his arguing would be unlikely to improve my mood.

'Domine,' the ugly spymaster said quietly, coming close so that only a dozen or so of us could hear. 'They did nothing wrong in answering a legitimate summons. There is fault somewhere, but it does not lie with these men who did their duty.'

I was trembling, but I bit down on my next harsh words and instead nodded my agreement. 'True. My apologies for my reactions, Quadratus.'

'None necessary, Domine. I understand entirely.'

I took a deep breath and clenched my fists to stop them shaking. 'Rest quickly, Quadratus, then turn and hurry back before Ruricius needs you.'

That look returned to his face and I felt the pit beneath me widen.

'Domine, there is no point. Constantine will be at the gates now. There is nothing we can do.'

My world suddenly fell apart. Ice flowed in my veins and I felt faint. Had my ears deceived me? I croaked something at him. It was probably simply 'what?'

'Constantine, Domine. Immediately before your summons word came of his advance. He bears down on Taurinorum. His army must have swamped Segusium completely, for no word came from there of his crossing the Alpes, and there was little warning of his approach at all.'

The injured scout. Taurinorum. Constantine. Ruricius.

Constantine...

'He advanced so *suddenly*,' I managed, still stunned by the news.

'Quite, Domine, and the enemy will already have invested Taurinorum by now. Ruricius had solid plans for its defence, though, with a ruse at the gates luring the enemy into the waiting arms of an ambush, and he has adequate forces to carry it out. I fear for their disposal without good officers, for we were to lead the ambush, but he should be able to hold off the enemy for some time.'

Constantine...

'But now we are here, Domine, it is more important that we lend our hands to preparing Verona. Constantine will come here if he breaks Taurinorum and Mediolanum, and if the scouts are even half right, Mediolanum will be little more than an impediment to him.'

'Ruricius will hold,' I said, though my voice cracked.

Quadratus nodded, though uncertainty clouded his face. 'Perhaps, Domine. If he does, then all is well, and he will send us a missive to that effect, but only a fool fails to prepare for the worst. We need to make Verona a bastion. Losing Taurinorum and Mediolanum would be a heavy blow, but if *Verona* falls then Italia is open to all.'

I stared at him, at the very idea of letting Mediolanum fall without so much as a blink.

'Mediolanum?'

'Verona is the key, Domine. We cannot afford to concentrate on Mediolanum or we risk losing Verona. Sacrifices must be made.'

How pale and shaken I must have looked. I couldn't quite believe my ears. All this time I had been so sure – *so sure* – that my old friend would not come. No matter what had passed between us, we would never be at war. Such foolishness was for men like Severus and Licinius, not the sons of Maximian and Constantius, and yet here were some of my best men telling me that my armies were engaged in Taurinorum and that that same Constantine was coming with sword bared.

My world had changed in a flash.

'G... go,' I managed, waving at him.

Pansa gave me a concerned look, then gestured to the prefect. 'Settle in and see to the disposition of your men. Familiarise yourself with the city and the camp and then be in the imperial domus at sunset for a meeting of the consilium.'

The men saluted and dispersed. I remained still. I was having serious trouble not collapsing in shock. As I steadied myself, my heart thundering, Pansa dismissed most of the entourage, both civilian and military, sending the fussy, buck-toothed Bishop of Verona packing with some difficulty.

I stood with my eyes tight shut, trying not to picture my old friend holding a sword to my neck. A few moments later, I snapped them open to find I was almost alone in the square. Just Pansa and the two centurion brothers remained.

'How did this happen, Pansa.'

'You mean the seal, Domine?'

And Constantine. All of it. But yes, the seal specifically. The seal that might well have lost me the north, drawing away Ruricius' veteran officers at a critical moment. 'Yes.'

'The seal would be very difficult to fake. Only a man who was truly familiar with it would be able to do so, and it would have to be perfect. Expertly done. No reputable artisan would work on such a thing, as discovery of involvement would mean a horrifying death. Also, Quadratus is more than familiar with the seal from his time at Albanum and Rome. He says it is definitely the imperial seal; I am content that he is not mistaken.'

'There are only two seals?' I asked, seeking confirmation. Two. One in the form of a ring, which I kept in my purse, since it had been my father's and he had huge fat fingers. I should have had it resized, I suppose, but somehow I had never got round to it. I was never a devotee of jewellery anyway. The other was a stamp seal with an identical design, which remained in my offices on the Palatine. Despite my arguments with Volusianus, I still recognised that he needed my authority in many things and so I had left him it. Two seals. One on my person and the other with Volusianus. It seemed farfetched that someone had faked them.

'Could a message have come from Rome in that time? Between the officers being deployed in Taurinorum and the letter arriving?'

Volusianus. I knew the man had a habit of defying me, but surely not *betrayal*? After all, if I lost, so did he.

Pansa was shaking his head. 'It is just about possible, but neither feasible nor likely, Domine. A fast *liburnian* could coast from Rome to Genua in perhaps three days. Then another day by horse relay. It could *almost* be done, but the disposition of the troops at Taurinorum was decided by Ruricius once he had ridden north. No one in Rome can have known where the officers were or where the peril lay. Volusianus cannot be the culprit, in my opinion, Domine.'

Who was I to argue with the judgement of a man who had run the imperial spy and intelligence network for a generation? If there was a man in existence who could say with a degree of certainty what treachery was possible and what was not, then that man was Ancharius Pansa. I nodded. Not Volusianus, then, and *I* had certainly not sent the letter. So it *had* to be the work of a traitor with a forged seal, regardless of the difficulty and danger in such a thing.

I looked up on an impulse to see Valeria at the balcony looking down at me. She would have something to say about this. I decided, for no reason I could identify, not to reveal the tale of the seal to her. She would rant and rage and begin a thinning of the ranks in order to determine a culprit. I could imagine half my good officers being hauled over the coals for it. It would be terrible for morale, especially given the sudden peril we were in. I would trot out vagaries about the reason for the officers' arrival. I would tell her of the real trouble. Of Constantine. That would be something for her to get her teeth into. She would have many an idea about that, and a number of 'I told you so's', no doubt, but I would weather that. I would also steel myself for tonight's meeting of the consilium.

For I was now at war with my oldest friend.

7

CONSTANTINE

Augusta Taurinorum, 10th March 312 AD

After four days of trying to organise my forces after our victory, I sank into the steaming hot waters of Taurinorum's bathhouse *caldarium*, my muscles softening, my skin tingling, the scent of burning incense sweet and soporific. I ducked under the surface then rose and smoothed my hair back from my brow before resting shoulder-deep at the poolside, head tilted back. Threads of clear water gurgled lazily from the mouths of sculpted satyrs set into niches all around the bathhouse walls, feeding the pool, winking in the shafts of sunlight from the high windows. The steady ripples on the surface of the pool were hypnotic, slowing and flattening as they gently glided out towards the fountain's edge. The steam rose in gentle puffs, partly obscuring the fresco of Neptune on the ceiling, the God of the Sea majestic, holding his trident high, surrounded by leaping dolphins. I closed my eyes and, for a moment, I thought of nothing. Pure, sweet nothing. It had been some time since I had known such blissful anoesis. A perfect contrast to the preceding months of marching through bitter winds and blizzards, enduring a constant wind of horse dung and the rank odour of unwashed soldiers, mind constantly turning over the great strategy and minor details of the campaign.

A sound, the slight shift of bronze scales, spoiled the moment. I half opened my eyes to see one of the two Cornuti standing watch at either end of the room, shuffling as he tried to scratch under the collar of his armour.

My eyes were about to close again when I noticed movement: a slave quietly approaching with a pot of oil and a strigil. I took the things from the young man, smiled and waved him away, for I have always preferred to wash myself. I moved to the poolside steps and began massaging oil into my scarred shoulders, then my chest and legs. Long, slow strokes that felt sore but soothing at once.

Taurinorum is mine! I thought for the hundredth time that day. It was a greatly satisfying thought, like the *clunk* of a heavy and well-oiled lock turning. One of the three bulwarks of the north had been secured. It was the adversity that made it most satisfying – we had not faced just a city garrison, but an ambuscade, and still we had prevailed.

In that moment of peaceful contemplation, I even forgot how Taurinorum was won. But not for long. First arose the memory of the stink at the western gates where the slaughter had occurred. Then the sights of the faces of the young men, green to soldiery, then grey in death.

Victory? I laughed inside without a morsel of humour. *No... a slaughter, a cull!* I looked down into the water's surface and saw my own reflection: listless, black-ringed eyes – not at all like the handsome and fine busts men raised across the empire... more like that old rogue, Diocletian, in the days when he began to shrivel and fester in his own horrific pool of guilt.

I pressed my thumb and forefinger together and tried to

focus my mind elsewhere. Unfortunately it didn't land too far away from the matter of the recent battle – specifically, the strange make-up of Ruricius' forces. I had had my suspicions that something was afoot even during the fray. In the moments after the battle, my army had acclaimed the thwarting of the ambush and the triumph over the enemy force as a great victory. However, as my men cleared the bodies and washed the gore from the city gates, I became certain that we had won mainly thanks to the terrible planning of the enemy. Yes, the ambush was well-placed. Yet that mass of soldiery had been led by novice officers and young men. I thought of the irate, puce-faced Ruricius on the walls, orchestrating the ambush from the battlements. He had a reputation for bravery and sound battle tactics, but that attack – throwing untried officers and recruits at my veterans – had been sheer folly. Had he simply kept his forces inside, they could have held the place for the entire spring, or at least long enough for a strong reinforcement to arrive.

Maxentius' problem, not mine, I thought, relieved to be able to forget the matter.

I glanced over to the *apodyterium*, and could see through the steam that the slave had, as I had asked, brought me a crisp civilian tunic and sandals. Apt, for here at Taurinorum I had temporarily broken off our march and set down the mantle of war.

There was no doubt left: Maxentius now knew I was here in Italia. Thus, every step from here on in would have to be cautious and watchful on all sides, and this place was ideal to halt and plan for such an advance. Time to take stock of our supplies – drawn upon more heavily than we had anticipated – and evaluate the number of able-bodied soldiers. Time to—

'Centurion, take your men to the gates – be quick!' Big

77

Batius' voice pealed from somewhere outside. A rapid drumming of hobnails on flagstones followed.

All sense of contentment and security drained away. A great dread seized me – had Ruricius returned with a new force? I shot to my feet, spraying water, instantly cold. I slipped and skidded along the poolside, soaking, still slick with washing oil, naked and lacking any grace. I grabbed the tunic the slave had left out and pulled it on... only to hear the *riiip* of tearing stitches. I gasped in disbelief, for it would have barely fitted my lad, Crispus! But there was no time to find something else to wear. I snatched for my swordbelt three times before I actually managed to pick the damned thing up. The sandals would take too long to tie. So, barefoot and still sopping wet, I staggered out into the bright city forum in a dramatic puff of steam. Big Batius was there, leaning by one billet house door, waving a century of his Cornuti legionaries out and towards the city's western gates, toying with a toothpick. He gave me one look, confused and slightly amused by my ridiculous attire, then informed me we were not in fact under attack.

'The first grain convoy from the north has arrived,' he explained.

Dread became relief, then delight. I had organised the grain wagons carefully: a convoy of mule-drawn vehicles were to steadily resupply us on the campaign, coming down from Gaul where the absence of the legions meant there should be a surplus. It was a sound strategy, I was sure; we could not come here and hope to rely solely on the provender available in these lands, lest we quickly turn the populace against us. 'The grain is *here*? So why the shouting?'

He beckoned me to a watchman's turret, mid-city, and led me up the stairs. We emerged onto the turret roof, and Batius pointed towards the western gates. On the grassy plain outside the city, two masses of armoured men were remonstrating with one another. *My* men. A thin line of wagons waited, halted, between them.

'I watched it unfold from the gatehouse,' Batius explained. 'The Thirtieth Ulpia were performing some drill exercise on the western plains, and the Petulantes were patrolling the countryside. They both saw the grain coming in at the same time, I'm told. Both rushed to escort the wagons into the city.'

I understood. This first convoy was an important moment – a validation of my campaign strategy. The two regiments probably hoped I might grant them an additional share of the rations for their unsolicited help. What I did not understand was why the foremost three wagons lay on their sides, the golden wheat they carried spilled across the earth and the mules braying like the soldiers.

'They started to argue about who would have the honour of escorting the wagons inside.'

'Both?' I said, bemused.

Batius smiled wryly. 'Ah, the old common sense, eh? Well, in the eyes of that lot out there, sharing wasn't an option. Quickly, it became about seniority, then rapidly it dissolved into slurs about heresy and false gods.'

I planted a hand on my face and dragged the fingertips down, slowly. This, again?

'The Petulantes seemed to think that tipping the wagons over was a great way of showing how much stronger Sol Invictus was compared to the Christian God,' Batius grumbled.

Well they certainly wouldn't be getting any bonus grain ration, I seethed. Neither would the Ulpia, I decided, seeing that some of them were brandishing swords at the lesser-numbered Petulantes. Something struck me then: 'You sent your Cornuti out to deal with the dispute?'

The big man nodded.

'Didn't you say they were beginning to become fractured in their beliefs?'

Another nod. Then a twist of concern. 'Aye... perhaps I should have through that one through a little better.'

We both watched as the feather-helmed Cornuti century flooded out into the plain, into the divide between the two regiments... and quickly began to shout and rage like fresh fuel added to a fire.

'Ah, testicles,' Batius muttered under his breath. Then he turned to me. 'Perhaps you need to address them.'

'You know where that will lead,' I replied quickly. 'They'll ask me which god is greater, a question I cannot answer if I want my army to remain cohesive.'

'Then send out old Lactantius,' he mused, pointing down to the nearby governor's gardens – a peristyled riot of colours: bushes of purple iris, spring jasmine and yellow mimosa, all washed in morning sunlight. From up here I could see my old tutor, reclined on a bench on the far side of the peristyled grounds, resting his ancient bones and reading over the latest portion of script he had written. A tortoiseshell cat basked on his lap, lazily clawing at a lock of his long white hair.

Batius was right, I realised. Lactantius was deft at guiding the men of the legions' minds when it came to matters of faith, at delivering impartial and calming advice to those who were about to brain one another. I descended the turret steps, hurried across the avenue and entered the governor's gardens.

Thrushes sang and moorhens chattered and clicked in the branches of a nearby olive tree. The sounds should have been pleasant to my ears, but given the crisis outside the city, every note was a distraction and an annoyance.

He didn't notice me approach – too busy talking to the cat and marvelling at the bees and insects that landed on him and buzzed in the air nearby.

'Stop,' he said as I approached.

I halted, for a moment fearing that an enemy archer had an arrow trained upon my back.

'Don't move,' he said, then slowly leaned to one side, extended a finger and enticed an olive-green and bright-pink moth to walk along his digit. 'An elephant hawk moth,' he whispered. 'A most beautiful creature, wouldn't you say?' He stared down his nose at the moth, examining it from different angles. 'You can tell he is a male from the breadth of his thorax. They are drawn to manicured gardens, because they like the more fragrant flowers. Yet it's very unusual to see this species in flight at this time of year. The creator is ever unpredictable.'

'Old tutor—' I tried to interrupt.

He held up a finger of his free hand. Like a boy in his class again I instantly fell silent.

'They who believe that there are many gods, unwittingly predicate their beliefs on dispute and contention,' he said, eyes tracking the moth as it moved along his finger. 'Homer represented the gods at war among themselves, some desiring that Troy should be taken, others opposing it. Thus, if we are ever to know harmony, we must move past that old way, see the truth: that the universe is ruled by the will of one.'

'Old tutor, now is not the time to teach me,' I said, exasperated.

'Only a poor pupil believes their learning is complete,' Lactantius said, moving his finger a little, setting the moth to flight, then swinging his twig-like legs from the bench to sit upright and wagging his vacated finger at me. 'The wise man knows that he knows nothing.' Then he beheld my state of dress and frowned. 'And the blind man walks around wearing his son's tunic.'

I gasped in further exasperation. 'I need you to guide my men, old tutor. The legions are quarrelling again, out on the plains.'

'But I have promised Lucia here a saucer of milk,' he complained. The cat shot me a sour look, supporting the argument.

'The matter is pressing; they have drawn swords upon one another. The grain is at stake.'

The old fellow's face sagged as he realised the gravity of the situation. With a wriggle of his knees, the cat hopped down and darted off, and he stood with his cane. I called over a wagon and put him aboard with a pair of Cornuti as an escort. With a crack of the driver's whip, the wagon trundled towards the city gates.

I climbed back up the turret to watch with Batius. It was incredible. The old man – merely a white dot at this distance – disembarked from the carriage and the quarrelling regiments quickly became less animated, affording him due reverence. They would have done the same for me, of course, but I would not have been able to assuage their anger in the way he then did.

He walked slowly around the quarrelling regiments, his old arms rising slowly, gesturing in a way that was neither aggressive nor lacking assertiveness, including all, alienating none. I could not hear what he said out there, but it worked. Gentle, measured and guiding words. Within the hour, Lactantius' wagon led the grain vehicles inside the city, while the Ulpia and the Petulantes worked together to shovel up the spilled grain and right the tipped-over wagons.

I vowed to myself at that moment that I would find a way to emulate him, to be both their emperor and the voice of all their faiths.

* * *

Later that day, under a dusk sky streaked with lavender light, I sat where Lactantius had been. Lucia the cat glowered at me from the iris bed, still injured by my interruption that had cost her a plate of milk. Outside the walled gardens, I heard the sounds of gaiety, men and women yammering, laughing, singing and flutes. The air was spiced with the scent of baking loaves, malting barley and roasting fish. Once again I felt assured and comfortable – helped no end by the fact I was now dressed in a loose-fitting and comfortable man's tunic and sandals.

A gentle rattling sound arose beside me: Crito, Governor of the Alpes Cottiae province entire and owner of this fine urban palace, shambled over to me, carrying a platter of silver cups all teetering on the tray. He had the vague appearance of some sort of carrion hawk when I first saw him on the city walls, holding up the olive wreath to me to indicate his loyalty, but up close I saw he most definitely resembled a vulture, his scrawny neck bent out and then up, his ring of thinning, grey hair and beaky nose completing the likeness. It was the first time I had had the opportunity to talk to him since the day of the ambush and our victory. He plucked a cup from the tray and handed it to me.

'The finest Ligurian – a toast to your victory,' he simpered, taking the other cup for himself and sipping it before theatrically releasing a decadent 'aaaah'.

I cocked an eyebrow, amused by his blatant toadying.

'I would like to reassure you, Domine, that I had no part in that terrible ambuscade,' Crito said. 'Indeed, it was only when messengers brought forward news that Ruricius had arrived at the docks of Genua that I realised legions were being moved from Rome to defend the north. Even when Ruricius arrived here, he told me nothing. He took charge of this palace and made it his war headquarters. When locals in the mountains brought in word of your approach, he held a council with his officers. I heard them mutter and curse your name,' he recalled, then his eyes widened in unctuous obedience, 'but not I, not I.'

I took a sharp swig of the wine, rolling it over my tongue and knowing it would not be the last cup I would have this evening. 'Crito, I wouldn't trade a mule-turd to hear what you might or might not have said about me before I arrived here. You wisely offered no resistance once Ruricius' army was beaten and he himself fled. You have secured your freedom and your life by doing so.'

The man's eyes relaxed a little, his panic over.

'You said Ruricius held a council with his officers?'

Crito nodded, top lip tucked over the bottom one like a man afraid to speak.

'Tell me about them.'

'Quadratus, Prefect of the Second Parthica, is the best of them. There were many others too. Men with long histories and famous names,' Crito said, then hastily added, 'but not as famous as yours, Domine. No name is as famous as yours.'

I held a hand up to slow his overwhelming servility. 'So why did he ambush me with such a weakly commanded force?'

'He used what he had, Domine.' Crito frowned. 'Only hours after he disbanded his officers from that meeting, he went to his quarters and they to the barracks. It was there the letter arrived – the messenger delivered it to Quadratus.'

'The letter?' I sighed, becoming tired of the conversation.

'The letter from Verona, calling Quadratus and the officer corps away to that city with a detachment of riders.'

'Why?' I snapped.

'To protect the empero—' Crito started then broke down in an obviously false coughing fit. 'To protect the *tyrant!*'

Every hair on my body stood on end. 'Then it is true: Maxentius is at Verona?'

Crito nodded, although it was more like a grovelling bow.

I stood, my every hackle risen, my eyes darting as I paced around the gardens.

Crito bleated on and on, following me, but I didn't hear another word of what he had to say. I think he must eventually have worked out that he was being a pest, because he drifted away after a time. I stopped my relentless pacing and rested the heels of my hands on the lip of an age-old travertine fountain. I took a deep, long breath, my lungs swelling, and dipped my head. The fountain's sun-bleached stonework was freckled with spots of cream and white lichen. Orange-gold fish swam below the surface, glinting like treasure. *Verona*, I repeated over and over. Maxentius had advanced from the viper's pit of Rome. The War for the West could be over far sooner than I or any of my generals had anticipated. Hubris began to surge through me. It was only then I noticed the reflection of the sharp sickle moon hovering in the water's surface, just beside the outline of my neck. *Indeed, the war could be over soon*, I thought wryly, *but for him… or you?*

It was only thanks to Lucia's sudden purring that I realised that another had entered the gardens. She had been crouching beside the cat for some time, I realised, watching me.

'Fausta?' I said.

She continued to stroke the cat's neck. The creature finally submitted, rolling over onto its back. 'So you and my brother will meet soon?' she said.

I frowned.

'I heard everything that you and Crito discussed.'

'You know he and I must face one another.'

'I know.'

We were silent for a time before she spoke again. 'Before we came to this city, I had never before seen the ruination of battle. In the nights since, I have been unable to sleep. Every time I close my eyes I hear their screams, see them fighting: cleaving each other open, soaking the ground with blood. So many bodies.'

I could have wept, for she described the very things that had haunted my dreams since my first experiences of battle. Estranged though we were, never in all my days had I wished those wild, fiery and tormenting visions to plague the mind of my wife.

She picked up the cat, cradling it in her arms protectively. 'What happened here is just the beginning, isn't it?'

I tried to answer a few times but could not. In the end I had to avert my eyes from hers, and could answer only with a stiff, reluctant nod.

8

MAXENTIUS

I was in the bath house. It was late afternoon on a damp and depressing day in Verona in which even the birds had given up hope and hid from the repetitive deluges. The only wildlife seemed to be a thousand snails crossing the smooth stone surfaces of the city, making for wet soil nearby. I had missed my usual early afternoon session in the baths as the seemingly endless bureaucracy ran on and on with a procession of po-faced clerks bringing me decisions to make and documents to approve. War, it seemed, needed as much administration as peace. Finally, feeling in need of relaxation as much as I ever had after a fight, I had strolled out onto the balcony, been subjected to a brief shower, counted the snails and then given up and headed for the baths.

It was the one place I was not disturbed. Ever. I had made that a rule both in Rome and Verona. My enforced solitude there was born of the need for peace and quiet, to marshal my whirling thoughts, yet the place reminded me unpleasantly of finding Anullinus in a pool of blood in his own baths. There were always two guards on the door these days. Better safe than sorry, but with two of Pansa's men on the door and no

SIMON TURNEY & GORDON DOHERTY

attendant, I could relax. Valeria was lightly scathing at the idea of an emperor carrying his own towel or applying his own oil and using his own strigil, but in addition to the peace it granted there was always the added sense of security in not putting my body in the hands of a man who could be in the pay of my enemies.

I had done a few exercises. Not enough, really, but I had cheated, counting twice for each push up in order to get into the soothing water faster. I had oiled and scraped and then slipped into the *laconium* then the warm bath. I should probably have moved faster through my routine, given that I'd started later in the day than usual, but I had no desire to rush into the cold pool, the warm water lapping about my chin and soothing away some of my myriad cares.

Thus it was that I was far from finished with my bathing when I was rudely interrupted. The guard who had been at the door cleared his throat from the next room.

'Domine?'

I frowned, pulling myself up and resting my elbows on the poolside. I was not interrupted at my bath. Ever. 'What is it?'

'Your presence is required in the *aula regia*, Domine.'

'Required by whom?'

'The empress, Domine. A force of men has returned to the city, led by Ruricius Pompeianus.'

A chill ran through me. Ruricius? My treacherous mind furnished me with an image of a field of bodies, crows pecking at sightless eyes, which was replaced by the equally unwelcome image of my old friend Constantine laughing from the walls of Taurinorum, garbed as a conquering emperor.

'Wait outside.'

I leapt from the water and very lightly towelled down. In the apodyterium, shivering with the sudden change of temperature, I wrapped my *subligaculum* around my nethers and threw on my tunic, belting it military-fashion in the old way so the hem was above the knee. I always felt it looked better to meet military types on their own ground if possible. Slipping into my soft, calfskin shoes, I exited, rubbing my hair and trying to smooth it down. I would never have thought of presenting myself in public in such a manner, but this was no state audience, and Ruricius' arrival too important for me to delay.

With the two guardsmen at my heel, I pitter-pattered through the extensive domus. A small crowd was gathered outside the door of the room I used as my aula regia, or chamber of state. Not members of the public, per se, but people I had no intention of passing time with at the moment: bishops, councillors, administrators, sour-faced politicians and the like. They turned toward me as I approached but I waved them aside, matching their expression, and the guards forged ahead, clearing them out of the way like the prow of a ship. I watched them bob and wash past, eddying behind me as the guard thrust open the door and I entered. The *ab admissionibus* hurriedly straightened to announce me.

'His glorious Majesty, Emperor of Rome, Father of the State, High Priest and Consul for the fourth time, the living embodiment of Hercules'—*who had slipped that nonsense in?*—'Marcus Aurelius Valerius Maxentius Augustus.'

I was already across the room and at my seat by the time the titles had finished and I sank into it, motioning for the door to be closed behind me, keeping that rabble away. Lictors lined the room to each side and the throne was flanked to the left by Valeria, seated, and to the right by Ancharius Pansa, standing and glowering.

Ruricius looked tired. He also looked dirty. I felt suddenly

SIMON TURNEY & GORDON DOHERTY

very conscious of the fact that I had clearly been called from my bath.

'The north falls like stacked boards, Domine,' he said with no preamble.

'Tell me.'

'Segusium must have fallen without a great deal of trouble. We heard no word of it. Constantine must have come fast and taken it without allowing word to escape. The treacherous dog sneaks into our lands rather than coming under a banner with a bloodstained spear and a declaration of war.'

But there *had* been word, hadn't there? One brave rider, wounded, hurtling south to warn us, but succumbing to infection and illness and dying on a ship without ever delivering his tidings, his very existence ignored by us all. Ignored at *my* insistence. Damn it.

'Tell me of Taurinorum.' *Constantine. Gods, but how often had I denied it?*

'Taurinorum should have held, Domine. It should have been the rock that held the north. I had the forces and the plan. I had the walls and the time. Moreover, despite capricious city folk, there are still men in the mountains loyal to your cause, and after Segusium word of his coming had trickled down from unseen sources despite all his effort to avoid it. With our forces, the defences and such warning, we should have held.'

I nodded sagely and motioned for him to continue. 'But I could not win, Domine,' he said. '*No one* could have won that fight, no matter the terrain, the plan or the mettle of the men. I was alone in command. One man trying to marshal an army in the field with just junior tribunes who had no experience and centurions doing their best but with no overall guiding hand. It should have been glorious. It was a disaster. The men broke and fled readily. Their centurions held them for some time, and I tried to coordinate everything, but without able officers it was an impossible task. Our cataphract charged the enemy. I could see the result coming. Constantine opened a door for them with a knife behind his back. They were riding into a forfex. I sent a tribune to stop them and he went to the wrong fucking unit. This is what I had to work with. A cataphract charging into oblivion and the ridiculous naïve little tribune goes off to warn some peripheral light cavalry unit who are more in danger of dying from boredom.'

I rubbed my temples. Taurinorum. Gateway to Italia.

'And all this because of your written command.' No 'Domine' this time. Just heavy, dripping accusation.

'Ruricius, back down,' I said flatly, carefully.

His eyes were blazing, angry. 'You were so sure he would not come, but so nervous of Licinius crossing the border that not only did you marshal unnecessary forces in the east, but you stripped me of precisely what I needed to hold the west.'

'Ruricius…'

'No, Domine,' he almost spat. 'You task me with something critical, ignoring the advice of your senior prefect – who, it turns out, was right all along – and then you remove my ability to carry out that task. No man has the given right to demand an explanation from his emperor, but I *earned* that right in blood and bone and shit at Taurinorum, Domine. Why take my officers from me?'

I felt that old anger rising in me at the manner in which he was speaking. Indeed, both Pansa and Valeria were looking at me expectantly, waiting for me to launch into him. Yet I bit down on it, forced a cold settlement on the rising anger and nodded. I would not do that. Because for all his manner, Ruricius was right. He did deserve an explanation.

'There are other forces at work here, Ruricius.'

Now he looked less certain. He had expected an argument or an admonition. 'Domine?'

'I wrote no such letter. I sealed no such order. Your officers arrived here entirely unexpected. I would have sent them back, for I know how valuable they are, but it would have been too late. Quadratus was certain you would be engaged long before he reached you. I had hoped... I had prayed that even without them you would have the resources to hold.'

He shook his head wearily, the fight gone out of him. 'Taurinorum fell. Constantine is now master of the north-west. Who could have sent the letter, Domine? Who would see us fail in the west?'

I sighed. 'We have been asking that very question. I have one seal in my chamber and the other is with Volusianus.'

'Volusianus did not have time, Domine,' Ruricius said.

'We came to that same conclusion, which suggests that however unlikely Pansa here believes it to be, someone must have forged my seal.'

My seal, stripping Taurinorum of its defences. This was truly an underhand world.

Ruricius almost slumped. 'Since then we have fallen back. There are a few defensible spots between here and Taurinorum, and I have small garrisons here and there, but the next true bastion is this very city. These walls. This is where Constantine will set his ballista sights next. I gathered as many of the survivors of Taurinorum as I could and brought them with me. I have no doubt that others survived the chaos, and there will be units and fragments of units all over the north now, but they will all turn east and come here. This is the next place, and we have to hold here, Domine.'

'What about Mediolanum?' I said, frowning. 'Stout walls, good terrain, excellent position.'

'There is not sufficient time to manoeuvre all the units we need there, and even if we could we would have to strip Verona to do it. It would be foolish. Mediolanum is now a necessary sacrifice in order to save Verona. You *want* to save Verona, Domine?'

'Yes.'

'Good. Because if we cannot hold Verona...'

My heart ached to sacrifice Mediolanum. It had been my father's capital for a while, and I had spent time in its gilded corridors myself. It was my city more than any other outside Rome, and to lose it was a heavy blow. Still, I nodded. I was well aware of the stakes in this particular game. If Verona fell, then the road to Rome was open. Not that it would matter to me, for I was here. If Verona fell then I would fall with it.

* * *

I took no joy in the rest of the day. Who could? My old friend was coming for me. Even when Quadratus had brought me word I still found a corner of my mind hoping it was all some kind of mistake. Because then there had been no war. No blood. Just an absence of news from Segusium and vague reports. But now there was no denying it. Ruricius had fought the man and lost. Constantine had taken an irreversible step.

Damn him. Didn't he know we were friends? The empire had been split for generations now. Yes, we both claimed the West, but perhaps we could have worked together, two old friends in concord against the armies of the loathsome Licinius and the despicable Daia; we might have been able to coexist and create a Rome to be proud of. Instead here we were tearing each other apart, both seeking alliances with a man we hated against a man we called brother. And all because of insults and bile spewed in anger. Was there really no plastering over the cracked walls? How stupid are emperors?

I rubbed my neck wearily as I trod the floor of the corridor back to the rooms I shared with Valeria. I opened the door and sagged as I entered, closing it behind me and slipping off my shoes to shuffle my feet gratefully in the thick carpet of the main room. Valeria was there, at her desk, busily penning letters. I smiled. I never seemed to have time for personal correspondence anymore. I only wrote letters of state through my secretary, while Valeria managed to write to Euna, securing word of our poor youngest son for me, and to my stepsister Theodora down on the family estate in Campania.

'This,' I said in a tired tone, 'has been a trying day.'

'It has,' she agreed, without looking up from her missive.

'Theodora or Euna?'

'Neither,' she replied. 'I find I am living someone else's life here, with the personal effects of my predecessors. That is not acceptable, so I am sending to Rome for a few of my possessions. No more than a single cart. I'm sure Volusianus will spare a detail of men to escort it north.'

'Valeria, by the time your favourite brush arrives, we will probably have won or lost the war. Either way I will be returning to Rome, with a wreath above my head and chin high, or in a jar, bound for a tomb.'

'You are too morose. A pessimist.'

'A realist,' I corrected.

'A pessimist,' she insisted. 'Constantine only won Taurinorum because of some stupid mistake. He will not win Verona the same way. You have adequate forces and adequate commanders. This is a bastion, unbreakable.'

'I wish I had your confidence, dear.' I sighed, and a frown passed across my face – a shadow across my soul – as she finished her letter and fastened it in the scroll case. 'Is that my seal?'

'Yes,' she said casually, gesturing with it as she dipped it in the wax on the case and pulled it back, leaving the imperial imprint.

'Valeria, that is the imperial seal. Only I and my secretary have the right to use that on pain of death.'

Valeria snorted. 'Tartarus would claim you before you had me beheaded for this. Besides, *Volusianus* has your seal.'

'Why? Why use my seal. You know the current importance of that? The controversy surrounding it? Pansa is supposed to keep that under lock and key in this room.'

'It is under lock and key in *this* room, Maxentius, and so am I. I use it for anything urgent. If I send an ordinary letter it takes too long, and sometimes the couriers lose them. Sometimes even on purpose, I am led to believe. But with that seal on, the letter moves like lightning and is guaranteed to arrive safely. It is just common sense, dear.'

I was wide-eyed. I suppose probably other emperors had let their wives use the imperial seal, and under normal circumstances I would have hardly blinked, but with what had just happened...

As she put the seal and wax away in the drawer, I found awful fanciful notions running through my head. Valeria writing demands for the withdrawal of officers. Her gleaming eyes seeking the fall of Taurinorum. I shook it off as she moved over to the bed and sat with a sigh of relief. No. Why would my wife do such a thing?

But had she not once been cold and distant – hated me, even? She was the daughter of a man I had called enemy all his life. She had not sought my hand and I had grudgingly taken hers. She had spent most of our marriage taunting me,

riling me, shunning me. Then, so recently, after the death of...
so recently had she turned to me; had become my wife in
more than name. Was it possible that had all been a ruse? A
long plan to ruin me? Could she have been that cold? That
calculating?

It was not a question I really needed to ask myself. She
could be all those things. I hated to think that might be the
case, but it was undeniably possible.

'Are you coming to bed?' she said, interrupting my
suspicions.

'I... not yet. I think I want a glass of wine. Perhaps more.'

'Then come in quietly, for I shall be asleep.'

I nodded and turned, leaving the room. Back past the
doors to the other rooms and along that corridor, out into
the more public areas of the domus. As I emerged from the
corridor, past the two guards that always kept a watch on
my apartment, I spotted Pansa crossing another hallway and
called for him, hurrying over. I joined the man as he was
moving towards the *triclinium* where I would find my wine
anyway, and walked alongside him.

'Pansa, could someone have made their way unnoticed
into my chambers?'

The commander of my guard, once the foremost spymaster
in the empire, shook his head. 'No, Domine. Since the day
I took on this responsibility from Volusianus I have been
concerned about the dangers of assassination. A dagger in
the night is an easy way to win a war, after all. I have kept
a careful watch on both you and your quarters, staff and
entourage. I would know if someone unauthorised were in
your rooms.'

'And authorised folk? Who are they?'

Pansa pursed his lips. 'Your body slave and secretary, your

wife and her slaves, but no slave or freedman or woman is at liberty in the apartment, Domine. Unless they are with you or the empress, they are always accompanied by myself or one of my men. I am very thorough, Domine.'

Yes, I knew that. Few men were as thorough as a man who had commanded the frumentarii. So no one had touched my seal other than Valeria and myself. And Volusianus? Even if he had been foolish enough to lose the one in Rome, there had not been time to use it.

In the end I drank a lot more wine than I had intended that evening, and even then sleep did not come easily.

9

CONSTANTINE

Mediolanum, 1st April 312 AD

Eyes, watching. Everywhere. The flagged way to Mediolanum was fringed with pine woods, and they gathered there, in the shade beneath the branches, to stare and whisper: countryfolk – farmers, goat- and swineherds – watching my silvery army flood into their lands. *Liberators? Conquerors?* I could only guess as to how they beheld us.

Just then I heard a rustling sound. My head snapped round to a landholding of emmer wheat on the right-hand side of the road. Just ahead, the high stalks were shaking madly, a golden cloud of chaff rising. Something was coming – *fast* – for the side of my column. The closest three centuries on that side bristled, they, like me, knowing this could only be one thing...

A boy, scrawny as a plucked bird, burst from the wall of wheat and onto the flagged road. There, he ducked down to scoop a stray goat kid up to his chest and then sped across to the other side of the road and took shelter under the pine branches with the others. My shoulders relaxed and I heard a murmur of curses and a gentle *hiss* of quarter-drawn spathae being slid back into scabbards around me. The boy shook as he watched me trot on past, as if he thought I might ride over there and slay the tiny creature. My heart ached for the boy, but at the same time I was angered that he and the others watching felt they could judge me. I wondered if I would ever be in a position again where I could explain my motives to the lad or to his father or mother or any of the workers who watched me. Whatever I was to them – a monster, a champion – I realised how much the events of the past fifteen years had shaped me into something different, calloused, suspicious, angry, laden with regret.

It was a curious thing which drew my thoughts next. Just as one only notices the softness of yesterday's garment when he dons a scratchier robe the following day, or appreciates the fire he had been sitting at after he steps out into the cold... I could *feel* a difference in my army. Perhaps it was the fractionally quieter drumming of boots on the flagstones – or maybe the absence of certain voices and contentious songs of faith from particular regiments. True enough, I was ploughing into my enemy's northern holdings like a spearhead. But, just as Maxentius' overambitious and poorly led cavalry had perished within my forfex at Taurinorum, my every stride forward across these lands had seen my forces shrink. Some generals might say the death toll was low – only four hundred casualties and two hundred wounded. Regardless, every loss troubled me... more so than in any barbarian campaign. In any case it was consolidation that had robbed me of far more men than any Maxentian blade. It had to be this way. No point in seizing the northern cities purely to disrupt Maxentius' affairs. Seize them and *hold* them – that was the way it had to be. My force had been whittled down to thirty-four thousand now. For every man of Maxentius' I had slain or captured, one of my own had been tied down in garrisoning the newly taken cities, and Maxentius – damn him – had far more men to lose than I.

The Third Herculia were now well established back at Segusium and since then, the Thirtieth Ulpia – one of the staunchly and boisterously Christian legions – had likewise been detached and stationed at the camp outside Taurinorum, tasked with ensuring no counterattack might rob me of that newly won city. Regardless, it was the thirty-four thousand still marching with me who mattered most. For within the light of this day, we would reach Mediolanum. The capital of the north. Once, before Maxentius had risen against me and claimed these lands as his own, Mediolanum had been the seat of his father, Maximian, the Western Augustus. Fitting it was, then, that I should come to claim it today as my own.

I heard crunching and splashing up ahead, and saw my vanguard riders walking their steeds down the gentle silver-shale banks of the River Ticinus, then into the shallows and across a ford – the waters opalescent blue in the golden light of noon, the currents creaming, foaming and chuckling around their steeds' thighs. The beauty of the riverbank was an odd thing in itself – the river, stretching north to south before us like a barring arm, would have been one of the first things I would have buttressed: blockade the fording points, make castles of the bridges and line the banks with ballistae and archers. *If* I were Maxentius. A dry smile wriggled its way across my lips as I realised I was doing it again: living in the past, when we both were young men, when we had shared wine and bread and talked like brothers.

Swiftly, the distant memories changed like molten bronze bursting through the charred scum floating atop a smith's urn.

Son of a whore! I imagined Maxentius scream at me,

seeing the strange shape of him now as a man, chin dark with bristles, face weathered with age, eyes red-rimmed and cruel with tyranny. My hands tightened on the reins. This false emperor had cast dark slurs upon my family line, tried to assassinate me, and had taken these very lands from me. Well, right now, I was taking them back.

'The river is undefended, Domine,' Ingenuus barked, riding to me then wheeling round to take the pace from his steed. His eyes flashed with courage and sincerity as he added: '*This* time I made my riders sweep an extra mile in every direction. There will be no ambush.'

I nodded once, faintly. I knew that Maxentius – or more likely the cadre of generals – would not be so foolish as to try the same thing twice. He had learned at least something from me, it seemed.

The rattle of hobnails rose and echoed as we narrowed into a thin front and climbed over a stony hump-bridge across the River Ticinus. On the opposite banks, Ingenuus' riders stood in clusters, forming a bridgehead while more lined the road ahead, eyes watchful. A vineyard fringed the road on both sides, well ordered, the spring budburst adding spots of purple to the dark green foliage. No enemy archers or riders could be hidden in these parts, I realised, eyeing the clay-soil in the gaps between the vines, seeing flatlands for miles. Ahead lay a hazy crescent of low, green hills, clouds rising like mountains into the blue sky. Hugged in the crescent of hills was a thin band of brick-red fortification. That was all I could see of it from here. The colour alone was enough to send a spike of malice through me: Maximian's red walls. The fat old bastard – whose shade I hated even more than his living son – had embellished Mediolanum with many things: theatres, a mint, the Baths of Hercules and a circus... but the treacherous cur's walls would be his last stinging swipe at me. Even in death, the bastard continued to infuriate.

I had my army slow as we drew closer, forming a battle line. Archers sped wide and Ingenuus and his riders made a circle of the city's countryside.

Batius grumbled, his flinty eyes on the chunky red walls of Mediolanum, the sweep of his gaze snagging every time it reached one of the many multi-sided towers studding the flat, featureless, unbreakable redoubt. Up there in those towers were glinting iron beaks: loaded ballistae – devices that could wreak havoc among my legions.

Was that sentries gathering above the gatehouse? Once again I fretted over numbers, doubted my plans and felt like a lost child. I pinched thumb and forefinger together, seeking calm. It arrived, in the form of a vivid, red petal.

The petal landed on my thigh, having drifted through the air. I lifted it, confused. For a moment, the scent of rose enchanted me – made me think of Fausta, riding her wagon safely with the rearguard. Then a pale petal fell, and then a yellow one. Batius' lower jaw jutted like an angered bulldog's as he looked up and around, his craggy face spotted with sweat and a few of the falling red petals landed on his cheeks giving him the look of a rather unsightly whore.

Krocus, riding just behind us, laughed like a bear. 'At ease, pretty boy,' he mocked. 'Rejoice, Domine,' he continued, turning to me, pointing to the twin-towered red gatehouse, where I saw the 'sentries' clearly. A pair of white-gowned Vestals, shovelling handful after handful of blooms into the air, the petals drifting in the pleasant breeze and raining down on us thickly now.

'Mediolanum has learned from the errors of the defenders of Segusium and the ambushers of Taurinorum,' Prefect

Baudio boomed in triumph, just as the gates of the city creaked and groaned open before us. The Via Decumana stretched out ahead, lined with people, eager if anxious like the countryfolk, but clutching wreaths of vines and more petals, jugs of wine and platters of bread and fruits to welcome us.

My officers took the initiative, Vindex and Hisarnis guiding their regiments forward and into the city first, to sweep the avenue ahead and confirm what every one of us wanted to believe. A handsome fellow with long dark hair flashed grey at the temples rode forth from the gates to say it aloud before my soldiers could. He slid from his horse and knelt before me, holding up a vine wreath. 'Domine, Mediolanum is yours. The False Augustus of Rome has bled these parts of every coin and basket of spare grain in this last year. He is not fit to rule us.'

It was like an iron mantle being lifted from my shoulders and my mind. Mediolanum was mine. Not a man had been lost. The balance of the north was tilting.

The handsome fellow and his retinue of officials led me inside. We came to a towering, loricate statue of the old emperor Aurelian. He wore upon his head a radiant crown. I halted near it, unconsciously, gazing up, a shiver racing over my flesh as I realised this was how my soldiers and my people saw me now – chosen by Apollo, Mars, Christ and Mithras. All around me the liberated populace cheered in a frenzy. But amidst it I heard the legions begin to squabble – again. It began when well-meaning city priests – of several faiths – had waded into the marching column to offer gifts and prayers. Each legion seemed either offended that they were not personally greeted by the priests or had been greeted by the wrong ones. My soldiers began shouting down the opposing claims of the others, insisting that I, they and the campaign was guided by *their* chosen god alone. Perfectly timed, the four bishops arrived on the back of an open wagon, standing tall, howling like wolves to whip the Christian regiments into a frenzy: 'The true Augustus has come. His thirty-year reign is nigh!' Bishop Ossius took things to a dangerous level when he swept an accusatory finger across select regiments. 'The heretics will suffer, in the flames of this world and then the next!'

I felt a horrible shiver pass over me, memories of the Persecutions flooding back. Then it had been the shit-sack emperors who had ordered the burnings and torture of Christians. Now Ossius threatened a reverse? Was he truly so blind to the dark irony of his words?

The Cornuti began whistling in derision at this and singing songs of Apollo. All too quickly the air of celebration was bruised with the sounds of an army – a huge army – creaking and splitting like a great vessel on a voyage it could not hope to complete.

I should have confronted the issue there and then, but what could I say? This was no moment for a pre-battle homily. *That* was my forte. The battle brewing before me was one of faith, ethereal, the ways of such a clash like mist to me.

With a great surge of relief, I saw old Lactantius rise from his wagon. He clambered up atop the vehicle with the help of two Cornuti men and set about crowing over the bishops, drowning them out, deriding their fiery lectures.

'You speak of flames, of fire?' he called to the bishops. 'Your bones are not as old and dry as mine, but neither are you young. *You* lived through the times of the Great Persecution just as I did'—he swept a hand around the crowd—'didn't we all?'

The swell of discontent ebbed, all hooked on his words.

'That day, the harbinger of death, arose, First cause of ill, and long enduring woes,' he sang. The grave lines brought near-silence to the streets of Mediolanum.

'Diocletian and Galerius sat on their thrones and watched men put to the scourges, iron claws, swords, ropes and various kinds of torture... to flame! To what avail? Did our cities not burn? Did widows not weep?'

The soldiers and the citizens of Mediolanum were rapt by Lactantius' words. I was as gripped as any of them. I watched as he then skilfully dismissed the few retorts that came from the legions of the old gods. All without resorting to threats or personal insults.

Before we reached the city forum, he had them laughing, distracted... together. Now the noises of festivity arose once more, unstained. My army and the people of Mediolanum enjoyed a great feast that filled the afternoon and all night too.

Yet later I heard that before Lactantius' intervention, a dozen soldiers had been injured in fights and three citizens had died too. The greatest tragedy of all was that these losses would soon pale into insignificance among far, far greater numbers.

PART 2

Deos fortioribus adesse
(The Gods are on the side of the strongest)
– Tacitus

10

MAXENTIUS

Verona, 8th April 3 1 2 AD

Mediolanum had thrown open its gates and welcomed my benighted enemy-friend into its great walls. From what I heard, the people there had branded me a tyrant, complaining about taxes and welcoming their flat-faced Moesian saviour. If the ungrateful bastards had any idea how much more the people of Rome three hundred miles south paid in taxes than the lucky ones up in Mediolanum, they would have blanched. I cursed them, and cursed them again, wishing them luck under their new saviour when they realised that he too had an army to feed and that their taxes wouldn't change.

To Tartarus with the lot of them.

Valeria wisely left me to rant and rampage around our rooms when the news arrived. Like a spring storm, the rage finally blew itself out and I emerged, probably haggard and grey, from the private rooms, full of purpose to move forward. Mediolanum had been more than a dent in both the defence of the north and my personal pride, but I had known it was coming. Had Ruricius not persuaded me that Mediolanum had to be sacrificed for the good of our campaign?

Our campaign. Hard to think of it as such, really. I was still waking every morning in a cold sweat, half believing that this whole thing had been a terrible nightmare and that my old friend was still lurking in Treverorum, waiting for a reconciliation. Every morning I returned to the real world with a shock and had to come to terms with the fact that I was at war.

My aula regia was busy, but I was prepared. On the way through our apartments I had stopped before a reasonably flat bronze mirror. I had adjusted the hang of my decorative white tunic with the gold-and-purple embroidered cuffs. I had donned the purple cloak, brushed my short hair and smoothed my neat-trimmed beard. I had made myself look every bit the emperor in control.

As far as I could.

There was nothing I could do about the eyes. Red-rimmed with poor sleep and worry, black pits beneath telling of my weariness. A man would look at me and think me master of the world. Then he would look into my eyes and find a frightened child, wondering why his friend was kicking over his wooden city.

Damn that man. Damn him to Tartarus – him and all his attack dogs.

I strolled out into the audience chamber and the clamour began. Like a gaggle of geese when someone throws bread they started up, honking and blaring. I tried to control myself. I was master of the world, not that frightened boy. As I reached my chair on its dais, I waved my hands for silence and was almost surprised when it worked.

Bishops, soldiers, courtiers, administrators and clerks all looked to me expectantly. There would have been rumour circulating, of course, since the news arrived, and my rage-filled seclusion would not have helped. Time to grasp the beast of State by the neck and wrestle it under control.

'Mediolanum is now Constantine's,' I announced, rather unnecessarily, but trying to focus attention on one matter. 'Do not judge its population harshly'—*the cheap, unctuous, treacherous reprobates*—'for they were left with little option. In order to secure Verona and thereby Italia as a whole, we withdrew our forces and sacrificed that noble city. What choice did they have but to submit or be butchered?'

Though the two cohorts we had left in the city to make it a living hell for any invader might have put up a fight, instead of denying me and clutching at Constantine's tunic hem in obedience, the ungrateful traitors.

The silence in the room took on a thoughtful air as the occupants considered this. It had been my great opening remark, planned at the last moment as I stalked down the corridor, wondering how to approach the matter. It seemed to have calmed things, as I'd hoped. Now to move on. I would instil order. I would command. I would not seek advice now, nor would I countenance it, for every time I took the advice of my great court, I lost another damned city.

'Ruricius?'

The tired-looking officer stepped forward from the crowd. 'Domine?'

'I have a task for you. It would appear that Licinius is not planning to invade after all. Likely he is leaving the matter to Constantine, since it would endanger him unnecessarily for the three of us to meet in war. Therefore, I intend to pull three-quarters of the force defending the north-east back here to Verona. A small border force should still be able to keep control unless Licinius fully commits. I do not think that likely at this stage, and I have constraints moving into place to ensure that he will not do so.'

I wondered where Zenas was now with my carefully worded overture for Daia. A deal with a monster to save me from another monster. When did the world become so unpleasant? I tried to push away the image of myself standing on the Capitol as my soldiers butchered Roman citizens. No, I was not a monster... was I?

Ruricius straightened and some of the weariness fell away from his face like flakes of plaster from a wall pounded with artillery. 'I believe that a wise course of action, Domine.'

Good. Oddly, despite any failures, I found Ruricius' support a relief. Would that Anullinus, Volusianus, Zenas – even my wicked old drunken father – were here to support me too.

'However,' I went on, sitting straighter in the seat, 'it will take time to withdraw those forces. Aquileia alone is over a hundred miles from here. Even with the swiftest couriers outbound and forced marches in return, it will take time. Constantine and his army are closer. Mediolanum is less than a hundred miles from here and the delaying tactics there failed spectacularly with the caprice of frightened soldiers. You appreciate my concern?'

Ruricius nodded. Everyone could calculate that problem. Constantine could quite easily be at Verona before my reinforcements.

'You wish *me* to delay the enemy, Domine.'

'Yes. Since the men we left behind failed, I want someone I trust to slow his approach. To make every step of the way from Mediolanum to Verona a laboured and troubled one. Buy us the time we need to assemble all our might at Verona. His army is smaller than ours even now, from what I am told, and if we bring in all our might from the east, we can simply sweep him away in a sea of steel. Constantine is a lucky man and a cunning strategist, but it is a rare general who can win a war against insurmountable odds.'

Ruricius tapped his lip in thought. 'Might I offer a thought, Domine?'

Here we go, I thought. *I'm about to lose another city in the name of strategy.*

'Go on.'

Ruricius gestured at the great map that hung on the side wall of the chamber. Two fat priests and a courtier with a face like a smashed egg scurried out of the way to clear the view. The cavalry commander strode over and began to illustrate his words by tapping at the locations on the map.

'Constantine is here in Mediolanum, or at least he was a day ago. We are here in Verona. Like the potential race between the enemy and our reserves to reach this place, I will encounter similar issues if I attempt to halt Constantine at Mediolanum. He may well have left before I can reach him, and there is a second problem. To comfortably march a full army at us, he would have to take one of two roads, either via Laus Pompeia or Bergomum. I would advise beginning our blockade of his path at Brixia, for whichever of those routes he takes, he will pass through Brixia, and I can certainly reach there before him and prepare.'

I peered at the man in concern. I'd not considered he might see more than one route, for on my map the main road went through Bergomum, but now that I examined it, there were several other great highways spidering across the region. 'Might he not come another route entirely? What if you are ensconced at Brixia and he sweeps around to the south via Cremona?' I was suddenly aware that I was publicly pulling apart my own plan and fought down irritation as Ruricius replied confidently.

'Constantine seems to be aware of our general disposition. He will no doubt be aware that the Padus valley is denied to him, for we have broken all the bridges and sealed the crossings. Ad Padum, Placentia and Brixellum will all put an end to him if he tries to cross the river there, and the same is true of Bedriacum. The river is a hundred paces wide there and the crossings are gone. Besides, with the history of emperors losing and dying at Bedriacum, I cannot see Constantine wanting to risk an engagement there. The place is cursed. No, he will have to come through Brixia, where we are still closer to the mountains and the rivers are narrow and shallow, and therefore less of an obstacle for him. Brixia is where we should begin to blockade him.'

I nodded, though my eyes picked off the names of potential garrison cities that meant sacrificing. I could count half a dozen on that great map even from this distance. Once again my advisors were costing me cities in the name of strategy, but once again, it all sounded too reasonable and logical. I suppressed a sigh.

'Very well, Ruricius. Take strong but highly mobile troops. Whatever clibanarii can be made available. The Sarmatian cataphracti. The remaining Equites Singulares. The strongest and the swiftest men.'

Ruricius was shaking his head and I once more had to fight down irritation. It always started that way. Good advisors shaking their head in the face of my plans, and soon they would be shouting denials at me and telling me what I was doing wrong. Anullinus, Volusianus. Now Ruricius.

'What?' I snapped.

'I should not take the singulares, Domine. Their task is to protect the emperor. It is the very reason for their existence.'

'And that is exactly what they will be doing when they keep Constantine from my door.'

'Domine, there is the very real possibility that someone in this city is working against you. Someone who sent that message stripping me of experienced officers. You need protecting.'

From Valeria? I still could not bring myself to believe that, and spent what free time I had trawling my memories for anything that might provide an alternative explanation. Now was not the time. Now was *war council* time.

'I have Pansa and his guards at my side. They can stop any traitor's knife, and I am safer in Verona than anywhere at this time. Our army here is vast, and still growing. Take the Singulares, and all the heavy cavalry. Ride to Brixia and deny Constantine. Buy us whatever time you can. Do not throw away men, mind. Deny him as long as you can, but withdraw before you are overwhelmed and fortify your next position. Your speed and flexibility will save many lives.'

Ruricius nodded and tapped the map again. 'Brixia. Clesus bridge. Sirmio bridge. Ardelica. Four places that can hold for some time. We can add a sizeable unit of infantry at that last, for Ardelica is only fifteen miles from these walls and there is plenty of time.'

'Good. See to it, Ruricius. Do not let yourself be killed. I have need of both your hand and your mind yet.'

The cavalry commander smiled and bowed before withdrawing. Soon I would have to turn attention to civic matters and general administration and deal with each of the other vultures that perched within that room waiting to pick at my bones, but first I needed to finish dealing with the business of war.

'Ancharius Pansa?'

The head of my bodyguard, and now the most senior military figure in the room, left his position close to my shoulder and walked around in front of me, bowing his head.

'Domine?'

'You are aware more than anyone of the disposition of my forces in the east. I need you to work through the records and select which units should be withdrawn. Once you have the appropriate details, have messages sent to their commanders via the *cursus publicus* on the fastest horses in the north. I want all those units at Verona before Constantine has time to breathe.'

'I will bring the messages for you to seal by the end of the day, Domine.'

I shook my head. 'This is a simple military matter and your own rank and position are sufficient. Have the messages sent as soon as they are written. There is no time to waste.'

'Very well, Domine,' Pansa bowed again and gestured to the senior of his Palatine Guard, who nodded. The commander hurried out of the room to bend to his task.

I paused, breathing deeply. It was going better than I had anticipated. I had been in the room for more than a hundred heartbeats and I had only lost a dozen cities. Now I would have to attend to the minutiae of rule. What did it say about my life that I had once relished the chance to deal with the administration of empire and shunned the sword and the ballista, leaving their handling to my generals, yet now I found myself dreading civil matters and wishing for the simplicity of a sword and an enemy before me.

Was I turning into Constantine?

Damn this war.

11

CONSTANTINE

Northern Italia, 19th April 312 AD

In a frenzy of flapping cloak, plume and stallion's mane, Batius galloped back down the marching column from the vanguard. For a moment, I feared the worst, but then he yanked on the reins, bringing his steed up onto its hind legs, and punched a hand in the air, sword gripped high. 'The road is clear,' he roared through gritted teeth, then swished his sword back down the highway whence he had come – the great road that scored northern Italia from west to east. 'Onwards... for the emperor!'

'For the emperor!' my army chorused. The air shook with their gruff acclaim, then the noise fell away back to the drumming din of clacking hobnails and hooves. Since leaving Mediolanum, town and city after town and city had welcomed us, showered us with gifts and supplies, told us of the terrible reign of Maxentius and the taxes that had left families hungry and destitute. Given these successes so far, my legions believed they were invincible. They were certainly not, but I let the tactical fiction go unchallenged to swell their hearts and stretch their strides. Now just a few more small towns lay between me and Verona – the last great bulwark of the north. The stony carapace within which Maxentius hid.

Just then, the four bishops began preaching behind me, regaling the column with Christian song, waving their hands up as if demanding all should join in. Within a few breaths, the Cornuti and the Petulantes began ancient chants of defiance, in praise of Apollo and Sol Invictus and of Mars.

I felt rage swelling in my chest. It was all I could do to bite back on the fiery tirade I wanted to give. Instead, I glanced over towards Lactantius, riding aboard one of the wagons with Fausta. The old man must have sensed my gaze upon him, because his weary eyes rolled up, meeting mine, reading my thoughts. With an exaggerated sigh, he rose and began to call to the disgruntled regiments, asking them questions about their shared pasts.

'You, Paulus,' he said, his voice amiable and light. 'When did you last see your brother?'

The one named Paulus stopped singing along with the bishops. 'Grypus?' he said with a faint smile. 'Not for years. He lives back in Massilia as a fisherman. The army was not for him.'

'And in those years since you last spoke, how many miles have you walked with the men you now try to drown out with your song? How many meals shared? How many battles endured where you both survived only because you were each there to protect the other?'

On he went, calling to individuals on both sides, and prominent soldiers. Soon, the voices and murmurings faded away. It was like a splash of cold water on a fiery itch.

My thoughts returned to Verona. I clenched my fists. Within days, I would smash that crab-shell of a city and before spring was out I would plant my standards all along

SIMON TURNEY & GORDON DOHERTY

the highways and cities here. From the Alpes Mountains to the River Padus – it would all be safely mine. It took much restraint to resist digging my heels into Celeritas' flanks, to break ahead in a canter or a gallop and ride with the van – to feel the clement winds in my hair. Finally, *now*, the time had come. The cur who had once been a friend, who had turned against me like all the others – slurring my mother, calling me a bastard and a pretender, all when it was *he* lodged upon a stolen throne – would answer for his crimes. I lost control, squeezed my steed's flanks and rode ahead. My men cheered at the sight of me at the canter, and I twisted in my saddle to look back and salute them all, bringing from them a greater clamour of hubris and excitement. Looking forwards again I spotted Ingenuus, the praepositus of the vanguard, holding a fluttering draco standard aloft. I would ride with him, I decided, as I guided Celeritas towards his position. Yes, I would have Maxentius answer for what he had done, I decided there and then with a seething ire, looking on down the road. A man needs that more than anything – reasons, explanations... cold, crisp keys to unlock those hot, spiky cells of doubt and injustice that burn in one's head. Maxentius would answer. Maxentius would pay.

Nothing blinds a man more than anger...

The thing came from nowhere. It was painted black, you see. A coward's trick. Disguised like this, the ballista bolt flew through the air unseen, and it ripped past me, slicing the leather strap holding my bear cloak on my left shoulder. Celeritas whinnied in fright and reared up, just as the night-black bolt whacked into poor Ingenuus' head. With a stark *crack*, skull shards, brain matter and a mizzle of blood flew in every direction, soaking me. His horse sped off the road in terror, breaking across a grassy meadow. My cavalry praepositus' headless corpse listed on the creature's back, arms flailing limply in a grim imitation of life, his black cape rippling like the bright tails of the mournful draco still clutched in one hand.

'Protect the emperor!' Krocus shrieked from somewhere behind.

Hooves and footsteps racing up behind me. The next thing I felt was a colossal blow to my side – Krocus leaping from his own saddle to barge me from mine. The move snatched me from the path of a second lethal bolt. We landed and tumbled in a heap, the entire column swarming forward to present a front around me and the disrupted vanguard riders, the Cornuti clacking their red-serpent shields together in a small cupola around me.

'The trees, they're in the trees,' I heard Hisarnis scream outwith the shell of Bructeri shields.

A drone of hooves faded and I heard a distant clash of iron... and then all was still. Rising as the Cornuti shield-shell parted, I saw the stain of slain men on the edge of a stand of ash a few hundred strides away, just on the left of the road from where the bolts had flown. Ingenuus' vengeful riders were wheeling round and away from the scene with bloody swords, coming back to me – others scouting the rest of the countryside fervently. Two men had ridden after their dead leader's headless corpse to calm the panicked horse and recover the body.

'Two ballistae, hidden in the brush,' seethed Vitalianus, Ingenuus' deputy, as he slowed before me, his face streaked with tears of fury.

'Then shield the flanks,' I demanded, instantly fearful for my column that armies were about to pour from the ash trees on either side of the way.

Vitalianus shook his head. 'There is no army waiting to spring upon us. It was an ambush designed not to destroy your army, Domine… but to kill you alone.'

I shook – but not with a speck of fear or shock. It was the heat of anger in me, like when a pan of water boils with a lid secured.

'Worse, Domine,' an archer said, somewhere unseen behind me. 'Look to the hills ahead.'

There, waving a bright, golden pennant, was one of my advance scouts. We all knew what the signal meant. More enemy forces ahead. The run of towns and cities throwing open their gates to me was at an end.

'Seems the bastard has stopped running,' Batius drawled.

A cold hand stroked my neck. I had seen many battles in my time, most petty and swift, some horrific and haunting. With every one, an invisible callus had grown around my heart, like a sheath of iron. Dulling my senses, diluting the rawness of fear, of pity, of mercy. Yet even just a short period away from the field of war – such as that between the ambush at Taurinorum and now – was often enough to allow the shoots of those boxed-away emotions to grow again. And they were back, I realised, feeling a hot pulse of fear, a sudden dryness in the mouth. That was not the only sense of my discomfort… something else wasn't right. I glanced at a nearby scribe, and more specifically at the leather tube hanging from his belt containing the map scroll. We were still days away from Verona.

Batius read my confusion. 'Brixia lies beyond those hills,' he clarified.

A first line of defence, I realised. An outlying rampart protecting Maxentius in his coward's lair at Verona. 'Then Brixia will fall,' I yelled, standing tall, stamping the heel of one foot to drive away my fears.

We advanced in a wide front to crest the rise, and saw it. Brixia, the white-walled metropolis: the city of Hercules, fed by a majestic aqueduct picking its way down from a mountain spur and into the city past a high-vaulted bathhouse. The marble Temple of the Capitoline Triad stood proud on a small hill, overlooking a warren of red-tiled insulae and workhouses which packed the rest of the space inside the city defences and spilled outside and around the walls too. Those walls were thick and high. Yet it was not the city defences that we would have to deal with here, I quickly realised.

The River Mella ran before the city's western side like a moat. My eyes settled on the remains of four bridges. Smashed, the craggy stone and timber abutments stretched out hopelessly like the hands of dragged apart lovers. There was no way across ...

... apart from the lone bridge my enemy had left intact. Built of stone. Wide. Strong. Perfectly adequate to take my army over the deep waters... were it not for the shimmering monstrosity that waited on the far bridgehead like a titanic, barring hand. It was a castrum of sorts: a wall of travertine rubble and timber – harvested from hastily demolished buildings, going by the tumbledown state of a small shrine nearby. It was thick and wide and as high as three men. Lining its top was a forest of iron spears and helms. Two more ballistae were mounted either side of the rubble 'castrum' too, pointing in towards the mid-section of the bridge, and the bridge's waist-height stone sides had been knocked away to deny any who might cross even a speck of cover – possibly even to encourage soldiers beset by missiles to jump into the waters in search of a watery grave instead of an arrow in the throat or eye. The perfect killing ground.

I saw one figure rise into view atop the castrum with a

few slow, purposeful steps. He stood there like a conqueror, cuirass polished, hands clasped behind his back, his red cape rippling behind him. For a trice, I saw Maxentius and my heart turned to ice, my soul to fire. But my eyes were deceiving me.

'Ruricius,' I said, seeing now it was the puce-faced officer who had 'coordinated' the failed ambush at Taurinorum. The cur-prince Maxentius was too weak to face me, it seemed, and so he had sent his deputy instead.

'He has a few cohorts of infantry over there at best, Domine,' Krocus observed, tugging on his beard. 'The rest – all cavalry. This isn't the main Maxentian army – but it's a stout one nonetheless and that crossing is...' He stopped and sucked air through his teeth, then spat on the ground.

A short way back from the castrum, a few thousand horsemen waited in broad wings – pale-skinned Sarmatians in steel vests and greaves, imperial horse guards too. The rubble castrum on the far end of the bridge had a double door of sorts at its centre. Potential for a frontal sally or charge.

'More shields to the front,' Tribunus Ruga snapped, seeing this possibility too, guiding some of his Ubii centuries there.

'No. His horsemen won't charge,' I realised. 'He knows I have the measure of him in the field.'

'If he keeps those riders over on the far side of the river then this will be easy,' Ruga growled.

I arched one eyebrow. Ruga was fire in the shape of a man. An inspirational tribunus. But, by all the gods, he couldn't half talk horseshit sometimes.

'Easy?' Prefect Baudio replied for me. 'A bridgehead siege?' He turned from the scowling Ruga to me. 'We will suffer many casualties, Domine, if we try to pierce through that... *mess.*' He cast a derisive finger at the rubble castrum.

I said nothing for a time, my eyes combing the land. One bridge. Certain death for many of my soldiers. *Too* many of my soldiers. To the south the land was flat and clear, but blocked by the river. To the north the countryside grew rugged, and a long tangle of gorse ran all the way upriver, the earth slightly darkened by dampness on the near side of the vegetation. My eyes narrowed, now examining the far side of the river once again.

'In Britannia,' I said, 'there was a black and white cat who ran riot around my villa. A fat sack of fur who would not be chased away.'

Baudio and others nearby twisted towards me, confused at the apparent non sequitur.

Only Lactantius, riding in the wagon with Fausta, seemed to know what I was talking about. He popped his head out of the wagon: 'Aye, it was a vicious brute! I tried stroking it once and it seized my arm with its front claws then started furiously kicking with its back paws. The worst bit was the monster was purring throughout it all – enjoying my torment!'

I slid from my horse, pacing along our army front, beckoning Batius and Prefect Baudio with me. 'The slave in charge of the villa *cucina* was at his wits' end about the cat's antics – stealing food every time his back was turned.' I then jabbed a thumb towards the wagon where Lactantius was still professing the wickedness of the cat. 'One day my old tutor brought a freshly caught trout into the cucina and asked the slave to mind it for him until evening. The slave sat in the cucina doorway – the only way into the cooking room. He ate tarragon and drank strong nettle brew to stay awake and sharp. The cat wasn't getting past him and it certainly wasn't getting Lactantius' fish.' I pointed towards two of the standards near our front.

Batius and Prefect Baudio read my signal and summoned a cohort each. I half-smiled at the pair's confused looks as I led them and the two cohorts through our lines, to our rear. 'But it did,' I explained. 'It found a way. There is always a way.'

★ ★ ★

Within the hour I watched from a distance as my Ubii and Bructeri legions walked in slow, careful steps, encased in shields at every side and overhead, onto the bridge. 'Hoo-hoo-hoo!' they chanted as they marched, like heroes, into the killing zone. What kind of leader must you think me, to send my men onto that bridge while I sat back and watched?

Thrum! went Ruricius' two ballistae. *Smash!* as the bolts ripped holes through my loyal Bructeri men. Next, and with a cry, Ruricius' infantry atop the rubble castrum launched a thick hail of javelins too. My Ubii soldiers toppled, skewered and screaming, into the Mella's churning waters. Still, the survivors rushed manfully at the castrum, trying to bring a battering ram to the redoubt's crude gates. Yet those carrying the ram were shot down and those who tried to pick it up were too. Some of my legionaries tried to scramble up and scale the rubble blockade, only to lose their hands or heads to merciless Maxentian blades.

On I watched… until Batius planted a hand on my shoulder. 'Go, Domine,' he whispered.

I turned away from the scene of combat, a half-mile downriver, and towards the Mella waters here before me. I laid my shield down onto the churning surface and lowered my chest onto it. The currents were like icy hands clawing at me, the waters, speeding inside my armour and soaking my clothes. I used my arms like paddles, crudely guiding myself across the river. Beside, behind and ahead of me, my men did likewise in a quiet ribbon of steel and shield.

My shield crunched onto the shale on the far banks, and I rose, soaking, shivering, more and more men rising likewise behind me like Neptune's children. We gathered, crouching, gleaming wet, under a natural scarp lining the banks on this side. It had been a silent and speedy manoeuvre: veiled from the eyes of the enemy behind the screen of my legions, we had moved away from the main body of the army at the fortified bridge and headed north. We had moved low, behind that long stripe of gorse for the rest of our speedy journey upriver. The damp ground there meant we cast up no telltale dust. The decoy charge of the Ubii and the Bructeri had distracted the eyes of Ruricius and his lot from our river crossing.

'So the slave caught the cat. Cooked the hairy bastard, aye?' Prefect Baudio asked, prompting me to finish my story.

'If only,' said Batius, shaking his head like a dog, water spraying from him as he rose from the waters.

I flashed a half-grin and shook my head. 'Lactantius returned that night, licking his lips in anticipation of his meal. The slave sitting in the cucina doorway sat up, smiling, announced that he had done as asked, then whirled on one heel to present... the cat, lying on the table behind him, licking its paws and cleaning the last morsels of fish from its face. The cat had squeezed in through a gap in the shutters, silently and carefully, and stolen right up on its prize.'

I pointed downriver. The scarp by which we were huddled ran parallel to this riverbank, obscuring us from Brixia's turrets. More, it hid us from the eyes of the Maxentian cavalry wings waiting outside the city. I gazed all the way south to a kink in the river. Beyond that lay the defended bridgehead. This channel led all the way up to the castrum flank. 'Every pair of eyes defending that castrum is on the Ubii and Bructeri attack. If we stay low, and approach with the minimum of noise...' I punched a fist into my palm.

'Domine,' they all rumbled as one, eyes glinting, all sold on the plan.

We sped south, the gentle *shush* of our armour, puffing of breath and the odd grunt the only sounds. In contrast, from downriver, the cacophonous song of the ongoing assault on the bridgehead castrum came and went in terrible echoes. When we rounded the kink in the river, the scene unfolded before me like a scroll. Ruricius' forces were engaged fully in the slaughter. My soldiers were now falling in droves on the bridge – but it was the only way. If we were not swift and decisive in this stealthy move, I would pay with my own life too. I glanced left and up at the scarp's brow, knowing the eyes of the massed cavalry ranks were but fifty strides back from that grassy ledge. Then I glared ahead, to the bumpy rubble slope that was the rear-right of the castrum. It was like a siege ramp, lined with ranks of legionaries ready to replace those defending the top. Up there near the rubble summit was Ruricius, back turned, oblivious to me as he strode, roaring and marvelling as he directed the slaughter of my men on the bridge. When he turned every so often and I could see him in profile, I noticed every flap of his jaws, the clouds of spittle, the triumphant and joyous cries he and his men emitted every time they loosed another ballista bolt into my forces pushing frontally on the bridge. I glanced left again: the scarp was tapering off. The Maxentian cavalry slid into view on that side like a blade quarter-drawn from a scabbard. Poised on our flanks but as yet oblivious to our presence. A moment's hesitation and they would see us, charge, and slaughter us all.

'With the speed of the gods!' I rasped, launching forward

across the short stretch to the castrum, the others coming with me like lions. We heard the gasps and shouts and whinnies of the cavalrymen – startled at this strange force suddenly appearing on their 'safe' side of the river. Their shock was their mistake, and it allowed us to storm into the backs of the Maxentian foot soldiers standing at the rear of the castrum – caught equally unawares. Iron smashed against iron, and steel drove deep into flesh. 'Get among them,' I screamed, knowing that if we could spill onto the castrum's steep and rubbly rear slope then their cavalry would be next to useless. I ran one legionary through then hilt-smashed another on the nose; Batius let out a tearful roar as he cleaved another from shoulder to chest – every Roman death was anathema for the big man, for me, for us all, yet each of us knew it had come down to one, horrible truth: us or them.

Baudio headbutted an archer who tried to loose close-range at me. While my Cornuti and Second Italica cohorts swamped the rest of the enemy, I sped on up the rubble mound, hearing from behind me the hasty and disorganised surge of the Maxentian cavalry coming then slowing and breaking down in a series of shouts as they realised they could hardly charge up the ruinous rubble slope of the castrum's rear, and that any javelins thrown would be as likely to strike one of their own legionaries as one of mine. The men running with me split off to fall upon and silence the two deadly ballistae at last. Me? There could only be one foe next.

Ruricius spun round with the look of a man meeting his own shade.

'You? How?' he stammered, drawing and swinging his blade in shock.

I caught his wild strike and struck back. *Smash, smash, smash*, I went at him and he slashed back. Not even a notion of surrender was on offer here for either side. It would be over only when one of our sword tips rested in the other's heart. I saw my chance: as he swiped and missed he left himself open to attack. I rammed my blade towards his exposed armpit. He bent away from the strike then teetered, one foot slipping from the castrum lip, his arms flailing for balance. He plummeted, his cape streaming behind him before he splashed into the Mella's waters. I glared down at the spot of churning water into which he had fallen. Drowning under the weight of one's own armour – a wretched end indeed. Robbed of my kill, but strangely grateful for it, I heard the bashing of wood as Batius cleared and unbarred the castrum's makeshift gate from this side. It was like the burst of quicksilver: my men pressing on the bridge finally flooded through the gap and spilled onto the enemy banks. I joined them and we clustered together there, shields in a wall, a maw of spears and swords jutting, glaring, panting, ready.

Ruricius' cavalry was now in disarray, some commanders calling on their men to dismount, some demanding an assault on us and marshalling thin volleys of missiles, others screaming for a retreat as my numbers on this side of the river grew rapidly. Within moments, most had turned to the latter strategy, the riders turning and breaking into a gallop for the east.

No sooner had they broken into a full retreat than I smelt smoke and then saw a tongue of fire rising into the air, and I realised that this was Ruricius' last riposte: handfuls of his riders were throwing blazing torches into the serried brick *horrea* near Brixia's southern walls as they passed.

The flames had taken hold of the horrea now and rose high into the sky. Grain to feed Brixia for a year, gone. Grain to refill our ever-lighter supply wagons, gone – and the next convoy from the north was late. My soldiers shouted and clamoured, gathering and taking helmetfuls of water to attack the fires once the enemy riders had departed, to salvage something, *anything*. But it was too late. I had seen such a blaze once before: on that day Maxentius' boy had been trapped in the burning grain silo in Nicomedia. That day we had been friends. Brothers. We had saved little Romulus that day and we had rejoiced together. My heart swelled with sickness.

'Now you will starve...' a voice spat over a rapid drumming of more hooves, just to my right. I swung to see Ruricius, sopping wet, purple-faced again, clinging to the back of a rider who had fished him from the river. He sped past us, shaking a fist, his features bent in spite as he repeated the words that had kindled this war: '... son of a *whore!*'

A cloud of arrows spat into the air and I willed them all to land in his eye. But he went unharmed, and sped away with the rest of his mounted army.

My heart turned to stone. Little Romulus was dead now, and so was my kinship with his father. Further to the east, rising from the trail of Ruricius' fleeing men like puffs of dust, came more smoke. The farmsteads too were being razed and put to the torch.

'The grain may be lost, but we have victory, Domine!' Prefect Vindex enthused, his face smoke-blackened, glistening red in places with smears of blood.

'How long will it take us to clear that bridge?' I said flatly.

'A few hours,' he estimated.

'Then it will take the rest of the day to filter our legions and wagons across,' I finished for him, glancing up at the sun. I looked up at Brixia's walls, seeing not a single sentry there. 'We have won Brixia,' I said. *An empire of ash?* I wondered, seeing that the flames were growing higher and had spread into the workshops hemming the city walls, then catching from the corner of my eye how the River Mella ran red in places, the bodies of so many – thousands – of my men who had died just to allow me a chance to take this castrum. 'But Maxentius has won precious time.'

'Time for what, Domine?' Vindex whispered, as if a god was listening.

I peered east like a man sighting a storm on the horizon. 'The answer, I fear, lurks at Verona.'

12

MAXENTIUS

Verona, 20th April 312 AD

The day began with a disaster. It was hard to see how it could descend from there.

The gates of Verona opened to admit the riders and, warned of their approach, I met them on the Cardo Maximus, just inside the great, heavy gatehouse. I was astride my horse, attired in my panoply with white leather *pteruges* at shoulder and waist and a gleaming cuirass embossed with divine images, all set off with my purple cloak and matching Pannonian cap. But for all the colour and glory of my attire, no one could mistake the utilitarian soldier's sword at my side for a thing of beauty. I had taken to wearing this ensemble at all times in public. It would do the people of Verona and the soldiers of my army good to see their emperor prepared for the fight to come. It made me one of them in ways that words could not.

Today I would have preferred to *be* one of them, blissfully ignorant of what the riders' arrival might mean.

Ruricius was a mess. He sat astride a good horse like a badly stuffed sack of wet straw, his uniform limp and clinging to him, discoloured and drab. Rust was already beginning to form on the armour he wore, but nothing about him was as grim as his face.

He was intact and unscarred, but had I thought that his was a peaceful visit the notion would have been instantly disabused by the sight of the men with him: perhaps a dozen soldiers, half of them wrapped in makeshift bandages, sporting bloodsoaked limbs or arms in slings. The remnants of the Equites Singulares. The most powerful cavalry in the empire. The best of the best.

'Tell me.'

Ruricius gave me a half-hearted salute and winced as he leaned forward in the saddle.

'Constantine is a devious snake, Domine.'

I had already guessed something of what had occurred, of course, but to have it confirmed in such simple words swept away any shred of confidence or humour all in one. Had I both or either, I might have quipped at the man's expense or demanded explanations. As it was I just waited, a dull languid melancholy slowly spreading through me. Somewhere a bell tolled, and it too sounded disheartened.

'We fortified Brixia, and we did it well, Domine. No man can be accused of not putting his whole heart and body into that defence. We tore down all the bridges for miles bar the one, and we made that uncrossable. We denied him the river. We built in days a fort of rubble and iron that could stop any army in the world.'

'Except Constantine's, clearly.'

Ruricius shook his head. 'The wretched dog sent men over the bridge in droves and we killed them in droves. Iron bolts, arrows, spears, swords. It was butchery on an unprecedented scale. For a time I even wondered if we might win the war right there, without the whoreson ever even reaching Verona.'

I flinched, and not at the news or the images, but at the casual way my northern general called Constantine a 'son of a whore,' one of my more unfortunate insults that had made the gulf between us unbridgeable.

'I had most of the cavalry lined up in reserve waiting,' he went on, bleakly, 'and was holding the bridge firmly with just my few infantry and scattered dismounted cavalry. We could have held for days. A month, even. We could have slaughtered every man he sent onto that bridge.'

'But?'

'The sly fox,' Ruricius snarled. *A snake, a dog and now a fox. How long before he was a camel*, I wondered wearily. 'The sly fox kept us busy killing his men while he took a legion upstream and crossed the river somehow. Don't ask me how, but they didn't cross on Mercury's winged boots for sure, because they were soaked to the skin. How they didn't drown, though, is beyond me. They used a gulley we'd not anticipated and completely bypassed the cavalry, falling upon my bridgehead from the rear. We couldn't maintain the hold on the bridge *and* fight an enemy to our rear. They overcame the defences and cleared the crossing for the rest of his men.'

'And you put out the calls for the cavalry to fall upon them?'

Ruricius shook his head. 'I never had the chance. I saw him, in the fight, you see. I saw Constantine, and I knew I had a chance. Just one chance. If I could kill the bastard there and then, the war was over. We fought. I actually crossed swords with the man, but he was tricky even then. Manoeuvred me to a treacherous part of the fortification and pushed until I lost my footing. The low trick of a peasant brigand. By the time they were in control of the bridge and I needed to have the cavalry ready I was in the water and drowning. Only

Vinicius over there saved me, dragging me coughing from the water and throwing me over his horse.'

'So what of the cavalry?'

Ruricius shrugged. 'They were in chaos. Some of the commanders led their men into the fray. Others turned tail and fled. Others still dithered and did nothing. It was like Taurinorum all over again. I managed to give the signal to fire Brixia's granaries and deny the invaders their supplies, but I was gone then. Half drowned and barely conscious, all I could do was lie across the horse and throw up for the next five miles.'

'So the survivors will have gathered at the Clesus? Sirmio? Ardelica? The officers will have regrouped and rallied their horse at the next defence, yes?'

'Perhaps, Domine.' He did not sound confident. 'I would not wager good coin that many escaped Brixia. Likely most survivors from the battle are now in small groups all over the region, hiding and hoping that Constantine and his army will be past and out of their way soon. Chaos.'

I shook my head in despair. 'So the other redoubts are undefended?'

'I presume so. We didn't have time to regroup, and I could hardly see straight anyway.'

'So there is nothing between Constantine and Verona?'

'Just a few cabbages and about five miles of my vomit.'

I glared at him. This was no time for humour, but then he did not look amused either.

'We have not had time, Ruricius. We are not prepared.'

'I did everything a sane man could, Domine.'

In fairness, even in my gloominess and anger at this latest turn of events I could see the truth of that. Would I have managed any better? Of course not. Ruricius had been clever, but Constantine had been more so. It had happened more than once, and not just to my northern general. 'I know,' I sighed. 'I assign no blame. I am simply weary of defeat, and worried as to the coming days. I will need your mind and your sword arm to save Verona, my friend.'

Rallying himself slightly, Ruricius sat straighter in the saddle. 'Both are yours, Domine, always. What forces have arrived?'

I tried to think back over the reports of the last few days. 'Not even half of them, and most auxiliaries and light skirmishers. Some Numidian cavalry, archers, various light infantry. Perhaps another ten or fifteen thousand men on top of the garrison we had.'

Ruricius' face fell for just a moment before he jacked confidence back into it. 'Sadly, we lost several thousand at Brixia, and good, heavy veterans, too, so the difference is negligible at best. What of the cataphracti from the east – the Equites Sagitarii Clibanarii and the Comites Alani? What of the Praetorians?'

I nodded and turned. Somehow I knew Ancharius Pansa was there even without having seen him arrive. He gave off an odd aura that was endemic of the frumentarii and spies the world over. He might not look quite so much like a greasy homunculus these days, with his gleaming uniform and well-groomed appearance, but his face still reminded me of a misshapen turnip, and his bad eye still stared at some point on the horizon while the good one swivelled towards me.

'Pansa? The heavy cavalry? The Praetorians?'

The man gave me a hollow, boss-eyed look and sighed. 'Of the Praetorian units there is no word as yet, but they were set furthest forward, so they have the furthest to travel to join us. The cataphracti are based in low-lying Venetia, and should have been with us by now, though I gather there was some issue with supplies and fodder that delayed them. With luck they will be here within the day. Other units are moving already. Two, perhaps three days and all our forces should have arrived.'

I looked at Ruricius, who shook his head. 'That will not be fast enough, if Constantine has the bit between his teeth.'

Pansa bridled slightly at what sounded like faintly accusatory words. 'Forgive me, General, but I was given orders to withdraw troops to Verona on the assumption you and your men would buy us adequate time. You have not done so, and unless you can persuade Mercury to bestow wings upon the army, then there is little more I can do. We will simply have to wait and hope.'

I watched the fire burst into life in Ruricius' eyes and felt the day slipping away from me. What was it with my consilium? Anullinus and Volusianus could not speak without arguing. Now it looked like Ruricius and Pansa were about to start emulating them. I glared at both of them and held up a warning finger.

'*Enough.* What is done is done. Pansa cannot make men travel faster than nature will allow, and Ruricius did as much, and more, as any man could to halt the enemy. We must make libations and pray and trust in the gods. There is still time.'

But there wasn't.

The day began with a disaster. It was hard to see how it could descend from there.

Now I saw it. Or rather, I heard it. The warning blare of horns from the gate top. I did not immediately understand what it meant, though I was not kept in the dark for long.

'The enemy,' bellowed a voice from the parapet as two lookouts waved down to us. 'Domine. Enemy scouts sighted.'

My heart froze. Scouts, and they would not be more than a few miles ahead of the army's vanguard. The enemy had moved with the speed of a hawk. Damn it, now *I* was assigning animals to him. *Him*. Not *them*. Suddenly, for the very first time, in my head Constantine himself had become the enemy. Or perhaps the enemy had become Constantine. Even through all the losses in the north, it had not seemed real – like some night terror from which I might awake – but I no longer clung to hope. Hope had been stripped from me one shred of flesh at a time, through my father's betrayal, my beloved son's death, the discovery that someone – *Valeria?* – was working against me. And now my oldest friend was gone, replaced with an implacable foe, a situation that would never now be reversed.

I hardened my broken, frozen heart. I may have lost almost everything I loved, but there was still one thing: Rome. I still loved Rome, and would see her dominate and prosper over all these provincial warmongers. I would save Verona and defeat my old friend.

Purpose flooded through me. I gestured to Ruricius and Pansa.

'We can hold Verona for months if we have to. Plenty of time for the reinforcements to join us, but we must leave the way open for them. We cannot make the mistake of the Gaul, Vercingetorix, sealing ourselves tight against Caesar's army and leaving no way for the relief army to join us. We must secure one of the bridges to the north-east of the city and hold it. Only then can any of the troops flocking to my banner join us, else they will find themselves trapped outside by the enemy. Pansa, you have Verona. Quadratus will lead the army as a whole. Ruricius, you have the crossing. Make me a bridgehead like your one at Brixia, only better.

Impregnable. Make a corridor for our reserves to join us, and hold it safe.'

Pansa gave me his odd half-salute and wandered off to see to the disposition of my guard. Ruricius saluted sharply, though his arm was still shaking with the effort. I asked so much of them but there would be more to ask yet, more to do. We had to hold Verona, else Constantine had a clear road to Rome, and I had to do my part. The days of peace and delegation were gone. I was as responsible as anyone now for the prosecution of the war.

And I would see my old friend die before these walls. I might wish him a quick and noble death, but now, whatever the method, I wished him death.

'Come Constantine. You dog. You fox. You snake. You hawk. Come find me at Verona and I will show you how much you taught me about building walls all those years ago.'

13

CONSTANTINE

Verona, 20th April 312 AD

Bucolic serenity, golden sheets of morning sunlight on green, lush lands, the air spiced with honeyed broom and dulcet spring birdsong. All riven by rolling thunder. A thunder of war, with me at its head, bronze scales clanking with every strike of Celeritas' hooves, my bear-fur cloak rippling in the wind of our advance, the cheek and nose guards of my jewelled, studded ridge-helm clutching my face and sparkling in the sunlight.

We spilled eastwards along the Via Postumia, the foaming currents of the River Athesis racing with us, eager and strong like us. Birds scattered, deer bolted, men ran from the nearby fields, though some stooped to one knee and bowed their heads in reverence. All souls in these parts knew I was coming this way. Then we saw it: Verona – an ancient bastion nestled in a tight loop of the River Athesis. The final hinge of the north.

Close enough for now, I realised, throwing up a hand. My officers called out in gruff tones, standards were raised and trumpets blew as my army slowed like a ship's sail sagging on a quiet sea. Once more there were just the beautiful sounds of the country as we saw what awaited us.

I studied the place carefully, hearing the rush of the river, the whirring song of the cicadas and the cooing of doves, feeling the warm wind stroke my skin. The walls and turrets were impressive, yet almost entirely unnecessary. For the rushing currents of the river, lapping against the very foundation stones of the walls on the northern, eastern and western edges of the city meant none could approach from those sides. The bridges were the key, rising on each riverbound side. And, damn him, my enemy had broken all of them – not even one left intact this time. That left just one viable way to tackle Verona: the land approach from the south – the open end of the river loop.

'Well that makes the tactical chat a bit easier,' Batius remarked glibly, before placing a finger over one nostril and blowing a massive blob of snot from the other.

'We always suspected that it would come down to a siege here,' Krocus remarked. 'We have the means to tackle those walls now,' he said, flicking his head back towards our wagon train.

I nodded slowly. 'Forward, at a walk,' I drawled. The trumpeters blew and commanders called out orders, and we rumbled on towards that land approach. We came to a halt again, far enough away not to come to harm from any missiles, but close enough to allow my forces to occupy the open end of the river loop and the city and to examine more closely the main and outer defences.

The Via Postumia stretched on through the almost apologetic white Arch of Gavi towards Verona's southern bastion. Before it reached that mighty wall the road's ordered flagstones became a mess of smashed slabs and deep, earthen scars, picked out with twinkling spikes of iron – he had broken the road, sewn the ground with stake-pits and strewn caltrops. Worse, a freshly dug, unbroken ditch stretched across the front of those southern walls.

Should any fool try to pick a path through that, they would simply come up against the city's famous Jovian Gates: two tall, white limestone arches, framed by expertly sculpted columns and pediments. Each was blocked by heavy timber doors, vertical bands of bronze giving them extra strength and the look of feral rictuses. Above the gates a gallery of windows loomed like the empty eye sockets of an arachnid cadaver, the paired archers positioned in each one like ants picking at the remaining flesh. The parapets were most dispiriting of all – lined with shuffling, bristling men encased in silvery armour, serried, spear tips jabbing into the sky like the asp-hair of Medusa. Three or more ranks of them up there, closely packed. Thousands in all. From the towers poked more glinting bolt throwers than I could count: ballistae and smaller scorpions. Wisps of steam and smoke rose here and there too: pots of boiling oil, water and sand heated until it was glowing, I realised. At the cajoling words of some commander up there, his massed ranks on the battlements exploded in a chorus of vitriol, pumping their spears aloft, their throaty cries amplified by the natural theatre created by the course of the meandering river.

'They were a little more welcoming at Mediolanum,' Krocus said with a wry grumble.

'He's in there,' Batius said, pointing to the purple banners flying high above Verona, emblazoned with golden eagles and the bold, arrogant lettering he claimed as his insignia: S.P.Q.R – as if he *was* Rome itself, 'and he knows we are coming. The time has arrived.'

My heart hammered. I thought of Mother and my dear lad Crispus back home in Treverorum. I thought of the boy

I had once been. Was this to be the moment? Then I thought of Fausta – here with the army, but back at the well-guarded supply tents with the other officials and non-combatants. I had no wish to subject her to the sights of what was to come, but equally, I dared not entrust her to the garrisons of Mediolanum or Brixia lest my enemy send some force around behind us in an attempt to recover those cities. The only way to guarantee her safety was to pulverise the enemy quickly.

I watched as the enemy roared on and on, gleeful and triumphant as if the day was already won. 'We should extend a greeting in kind,' I rumbled to myself. I glanced across to my wagon train. Already the men there were poised, hands on the hide sheets covering their contents. The faintest of nods from me set them to work: they whipped the sheets away, hauling timber, rope and steel from the vehicles. A rapping of hammers on pegs, of sawing and the straining of ropes fought against the gradually dissipating Maxentian cries. I had not been wasteful with my extended stop in Taurinorum, you see. Men had been sent into the pine woods nearby. Huge teams of them. The city's smiths too had been busy, forging great bolts, and stonemasons shaping balls of rock.

Wood groaned, and the first of the onager frames rose under the power of my men's efforts. The bulky stone-throwers would ruin swathes of the legionaries up there on the battlements. They would weaken the walls too, and maybe even smash the bronze teeth of those twin gates. Another chatter of straining ropes, and a war tower – the first of three I had commissioned in Taurinorum – began to take shape. High enough to meet Verona's battlements. Brave legionaries would run ahead and lay planks to bridge the ditch before the walls so the giant city-takers could reach them. The bold cries from the Maxentian troops on the walls fell quiet now.

Then I saw it. A shape. Yes, a mere shape of a man, rising up to stand atop the southern gatehouse.

Maxentius!

I saw nothing of his features at this distance, just his cloak, billowing behind him in the breeze. Yet in my mind's eye I saw that shadowy mien that had twisted and soured with every new rumour of his deeds. The tales of my one-time friend's massacre of the people of Rome had been confirmed by the citizens we had liberated on our march. His crimes against me – the lands he stole from me and the cold killer he sent to open my throat – flashed through my thoughts. Worse, the echo of Ruricius' parting jibe back at Brixia came back to me, and my mind's-eye image of Maxentius jerked, the tight, colourless lips spitting the words with a venomous mist of saliva. *Son of a whore!*

More soldiers arrived on the battlements to swell the defences. I saw just how strong and numerous his defensive ranks were. Doubts scratched at me from either side where, in my peripheral vision, I could see my own forces stretched out in a line to block the city's land approach. *Too few?* Now only twenty thousand marched with me. I had entered Italia with seventeen legions. I only had twelve here with me now, along with my cavalry wing under the new leadership of Vitalianus. The losses at Brixia had been heavy – over three thousand men dead and another twelve hundred maimed, and I had been forced to detach another eight hundred of the Seventh Gemina to ensure that burning city could be saved – its people restored to some kind of order after the tyrant had ordered their homes burned. My generals thought me insane when, only hours after that original decision, I detached a further three entire legions there: the Second Italia, the First Martia and the Eighth Augusta. They didn't understand: why would

I dispense with nearly nine thousand men? Brixia needed no such garrison. I told them that they would soon understand, that if they believed in me as they claimed they did, then they should have faith in my choice.

'Domine,' Krocus said in a whisper, clearly still unsettled about the nine thousand men I had 'unnecessarily' left behind at Brixia. 'Perhaps we should rethink. The numbers on those walls are many more than we expected. They match almost what we have here. Worse, we do not know how many they have inside the city.'

'Not enough,' I said instantly, denying my doubts. 'He sought to slow me at Brixia because he needed time to draw reinforcements here.' I raised my voice so my legions would hear. 'Maxentius barely slowed us at all at that burning city of Brixia... and his reinforcements are *not* here.' I swung my arms wide, then pointed up at the walls. 'And *those* men are not your equals,' I boomed. 'They are farmers and city watchmen in the garb of legionaries. Sentries who have been patrolling quiet hinterlands for generations. War to them is like ice to a Nubian.'

My men erupted in throaty laughter.

'The only downside to this is that you will have to buy fresh whetstones to re-sharpen your blunted swords after you win this city. But fear not, for I will take no spoils for myself. The riches in the palaces will be *yours*.'

My men smashed the hilts of their swords on their shields, voices rising like the swell of a storm. 'Con-stan-tine! Con-stan-tine!' they chanted. Lactantius was our shepherd on the march and in camp. Here, on the field of battle, I was their champion.

The pleasant spring morning grew glorious as my men made their final preparations. The legions stood in a *triplex acies* – a triple band of soldiers – facing the city's southern walls. Four regiments – the Regii, the Cornuti, the Fourth Jovia and the Lancearii – formed the rear band, our anchor; the Second Augusta, the Bructeri, the Petulantes and the Ubii stood in the middle band; four more stood in front of them: the Sixth Victrix, the Twenty-second Primigenia, the Seventh Gemina and the First Minervia... these brave souls were ready to surge for the walls, armed with long ladders and sharpened steel. My three war towers stood, ominous and silent bar the occasional creak and groan when the warm spring breeze sighed around the timbers. The roofs were packed with archers and slingers, poised behind the timber parapets, the lower floors jammed with legionaries who would act as ballast when the huge wheels eventually rolled and then, when these city-takers reached Verona's walls, would ascend the stairs inside and spill from the hatch at the top and onto the city battlements. The onagers were loaded, the legions were ready. All of them looked at me. This was it. *This was it.*

'Domine. The hairy bastard is right,' Batius said as if swallowing a disgusting mouthful of food, flicking his eyes in Krocus' direction. 'About our numbers. If we attack, we will probably bring those damned gates down, slay most if not all of the men atop the walls, and perhaps even force our way into the city's interior wards. But...'—the big man was locked in a battle of wills with himself—'but that will be it. We might reach the heart of the city, but the campaign will die here too. This place will be the grave of our men and his. Maybe of him and you also.'

I felt something clutch at my heart, a stinging behind my eyes. 'This *has* to end, Batius.' I stamped on my emotions, straightening. 'Perhaps it *will* end today, but not as you say.

You know me better than most. You know I would never throw my men against enemy stone and steel blindly, with only hope as a strategy.'

Batius' forehead creased.

I looked up to see the sun, directly overhead. It was noon. It was time.

'See the far end of the city, old friend,' I said, pointing across the city's southern defences and jumble of inner wards. From the small hummock we stood upon we could see it: at the far end, the northern gatehouse stood proud of the walls – not quite the marvel like the Jovian Gates before us, but stout nonetheless. The battlements there were lined with a smaller bank of men too. Perhaps a cohort's worth.

'I didn't believe our scouts when they told us; why does he waste a cohort to guard a gate that opens onto a broken bridge?' Batius muttered.

'Quite,' I said. 'Now look further north, on the riverside opposite that broken northern bridge. See the theatre, part-cut into the rising northern banks?'

Batius' eyes rolled back and forth across the white, stone theatre, then snagged on the ant-like iron garrison patrolling its upper rim. Watching the north. 'A bridgehead. For a broken bridge – why?'

'Look again at the northern gates: notice the timber platform that stands proud there.'

Batius' gaze ran over the jutting sheet of timber planks standing vertically there, held high by ropes tied to the northern gatehouse towers. 'A drawbridge?'

'Aye, controlled from the city side. Maxentius' reinforcements and his supplies will come from that direction.'

He bristled in alarm. 'Then we must send a force back to the bridge downriver at Parona, cross and assault the northern side,' he said. 'We might only have hours before Maxentius' reserve legions arrive.'

I raised a hand to calm him. 'Watch, old friend,' I said, my gaze flicking from the noon sun to the theatre on the northern banks.

The silvery forms of Maxentius' bridgehead guard there were strolling along the theatre's upper lip, untroubled by my forces here – the city and the river between them and us. Time passed and I began to feel creeping doubts. Then one of them halted, pirouetted, and plummeted into the theatre's grounds. Another sank to his knees, shuddering. Then a third fell and in a flash, scores were toppling, small puffs of red rising from their bodies. Silent, lethal javelins, arcing from the trees just to the north. A tight, hateful smile tugged at the corners of my mouth.

'Baudio and the Second Italica,' Batius said, realising now. 'Vindex and the Martia... The Eighth Augusta.'

'They did not stay at Brixia – they crossed the river shortly after we left and marched parallel to us. I couldn't risk telling anyone. Not even you, oldest of friends.'

All along my legions, necks stretched, peering to the sudden attack on the northern theatre. On that far side of the Athesis loop, the trees near that theatre bridgehead shook. Another volley of javelins soared out of the green and despatched another swathe of the theatre bridgehead guards. Then my detachment surged from the woods and into view, bright and numerous, their roar rising like a rowdy audience as they stormed the theatre, flooding into its archways, throwing ropes and ladders up its walls, climbing, slashing down the few remaining Maxentians up there then dropping down into the arc of seats to clash in combat with the remaining defenders. In moments, the white stone steps of the theatre were streaked with red runnels as my three legions battled hard against Maxentius' contingent for control of the theatre.

The Maxentian forces here on Verona's southern walls were suitably quietened by this, the thick lines of men up there twisting to look backwards and see their one route of reinforcement and supply being snapped off. My men controlled the northern banks; I had the southern approaches. Any ships which might try to bring men or grain to the city would be shot through with onager rocks. I imagined my forces moving like the hands of a strangler around the throat of a victim. *No, not a victim*, I corrected myself, once more seeing the dark, twisted creature Maxentius had become, *a murderer like Galerius, like his bastard of a father… a tyrant!*

'Maxentius will have no relief,' I said to Batius, 'neither from legions nor from supply boats. He has no way out. It *will* end… here.' I eyed my ranks, the waiting war towers, the horsemen. All ready. So I took up my battle shield and rested my other hand on my sword pommel, then sucked in a deep and full breath and boomed so Batius and all my highest officers would hear: 'To battle!'

The clarion call of many hundreds of buccinae and a thunderous explosion of war cries filled the sky above Verona, and we advanced to begin the final battle for the north.

14

MAXENTIUS

Verona, 20th April 312 AD

'The bridgehead. Domine, the bridgehead?' yelled the centurion, gesticulating wildly to the north. All was chaos, the din of battle at such a horrendous level that it surpassed any noise I had ever heard. Thousands of men within the city were shouting and screaming. Thousands across the river were fighting and dying, but also shouting and screaming. Thousands more were still on the far side of the city whence the enemy had initially come, all shouting. All screaming. If Tartarus could be experienced by the living, we did it at Verona, and the voices were just the main instrument in that cacophony. Animals. War machines. Missiles. Things boiling. Things breaking. Things falling. Things exploding.

Yet to me, it was all oddly distant, like a noise heard through a door. Because I had seen him. From the walls. I had seen Constantine.

I had been ready for the fight. I have said before that I was becoming a son of Mars, my civic, peaceful ways wrapped up in the toga I now never wore and put away in a cupboard against the day my realm might once more be at peace and allow me to breathe. I was a soldier. I wore the armour and

I swung the sword, more deftly than many expected, I might add. I was ready. I knew the enemy was coming and as far as we could be prepared for it, we were. I was standing on the walls and I saw him, plain as day, gleaming on a powerful horse with a helmet so clagged with gems it must have been like wearing an onager on his head. What had become of the plain-speaking, martial, honest and dour warrior I had known?

But somehow the very sight of him shattered everything I had felt. I was no longer prepared. It all flooded out of me at the sight of my old friend coming for my head. Suddenly I was the boy with the wooden blocks again in the palace in Treverorum, only now it was not the thug Candidianus trying to kick me to a pulp, but the boy who had saved me that day.

I actually ran. I did not know what the men on the walls thought, and I really did not care. All I knew was that I could not be there, looking at Constantine. Probably, given the chaos and the noise, they all thought I was responding to an urgent call. That I ran to something and not from it, which I should have been doing – there was a plan but I was too wrapped up in myself to remember.

I wandered around the city's defences aimlessly, like a lost sheep. I felt utterly empty and confused. All was noise and death and destruction and pleas and commands and blood and fire and flesh and the grating sound of metal raking metal, and I walked through it like a man in a dream. A nightmare, more like, and that was how I came to be at the very furthest side of the city to the shining, bejewelled figure of Constantine, as far from him as I could get, my legs having subconsciously carried me thence.

The centurion sounded so urgent. So desperate.

'The bridgehead, Domine.'

He was pointing wildly. The plan... I strayed to the wall's parapet and looked over, quiet, dreamlike. There was fighting in the theatre on the far bank. My safety net. My secure route for the reinforcements, for we had demolished all the bridges. The two that touched the city to east and west gone, their stones moved to the bridgehead, their timbers now shoring up gates, and the two that crossed at the north and alighted on the far bank to either side of the theatre? One much the same, gone and reused. The other remained only as a stumpy truncated structure that ended some fifty feet short of the city gate. The theatre and the small, walled suburb that housed it on the far bank were cut off as long as we kept the drawbridge up.

Ruricius had examined the state of the suburban walls and had pronounced both the suburb and the area about it indefensible. Instead, he had used his engineering and strategic nous and decided to fortify the theatre. High walls, small entrances. Perfect. He had also constructed a short wall that connected the drawbridge to his theatre castrum where he held, though not for much longer by the looks of it.

Across the river should have been a solid fortress, awaiting new troops, but instead it was a seething mass of men and blood, cries and screams. I knew I had to do something – the plan – but somehow my mind was filled with fuzz and confusion. That jewelled helm. Constantine. Candidianus was here for my head. No, not Candidianus...

The centurion's slap came like a thunderbolt from the gods. He lurched back, ashen-faced. No man even gainsays an emperor. To *raise a hand to one* is an executable offence. Some emperors would have had the torturers keep the centurion alive for months to regret his action, and it was clear that everyone else was as shocked as he. Wide, staring eyes, all around the wall-top. Every man paused in the middle of his task, watching in shock as a low officer slapped an emperor. My head had snapped round to the side. It had not really been a heavy blow, but the shock had carried more weight than the slap. The centurion was now staring at his hand as though it had taken on a life of its own and disobeyed him.

I stared at him, but there was no anger. The ire I always felt, the last – perhaps the *only* – true gift from my father, was not there. The man had been in the right and had it been any other man on the receiving end of the slap he'd have been applauded.

The strange spell was broken when one of the watching soldiers suddenly cried out as an arrow thudded into his neck, sending him plummeting from the parapet.

The noise broke over me like a wave. The ethereal door that had blocked it out had been opened. I was the emperor. Slapped or not, I was Emperor of Rome and fighting for my realm. Damn that beautiful centurion. I fixed him with steely eyes, now focused on my world rather than some lost, long-gone domain.

'How?'

The pale, terrified centurion croaked. 'Three legions. Came from the north, along the bank. Must have been travelling parallel to the enemy for some distance, for they did not cross anywhere near our pickets.'

'They crossed the river upstream and we fell for it again. *I* fell for it. I chastised Ruricius for allowing such a thing to happen at Brixia and entirely failed to learn from his mistake. Gather my Palatine Guard at the gate alongside the reserve and have the Sardinian archers moved to the gate top. Hold all missiles until I give the signal. Go.'

As the centurion scurried off about those tasks and the

world returned to horrible normality atop the wall, I hurried around to where I could get a good view of the theatre.

Ruricius had held the outer wall with archers and guards, but they had fallen and now the foe were swarming over the outer edge and down into the seating, where disordered sections of Ruricius' cohort struggled to hold them back while their commander gathered the bulk of his men down near the stage and the orchestra. The enemy in the great structure outnumbered us by quite some margin. We had lost control of the walls of that great half-moon complex and soon we would have lost all the forces therein, which included some of my best veterans and Ruricius himself. *Hold on*, I urged him silently. *Hold on, Ruricius. Help is coming. I remember the plan.*

Moments later I was down the stairwell and emerging into the arming square behind the gate where my guard were already assembling. I could hear the Sardinian archers moving into position above, where I had just been. There were not enough of my guard to make much of a difference, but I knew a cohort of Cyrenaican heavy infantry were kept here in reserve, too, and I gestured to their commander. 'Form up your men. You and I and the guard are going to make a sally.'

The man's eyes widened, but he nodded his swarthy head and began issuing orders to his musician. In a hundred heartbeats, each one counted with the imagined failure of a heart on the other side of the river, my small force was gathered.

'Guards and men of the Fourth Cyrenaica, hear me. Our hopes for reinforcements are being dashed as I speak by our wily enemy, who has sent a second force to secure the bridgehead. Ruricius Pompeianus and his men, our brethren, are being slain there. There is no hope now of securing the theatre, but with enough vitriol and enough mettle, we can halt the advance of Constantine's men at the waterfront and save our brothers. I want you interspersed to make the most of your different styles and armaments, fighting as one unit, a century of each beside a century of the other. As soon as the bridge is lowered, we cross. We enter the theatre, engage the enemy and save our friends. When you hear three short blasts and one long, pull back to the bridge and then the city, but until then, kill like demons, my brothers. Like demons.'

There was a roar from both units and swords flashed into the air. Their officers had momentary trouble cutting through the cheering and the chants to give the orders to re-form. I left them to it, instead delivering my commands that the gates be opened and the drawbridge lowered. As the doors began to creak wide with a sound like the bones of giants grating and the chains of the bridge began to rattle in their housings, the swarthy officer was suddenly by my side.

'Domine, you cannot mean to lead this action.'

'On the contrary, I must.'

'What would happen should you fall, Domine,' he implored.

I fixed him with a steady gaze. 'Then there will be only one emperor in the West and the war will be over. Ready your men.'

I drew my blade and examined it. I'd had one of my slaves put an extra keen edge on it last night in anticipation of the battle to come. It would split an eyelash, such was the sharpness. We waited as the doors finished opening, and the brightness of the world beyond the walls began to leak in over the top of the lowering drawbridge. I realised I had the two officers beside me now.

'I want half the men breaking left and securing a perimeter for our men to fall back to. Be prepared to form testudo as soon as the archers loose. The other half need to be split between centre and right, but with the weight at the centre – I need manoeuvring room at the right. Space your men carefully, as I want our forces to appear evenly distributed. There is something I need to do there. I will take the first century of the guard independently and seek out Ruricius. Once we've got him, here's what I want you to do...'

The two men nodded, listening to my plan, then momentarily discussing the matter and assigning positions. Then the bridge was almost down and I gave the nod to my musician, who lifted the heavy, curled cornu to his lips. The cadence blew and we were running. There were almost a thousand of us. The hiccup in my plan occurred straight away and betrayed my lack of strategic skill, I suspect, as the men were slowed in a bottleneck. A thousand men cannot quickly issue from a single gate, no matter how big. It mattered not. As soon as they were through, the men were forming again and running at pace. The bridge was still not quite lowered and it felt odd running up a slight incline toward a lip, below which deep water churned.

We were two-thirds of the way across when it finished its descent with a crash. Men struggled to keep their footing as the reverberation shuddered along the length of the timber. Then we were onto the part of the original bridge we'd left intact, solid and strong, and we were bellowing war cries and hurtling towards the defended enclosure of the theatre. We raced from the bridge onto the river bank, past the short temporary wall Ruricius had built out of ruined bridges and which kept this area separate from the suburbs, and finally through the gates and doorways at the rear of the theatre, emerging within and quickly taking in the scene.

Already the newcomers were in danger of taking control.

Having used missiles to pick off the men on the theatre's upper tiers, and unable to breach the heavy, barred doors that had been blocked with rubble in order to enter the theatre, the enemy had used grapples and ladders and climbed to the top at the outer curve, and then over into the theatre itself. Yet the Constantinian legions died in droves as they passed inside. Ruricius' carefully placed archers had not just been on the top tier to keep attackers out. We had learned never to rely on just one wall, after all. More archers were secured behind screens and in doorways in the theatre stage area, and their missiles were picking off enemy legionaries even as they tried to form up. It was valiant, and men were dying, but it was like trying to use a net to hold back a wave and the odds were about to tip the scale.

The insurgents had finally achieved a solid shield wall up in the seating area and, while some of their number still fell periodically, more and more men were joining in as it slowly descended the seating like a wall of death, pushing in on where Ruricius waited, stomping over corpses. The seating area and the orchestra were littered with bodies from the initial attack over the walls, the men both enemy and ally, horribly alike, brothers again in death. Ruricius had now pulled what was left of his men back to the stage to prepare for a final stand, though small pockets of his soldiers still struggled here and there on the seating, trying to hold back the growing Constantinian tide.

The enemy were gaining morale now and starting to advance carefully downwards towards Ruricius, since the arrows had stopped flying from the walls. I was allowing them a clean advance, but there was a reason. I had my plan. In that mad fluster when I'd spotted Constantine and almost lost my will to fight I had almost forgotten it all, and had nearly left Ruricius here to die as I meandered vaguely, ignoring the plans we had made over spiced wine in dark rooms over these past few tense nights.

Bless that centurion and his stinging slap.

I had been one of the first through the archways and into the theatre with my century. Guards and Cyrenaicans flooded through, bolstering the forces there, helping hold against the advance of Constantine's men.

Any moment, but hold for another heartbeat...

I saw Ruricius. Saw him recognise me among the new arrivals. *Yes, my friend. This gamble has failed, so we must fall back on our secondary plan, and I have come as I said I would.* I motioned right with just a flick of my eyes. He nodded.

Now I needed chaos. Ruricius had to be ignored. I motioned. The horn sounded. The arrows from my Sardinian archers came, finally.

With a hiss like a thousand angry adders, arrows thrummed into the theatre, finding targets or just clacking menacingly off marble. Pre-warned, my officers gave the order for testudo, a somewhat old-fashioned manoeuvre, but still a good one, because at this distance and with the two forces only now twenty paces apart, the arrows were almost as likely to kill my men as theirs. But mine were now under a roof of shields and arrows were thudding into them which would otherwise be thinning out my forces. The enemy tried to do the same, turning their shield wall into a square box of wood using the second, third and fourth ranks. They were staggered up the slope of steps, though, and it was impossible to seal the gaps. Men continued to die even as they tried to create a roof. I had timed my archers carefully. Hold off long enough to give them the confidence to move, then release in a cloud at a moment we could protect against the shafts and they could not. It was as I had predicted – *hoped*; *planned* – chaos.

The enemy were distracted.

I gave the orders. Whistles blew. My force, which was heavily weighted to the left, now spread themselves out to the right, evening out the numbers and creating a solid front of uniform strength. But where it had been weak they had left enough room to manoeuvre. Ruricius had moved half a century of men through the front line and was even now making for the *aditus*, the arched tunnel that led out between seating and stage, unnoticed by the enemy in the chaos. My men were there too. As I reached the shadowy tunnel, I was suddenly next to Ruricius.

'You are free. Go.'

Ruricius nodded and clasped my hand momentarily, a curiously brotherly gesture to which I was not used, and which touched me deeply. He smiled. 'I'll be back, Domine. Try and stay alive until I do.'

I grinned. 'Have you not yet learned how hard I am to kill?'

I turned and called my men, and we moved back along the aditus into the orchestra where, there was now a proper fight breaking out. We had to hold for only moments, then we could run. We'd saved Ruricius and bought him time to slip away unseen, for my wily lieutenant had left one tunnel free from the theatre – a slave's entrance. He and half a century of men were even now emerging from the outer wall and navigating to safety. With the aid of Fortuna he would be successful and all this living Tartarus would have been worth it.

I hurried back into the theatre and found that the enemy had forgone their shield wall as inadequate protection and simply charged my forces. They were relying now on weight of numbers. Thank the gods the archers had ceased their barrage when the armies met. We could probably have gone then, but I needed to buy Ruricius time. He had managed to slip away unseen but we needed to make sure he stayed that way. Consequently I spent two hundred heartbeats experiencing what it meant to be a soldier of Rome. I fell into position with my force and I had honestly intended to stay out of combat and cheer on my men as one of them, but the casualty rate was appalling and suddenly I was facing men of the Second Italica – I knew their insignia somehow.

My sword stabbed and pulled back, stabbed and pulled back, stabbed and pulled back. I had no shield and in one mad, spare moment twirled my cloak around my arm, using it when necessary to parry.

I was now a soldier. I was no longer that civic, toga-wearing boy. I was a warrior of Rome, defending my homeland. I hewed flesh and bone with the best of them that day, and whatever else has happened in my life, I will always be proud that I stood with my men at Verona and fought Constantine's legions with my own muscle and steel. And I killed. I would like to claim that it was my martial prowess at work. In retrospect, almost certainly half the men around me were devoting their every effort to making sure I survived the engagement.

I had meant to order the signal but I was so busy glorying in the killing that it completely eluded me and I count myself lucky that I had such men around me as the commander of the Cyrenaicans. *He* had given the signal. The men began to fall back. The enemy, having fought too hard for such little gain, allowed us to pull back. We retreated across the stage, leaving our dead where they lay. We passed through the theatre doors and passages and, as soon as we were clear, men barred them and pushed up stones against them to prevent speedy pursuit.

We ran past that makeshift wall again and onto the bridge. I was one of the last few as we passed onto the drawbridge. The archers above began to release again, keeping the enemy pinned down. It mattered not. We had survived.

Even as we crossed, we felt the great drawbridge shudder and begin to rise, the last few men cursing as they skittered and slid with the increasing incline. My men on the walls were taking no chances, especially with their emperor among the fleeing bodies.

The bridgehead had fallen and we were besieged, but I had won three small victories in the chaos. I had managed to slip Ruricius and his men out of the city to the north. I had become little less than Hercules himself to my men, streaked with blood and gore, my blade wet and notched, my eyes holding that heart-stilling sight of men dying. I had put aside the dreadful spectre that Constantine had raised against me. He was just a man in a fancy helmet. We would win.

We had to.

Run, Ruricius.

15

CONSTANTINE

Verona, 23rd April 312 AD

Three days of bloodsoaked Hades ensued. No sleep, no rest, no way to break inside the stony carapace of Verona. The struggle swung like a corpse on a rope, the bulk of my legions savaging the southern walls but so far to no avail, and the three legions in the north engaged in a desperate battle of wills: they on the lookout for Maxentius' supplies or reinforcements which would be coming from the north, the small enemy watch perched on the city's northern gatehouse, raining long-range missiles on any who came too close to the drawbridge-gap. All the while, Verona had remained locked to me.

On the third night, on the latest surge for the defences, arrows sped around me in both directions – unseen in the near-blackness, then a thick volley of blazing shafts whacked into the red shield-shell thrown up around me by my black-armoured Cornuti. We merely shouted all the louder and drove forward even faster. This was my dozenth foray, each interspersed with spells of rest behind our lines – hastily gobbled-down food and fitful rest that could barely be described as sleep. It was reckless to throw myself into the killing ground, but I could not stand on the grassy monticule beside my command tent and watch while scores of my men were butchered. My forces were close to exhaustion and beginning to doubt that they could break the mighty city's defences. The triplex acies had rotated over the three days, the men assaulting the walls falling back when they reached exhaustion and the lines behind them taking up the mantle. Yet that system was now smeared and spoiled by the fray – great gaps in legions where men had fallen, and the lines ragged and uneven. Yet when they saw me emerge from the command tents and advance again, their doubts vanished like mist in a breeze. Our testudo of shields and three more like it guarded a knot of ram-bearers. The bronze-headed battering post would surely shatter even Verona's mighty bronze-strapped Jovian Gates – if only we could bring it to within striking distance of those colossal doors. My head flicked to the sides every few strides to see the ram-carriers stepping over potholes, dodging round the corpses of dead men, drawing ever-closer to the Jovian Gates. All the while my onagers were hurling volley after volley of burning, oil-soaked rocks above our heads and into Verona's walls, shaking and scarring the stonework – anything to draw the enemy attentions from the ram.

Up ahead, a group of spry runners carried rough planks. They were faster than the gatehouse archers, deftly dodging the rain of shafts. They were almost there...

Yes... I willed them on as they threw down the planks to bridge the death-ditch before the gates – a bridge that would allow my men to bring the ram to bear. No sooner had they completed their task than bubbling oil fell in a sizzling deluge, drenching them and cooking them inside their armour – skin sagging from their faces and hands as they screamed their last, pitching over into the ditch.

Yet I could not afford even a blink of time to pity them, for the oil vases up on the battlements were now empty, and we and the ram were nearly at the gates. Moments from contact. Moments from breaking into Verona.

Whack! An arrow from the galleries took one ram-bearer in the eye. He sank like a dropped robe. But twenty-four more men were there to bear the load – twice as many as were needed.

Whack! Splat!

Two more spun away from the ram, screaming and groaning as their lives spilled into the churned blood-mire. 'Protect them, take up the slack,' I roared to those in my testudo and the other such units, who drew closer around the ram, only for four more carriers to vanish into the earth. Thick crunches sounded from the deep and disguised *lilia* pits – an array of spike-traps dotting the ground like plague scars before the ditch – into which they had fallen, along with screams the like of which I knew would never leave me. Then a shrill smash of thrown pottery sounded from the rear of the ram and a fireball erupted across ten of them. Like human torches they flailed, dropping the ropes, the great ram thumping down onto the earth. The stink of burning meat and hair sickened every man left alive in the doomed push. Now I heard the groan and clank of cogs as the ballistae up on the walls dipped down towards me like the beaks of vengeful carrion birds.

An instant later a bolt shredded through our shield-shell, destroying three shields and pinning the Cornuti legionary by my side to the ground, where he shuddered and remained standing like a living shade, vomiting blood. The ram was lost and our cover was in pieces.

Exposed, an arrow streaked across my upper arm, the

shaft ripping the bear-fur cloak, shearing the dark leather pteruges and gouging deep into my flesh. I roared, seeing the undamaged Jovian Gate and those damned archers in the galleries above. They simply would not yield, and now more than a dozen of them had me clear in their sights.

Creak... went the bows. *Thrum!*

I watched death speed for me. Then... *whump!*

A great weight hammered into me from the side, bowling me down into the stinking mire. Mud, blood and a slick grey-blue bile of some poor legionary's spilled innards spurted up as I skidded through the filth. 'Batius,' I croaked, seeing it was the big man who had saved me.

'Back, back – protect the emperor!' Krocus howled from somewhere nearby in the blackness. A fresh group of Cornuti raced forward to erect a new screen of shields over and around me, Batius and Krocus helped me to my feet and the latest grim retreat from the walls ensued. As we went I saw too much: hundreds of my men, dead in the ditch running the length of the walls, gawping faces and broken limbs jutting like vile roots. The ram would never break the gates. Two of my war towers lay ruined too: the first had fallen foul of one of the disguised pits, shuddering to one side then moaning like a downed giant as it toppled onto its side. My bowmen and slingers atop that one had been dashed like eggs on the ground, necks and limbs snapping, and the legionaries inside were crushed – many dying under the weight of their comrades, others knocked unconscious. The second tower had been set ablaze by Maxentian fire archers, all inside dying a horrific death – and the black skeleton of that contraption still stood like the remnant of a pyre where it had been halted, a little way to my right.

Death all around me. How many more would fall before

night slid away? Before the flies and vultures descended upon the feast? Before dawn shone an angry finger of light upon the city walls – the clay-red surface now obscured in bursts of stinking, drying blood and pockmarks where my onagers had battered at it in futility?

We backed all the way to the command tent and the grassy monticule, at last safely distant from the battle for the walls and the enemy missiles.

I staggered into an open-sided tent. I had no clue that I was in the *valetudinarium* until I heard the rasping of surgeons' saws and screaming of wounded legionaries. I looked around, the interior weakly lit by the pale glow of a few dozen oil lamps. Buckets of vomit, piles of trimmed flesh and even sawn-off limbs lay scattered like the toys of some terrible monster. A medicus, black around the eyes from lack of sleep, stumbled from one wounded soldier to the next, his apron – white at the opening of the battle for Verona – now black with blood. Hundreds. No, *thousands* of men here, most of them lying still, their cloaks drawn over their lifeless faces. Old Lactantius knelt by one man shuddering in death spasms. He held the dying one's hands and muttered words of prayer and solace.

What had I done?

I staggered backwards from the sight.

Just what had I done?

I almost trampled her in my backwards retreat. She was bloodied to the elbows like the surgeon, her beauty sprayed with red, her hair hanging in gore-soaked tangles. Back in the gardens of Taurinorum when she had lamented what she had seen in battle, I had assumed she would shy from it here. Not so.

'Come to admire your creation?' Fausta said.

My lips flapped uselessly.

'Are you injured?' she said, peering in the gloom at my bleeding arm.

'The wound is a decoration, nothing more,' I snapped. I noticed now the way she held a scalpel in one hand. It was the way a slum thief might wield a knife. I recalled then the night when she had last borne steel before me: when she had threatened to kill me lest I let her wretched father live. She couldn't do it then. Now? Now I was not so sure.

She must have read my crazed thoughts, because she threw her head back and laughed. 'This? No, this is to be used on someone worthy,' she said, handing the scalpel to a passing surgeon.

'You could have stayed in Treverorum with Mother and Crispus,' I hissed at her. 'Safe, far from this red hell.'

'I can think of nothing better than to be in Treverorum's halls with your mother and our boy... and nothing worse. A long, horrible wait for the stony-faced herald who would bring news of death? That my brother or my husband had been killed? That is how life is with you, Constantine, a game of swords, the prize: loss, grief. It was either you or my father who had to die. Now it is you or my brother!'

'Fausta, I have no time for this. Anyway, *my* death would not trouble you.'

'It would crush Crispus.'

I nodded silently, feeling like a fool for forgetting about the boy. It was something I was unfortunately skilled at. 'But you would not grieve my passing,' I muttered. 'You hate me.'

She seemed reluctant to reply. So when she did, it was like the kick of a mule. 'There cannot be hate without love,' she said, her voice thickening, her eyes shining with wetness.

'There is still love?' I said, knocked sideways by the notion.

'A seed of it,' she said quietly. 'Yet with every body that is carried in here, with every man who topples from Verona's walls, riddled with arrows or smashed through the head with a slingstone, that seed turns grey, and the shoots retract and wither.'

'Tell me what I must do,' I said, taking a step towards her, arms outstretched.

She backstepped, shoulders rounding, one hand rising to ward me off.

'Domine!' A cry sounded from somewhere outside the tent, amidst the chaotic discord of battle. I ignored it.

'Fausta,' I pleaded with her.

Again she stepped back. 'This war. It will end here, won't it?'

For a moment I saw everything at the corners of my eyes. It felt as if there were more men dead than alive. 'If Verona falls with Maxentius inside, then the war is over.'

'And Maxentius?' she started, her face twisting sourly in anticipation of my answer.

'He will kneel to me!' I barked, angry that she should assume I would not offer him the chance to surrender and relinquish his imperial claims.

'*Domine!*' the officer yelled at me again. Again I ignored.

'He will kneel to me,' I repeated more calmly to Fausta, 'then the war will be over.'

'Then go, take victory. Do not be reckless, lest you leave Crispus fatherless,' she said in emotional bursts.

I could see that she was using Crispus as a shield of sorts, projecting her own fears through him. There was a seed of love indeed. It lifted me at that moment – more than any cup of wine or hot meal might have reinvigorated me. 'I will not fail,' I said, pointing through the tent in the direction of battle. 'This is my destiny.'

'*Domine!*' the persistent officer screamed now.

I left the medical tent and saw that it was Tribunus Scaurus making all the noise, his big, sweaty head switching this way and that in search of me. When he spotted me, it took him a moment to recognise me. I realised why when I saw my reflection in his polished helm: for I wore a mask of dark blood.

'The last city-taker is at the walls!' Scaurus roared as he lumbered over to me.

My eyes swung towards the city, scanning the walls until I saw the wheeled wooden tower: like a great talon rising out of the earth, rocking and swaying as it rolled across another plank-bridge thrown over the ditch by brave runners. The sides were billowing with weak smoke where fire arrows had pierced the dampened hides draped there but had failed to take light. This tower would not topple into a pit, nor would it burn. This tower would be the end of Verona's stout resistance. Then, inside, I would face... *him*.

The war tower came to a halt. Then with a deep crunch, the small drawbridge at the top of the great device groaned and fell forward, clawing onto Verona's parapets. My legionaries spilled forth and into the massed Maxentian defenders with a chorus of war screams. The argent moon cast the fighting men up there in stark relief, blades swinging, blood mizzle falling like rain, bodies and hacked-off parts of bodies plunging down with a horrifically steady rhythm. Then I spotted a fresh wave of Maxentian legionaries: an unblemished steely cohort, surging to support the compromised spot on the battlements.

Then *crash!* went another ball of rock from one of

my onagers, exploding against the section the running reinforcements occupied at that moment, sending mortar and stone and pieces of Maxentian soldiers in every direction. A huge section of the southern walls sloughed away then, and a century or more of his defenders screamed as they went with it, plummeting into the very ditch they had built to snare my men. Yet in less than a breath, a concerted volley of flaming ballista bolts from the city's towers converged upon the offending onager, which burst into a storm of kindling, fire and blood, crew and machine ruined at once. Everything seemed set for a stalemate on the walls now, my men in the war tower unable to make headway onto the parapet thanks to the many defenders. If the war tower could not pierce the defences then nothing could. A great sense of despair began to settle upon me.

What now?

I thrust my sword – my father's before me – down into the blood-wet earth and turned to stride up the grassy hummock and into my command tent, Krocus and Batius following me.

Vindex and Hisarnis stood inside, within the pale bubble of lamplight – wet with battle-filth, steam rising from their shoulders. Where were the rest of my officers? Dead? In that vile ditch? Was this how it felt in the moments before a catastrophic defeat – the realisation that your army is all but gone? I looked through the open tent flap: the indigo band in the eastern sky was growing brighter. The first beams of dawn would come soon and show me the true state of my forces.

Despite my insisting again that I was not badly injured, a roaming medicus tended to my arm wound as I gathered my few trusted men around the table within the tent – he wrapped a length of white linen around my wound, the blood quickly blossoming to soil it. Likewise, the parchment plan we had drawn up became spotted with drips of my blood and sweat as I looked it over.

'The north, Domine,' Tribunus Ruga began.

'No,' I chopped a hand through the air, 'forget the north. That last war tower is our best hope.' I jabbed a finger into the line of the walls on our map. 'Gather what reserves are recovered enough to enter the fray again, concentrate what cohorts we can on the tower, press as many men inside it as we can.'

'But the north,' Ruga repeated.

I felt my temper flare. Damn the northern gate and the drawbridge. The city-taker was the key. '*Forget* the north! It is secure. Maxentius might hold the gates and the drawbridge, but my three legions have that grape-faced cur Ruricius and his forces pinned down on the theatre bridgehead. Without the theatre, the drawbridge is useless. We have the upper hand there.'

Ruga's face told me I was wrong. 'That's what I'm trying to tell you, Domine: Ruricius is no longer fighting in the theatre battle.'

'He has fallen?' I said, taken aback. I was sure after his escapes at Taurinorum and Brixia that Ruricius simply did not know how to die.

'Worse, Domine, he was spotted by one of our Second Italica men – a fellow who had been knocked unconscious in the theatre-struggle three days past, but awoke moments ago in the medicus' tent. He saw Ruricius being ushered from the theatre – alive and well – and not into Verona... but out into the countryside where he took horse and sped away.'

My heart slowed. 'Away? To where?'

Nobody answered. For all heads had swung to the tent flap, frowning at the two fire arrows that sped from the city walls and across the sky. Signal arrows. I staggered from the tent and stared at the sky, a terrible sense of dread rising within me that those blazing missiles were the answer to my question.

16

MAXENTIUS

Verona, 23rd April 312 AD

Torches burned around the walls, and not just for lighting flaming missiles. Dawn was still but an approaching hope as an indigo glow began to suffuse the black. I stood on the walls in my panoply, purple cloak whipping behind me in the wind, matching the pennants and flags snapping straight across the city. It might have looked heroic at some other time. Probably did that day, to the right people. I did not feel heroic. I didn't feel grand or imperial or commanding. What I felt was numb. Numb and tired.

I had seen the ugly face of war before, but still I had experienced nothing like Verona. Nothing like a siege on this scale. I had, over the preceding days, become acutely aware of just what Ruricius had been through, for which I had grumbled and upbraided him. If he'd felt half as broken at Taurinorum or Brixia as I did in Verona, then he'd done well to manage what he had, let alone what I'd expected of him.

Verona was a scene of Tartarus played out in the living world like some dreadful old tragedy on a grand scale. The weather high above was good, with cloudless, silvery-moonlit skies, and yet we only knew that from momentary flashes of clarity, for the air above the city and for a mile in every direction out over Constantine's massed ranks was a constant roiling mess of smoke and sweat and flies and blood. I had never seen the like. It was a miasma of war that had settled around Verona like some Hadean mantle, as cloying and obfuscating by night as it was by day. The noise had become a constant drone in the background. A single sound composed of a thousand threads at any one time, all of them screams or thuds or metallic rasps, whistles, shouted orders, death rattles, cracking stone, surgeon's saws, fiery explosions, neighing, struggling. Death, death, death. The smell was acrid and sickly-sweet like a bloated, part-burned corpse, and there was no way to escape it. It lurked in every home and in every tower and sat like fog around the city.

The strange thing is that the longer I breathed it in, saw it happen, listened to its jarring melody, the more I became comfortable with it, safe in the knowledge that as long as I could smell death, I was still alive. As long as the sounds of war rang out, it meant the city still stood.

The garrison was doing extremely well, or so my officers continually informed me. They were convinced that Constantine was losing more men than I on some grand scale with each passing hour and that attrition would get the better of him. Eventually he would not be able to maintain the siege and would have to run back north to gather supplies and lick his wounds.

Our supplies were holding well. Of course they were. We'd been stockpiling at Verona for over a year against this very possibility, or at least in the expectation of an invasion by Licinius. We could feed Verona even if Constantine determined to stay until the last man fell.

I worried more about the walls. The enemy's last siege

tower was being held at bay, and his ladders were proving worse than useless, but his bombardment was having an effect. Here and there we had suffered structural damage to the defences. My very capable engineers were constantly at work repairing damage, and every stretch still held strong, but every time a crack appeared, my mind's eye saw it open to a breach through which poured screaming legionaries hunting my head.

Still we held.

Some tribunus I didn't know by name hurried up to me along the wall, gesturing behind him. 'The last siege tower is coming dangerously close, Domine. They seem to be putting all their effort into it, pinning all their hopes on it, and there is a danger, albeit a small one. I would like your permission to draw reserves from the north to help. We can overturn it with enough strength. I already have the oil heating up to repel the next push.'

I nodded. 'Whatever you think best, Tribune. Just keep them away and buy us more time.'

Keep them away. More time. I'd been telling them to keep us safe and buy us time for days. Time for what, they all wondered and, given the way this was stretching out, I was starting to ponder that myself.

'You need a bath.'

I turned to see Valeria standing behind me like some wingless victory, pristine white and glorious amidst the carnage and the stench and the blackened world. She looked disapproving.

'It is a sad fact that war is not the cleanest of hobbies,' I said with exaggerated hurt. She did not smile as I'd hoped she would.

'The people of Verona and the soldiers who fight here,' she

said quietly, 'are all filthy and exhausted and their spirits flag with every passing day. Nothing destroys the mood of the hoi polloi like finding their betters in the same condition as them. They look up to you and the nobles and officers. You are supposed to be above grime and above squalor. You are supposed to be a god ruling in the mortal world.'

'Hades, presumably.'

'Do not be facetious, Maxentius. I am quite serious.'

'I know you are,' I sighed. 'I will bathe when I return to the palace. Until then I am a soldier, not a god. Look,' I added, gesturing out across the wall. 'Is *Constantine* a god?'

'Of course not.'

'But his people fight for him as though he is, and yet he is grimy and bloodsoaked and swings a sword among them, rather than being some immaculate, glowing deified nobleman.'

'You are not Constantine. He attracts that sort of martial, base adoration because he himself is martial and base. He is a peasant from some provincial backwater and that is the very reason why he must not be allowed to rule. It is not his right. It is *your* right. You are Roman, not Illyrian. You should be glowing and golden, not bloodsoaked and dark.'

I struggled then, forcing myself not to point out that though my father had risen to the apex of Roman power, my forebears had been shopkeepers in Sirmium, out in the provinces. Sometimes Valeria, like all noblewomen in my experience, preferred to forget what was inconvenient.

Further interaction was prevented by another arrival. Ancharius Pansa, as hideous as ever no matter how well he turned himself out, strode across from the nearest tower's door. At his heel were two soldiers of my guard – the two I had got to know and often found standing outside our chambers in the grand domus that had become my palace in Verona. Men that I had come to think of as my most personal guards.

'Florentius and Herodius, stay with the emperor and make sure he remains out of danger,' the squat officer said, gesturing at me, or possibly *to* me: 'Domine, if you insist on standing openly upon the walls for any opportunistic archer to try for, I must insist in turn that you have adequate guards at your disposal.'

I shrugged. I was surrounded by my army and was fairly sure that any man on these walls would leap forward with a shield to save me if Constantine proved to have Herculean archers with giant arms who could send an arrow this high and this far.

'And Valeria wants me to be escorted everywhere by an appropriate number of lictors,' I replied. 'This wall would be damned crowded if I listened to you all. It would probably collapse under the weight of my companions.'

'What was that?' the squat imp said suddenly, holding up a rather impertinent silencing hand as his head snapped around at some sound I had not noticed.

My brow furrowed at Pansa's words and I scoured Verona. Nothing had changed. The great tower was still disgorging men onto the walls, and Constantine's vicious motherless bastards swarmed like ants, heedless of their heroic losses. Their artillery still battered the walls pointlessly, unable to do more than give useful work to my engineers. I could even see the bejewelled-helmeted bastard himself – my heart still lurched at my only true friend turned enemy – struggling back through a wake of melted men and pinned corpses, ready to command his next legion of poor miserable shits against the wall.

That first day, the sight of my former friend, the pretender, had rather unmanned me. Now, on the cusp of the third day's dawn, I had become inured to it. He was *always* there. Testing. Pushing. Trying.

My eyes settled on the new factor in the gloomy tableau that had caught Pansa's attention, and it drew from me an odd smile.

A fire arrow. A single shaft shooting up to the heavens, still highly visible in the pre-dawn light.

'Thank the gods.'

'What, Domine?' Pansa asked, confused as he hurried toward me. Valeria was there too, now, brow creased.

'What is it?' she echoed the soldier.

'That, my love, is our salvation. Watch and rejoice.' I waved to the tower nearby, where a man bearing my standard stood. He saluted back at me and an unusual cadence blared out from his horn, which was picked up around the walls.

'What is happening, Domine?' Pansa asked, confused.

'The arrow was from Ruricius. Here comes my reply.'

Moments later more fire arrows streamed out from the walls, seemingly at random to the casual observer, but they were not. They were, in fact, *far* from random. Each arrow fell to earth in its designated spot, and each archer – the best in the city – repeated the shot twice, landing their missile with precision and care.

'What does it mean?' Valeria asked.

'It means that now Ruricius and his reinforcements know Constantine's weak points. My old friend is about to have a very bad day.'

17

CONSTANTINE

Verona, 23rd April 312 AD

As the fiery arrows faded to nothing somewhere east of my siege lines, a streak of golden light shone from that direction – dawn piercing the sky. I stood outside my command tent and stared into that blinding light, heart pounding. I prayed my fears were false. When a paean of trumpets blared from the eastern horizon, I knew they were horribly real.

My soul froze when I saw the shadowy, infinite mass rising with the sun, here on the river's southern side, arcing around towards the back of my unprepared and exhausted lines. They came at us like a tide – a churning, argentine tide that would smash into us, drive us across the swell of battle and surely pound us against the base of Verona's walls. I stared, shaking with exhaustion, at a loss, mud, sweat and blood dripping from my armour, my skin and my hair. The battle that felt like it might just be tipping in our favour thanks to my third and final war tower now rose against us like a nightmare from behind. Nearly forty thousand Maxentian reinforcements, with that *bastard* Ruricius at their head. Three days ago, he had vanished during the theatre battle. Now he was back and, for the first time since we entered Italia, I was outnumbered. He came with thick wedges of ironclad cavalry, serried blocks of legionaries, archers, slingers, javelin throwers.

Batius stumbled over next to me, staring too. The sight of him – his wiped-clean face as white as snow and gawping at what was coming for us – hammered a nail through my heart. The big man was everything I ever wanted to be: courageous, dauntless, unyielding. In the dawn light, in the face of that, he looked like a diffident recruit.

'Our lines, Domine,' he croaked, 'we must turn them around.'

Just then the earth spasmed right behind us and we were both thrown forward, earth pattering down nearby. A stone thrower up on one of the city's corner towers had somehow found a few dozen strides of extra range and had nearly ended everything – the huge ball of granite having flattened my command tent, pulverising one of my highest officers in the process.

I scrambled to my feet, head switching from the city defences to the wall of living death coming for us. If we turned our backs on Verona, a sally – ordered by Maxentius – would end us. If we did not turn our backs, Ruricius would. Snared on the horns of my oldest friend… my killer… I knew the greatest folly would be to writhe on the dilemma. *Make your choice, make it clearly, and put your heart and spirit into it*, Father whispered to me from somewhere in Elysium.

'Pull back,' I snarled to the rear band of my triplex acies. The Regii, the Fourth Jovia, the Lancearii and the Cornuti were positioned there. Five thousand men altogether – losses having robbed centuries' worth of men from each. Not nearly enough.

'Bring your spears around,' Batius screamed, loping

along lines, slapping the stunned ones who had seen what was coming for them and shaking those who had not yet understood what was about to befall them. Trumpets blared, whistles too. Dracos and standards swiped madly like the arms of drowning men, bright ribbons flailing.

'Batius, bring the middle rank round too,' I rasped, leaping onto Celeritas' back and riding along the back of my now rapidly roused forces. Another four thousand men. Not enough, simply not enough. Then I cast my frantic eye at the city walls and the churning mass of my legionaries pushing and jostling to pour into the low door on the rear of the remaining siege tower, ready to ascend the wooden stairs and ladders within and spill out to reinforce the many already tangled in combat up on the walls. Positioned not far back stood the front rank of the triplex acies, another seven thousand men. 'Pull all but one legion from the front, we need everyone.'

'But... D-domine,' one centurion croaked from nearby, 'the defenders on the walls are close to breaking. If we pull back we will surely lose our grip on the parapets. And if the defenders then come at us...'

'*Everyone!*' I screamed at him. Horns howled and whistles screamed. Like a field of wheat bending to face the sun, the three bands of the triplex acies creaked to face south-east, leaving just one regiment to support the war tower and the assault on the walls. Shields clacked together – a panoply of capricorns, hawks, hounds, Christian Chi-Rhos and more. Breaths puffed in the cool dawn air. Exhausted voices rose in moans and curses. Ruricius' storm was half a mile off, but already the ground was shivering under the hooves of his cavalry. I bawled to Vitalianus and the heavy cavalry. 'Cataphracti, ride left, make as if to charge but do not engage

– slow them if you can. Equites promoti, to the right, do the same.' Banners chopped and swished to pass the orders to my flanking riders.

They sped off at a gallop, spreading like talons to harry and slow the enemy approach. Brave riders, fresh too – having stood back while my foot soldiers assaulted the city. But by all the gods, what could they do against this deluge of steel coming for us? I saw them circle and mock-charge out there, saw their javelins fly, glinting in the sun. They did as was right: never veering too close to Ruricius' army, always darting wide whenever a unit of enemy cavalry came shooting from the oncoming ranks to try and engage. Perhaps they slowed our would-be killers by moments, but to what end? We, the besiegers, were now the besieged. Flashes of childhood tuition sped through my mind – of Caesar at Alesia, caught between the jaws of the Gauls in the enemy town and more hordes flooding in from the countryside to attack the attackers.

I felt the sheer scale of them, dozens of men deep, coming at a quick step. I heard them rumble in the beginnings of a roar. At that moment, I saw them speed up, and their flanking regiments racing proud of those in the centre. I glanced left and right – at the gaps between the flanks of my triple layer of men and the neck of the River Athesis loop. If the enemy came around on our sides, we were doomed. One line. One wider, *stronger* line, I realised.

'Sound the horns, *simplex acies*, stretch to the riverbanks,' I screamed, riding up and down furiously across the shield-and-spear front of my army. Trumpets blared again. I heard the clamour of boots, shouts and cries as the rear band of four legions surged forward to join the first, deepening and widening our ranks. Next, the men recalled from the war tower came too. Sixteen thousand men. Dozens deep, either end now touching the loop in the river. Ruricius' deadly tide could not outflank us now. A chance?

I slid from Celeritas and slapped his grey rump, sending him racing off to the western banks of the Athesis, then backstepped to take my place within the Cornuti ranks, front and centre of my army. Batius and his *primus pilus* parted then pressed their shoulders against mine. I glanced backwards at Verona's Jovian Gates, fearing that they were about to swing open for Maxentius to sally. Then I caught sight of Fausta again, in the tents immediately behind us. Thanks be to all the gods that young Crispus was back in Treverorum, but why – *why* – was she here on this damned campaign? It seemed like a cruel trick – for her to have talked of a surviving seed of love only moments before she, old Lactantius, I... all of us might be slaughtered.

'Domine, it is time,' Batius growled.

Twisting my head forwards again, I saw that Ruricius' relief army was but two hundred paces distant now. They slowed for a moment, perhaps a little cowed by the solid line awaiting them, even though they had two men for my every one? No... not cowed, merely slowing to unleash a storm upon our heads – for I heard a band of officers cry out over there and the dawn was stolen away by a swarm of missiles – arrows, slingshot.

'Shields!' Hisarnis bellowed, every other commander joining the guttural refrain.

Up went the bright discs like a roof. A blizzard of rattling death whacked down upon us. An arrow plunged into the collarbone of the Cornuti primus pilus and a lead sling bullet plunged through the forehead of another as if it was dropping into a pond. Their blood soaked my days-unshaved, numb face. I heard hundreds of death screams from around and behind me. My line swayed, panicked. Ruricius – I could see him now, on horseback in cape and helm, directing his bowmen and slingers – now ordered his men on at haste. We had no time to organise our archers, but a few pockets managed to send back weak ripostes before Ruricius' lot slowed again, this time eighty paces away – their armour and insignias clear as day now, so many of them.

'*Spiculaaaaa!*' I heard the bastard scream.

Now darts and javelin sailed across the short distance, thundering into our shields. I heard shredding wood, crumpling armour, tearing flesh and snapping bones. One such missile sped between me and the fellow on my right. Two behind me slid away. And then the enemy tide sped forward once again.

Seventy paces...

'Stay together,' I boomed, sensing my own nerve wavering, knowing my men would surely be feeling the same. 'For me, for your brothers, for the empire!'

I heard a small number of them bawl in a throaty, exhausted song of defiance. It was not the roar of men intent on victory. It was the feeble cry of those about to be vanquished. I glanced along our front. I saw Batius; he realised it too.

Sixty paces...

Something rose in me then. A blazing defiance, the likes of which I had only ever felt at the edge of death, a strength that comes to a man only when he knows he is at his last ebb. My chest swelled with breath and I cried out to my soldiers: 'One day I was on a mountain in Persia. The Shahanshah stood before me with his immortal guards.'

Forty paces...

'By dusk I had proved the guards were mortal, and the Shahanshah was in flight like a mouse. Stand shoulder to shoulder with me here, today... and we will win a victory to outshine even that one.' The men seemed stunned, but from them I heard the rise of a growing, guttural roar of hubris, kindled by my words.

Twenty paces...

Next, Batius added his part: 'This green-skinned mass of recruits is good at squealing and throwing sharpened sticks,' he snarled, spittle flecking the air, his granite-features lined with passion as he drew his spatha with a *hiss* that somehow sounded over all the clamour of shouting, rattling chaos that was coming for us, 'now let's see how they fare against the finest legionaries of Gaul, of the Rhenus borders, of Britannia, of Hispania...' The rising hubris exploded from the various legions as they heard the names of their homelands spoken aloud.

Ten paces...

'... of *Rome!*'

I swear I shed a tear at that moment, as the loudest cry of battle I had ever heard poured from my army, a rampant and swift barritus, just as Ruricius' relief army came to within five paces, just as we saw their snarling maws, their swishing plumes, the whites of their eyes. I swear I saw fear in them.

I felt my body shudder as the wall of onrushing enemy shields battered against mine in an almighty clash of iron upon iron upon wood upon leather – like thunder rolling from every direction. I felt our entire line stagger backwards, the air being crushed from my lungs, my arms pinned to my sides. There would be no forfex here, no ruse. This would come down to the sheer vigour and will of my veterans against that of Ruricius' lot. Spears licked like lizards' tongues between me and the Cornuti legionaries by my sides, sharpened tips skittering and scoring against shields and metal. I could barely breathe, the weight of many thousands pressing behind me and before me. I heard the enemy's gleeful cries. 'He is here. Constantine is here.' And Ruricius' blaring voice: 'Take his head, bring it to me,' he said as if it was a mundane task with no other possible outcome.

His troops seemingly believed so: a flurry of weapons flashed out towards me. With a great heave I freed my sword arm, forfended one blow then drove my spatha into the eye socket of some screaming enemy, then battered the hilt down, hard, on the unhelmed skull of another. The bone popped and the skull split, a bulge of grey-pink matter swelling from the fissure and the legionary suddenly staggering back from battle, lips moving in some nonsense utterance. An enemy javelin hammered down and stuck fast in my shield. I swept the shield before me to clear a modicum of space, relieving the intense pressure. A knot of Cornuti – heroes – leapt into the gap, making the front line whole before me, shielding me with their very lives. All along the long lines I saw blood leaping and steel flashing. At either end Vitalianus and my cavalry were pinned now by Ruricius' vastly more numerous riders. My infantry line began to sag. Scores of men fell, run through, robbed of their heads or limbs, ripped open. Heroes or not, we were simply too few. When I heard a ripping of cloth I saw that we were being driven back over our tents. *Fausta?* I fretted. Worse, I heard cries from somewhere behind Verona's Jovian Gates.

Then I heard it, just as at dawn: the wail of trumpets. My heart fell into my boots. This was it: Maxentius' ultimate riposte – a sally from the city gates that he would lead, hammering into the rear of my lines, butchering us. Failure pressed upon me like an iron cloak... until I heard the cries of those soldiers coming from somewhere to our rear.

'Second Italica, come round through the shallows, strike the Maxentian flanks!'

'Eighth Augusta, on the left! First Martia!' Prefect Vindex bellowed.

My veins pulsed with hot fire. The three legions in the north, who had been holding the theatre. Nine thousand soldiers. They had witnessed what was happening and they had raced across the ford just west of the city, braving showers of arrows and ballista bolts from Verona's walls to do so, coming to us when we were on our knees. They spilled into the western end of the Maxentian relief army. It was as if a giant had swept his knuckles against the enemy right. They staggered, tripping, men falling out of line, order collapsing. Before their commanders could shout them to their feet again, my centre surged at them in a storm of steel. Helmets split with the sheer ferocity of my men's strikes, ringmail exploded in clouds of iron loops, foes fell in entire ranks. First, I saw the enemy horsemen breaking away, and the legions on their flanks too now began to fall back, their war cries conspicuously fading.

A salvo of javelins sailed from my lines and wreaked havoc among theirs. I saw entire centuries topple – stricken or cowering in fear. Hundreds fell, then hundreds more.

'These soldiers are no match for you,' I roared. 'Push... *push!*'

By the gods, did we push. The dawn rays streaked across us, bathing me as it had done upon me that day at the Temple of Apollo, when I had become – beyond all doubt in my men's eyes – the one chosen by those very same gods. It was like a fire turned back upon the burner. Our lines kept some semblance of shape but we ran at them. Soon the backstepping foe became a wall of backs, shields and spears thrown down as they took flight. Once again – just as at Brixia – I saw

Ruricius amidst the heart of yet another defeat. This time, he would not live to try again.

My eyes met those of Maxentius' finest general, mine narrowed, his widened like moons. His red cape *swooshed* round as he elbowed a fleeing cavalry archer from his horse and vaulted onto the beast, taking it for himself. I sprang forward before his horse could pick up into a canter and a gallop. Just as he had done to his own man a moment ago, I leapt and barged him from the horse's back. The pair of us rolled together in the churned, stinking earth. He leapt to his haunches, his breath short already thanks to his stocky frame.

Hiss, went his sword as he drew it.

'These legions may have failed'—he gestured with jerky arms to his army—'but they are merely a fraction of the forces the true Augustus can muster. In the south, legion upon legion of hardened veterans stack up in preparation to crush you, and they *will* crush you if you dare venture there. Better you stay here, lumbering around the north, far from the heart of Italia with the tattered remnant of your invasion force. Rome will never be yours, you...'—he lunged for me, thinking I had not been watching the movement of his feet—'...son of a wh—'

My shoulder dropped to dodge his strike and my sword shot up and under his chin, the tip bursting through the back of his head. His face took on a strange look: lips still pursed in enunciation of the curse that had triggered all of this, but his eyes darting over my face, confused, then rolling down mournfully to see the blade that had ended his days.

'Rome will belong to the strongest, you dog, just like this day.'

He slid from my sword just as my forces overtook me, flooding on in pursuit of the fleeing Maxentians. The relief army had come. I had smashed them. Now, I thought, turning back towards the city, it was time to face the man who had once been like a brother to me.

With a groan of timber, the Jovian Gates swung open now when they should have opened at the same time as Ruricius' charge. *I taught you about walls, Maxentius*, I mused, *but not about the importance of timing during battle.* The faces of the sally force were sheet white as they realised the consequences of their ill-timing. Instead of flooding out to attack us, they halted there, some peeling back, some outright fleeing, the rest hastily dragging the gates closed once more.

I thought of sheathing my sword, but did not, instead waving a cohort of the Cornuti with me as I rushed towards the war tower – our route inside the city. The battle for Verona was almost over, the war too, and I would be there to see it finished.

18

MAXENTIUS

Verona, 23rd April 312 AD

I watched in horror. Somehow it was not the utter destruction of the swathes of ironclad heavy cavalry or my own imperial horse guard that tore the breath from me. It was not the sea of writhing corpses or the flood of fleeing men that had moments before been an unstoppable tide of victory. It was the sight of Ruricius swept from his horse by Constantine and then the pair brawling in the mud like two legionaries. It was the sight of them snarling at one another, covered in the muck of battle. It was the sight of Constantine's blade projecting from the back of my greatest general's head.

Ruricius. As he juddered and slid from the usurper's sword, images of the man flashed through my mind, right back to that day on the Palatine when he had been sweating and grinning, exhausted from sword training with my boy Romulus. The body that was now slumping down into the blood and shit of the battlefield had once been a friend to my son. He had been many things to me: confidante, general, friend. Now he would be a memory.

I moved through the world like a plague. Wherever I went, they died. Those I loved. Romulus. Anullinus. Ruricius. Even my father, I suppose. My heart grew bleak. The battle was lost. And if the battle was lost, then Verona was lost. And if Verona was lost, then the war was lost. I had lost. All that remained was for Constantine's victorious forces to clamber up these walls and take my head.

Would he do that, I wondered? It was common practice in war but for everything that had happened we had once been friends. The *best* of friends. Would that bloodsoaked figure down there, wiping Ruricius' brains from his cold steel, parade my head on a spear, gloating over his great victory? Not that I would care. I would be dead, and these days I made certain to be ready for the boatman. I wore a simple leather thong around my neck, thin and fragile, with a gold *aureus* upon it. When danger loomed I could with ease slip it into my mouth and bite through the thong. I would not drift around the world as some sort of ghost. I would pay the boatman for the final journey and be with my beloved Romulus in Elysium. Even if my head danced the jig of defeat upon a spear, I would be with my son.

There was an odd comfort in that thought, and I was calm and composed as I turned to Ancharius Pansa.

'Bring up the heated sand and the boiling water. Have the Corsican spearmen brought to the walls above their tower. If they want the parapet they can pay for every brick in blood. Have the archers deployed such that they can kill anything that moves on this wall when we fall.'

Pansa frowned. 'Domine?'

'The battle below is lost. Verona teeters and may be beyond saving, but we will make them pay for it. Issue the orders.'

I ripped my sword from its scabbard and unclasped my cloak, letting it fall ingloriously to the ground, where it would be less of an impediment in combat.

'Domine you must…'

'Must what? Run? Sue for peace?'

'Perhaps a careful negotiation? Constantine has a history of almost Caesarian mercy. He even took in your father.'

I stared at the man. 'He also murdered my father in prison. Gods, but you sound like you *admire* him, Pansa.'

The strange man shifted uncomfortably. 'I am thinking of your safety, Domine. Perhaps we can be permitted to withdraw? Surely that is better than a brutal death on the walls of this place, only to have your corpse defiled by a howling mob of Constantine's men?'

A powerful argument, it had to be said. But I knew that I could no more ask for clemency than Constantine could give it, and it would have been exactly the same the other way around. The tower of our conflict was built on powerful foundations of insults and anger, and no matter how much either of us might regret what had come to pass, it could no longer be undone. We were set upon a path of destruction now and there was no turning back. One or both of us would die before this war was over.

Pansa gave me a helpless look, and then another voice cut in on our awful discussion.

'You will not fall here, Maxentius.'

I turned to see Valeria standing like some goddess in white amidst the carnage. Somewhere nearby a man screamed and plunged from the wall, felled by an arrow from the wooden war tower that would end it all.

'There does not seem a lot of choice, Valeria.'

Another bellow nearby, this time of fury as a dozen legionaries appeared from a tower door and ran toward the struggle for the walls, roaring their defiance.

'I will not let you die here, Maxentius. You are the emperor of Rome and I am the empress. We will prevail, and in the grand palaces inside the great impregnable walls of Rome. I will not perish in some provincial latrine. I have the *equisio* below. He has horses. There is a century of men waiting to escort us.'

I blinked. We were under siege. Even if it were acceptable to flee with my tail between my legs, how could I manage such a thing? I had been prepared to die here. Accepting, even. Valeria was robbing me of my certainty. Out of the corner of my eye, I spotted an owl rising from the city. Minerva's bird, the very epitome of wisdom. Wisdom was what I needed right now.

'We are trapped,' I mumbled, watching that majestic creature as it climbed through the stink to the open air.

'There is a way. The bridge.'

Pansa nodded, eyes now gleaming. 'The bridge,' he echoed. 'The enemy are devoting all their strength to the tower. The legions they had on the other side of the river concentrating on the bridge approach were drawn away to face Ruricius. There are but a few units there now. It is almost overlooked. A rat-run out of this place.'

I shook my head, in disbelief rather than refusal. I had staked everything on Verona. The linchpin of the north. The bastion that protected the way to Rome. Verona had fallen and I expected to die here. For the whole war to end here. Was it possible? Could it be?'

'If we could flee south...' I said, almost a whisper.

'We can still win,' Valeria finished for me. 'There are garrisons all the way south who can hold Constantine up while you prepare, and the force you can muster at Rome will still outnumber Constantine's. Plus Volusianus is there. Ruricius has fallen, but Volusianus remains.'

I nodded now. The walls of Rome were the most powerful in the world. There was no way he could take Rome out from under me. Rome would prevail and I would prevail.

I would *not* die in Verona. I would *not* fall here and dance the spear-jig for my enemy's entertainment.

I opened my mouth and gave the orders. They went unheard, for just two hundred paces away, a fresh wave of Constantine's men spilled onto the wall-top like floodwater over a dam. Men were killing and dying. Screams, blood and gleaming metal. The battle for Verona's walls was done. My gaze dropped to the land beyond the walls and scanned the seething masses. I spotted him then, a bloodsoaked gleaming mess surrounded by hairy barbarians and banner-men, hurtling for the tower, determined to be part of this victory in person, perhaps determined to take my head for himself.

'Sorry to disappoint you, old friend.'

I turned and began to take the wall stairs two at a time, Valeria and Ancharius Pansa at my heel, along with the ever-present Valerius Florentius and Valerius Herodius, the pair of brothers who had been my closest guards now since the day I set foot in Verona. We reached the bottom of the wall and I recognised the banner flying among the men waiting on horseback to save me. A Praetorian banner, proudly bearing the ancient scorpion emblem. I knew the flag and the number on it. These were the men who had been with me when we stormed into the governor's palace in Carthage and put an end to Alexander, and now they were with me again here. How Valeria had managed to drum up a unit of Praetorians when most had perished and those who had not were still in Rome, I did not know, but I was grateful for the sight. I took it as an omen as favourable as the owl I'd seen flying in the early morning light, and I now realised it had been heading south, making for Rome. Minerva's own bird was drawing me back, leading me home.

We mounted and made our way through the panicked, screaming city, soldiers barging aside anyone who got in the way, riding down the defenceless and the innocent in the need to get their emperor to safety. I felt for the victims, and for all those about to perish in Verona. They would suffer badly, I knew, but I simply did not have the energy to mourn yet. We pushed and rumbled through the crowds. Valeria sat proud on a soldier's horse, astride it like a man, rather than lounging in a carriage as was the custom. It should have been an odd, jarring sight, but somehow there was always that about Valeria that made her commanding, and in a military saddle she could easily have been a general.

By the time we reached the north gate, the city had fallen. There is a curious change in the noise of a city between beleaguered defender and conquered foe, and now that latter sound was moaning out across Verona, a tone of despair with jangling chords of panic. Somewhere back there Constantine would even now be moving through the streets seeking my headquarters, looking for me. His men would be demanding of any officer they found where the pretender emperor was cowering.

The gate was already creaking open as we neared it, the drawbridge descending with a rattle and clatter. Somehow someone had sent word ahead and the rat-run was prepared. My heart leapt to see Quadratus here, once a tribune of the Third at Albanum, one of the men who had draped the purple cloak about my shoulders all those years ago. He had gathered together a vexillation of several hundred legionaries and was preparing to sally forth.

'Imperator,' he shouted across the heads of his men.

'Quadratus,' I smiled in relief.

'The enemy are reacting. They move toward the theatre and the gate to prevent any flight. You must get through. Your horsemen will escort you. The Third will watch your back.'

I felt that relief crumble at the realisation. Quadratus was not here to ride with me, but to hold back the tide while I did so myself. I had no time to argue, though, for the gates were open and the bridge lowering. Half a dozen riders were moving immediately, racing over the timbers even before it clonked down flat. As Quadratus had the horns sound and moved his men out at a run to repel the advancing enemy, those few cavalry secured the way through the hastily constructed defences we had created. To our current benefit, Constantine's men had broken down most of the defences for ready access to the bridge, which gave us an almost clear run. As those half-dozen men killed the few sentinels at those defences, Quadratus and his legionaries flowed out like a crimson tide across the far bank, throwing up shield walls and casting pila heroically, facing certain death like the Spartans of Leonidas so that I could survive to hold Rome.

Tell the Spartans, passer-by, that here, obedient to their word, we lie.

'I will tell them, Quadratus. I will tell them.'

As we raced across the bridge and towards tantalising freedom, I watched the sickening scenes as Constantine's legions, feral and howling, swept into the shieldwall of my saviours. I never saw Quadratus die, though I knew he did, for every soul who ran to their doom that day died. They died to save me, may the gods watch over their future in Elysium, each and every one.

My own peril was far from over, though. We raced through the ruins of the defences we had put together when the enemy was still a distant threat, and we made for the suburban city wall there, which had been breached in many places, the gates broken and open. But there were still men on the walls and still Constantinian riders here and there, trying to gather into units to stop this sudden and unexpected sally. They were not large forces, but then, neither were we.

Then there was true danger. A small unit of riders – lightly armed and armoured, fast and determined, rounded a wall and came for us. Spears were levelled among my companions, and dozens of swords hissed from their scabbards. I did the same, my sword ready to take their blood in order to ensure the freedom of Valeria and myself. I was surprised to see a hand suddenly on the wrist of my sword arm, and I turned, wide-eyed, to see Ancharius Pansa. 'Not today, Domine. Ride for freedom.'

I thought for a moment that the homunculus meant to sacrifice himself just as Quadratus had done. I couldn't countenance that. Not another one. But no, he gave orders to half a dozen men, and those men raced off ahead, breaking their horses in desperation to head off the danger. As they pulled ahead I noted with dismay Florentius and Herodius, my long-time guardians, kicking their horses, swords levelled. They hit the enemy horsemen like a hammer, and the combat was short and brutal. I saw both the brothers fall to chopping blows, screaming out their defiance in the service of their emperor. How many more would have to die? How many?

But Hades had not gathered his full harvest yet. Those half-dozen were not enough. The enemy were still coming. More men peeled off our small and ever-diminishing escort, racing to stop the enemy.

There were some thirty of us left when we crested the hill

and the scene of my greatest defeat was finally lost to sight. We could not stop, though. No matter how many we had beaten to reach this place, there would be more. They knew we had fled, and as soon as Constantine became aware of that the entire north would be flooded with men seeking me.

We paused by a stand of pines, and I wondered why. Pansa then ordered half the party off their mounts. I stared, bulge-eyed as our escort halved. Twelve Praetorians remained in the saddle to escort Pansa, Valeria and myself south. I knew why, of course. We had ridden hard, though it had been just a short distance. We could not risk ruining the horses before we were a safe distance from Verona. Now we would each have a spare horse, while that dozen brave soldiers would straddle the road to slow any pursuit.

'What now?' I breathed, anxiously, as the riders took the reins of the spare horses.

Pansa pointed south. 'There is a small cavalry unit at Hostilia. Once we are safely away from the battlefield we angle back south-west and make for it. There we can pick up supplies, fresh mounts and extra men. Once we pass Hostilia we will have a safe ride to Rome, Domine.'

Safe.

Was anywhere in the world safe now?

I had turned northern Italia into a massive fortress against my enemies and it had crumbled, one bastion after another. Where we were sure of victory we suffered defeat. Where we were cunning we had been outmanoeuvred. We had every advantage and we had outnumbered Constantine by some three men to his one when he crossed the mountains. And yet we had lost. The north had fallen, and it was not *all* through the ill favour of Fortuna. Nor was it lack of spirit or cunning. Ruricius had shown both. Someone had interfered with the defences at Taurinorum, which had started the fall of the northern cities and changed the course of the war. Someone had ruined our chances. Someone had lost me the north.

I would find out who, and I would have them skinned.

'All is not lost, husband,' Valeria murmured close by. I started, turning to her. Ancharius Pansa and his riders were both ahead and behind, playing van and rearguard, and only my wife and I rode together. I felt a bitterness fill me at her words.

'Perhaps, but by the gods, it feels like it.'

'You still outnumber Constantine, and you have the strongest walls in the world to hold against him. Crush him at Rome and then watch these paltry northern holes proclaim for you in cowardice as he flees past them with his Moesian tail between his legs.'

I sighed resignedly. 'It sounds perfectly reasonable. Every plan brought to me always sounds perfectly reasonable. Yet somehow, between the planning and the execution it always ends in disaster and loses me yet more territory.'

'It matters not if you have to fight back north from Rome. You can do it, and Daia might yet weigh in on your side.'

I nodded sadly. 'Constantine's force is just too strong. They are small, but they are veterans and powerful. Several times now we have thrown vast arrays of men at them and watched the ensuing disaster. What we lack is veterans.' I thumped my saddle horn in irritation.

'You *have* veterans. African legions at least.'

'The African legions have done little more than club a few nomads and build the odd aqueduct for centuries, but yes, I take your point. The bulk of the forces, though, are garrison troops or recently recruited, unlike Constantine's, who have been forged in iron on the northern frontiers for decades. I might have had more time to prepare such troops had I not spent the last year arguing with Volusianus over how to deal with the mob and putting endless Christian priests in their place.'

There was an odd silence. It felt as though something had changed, and I saw calculation in Valeria's face. I waited. She was shrewd, and I was intrigued.

'Religious difficulties.'

'What?'

She smiled an unpleasantly feral smile. 'You have suffered endless difficulty holding a single city together with conflicting beliefs. Your army suffers schisms, but to Zenas and Volusianus' credit they have kept the Christian units separate from the rest, preventing too much unrest. This is the bonus of having such a large army. Constantine does *not* have such a large army.'

'What are you saying?'

'I stood on the battlements of Verona long enough to get a good look at his army, as did you. There were legions who knelt for the Christian song in the morning, and there were men who praised Jove. There were even men hollowing out a chamber to worship Mithras during the siege. And there were fights. I watched the ebb and flow, for a woman can but observe in war, and you know that we are as a species more subtle than you men.'

'So his legions are divisive over their gods? It does not seem to stop them in battle.'

'I suspect because they are not divisive *enough*. Remember your own city. How little it took for the Christians to burn down temples and for the rest to call for good-old Christian living torches to light the streets? Discord. Discontent. Trouble.'

My lip wrinkled. 'How in Jove's name might I influence that?'

'They are Roman. Our men are Roman. You have seen what happens on the maps? At the Castra Peregrina where visiting troop units move in and out, reinforcing one frontier or another? You have seen how easily your enemy's armies have pledged to you, and how simply your men in turn have panicked and pledged to Constantine? Getting men into his camp can hardly be troublesome, and Pansa is the subtlest spy in the world. You have ex-frumentarii working for you. I know half a dozen of them myself, three in your personal guard.'

I blinked. 'You do?'

'What do you think I do all day? Plait my hair and read the spicier passages from Catullus? I plan and I plan and when I think I have planned enough, I plan some more.'

'You think you have men who can infiltrate Constantine's army? Who can pull his army apart from the inside?'

Valeria laughed coldly. 'Oh, my husband, you have simply no idea.'

For the next hour I rode with her and we planned. Once we had security and my guard about me, we could start a new campaign, but for now, we had to ride and garrison the south. The enemy was coming. I would make them pay dearly for every pace they took on the journey south, and then crush them before the walls of the greatest city in the world.

Rome.

PART 3

Inimicum quamvis humilem docti est metuere
(A wise man fears every enemy, no matter how small)
– *Publilius Syrus*

19

CONSTANTINE

Ravenna, 8th August 312 AD

When the smell of death creeps inside your nostrils, it never leaves. It infects your mind, your heart, your soul. The sights too: of dying men with maddened eyes begging you, their leader, to put them together; of weeping widows; and of war-prisoners being marched to faraway mining colonies to see out their lives in dark misery.

That was how it had ended at Verona. The captured had been unruly, even after their defeat, and I had been forced to send the Maxentian soldiers to the deep pits of Britannia. So short were we of even basic supplies that I ordered their swords to be hammered into makeshift manacles. It was a grim sight: legionary wrists shackled by legionary steel. Brutal times.

Mercifully, after six moons of such frantic battle in Italia – Segusium, Taurinorum, Mediolanum, Brixia, the taking of Verona, and of the swift capture of Aquileia and of Mutina since – my great, rolling war machine slowed to a halt at Ravenna. The north – the thigh of Italia – was mine.

Now it was time to rest and take stock. Everything felt good for those first few days of respite. Every morsel of food prepared by Ravenna's palace cooks tasted like honey, every sip of water like wine and every sip of wine like... well, very good wine.

This afternoon, like several previous, I relaxed on the high balcony of the city's imperial residence, looking out over the peaceful wards of the city, my belly full and my heart content. Ravenna's wide streets were washed in a molten gold sunshine, off to the east the turquoise waters of the *Mare Adriaticum* sparkled like an infinite treasure trove, and the calm lakes and marshes north of the city walls rippled gently like sheets of dark silk, spotted with coots and moorhens. Gentle chatter and birdsong from the gardens below the balcony mixed with the incessant – yet soothing – cry of gulls and the *tap-tap* of chisels upon marble from the sculptor's shop. The city's imperial tailor had brought me white trousers, a tunic and cloak, and like every other sensory delight, these garments felt good upon my skin. My fingernails were clipped and clean of dirt and scum – for the first time in moons. I wiped a hand across my clean-shaven jaw and smoothed my hair – newly trimmed and still cool, damp and scented with perfumed oil. My skin had been well-soaked in the private bathhouse, my muscles rubbed free of their rope-like knots by the slaves there, and the rather grim-looking wounds on both arms and my flank had been bathed in some paste and dressed with clean bandages. I let my eyes slide shut, basking in the heat of the late day, almost reaching that deep, warm inner well of perfect tranquillity that we all seek but rarely find. Almost.

For just before my eyes closed, they snagged on the city wharf... and its long, empty berths. Docks where the *Classis Ravenna* should have been moored. Instead, there was nothing but a few dozen fishing skiffs and a couple of private boats. My foe had been chased from the north like a kicked hound, but he had been shrewd enough to organise his retreat, withdrawing the Ravenna Fleet with him.

Let me explain: the missing fleet was no mere cluster of simple galleys, it was a mighty flotilla that dominated the Mare Adriaticum and the eastern coast of Italia. Thirty triremes, six huge quadriremes, and two enormous quinqueremes each with five banks of oars like the spines of a porcupine and the high decks rigged with ballistae and archer platforms. Had we acquired it, such a navy would have been like a scalpel, the boats cutting south, screening us as we moved along the coastal roads, resupplying us as we went, warding off any Maxentian attacks and blocking the enemy ports – starving him of troops and grain.

I worked my fingers together, anxiety rising.

And then some cur down on the streets spoiled things thoroughly, standing on the base of a column of Neptune, beseeching passers-by in a tone that reminded me of my commanders' calls during battle: 'Arise, shine!' he bawled. 'For thy light is come and the glory of the Lord is risen upon thee. *Arise!*'

I rose, most certainly, but only from my chair to stride over to the balcony edge and peer down at the irritating fellow: a man dressed in loose robes, his face scarred and one cheekbone sunken. He preached and yelled, throwing his arms skywards every so often as if pitying the passing people who couldn't see the obvious answer up there in the blue. One of Batius' Cornuti on furlough, I realised, my irritation fading: I could hardly be irked by this one – he like every man in my ranks was a hero. Still, it was interesting to see that this soldier from the finest legion in my comitatus – a legion that had been solidly devoted to Apollo in all the time I had been with the army – was turning to the way of the Christ. Just one man, I thought… and the notion conjured up childhood memories of the lone legionary on the walls of Naissus that night during the storm. Clutching his Chi-Rho, tranquil, content that he had completed his journey to find his god.

'He changed his ways the day you rallied him and all his comrades at Verona,' a voice said, right behind me.

I almost leapt from the balcony, such a fright I got. 'Batius, for a man built like a bull, you move like a cat wearing cushions on its paws.'

His brutish face wrinkled in mischief. 'And in the whorehouse, I rut like a rabbit with a two foot—'

'Arise!' the converted soldier's cries rose to new heights, drowning out the remainder of the simile.

'Close your trap,' a drunken voice howled from the far end of the street. There, outside a tavern, stood a cluster of First Martia legionaries in their soldier tunics, each sporting bandages and scars like the cryer. So similar in everything but their faith. 'You turn my wine bitter!'

The Cornuti man gave the Martia soldiers an unhelpful look of simpering superiority, then stared skywards again. 'Arise!'

One of the Martia men tossed down his cup, wine splashing across the flagstones like weak blood, and stomped up the street towards the Cornuti fellow.

I felt that burning sense of impotence. Why, *why* was it that I could unite my men on the field of battle as a smith could blend tin and copper into ultra-hard bronze… but in the long days between the madness of battle, they seemed to find reasons to disintegrate, to turn against one another. I sucked in a full breath to shout at them, but Batius put a hand on my shoulder.

'Wait,' he said, sticking out a meaty finger.

I saw the third figure he was pointing at. Again, as with so many times before, Lactantius came hobbling from the side of the street with his cane. Even the way he walked across the bullish Martia man's path was subtle – seeming almost accidental.

The Martia soldier cursed at first, then – seeing it was Lactantius – apologised, and bowed sharply from the neck to the old tutor. They respected me as their general, their emperor – even as the chosen one of their differing gods, but they *loved* Lactantius like a father. I watched as the old goat stuck out an elbow, and the Martia soldier linked his arm through, helping Lactantius climb the slight incline of the street. I could not hear what he was saying as he went but his gums flapped away, and the Martia man seemed entranced. Lactantius pointed to the sky, then patted the Martia man's chest. As they passed by the preaching Cornuti soldier, Lactantius said something to him as well. The man's haughty expression changed with that one sentence, softening. He stepped down from his makeshift pedestal. He and the Martia man beheld each other for a moment, before sharing a nod of truce, then both parties went on their separate ways. I watched the Martia fellow part with Lactantius, and then watched the tutor, impressed and envious. The old fellow was as vital to me as Batius and Krocus. I realised then that I too loved him like a father.

A grumble of hungry guts sounded behind me, reminding me Batius was here.

'What brings you?' I asked.

'The generals of your consilium ask for an audience with you,' he said with a stern look. 'They are gathered on the southern gatehouse.' He tipped his head in that direction, across the great marble bowl of the city arena to Ravenna's stocky, southern perimeter. A light smog hung over the arena and the wall – remnant from the feasting and games held there the previous day in my name. I had not attended, such was my exhaustion, but Prefect Vindex had assured me it had been a fine spectacle: he had personally instructed the cooks on which spices to season the meats with and which wines to pair with each dish. Batius had overseen the games, organising the delivery of fearsome creatures from afar. The great beasts were paraded before the audience, with dancers and acrobats leaping and twisting alongside them. Now, it seemed, a group of even fiercer creatures awaited me: my surviving generals – all eager to know our next steps, no doubt. The thigh of Italia might well be mine, but the muscular, long leg and all its sinewy and ancient routes and bony, mountainous ridges were not. I looked past the southern walls, towards the great camp of my army, sprawled across the countryside: battle-stained tents, row upon row of medical pavilions, countless men hobbling with the aid of sticks and crutches. This was the price of my winning of the north: a broken force, facing a Herculean task. Yes, I had set in motion plans to draw fresh forces from Gaul to bolster my numbers, but I knew it would be akin to wringing out a nearly dry rag. Ruricius' final gibes echoed in my mind:

In the south, legion upon legion of hardened veterans stack up in preparation to crush you, and they will crush you if you dare venture there. Better you stay here, lumbering around the north, far from the heart of Italia with the tattered remnant of your invasion force. Rome will never be yours!

Each remembered word was like a splash of molten bronze on my chest. The spell of palatial idyll was over. 'Come,' I beckoned the big man in a clipped tone.

We went with the click of my hobnails striking the travertine floor.

★ ★ ★

A boar sizzled and crackled on a spit atop the broad, flagged gatehouse as I stepped up the stairs and onto those heights. I knew not which of my officers had chosen this place as a meeting point, nor who had ordered the boss-eyed cook to bring and roast a hog up there. Probably Vindex, I guessed – the man seemed to be something of a gastronome. They stood in an arc, backs turned, the fading light dully reflecting from their patterned capes. Seeing them in battle regalia cast my mind back to the horrors of Verona. The screaming, the weeping, the stink...

A loud, phlegmy and tactical cough from Batius snapped me from the spiralling thoughts and alerted the arc of officers to my presence.

'Domine,' they rumbled in a variety of accents as they swung round, the arc now facing me.

Krocus stood with the leaders of my comitatus legions: Ruga, Scaurus and Hisarnis. Prefect Vindex and Praepositus Vitalianus stood either side of Baudio. Baudio looked nervous, while the pair at his sides were beaming like proud parents. For a moment I was confused, and then I saw the edge of a thick bandage under the neckline of Baudio's pale robe – a burn wound from glowing hot sand. It slapped the suspicion from me as I remembered: that moment at Verona. On the second day of the fighting, my chief siege engineer and his team were spotted by the enemy as they tried to scuttle along the ditch below the city's walls in an attempt to take bridging planks to a spot near the gates. They were bombarded with arrows and thrown rocks, killed to a man apart from the chief engineer, who lay there, one leg shattered, screaming. The Maxentians on the wall left him there like bait, eyes baleful, waiting for some effort to rescue him. Before I could even organise a response, Baudio sprang forth, alone, all the way towards that ditch, shield overhead against the rain of missiles and then buckets of hot sand. Alone, he had stooped to scoop an arm around the chief engineer and brought him back to us, bringing a huge swell of cheering and defiance from my exhausted lines. It had been like a tent pole, lifting our sagging spirits.

As I stepped up onto the Ravenna parapet, Baudio continued to stare at me like a proud son. I realised then that I had forgotten – entirely – to prepare for this moment.

Another cough from Batius, who handed me a small linen sack. I took it from him. It was heavy, reassuringly so. He had remembered. He had prepared for me. *Thank you, old friend*, I said to him by way of a look, then tipped the sack upside down and caught the heavy, wondrous and gilt torque it contained – like a band of molten sun.

'Florius Baudio, Prefect of the Second Italica Divitensis,' I said. The man grew taller with pride, his eyes brimming with tears. 'For your courage, your selfless devotion, to me, to the cause... I name you as a Protector, a golden one.' I fitted the torque around his neck, taking care not to disturb his bandage. Despite the considerable weight of the piece, he stretched another few finger-widths higher, like a banner atop the gates rising on a soughing wind.

'Domine, if I had died for you that day at Verona, I would have passed into the paradise that awaits knowing it had been a just death,' he said, falling to one knee, lifting the Chi-Rho necklace that hung between the torque's open ends and kissing it.

Then, like tall grass blown flat in a breeze, the rest did likewise, drawling oaths of their own to each of their gods and to me. As one, oaths reaffirmed, my generals rose around me with a gentle *shush* of mail and scale.

'How is the mood in the camp?' I asked the group.

Krocus' nostrils flared, in the way that I had come to recognise as an indicator of trouble. 'Tense. Squabbling and fights here and there between the regiments – usually when the Christians sing in prayer or the men of Mars perform a sacrifice. And those bishops...'

'You appear to have mispronounced "arseholes",' Ruga muttered with a mischievous grin.

'Lactantius passes through the camp once a day,' Batius interjected.

'Aye, like a calming breeze,' Krocus smiled.

I smiled too. My old tutor had almost competed his latest script, one he assured me was his greatest yet: reassuring Christians and persuasive to non-Christians. He had promised me he would not deliver its content to the legions, knowing himself that things were still too fractious. Besides, it wasn't complete because he hadn't yet worked out the last part. *The future, Constantine, it seems blurry. In all other matters things are so clear to me: Jesus will return, Christianity will prevail... but what will become of the sinners, the wicked? I simply can't see it clearly.* I smiled again, this time wryly: it was probably a good thing for the old goat to have this conundrum to chew over.

'There was the matter of the runaway,' Prefect Vindex said, snapping me from my thoughts.

'Deserters?' I said, suddenly tense. Even one such man was a sure indicator of a toxic mood.

'He *wasn't* a runaway,' Baudio insisted with a disdainful

shake of the head – and it was clear this was not the first time he had protested so.

Vindex scowled at the man. 'This, again? How can you be so sure?'

His tone was scathing, and for a moment, I thought these two – one Christian and the other a Mars-worshipper – were about to raise their fists.

'Because he was shot,' Baudio scoffed. 'Shot climbing through the palisade at *our* section of the camp, then running and hobbling across the southern plain with arrows in his thigh until another six arrows killed him.'

'Exactly,' Vindex snorted. 'He was running. Thus, he was a runaway,' he said, staccato as if speaking to a dim child.

Baudio smirked at this. 'Yet he wasn't from my Second Italica ranks. He wasn't from yours… none of the commanders could identify him.'

My eyes grew hooded. 'What are you saying, Baudio?'

'He was a spy. He wasn't deserting our camp, he was running *back* to his paymaster.'

'Even if he was a spy, it doesn't matter,' Vindex shrugged. 'He's dead. Whatever news he might have been taking back to Maxentius died with him.'

I stared at each man in turn. 'Who did he talk to while he was here?' I shot a look around the city, thinking of the preaching Cornuti man on furlough. Swathes of my soldiers had been given time away from the camp like that. 'Did he take leave from the camp at any point?'

All of my men wore apologetically blank looks. 'He was as much of a shade when he lived as he is now that he is dead,' Scaurus said.

Doubt. Such an uncomfortable state of mind. Straight away the whole matter began to itch and burrow into my mind. Maxentius had once before sent an assassin to kill me. This time, I had faced no hired blade… but I had a terrible sense that whatever that man might have been doing in my camp, the consequences might be far bleaker. Was he alone? To whom had he spoken and which conversations had he stealthily listened in to? Agitated, I stashed the matter away in my mind, although it felt untidy, ragged, troubling.

'Apart from that, all is quiet in the camp,' Krocus finished.

'So… autumn looms,' said Vindex, broaching the greater question first. 'We have tarried here for some time, Domine. Long enough, I would say.'

All heads gazed beyond the camp and to the southern blur where land met sky. The way to Rome.

'We should continue to wait here, allow the cold season to come and go,' said Krocus.

'And allow Maxentius to double his already swollen forces?' Batius scoffed. 'What if he has sent that missing fleet to Africa, to ferry over yet more legions to bolster his armies?'

'Yet waiting would allow our army to heal and swell too,' argued Vitalianus. 'Less than twenty thousand men are camped out there, Domine. The losses at Verona and the many more since, plus the garrisons we have left at each city, have more than halved your manpower. By now the Gaulish recruiting grounds should have completed their work in training new legions and mustering fresh auxiliary bands. We should wait for them to come here with the latest grain convoy before we advance south.'

I nodded slowly. The logic was sound. A steady, strong advance. 'Six thousand fresh men. We need them and—'

The look in Vindex' face and the way he was busily smoothing a finger up and down his long, aquiline nose was enough to stop me: it was the same as Krocus and his flaring nostrils – a sign of trouble. 'There has been a problem, Domine.'

All turned to him.

'The news came in just an hour past. I didn't want to spoil Baudio's presentation so I—'

'Spit it out,' Batius snapped.

Vindex shuffled in discomfort. 'First, there has been a riot and a strike in the fabricae of Treverorum – where the workers are holed up in the factory like men defending a fort, refusing to give up the iron coats and blades the new recruits need. Next, there was a mass desertion along the Lower Rhenus forts – men who had gone too long without pay.'

I heard the sound of rocks grinding together, then realised it was my teeth. I had assured the watchmen of the Rhenus that they would be paid a generous donative once my Italian campaign was over. I had assured the Treverorum workers likewise. My words had meant little to them, apparently. I then thought of the promises I had made to the residents of Mediolanum and the other Maxentian cities that had declared for me – promises that I would relieve them of the tyrant's tax burden. Promises that I would unlikely be able to keep.

At that moment, the cross-eyed boar-cook chirped: 'Meat's nearly cooked.' He was just being helpful and attentive, but at that moment – snared on the horns of a dilemma and angered once again – I wanted nothing more than to press his face, hard, into the red-hot coals. It was all true however: my nearby camp housed twelve legions of varying strengths. The colossal force I had brought through the mountains had been winnowed away. The plan to ready six thousand fresh men in Gaul and have them march south to join us here had been waylaid by sedition. That meant I was stuck with the forces I had here. Less than twenty thousand strong. The figure bounced around in my head like the clapper inside a bell, pealing incessantly. Even *less* men than Severus and then Galerius had led in their failed attempts to take Italia and Rome from Maxentius years ago. Was it not a fool's game to repeat their mistake? I gazed into the southern haze and couldn't help but imagine my charges being further chiselled and reduced with every next step we might take, gradually being whittled down to nothing, turning to dust before we could even sight Rome's walls.

'We don't know for certain how many legions Maxentius can still call upon,' mused Tribunus Scaurus. 'Desertions always follow a heavy defeat.'

'Still,' said Hisarnis, 'even taking into account his losses in battle, and assuming that a few regiments fled from his side, he had more than one hundred and twenty thousand legionaries to begin with.'

The bell inside my head now clanged as if struck by Vulcan's hammer.

'At worst, he still has half that number remaining,' Hisarnis continued. 'If we give him any more time, he will not just bed into the defensive positions all down the length of Italia – all the way to Rome – but turn them all into fortresses. One man on a sturdy parapet is worth four trying to scramble up the walls just to get close enough to attack.'

A wry grumble fell from my lips and turned into a wretched, humourless laugh. I looked at each of my best men, willing… *daring* one of them to give voice to the only remaining option.

Ruga flicked out his tongue to moisten his lips. 'What about… '

Brave man, I thought, staring at him.

'...what about sending a despatch to the east, up past Aquileia to... Licinius' border camps?'

'What about popping your balls onto the hog roast?' Batius grunted, his look as dark as night.

The cross-eyed chap tending to the coals scowled, holding up a shielding arm over the sizzling meat.

'But Licinius has legions, Domine, *many* legions,' Ruga persisted.

'He is also the most mendacious prick I have ever known,' I said, 'and I have met one or two.'

'Yet he could double your army in one swoop, Domine,' Vindex spoke up in defence of Ruga's suggestion. 'With his men, we could press south for Rome before autumn comes. Those ancient gates could be prised open and the city might be yours before the snows arrive.'

I shook my head slowly, sincerely. 'If victory came then it would be sweet. Yet I would forever be beholden to Licinius – and he would be sure to draw his likeness on every triumphal relief,' I said. 'When last we were apparent equals, he invaded my lands and tried to overthrow me. Instead, I crushed him. He fears me now, and I want it to stay that way. Licinius is *not* the answer,' I reiterated. 'If we are to push for Rome before the cold season comes,' I concluded, 'before every fort and wall on the way south is built high enough to scrape the clouds and packed with shield and spear... then we do so with the battered, weary numbers we have and no more.'

* * *

Later, in the dead of night, I sat once again on the balcony, head swimming with wine. A sickle of silvery moonlight sparkled on the calm sea, and the balmy night air left a patina of sweat on my skin. I stared at the marble bust that had been placed on the table in my absence, then reached out and stroked a finger across the likeness, coating the tip in white dust. The sculptor had seemed an honest type and had been glad to craft the piece for me, and I had insisted on seeing that he was paid well for it and that any customers whose work had been delayed were compensated. I could not kid myself, though: it had all gone so graciously only because I had come here as a conqueror, a victor, a liberator. What would transpire were I to blunder south with half an army and be trampled then chased back here? Would I find artisans waiting to offer me their services? Slaves eager to rub my shoulders and cooks keen to serve me pheasant and garum? I remembered the wretch, Galerius, on his graceless flight from Italia after such a defeat: his men were gaunt and ill, all discipline and order gone from them – all quarter denied them by local peoples. There was no dilemma now. South, to glory... or death.

I lifted my wine cup and drained it.

'You lied to me,' she said.

I almost choked on my wine and fell from my chair, turning to face her as I stood.

Fausta slinked towards me, her hood hanging around her shoulders, her hair loose. Her beauty was stained by lips thin with anger and eyes glinting with disgust. We had not spoken since that manic time, mid-battle, at Verona. 'You swore to me at Verona that the war would end.'

I spluttered, almost laughed. 'I swore to you that I would try! Did you not see me and every one of my men try until our hearts almost broke?'

'You let my brother escape. Now I hear your men talk not of deposing Maxentius, but of "parading the cowardly tyrant's head on a pole".'

'The men grow frustrated just as you do that another leg of marching and campaign lies ahead.'

'How many of them will even see Rome, Constantine?' she said flatly. 'How many graves will be dug along the road?'

I felt cold then, for I knew she was right. 'I cannot turn back. I must not tarry here. The war is not over, and I must march south to end it.'

'It will be long, it will be terrible,' she said in almost a whisper, her eyes glistening.

'I know, Fausta. I know,' I pleaded with her. 'Yet I have no choice. The war must go on until either Rome is taken or my advance founders.'

She stared at me for a time. A horrible silence. 'Then I will advise the surgeons to sharpen their saws and wind many sutures, and the gravediggers to bring good spades,' she said softly, before drifting from the room like a shade's breath, her gown trailing on the floor behind her.

20

MAXENTIUS

Maxentius' villa on the Via Appia, outside Rome,
15th August 312 AD

'The medicus has only bleak news,' Valeria said wearily,
sinking to the marble bench beside me.

'The *world* has only bleak news,' I replied, a little harshly.
Such despondency that summer came from a three-fold
source.

The medicus of whom she spoke attended upon young
Aurelius, our poor, twisted boy, who had taken ill during
the summer and, despite the best efforts of the greatest
medical minds in Rome and donations of a small fortune
to the temple of Aesculapius, continued in a steady decline
that looked sure to have only one outcome. It was torture
and, though he undoubtedly wanted nothing more than the
comfort of his parents at such a time, I simply could not
bear to watch it happen.

Aurelius could not express himself adequately to be fully
understood by any of us, and he must have been suffering
appallingly, fading away and unable to communicate what
he felt. It was partially my helplessness that drove me from

his bedside, and I would like to say that was largely all there was to it, but the truth is that I still mourned Romulus every moment I lived, and the notion of watching my other son follow him into Elysium was simply unbearable.

That being the case, you might think it strange that I came here of all places, and I cannot truly explain why I did, but sitting on this bench with its decorative triton carvings, facing the implacable, featureless door of my eldest son's mausoleum left me feeling calm. Hollow, but calm, in the same way as a dried-up reservoir is a piteous thing, but might still be better than a raging stormy sea. To me, morose and maudlin was better than to be shaking and sobbing, racked with impotent grief.

The mausoleum stared back at me, its skull-mouth the dark door, its eyes two of the grille-barred windows that I could see from this angle. Even my imaginings were becoming charnel. The world seemed to have taken all the hope of my youth and dashed it against the Tarpeian Rock until all that was left was horror and misery, hanging from my hands like a year-old corpse.

Valeria was faring no better. Despite our burgeoning relationship, which had been troubled a little by suspicion in Verona but was still a thing of strength, we often found it difficult to come close, especially at times like this. We had both lost so much. I had witnessed the passing of a father, a son, a friend. Valeria had also lost her father and then a son who, while she had never truly seemed to love him in life, had left a distinct hole in her heart with his passing. And she had seemed to *hate* poor Aurelius, yet now, faced with losing him, his significance had surfaced at last. He represented the last bonds of family either of us shared. Once he was gone, all we would have was each other, and I was fairly sure our tremulous relationship could not survive long under those conditions.

Oh, I had sisters, of course, and a mother, still. I had not seen Mother in years now, and I would not see her until this was all over, perhaps never again. The same with Theodora. My wonderful, beautiful elder sister remained in obscure comfort on the estate in Campania, and Mother in a palatial villa in Sicilia. To even contact either of them in these treacherous times was to put them at risk. I kept their locations a close secret, held only by the more trusted few, and I most certainly wouldn't bring either of them to Rome.

As for Fausta? Well she would almost certainly be coming to Rome soon enough, in the retinue of a soulless bastard I had once called friend.

Therein lay my second source of hollow misery.

The north had fallen. Through a seeming combination of treachery and ill fortune, I had lost the three critical bastions of northern Italia, and now I could almost feel Constantine's fetid breath on my neck. While my consilium reminded me repeatedly that my enemy's tarrying in the north was a boon, it felt to me like a sword blade hovering, waiting to fall.

We used the time well, of course. Italia was prepared for him. He had, I think, missed a chance in not following up on his dreadful victory at Verona and harrying me south, though that was almost certainly through lack of available manpower. Instead he had tarried, to heal and reorganise, and therefore so had we.

The Adriatic Fleet had been moved south from Ravenna, out of danger, and had been relocated at Ancona. If Constantine came south along the Via Flaminia he would be in for an unpleasant surprise, and my admirals were the best in the empire. The Misenum Fleet was mustered at the great harbour of Portus at Ostia, ready to deal with anything on the west coast, should Constantine for some reason double back and come south there. They also secured my supply lines from Africa there.

Every city and town along the route from the north had been turned into a fortress of implacable stone and steel. Constantine would pay in blood and pain for every mile he travelled. Bridges were ready to fall at all the critical junctions and crossings, undermined and left with just a tiny support that the local garrison could collapse in a heartbeat to deny the enemy. Passes were blocked. Rivers were dammed. Every farmhouse had a small party of men to deny him easy forage. Constantine would hurt as he moved. His army would be abraded like a man crawling slowly across cheese graters. I would make him pay for his sneak attack and the debacle at Taurinorum that snatched the north from me. If he ever reached the walls of Rome, his remaining pitiful force would dash itself against them like a shallow wave.

For despite my apparent failure at every juncture in northern Italia, the fact remained that my forces outnumbered Constantine's considerably, now that we were consolidating, and despite my fears as we fled Verona, on closer examination, there were a lot more veteran units there than I had expected, for we had, after all, acquired them without a fight from Severus during his failed invasion. No, our forces were strong and numerous, and I had no fear that we would be easy prey on the field of battle.

And then there was Daia.

Word had come back with Zenas in the early spring. That slavering animal, who was the least trustworthy man in the world and in whom I had been forced to place my trust, had accepted my proposals. He pledged support to defend Italia against Constantine and Licinius should that evil cur decide to involve himself. Daia would enter into alliance with me. He had plenty of troops and would keep them in his own lands, but close, ready to respond to any move by Licinius. According to his missive, twelve legions were moving to Cyrene, just ten days' sail from Italian soil, where a fleet was gathering in preparation. Similarly, another twelve marched to Ephesus in Asia, also but ten days' sail away. In less than fifteen days I could have another thirty thousand men or more on the plains outside Rome. Of course, if they helped me win the war I would be obligated to that bastard, and there was the ever-present worry that they might just turn on me and attack from within, for I could trust Daia's men no more than I could him. But the simple threat of their arrival to bolster my forces had been made very public, and word would soon reach Constantine. That threat would worry his men at least. There would be nerves. Dissent. Even desertions.

Italia was a line of redoubts against Constantine's approach, surrounded by navies, with a huge force of men and more in reserve, Rome as secure a city as any in the world and, even if the worst came to the worst, the Milvian Bridge across the Tiber could be cut, denying him at the last.

I knew all of this because Volusianus hammered the details into me on a daily basis, confident in his preparations. These days he wore a permanent look of discontent at the way I had treated him, yet he continued to fulfil the roles of military advisor and commander admirably. Still, worry and anger gnawed at me.

The north had been impregnable. It had been strongly garrisoned, as full of redoubts and denied crossings as every mile about which Volusianus told me, yet it had fallen in a few short months, regardless. That flat-faced bastard from Illyria whom I had called friend had rolled across my staunch defences like a runaway wagon, crushing all before him.

What use, then, to do the same to the Via Flaminia?

When I had voiced this opinion to Volusianus, he had pointed out that such a system had been instrumental in preventing invasions by both Severus and Galerius. I had nodded and accepted the point. Inside I had thought sourly *but neither of them was Constantine.* Somehow, no matter how it looked, and on parchment it looked excellent, I felt none of it would be enough to stop him.

I think perhaps Valeria had not helped matters. Oh, from the time we began our flight until we were once more settled in Rome, she was nothing but activity and strength, and it was partially her doing that I made it back at all.

I had, in my dejection after that terrible defeat at Verona, given her an open mandate to do what she wished to cause trouble in Constantine's camp. I think she'd sent five men, for I had come across her in a clandestine meeting with them on our journey south, two days from Verona. They were all soldiers, two of them officers and one high enough to wear a prefect's uniform. Two I saw wearing the Chi-Rho of Christians, and one had a tattoo of Minerva on his forearm. I could almost imagine the shorter, darker one in an animal costume deep in the bowels of a Mithraeum. She was sending men to tear apart Constantine's hastily stitched-together army. It was odd, given that these five men were so incredibly disparate, and yet they were all frumentarii, if Valeria was to be believed, and therefore their oath and their loyalty created an unbreakable bond that even their gods could not test.

She had given me a devious, cold smile as she dismissed

them, and I had felt a weird pride, and perhaps even a little sympathy for what Constantine had coming. As the time rolled by and we returned south, I heard nothing of what she had achieved, though tantalising hints abounded.

A single tent party of Constantine's army appeared seemingly from nowhere as we retreated. They had braved and barefaced their way through all our redoubts. They had entered our camp with a pay chest from one of Constantine's legions, proudly proclaiming their devotion to Mars and refusing to let the pay fall into the hands of their Christian 'brothers'. One morning, Valeria took receipt of a single parcel and opened it to find a bloody Chi-Rho inside. From the look on her face I deduced that one of her agents had met a grisly end. Still, she seemed satisfied. Odd little hints continued to come. One of the most fascinating was a missive, apparently sent by one of Constantine's senior officers to the pope, the chief priest of the Christians in Rome, begging him to proclaim Constantine as 'God's chosen'. What he did when Miltiades replied that *God* had invested his power in Rome and in Maxentius, I have no idea, but it could hardly have made Constantine's day, whatever it was. Gradually, activity began to dwindle, as her agents fell one way or another, and when one man limped back into camp, refusing to see a surgeon until he had reported to the empress, it transpired that he had been one of only two left. His counterpart would continue to work, though. Such was Valeria's campaign of divide and conquer. I left her to it, for she was wiser than me, stronger than Volusianus and craftier than Pansa at every turn.

But now we were back in Rome, she had no new campaign to oversee and Aurelius had fallen ill. Suddenly all the life and fight had seemed to go out of her. She attended the briefings still, but no longer put in a useful thought. Titbits from her agents arrived and she brushed them aside.

It was as though she had given up.

And if strong, proud, defiant *Valeria* had given up, why would *I* still fight on?

Another me might have given up, but two things kept me going.

Bloody-minded anger was one. I was the son of Maximian, and the blood of that wicked, raging old monster flowed in me, giving me the urge and will to soldier on to the bitter end. Then there was Rome. I had pledged myself to Rome all those years ago with Anullinus, taking the purple as its protector and champion. In an age where the emperors of Rome cared little for the ancient heart of the empire, preferring their rural palaces in far-flung barbarian lands, I was the only man to claim power and seek the survival and benefit of this ancient cradle of culture. Oh, I know some would say I was every bit as provincial as Constantine, for my great-grandfather had been a shopkeeper from Sirmium and the family nobodies before my father's meteoric rise through the army, but *I* had been born Roman and I had taken that fact and wrapped my soul in it.

Like the emperors of old, I was Rome, and Rome was me. If I gave up, then Rome would fade, so I would fight on, for blood-rage and the survival of my world.

I stared at that door in the tomb and contemplated all that had brought us to this dreadful situation. I wondered momentarily where the key was to that portal, for I had not opened it in a long time. Soon, it seemed, I would have to do so once more, placing another urn in there.

If we lost, I wondered, would Constantine have enough courage to acknowledge my claim in death and see my ashes placed in there with my children? Would I extend a similar courtesy to him? I wondered idly where his father was buried. Treverorum probably. Come to that, where was *my* father buried? *Had* he even been buried?

That thought further soured me and brought forth a fresh wave of ire at my enemy.

'When you kill him,' Valeria said suddenly, 'you must treat him as a vanquished usurper.'

Gods, but was my mind so easily read?

'I think it would sit better with the people of Rome to see me do honour to an enemy. To have him treated as a ruler and his ashes sent to his family tomb.'

'No. Do you think he would do such a thing for you? If he somehow managed to break through these walls, he would have your head on a spear, dancing through the streets in victory, and mine shortly after. He is an animal. A barbarian. Treat him as such.'

I sighed.

In truth, I suspected that whatever I did, the Roman people would find fault with it, for the populace was the third source of my melancholy. In addition to my endless family woes and the threat of Constantine's advance, I had also to acknowledge that the Roman people were starting to take against me, and there was little I could do about it.

I had been their champion. Their golden emperor. Even through all the difficulties with war and a diminished treasury and hunger I had managed to maintain my reputation among them as their defender against foreign emperors. But that reputation had fled me in tatters the day my Praetorians butchered the people in the forum and Rome had acquired a second river, this one crimson and glistening. It mattered not to a poor fishmonger in the city that the order had been given by Volusianus and that I had watched in horror. They were *my* Praetorians, and that was what the people saw: the emperor's men killing the people.

I taxed them within a hair's breadth of poverty and my soldiers killed them when they protested. There was dissent now, and ill feeling. Not quite hate. Not the way the people still hated Constantine and the other bile-sack emperors who cared nothing for this grand metropolis, but definitely not the love they had once borne me.

The threat of war was not helping matters, mind. No sane man hungers for that. While the Roman people might have been supportive of their glorious emperor and his legions imposing his will on rebellious Africa or garrisoning the north to protect Italia from rival powers, having the bridges outside the city prepared to be taken down swiftly, lining the walls with stacks of weapons, and hoarding food in the granaries against a possible siege was another thing entirely. The people wanted golden distant victories, not battles at their own threshold.

Much as the actions of others and simple bad luck had brought about the bulk of this situation, I did worry that I had brought *some* of it on myself. The north had fallen because of treachery and luck. Ruricius had done everything a good man could against the surprise attack of a rabid enemy. In the dark of the night, though, when I lay awake in thought, I found myself wondering if things in the north might have gone rather differently if I had heeded warnings earlier in my blindness, and garrisoned the north; if I had not become so angry at Volusianus and left him languishing in Rome.

Certainly *he* thought so. Upon my return he had been incensed, raging, as insolent as ever before and then some. I had not the fight in me to argue any more, and he vented opinion at me like a severed artery. Had he been allowed to lead a contingent north, he claimed, we would be drinking wine from Constantine's skull in Mediolanum now like some barbarian victor.

Was he right?

I looked across at Valeria, whose gaze was distant and hazy.

I needed her now more than ever before and she was not there. A pale shell of a woman sat beside me on the bench.

Damn it, but doubt surrounded me like a sea. I had every reason to think Rome safe. We outnumbered Constantine, and even if Licinius joined him then Daia would come and redress the balance. We would always outnumber him, and we had every advantage. Redoubts, fleets, topography, high walls, endless supplies. A *child* could defend Rome with what we had.

So why did I still worry?

I closed my eyes and in the darkness of my head I saw that room in Treverorum so long ago. My city of wooden blocks, and I saw Constantine smashing them aside to make a point. I had built those high walls now. Would they be enough?

I opened my eyes once more and gazed at the mausoleum before me. Slowly, in the sad silence, a strange, repetitive noise insisted itself upon me. Frowning, I tilted my head, turning my ear. A battering. A fluttering. Then I saw it. In one of the narrow apertures of the mausoleum that let in a sliver of light, which were shut off with grilles to prevent just such unwanted wildlife, I could see a shape. A bird, flapping desperately, somehow trapped in my son's eternal house, unable to escape.

I stared.

A bird trapped in the house is a terrible omen. I remember

Mother once actually selling a townhouse she had owned because just that had happened there, and if a bird in the *house* is bad, what of a bird trapped in a tomb?

I shivered, for I knew precisely what it meant. The gods had odd ways of making themselves known. I was in my villa, an emperor trapped within its walls, like a bird in a tomb.

I turned to Valeria.

'Gather yourself. We are returning to the city.'

She turned a questioning look to me and I set thin lips in a tight line.

'Constantine is coming.'

21

CONSTANTINE

The Coastal Road, 12th September 312 AD

I twisted in my saddle and looked back upon Ravenna's parapets. The time of recuperation and planning was over, and the journey was afoot: my army was on the coast road now and there could be no doubt – Rome was the prize. The only thing left to be decided was who would be the victor and who the vanquished?

'Come on, full step!' Batius screamed at them – over seventeen thousand steel-clad legionaries and nearly two thousand lancers. I believed in them, and they in me. I had spared a small garrison of two cohorts to watch Ravenna, ever uncertain of Licinius' motives. One thing was for certain, however: that bastard would have no share in my victory! I dared leave behind no more than that two cohorts, for I would need as many soldiers with me on this advance as I could muster. The rumours had grown stronger since this morning: the armies of Daia – that stinking vulture – had been sighted on the move, taking ship towards southern Italia. Was this what my one-time friend had stooped to? Bringing creatures like Daia into play?

I shook the thought away and sat tall in the saddle, looking ahead. The Mare Adriaticum stretched out on our left like a splendid cerulean infinity, spotted with gentle crystalline peaks, bright and fresh like the early autumn sky. We marched that day in good time, the vanguard riders and foot soldiers encased in steel, but the rest wearing just helm, spear and shield, having loaded their heavy ring and scale coats in the wagon train. I too wore just my old red military tunic and a white cape, the jewelled battle helm once given to me by Hisarnis resting on one of my saddle's horns.

We saw nothing and nobody for three days: no armies, no scouts watching us and scattering back south to tell their master, no impediments – neither broken-up roads nor smashed bridges. Italia was stretching her arms to welcome me like a wanton lover. If we could make use of this road to forge as far south as possible, then we could pick our way across to the western side of the peninsula via the Capanum Pass – a short and direct route to the region of Latium. The men's mood soared, sensing with every day unopposed the growing closeness of a golden triumph. Some even spread rumours that Maxentius had abandoned Rome and fled to the south of Italia, to hide in the toe of the peninsula with his new friend Daia like that ancient gladiator-rogue Spartacus. Others claimed he had taken ship to Africa to hide behind dune-ramparts and muster elephant brigades. Some swore he had been cut down by his own men – and given the Praetorians' history, I suspected that this might just be the most plausible rumour. In truth, I realised that none of these things were real. I simply knew that our great game was not yet over, and in the pit of my heart I knew that the bleakest part of it had yet to play out.

On that third day of the march, Batius – tired of berating the men – took to regaling them with stories of past campaigns.

He told them of our sorties in Persia. The men loved those tales of desert adventure and highly improbable feats in the wadis and baking wastes, and Batius was an expert at embellishment, insisting at one stage that he had ridden at speed upon two camels – one foot on either creature's back – through the avenues of Ctesiphon, under a hail of Persian arrows. Of course, he had even cut down an entire band of the elite pushtigban guardsmen before duelling with the Shahanshah himself. That last part, I thought wryly, was almost true, for it was the big man and I who had faced the King of Kings and sent him running.

Come late afternoon, we saw on the horizon a town perched on a rocky cape, ringed by the glimmering sea. In the centre of the town was a mound, topped with an ancient shrine.

The sight brought a broad smile to my face. What a fine omen.

'Fanum Fortunae,' Prefect Vindex said with a throaty laugh, recognising the place too. 'The Goddess Fortuna is with us.'

I declared this to be our stopping point for the day – in sight of the distant shrine, its presence reassuring to all of my men. We made camp in a sheltered bay near the roadside, enjoying a fine evening meal of roast fish that had been caught by the baggage slaves, wrapped in charred flatbread and washed down with either goat's milk, wine or stream water. As I ate, feeling my belly swell and my blood grow pleasantly hot from the wine, I wondered if the rumours of Maxentius' flight were in fact true. It seemed as if we were marching through an abandoned land.

My consilium decided to eat together that night. Prefect Vindex – ever the epicure – insisted on cooking a herb-rich fish broth for them all. Drunk and content, their laughter filled the night air.

I slept like a rock that night. I only woke once, and it was for the strangest reason. Fausta was there, in my tent. I pretended to still be asleep, keeping my eyes almost shut, but I could see her. At first I hoped she might lie with me for the first time in so long, but she did not. She merely knelt near me, looking over me as one might stand vigil over the body of a loved one. Come morning, I was not sure if it had been a dream or not.

I emerged from my tent to the sound of confident chatter among my men. I walked among them, talking to those nearest, always sure to address them by name. I remembered how my father had always done this, and how his charges had grown an extra inch taller with pride. I took an offered bowl of wheat porridge and lifted the spoon to my mouth, but a groan stopped me from eating.

'Leave me,' Lactantius moaned. 'I have my walking stick, I do not need anything else.'

The old goat was waving away a pair of legionaries who were trying to help him rise from the tree stump upon which he sat. One was of the First Martia and the other of the Lancearii. It was an apt scene, the old tutor the focus of worshippers of the old gods and the new.

'Old tutor?' I said, seeing him clutching his sides, face racked with pain.

He saw me and stood, defiant, hands leaving his flanks. 'Constantine,' he snapped, 'finish your meal and get on your horse. It is the marching hour already!'

The men laughed at his fond admonishment, and he strode away, his stick clacking. Yet I could tell it was a mask. That groan of pain had been genuine.

'Something he ate, I reckon,' said the Lancearius.

'Up all night trying to finish his script, no doubt,' the Martia man smiled.

'Have a medicus ride near him,' I said, dissatisfied.

Apart from this, we were refreshed and buoyant, and continued our speedy advance south, on towards the Capanum Pass. On those last few miles as we passed Fanum Fortunae, Batius' tales turned more poignant and heartfelt.

'In the sands near Ctesiphon, I spent the night with a Persian beauty: neck of a swan, hips of a tigress. She cooked me the most succulent meal of lamb, olives and apricots, then plied me with the richest wine. She sang for me, danced for me, whispered tales in my ear... then we made love, more times than I can remember. It was the most beautiful day of my life.' The men grinned and smiled fondly, each no doubt thinking of their loved ones in the north. Then Batius snorted, spat and shrugged. 'Of course, I woke during the night with the most rampant diarrhoea. The lamb, you see, it was bad. Spent the next moon on the latrine. I didn't know a man could shit out quite that much...'

The ranks roared with laughter, some wincing and mock-retching. For that moment I felt like a young soldier again, in those far-flung sands with the big man. When times were so different, so much simpler.

'Vitalianus – it's Vitalianus!' a voice said, breaking the spell.

All necks stretched, peering south. There, bursting over the brow of the headland, was a troop of riders: Praepositus Vitalianus and the cavalry scouts I had despatched south as a vanguard. How wretchedly high were our spirits at that moment, poised for the most horrific of falls.

Seabirds, speeding low across the bay. Not seabirds. Speeding rocks.

Whack!

The rearmost knot of Vitalianus' scouts jerked up and away from the coast, like game pieces flicked by the invisible fingers of a god. They fell into frantic tumbles of dust, colour, blood spraying, and all with the most horrific chorus of screams and whinnies. Eight of them shot through with artillery stones. Vitalianus broke into a crazed gallop, hanging onto his horse's neck in panic.

Now I realised what was going on. Now I understood whom Fortuna favoured on this day, even before the great shadows of scores of warships slid sharply around the headland: a forest of masts, creaking hulls, centipede-like banks of oars working hard. The missing Ravenna Fleet! Half-cloaked in the late afternoon shadow the flotilla dominated the waters. Many triremes, the giant quinqueremes... everything. With a rumble like distant thunder, the bright purple and gold Maxentian sails were unfurled on those ships, billowing like the chests of proud giants. A creaking of ropes sounded, bringing the fleet cutting round towards us. With a thrumming of distant artillery, the biggest vessels spat forth another volley of ballistae rocks.

Vitalianus was there one moment, and gone the next – a rolling mass of hooves, limbs, armour, thrown-up earth and sand and torn flesh.

I saw a blur of movement – the smaller liburnians sped close to the shore, coming alongside our column. I saw the packed marksmen aboard. I heard the burr of spinning slings and then the sudden cessation of that haunting sound. A heartbeat later came a chorus that chilled me even more: the heavy rain of slingshot battering down on our shields and plunging through unarmoured flesh. Snapping bones, wet innards being thrown free of bodies. All sense of balance and reality left me as I twisted to look back: the Second Italica and the Fourth Jovia ranks were peppered with gaps, men lying in broken heaps, screaming, clutching shattered limbs or gawping down at black holes through their chests. I saw Batius, rearing up on his horse, his mouth wide and contorting in some frantic command. All along the line, the men were struck with panic. Some threw up their shields, but in poor order – all knew how to form a shield wall against an enemy legion, but none had expected this, death from the waves.

The slinger-liburnians sped on past like gulls having stolen their scraps, and behind them, the giant vessels of the fleet – the artillery-bearing ones – were now adjacent to my column and began to stretch out into a line. I saw the beak-like line of ballistae trained on my disordered column's flank. Dozens upon dozens of them...

Creeeaaak... thrum!

I leapt down from the saddle just as a rock the size of an apple sped through the air where my head had been. I heard the most terrible sound then – Celeritas, the beast who had carried me faithfully for so many years – screaming, falling to the earth, chest crushed by one of those rocks. *No*, I mouthed, crawling back to him, seeing those glassy, black eyes gaze into mine as they had done so many times before. This time it was the last. I kissed his muzzle and felt a strangling knot of sorrow in my throat.

Not a tear had time to escape.

Creeeaaak... thrum!

'Shield wall!' Krocus and Batius roared over and over, scuttling to and fro along the line, barging men into place. But a shield cannot stop a rock shot from a ballista, and these poor men took the next volley face-on, the projectiles punching through their shields and taking their heads, bursts of red erupting all along the coastal road.

'Armour,' Ruga yelled to his Ubii legionaries. Men from the mule train hurried to and fro, throwing ringmail and scale shirts to the crouched and weary. One man dropped his shield, pulled on a scale jacket hurriedly, then fell back to his haunches to shelter behind his shield again, only for another rock to streak through it all – shield, armour and man – like a spoon breaking the wax of a honeycomb.

Now the smaller liburnians had drawn back along the shoreline, staying out of line of the artillery ships, but coming close enough for the massed archers on the decks to tilt their bows skywards. It was like a hail of fury. Hundreds upon hundreds of shafts plunged down upon my men, who jerked and spasmed, crying out, clutching at the spines jutting from their shoulders and legs.

'There is nothing we can do,' I cried, eyes darting across this mess, still on the ground with my dead stallion. I experienced an absurd image – like one of Batius' tall tales – of us somehow sailing or swimming out to those wretched galleys, climbing aboard and taking them for ourselves... but that was pure fantasy. Then another thought, of shooting back at them from here on the shore, tearing deep wounds in the hulls. If I could not have the fleet then I must deny its use to Maxentius! But our artillery was disassembled on our wagons. Useless! We had no means of assaulting this powerful fleet... no means of shielding ourselves from the bombardment. Our mighty horsemen could not charge across water! In the mere heartbeats it had taken me to come to this hopeless conclusion, a tranche of the Ubii legionaries had fallen and two dozen more from Baudio's Second Italica. The answer, I realised, was one I had never contemplated before

– never against the Goths, in Britannia, nor in Persia, nor at any time in my station as true Emperor of the West.

'Retreat!' I heard myself rasp as arrows and rocks whizzed around me. 'Pull back from the shore road!'

It was our only option. Those boats could do us no harm if we peeled away from the coast and into the countryside. My column was stunned at first, heads switching back in my direction to make sure they had heard correctly.

Batius and my other generals made sure. 'Get your arses up and get back from the fucking sea!' the big man hinted.

They moved like an uneven wave, stumbling, tumbling, some speeding ahead of others, scores more falling with arrows in their backs or dropping to the sound of rocks breaking their spines. I ran too, like a wretch, through marram grass, thorns and pitted dunes of earth and sand. I jarred my ankle, falling and scraping the skin from my elbows. Up and over a low rise we went and only then in the lee of the far side did the wicked song of speeding stone, wood and steel fade. We crouched, panting – a ridiculous sight, an army as mighty and numerous as mine pinned like children hiding from a bully. A few rocks and shafts bit down on the brow of the rise, throwing up puffs of sand and earth, and more sped on over our heads, but we were out of their line of sight now.

'What if they land?' Krocus spat. 'We need to find a defensible position.'

'They will not land,' I said. 'There were only archers, slingers and artillerymen on those boats. That fleet has served its purpose – to seal off the coast road before we might reach the Capanum Pass.'

Batius' eyes narrowed. 'We cannot retreat. They would rip us apart, all the way back north. So if we are to march on for Rome,' he said, his words trailing off as he looked west, along the inland stretch of the Via Flaminia. Many miles away rose the Apenninus – the ancient jagged, mountainous spine of inner Italia, hazy and blanketed in snow. 'Then it must be along the ancient road... and its high, tight passes.'

I stared at the old road: fine for travelling in times of peace; deadly for those who dared to walk it in the name of war. Italia, that wanton lover, was now a snake-haired demon, gnashing its fangs. 'Aye, and that's just where he wants us.'

A stark cry sounded from somewhere among my sheltering men. 'Domine! Domine! Come quickly!'

I ran towards the sound and saw the medicus who had shouted, crouching over old Lactantius. The old man lay, clutching his belly, delirious. There was no wound, but the pain and illness from earlier was all too real.

'No,' I said, my voice tight and weak like a boy's as I knelt beside him and cradled his old head. 'Not you as well, old tutor. I cannot lose you too.'

22

MAXENTIUS

Rome, 27th September 312 AD

I strode along the walls on the slope of the Collis Hortorum.
Like every foot of stonework surrounding this great city it
was the product of four men's wills. The bloodthirsty soldier-
emperor Aurelian had begun these strong walls some forty
years ago in response to a new threat from the north. Like
most of the hard, warlike emperors of those days before
the tetrarchy, Aurelian had died with Roman swords in his
back. Tacitus had taken the throne then, lasting but a year
before being butchered while thrashing around in the grip
of a fever. A few more courses of brick had gone up under
his aegis. Then his successor, Probus, had the entire circuit of
walls completed satisfactorily before a gladius slid between
his ribs to announce that his tenure was over. They came and
went like sacrificial animals in those days. I was determined
to arrest that run of luck.

And I was the fourth. I was the latest man to build these
walls. For Aurelian, Tacitus and Probus had built strong brick
walls with a walkway atop and in places a covered gallery.
They had ignored centuries of propriety in their intense desire
to see the city defended, incorporating Trajan's amphitheatre,

a burial pyramid-tomb, even the mausolea of the more noble emperors, as part of the defensive circuit. Heavy, squat towers and gates punctured the line, allowing access and providing platforms for heavy artillery. I had looked at those walls, I remembered Constantine and the wooden model back in Treverorum, and I had pronounced them inadequate.

Aurelian and his successors had been facing the threat of rabid Germanics from across the northern rivers. Men who were flummoxed when faced with adequate defensive systems. But I was facing a different kind of foe. A Roman foe. A foe who had all the great knowledge of siegecraft, who had smashed through my northern bastions as though they were kindling. Stout, low brick walls might be enough to frighten the Boii or the Iazyges, but not the armies of Constantine. If I wanted to protect Rome, I needed them to be better.

So my walls had risen further. The height had doubled in almost all places, an extra gallery for archers running throughout and a new great height above with a stronger wall-walk, with better merlons. The gates had doubled in height with a new archers' arcade. A barbarian launching himself at Probus' gate had to scale perhaps thirty feet of wall, facing two artillery pieces atop, and however many archers and soldiers could fit on the parapet, with perhaps half a dozen more at the windows. Constantine, when he came, would have my walls to contend with. Sixty feet high, crammed with missile galleries, with soldiers atop that still and more artillery on the interspaced towers. Swathes of men would lie dead before they touched the wall at all.

'Your city lacks walls. High ones. Strong ones. Walls that might have stopped my hand. Commission your carpenter to make you new blocks, with turrets and buttresses, gates and watchtowers.'

That was what Constantine had said to me all those years ago. Well, my new walls were ready. I had commissioned masons and engineers rather than carpenters, but I had done just that. Rome's defences were ready for a siege.

But was the city?

I had been looking north along the Via Flaminia, which issued from the new heavy gates and marched off toward the Milvian Bridge over the river, across which Constantine would have to bring his armies if he wished to besiege Rome.

Now I changed my focus and turned, looking inward across the roofs of a million souls, crammed into this, the greatest city in the world.

I had tried. I had tried so hard. All I had ever wanted was to be the emperor Rome deserved. To be a servant of the city that had spawned Scipio and Caesar and Trajan. To be not a despot but a binding and supporting force. To rally this fading city that had been all but forgotten by the emperors who yet held and revered her name.

I had rebuilt her armies. I had built grand new structures. I had restored her grain supply. I had held her against two invasions and a rebellion. I had reconciled a religion that could not be reconciled and made them my people alongside those who still worshipped the true gods. I had fought to make Rome great again and despite everything I had done I had slowly, inevitably, watched my success slip through my fingers like fine sand.

Had I been a man more given to maudlin thoughts I might have worried – I had been just that the year Romulus died – but my need to hold Rome together was too strong. Just as my personal world had declined, so had that around me. I had watched my son die, and my father die, my oldest friend become an enemy and now, towards the end, even my poor youngest son seemed destined to walk among the fallen. Oddly, Valeria had somehow moved closer to me as all others had fallen away, and with the unthinkable, yet unavoidable possibility that she had somehow betrayed my trust with the imperial seal, it was difficult not to see our recent closeness as a means to a nefarious end, despite her avowed efforts to sabotage Constantine's force. While all this had happened with my family, so Rome had fallen away. I had been forced to rely upon a dog with whom I shared a mutual loathing: Daia. To save religious schism that threatened to tear my city apart I had taxed the people to an unreasonable level and when they complained, Volusianus had unleashed his Praetorians and butchered them in the streets. Rome seethed. My name was a black word on the tongues of the people I had striven so hard to protect. Each roof I now looked upon harboured vile talk against me.

But what could I do?

People expect an emperor to be Midas, making gold from touching grapes, but the sad fact is that past emperors who did not levy unpopular taxes had left a deficit and an empty treasury cellar in the temple of Saturn for their successor. Those emperors who had taxed hard and left a healthy treasury – Caligula, Domitian – had been damned for their efforts.

There was only one solution and it was one I had come across as a conclusion on my own. I had to finish this. I had to end this stupid and dangerous conflict with Constantine, and then I could change everything. I would have the silver mines of Hispania then. I would have the fields of Gaul and the mines of Britannia. My border with opposing claimants would drop from being thousands of miles long to being a short land border across the Alps. That meant I would be able to disband perhaps four-fifths of my army. Imagine how much money would be freed up for the people of Rome if they did not have to support such a vast field army.

The people seethed, and the only way I could heal it, to return their wealth, their pride and their faith, was to destroy my old friend and consolidate the West under my command. I had to kill Constantine.

Despite everything, looking out across those roofs, all I could suddenly see in my mind's eye was my boyhood saviour.

The door from the ambulatory and the main hall seemed to be open once more, admitting a white-gold glow and, haloed in that brilliance, was a tall, bear-shouldered figure, seeming to me like Hercules himself.

Hercules indeed. If he were Hercules, then I would be the blood of the Lernaean Hydra, and I would be the burning tunic smeared with it, robbing the demigod of his life.

I had loved him as a brother, but then had not Romulus and Remus been both brothers and fratricides? And if I wanted to found a new Rome as that infamous pup had done, I too would have to kill my brother.

The gods can be cruel.

And perhaps I needed to overcome my aversion to brutality, too. I was no coward, and baulked not at a fight, for sure, but I had always seen violence as something with a place and a time: on the field of battle, and when both armies were prepared. Constantine had already taught me the harsh lesson that perhaps any time is the time for violence as he sneaked over the Alps in the middle of winter and fell upon me unexpectedly.

And while I had approved of Valeria's efforts to sow discord in Constantine's ranks, when tidings had come that the someone in the enemy camp had poisoned his frail old tutor, I had been incensed. An innocent old man? Valeria had briefly shaken off enough of the shroud of insouciance to remind me that Lactantius was still very much a steadying and guiding hand in the enemy's consilium, and notably one of the most respected Christian teachers among them. Still, I did not approve.

Her agents had clearly been sighting their targets high, but would the end justify the means? Or had we all now sold our morals to pay for our laurels? I berated Valeria for allowing her agents to murder an ageing civilian, regardless of his position. She told me in no uncertain terms that this was not the work of her one remaining man, but some problem of the enemy's, though she also acknowledged that it played well for us. Moreover, she held that had the notion occurred to her, she would have been content to order it.

Who, not in my pay, would have such reason to turn on Constantine in his camp?

I tore my angry gaze from the roofs and cast a quick look to the distant north, as if I could see that traitorous bridge that would bring Constantine to the city, then I strode off to the Porta Flaminia and descended to the ground, clacking down the steps, new and old, of the two storeys of defence that would save Rome.

I cannot say I was pleased to find the deputation awaiting me. Zenas, Ancharius Pansa and my hapless *cubicularius* Meno. Alongside the capable but currently absent and always troublesome Volusianus, they represented four difficulties central to my life. Zenas had been my political tool in bringing to my side an ally I hated and distrusted, and therefore little he might further report would be comforting. Pansa was my spy chief, my eyes and ears on the world, who had failed repeatedly to warn me of trouble and had yet to produce even an inkling regarding the traitor in my midst. *Not Valeria*, I still hoped. Volusianus represented the military and our preparations for war. None of them could bear tidings that would bring joy or ease to my heart. That left Meno. Meno could carry a plethora of news, and might even be a bright spot in my day, but the look on his face was enough to tell me that he also bore only gloom that day.

'Go,' I said, pointing at Zenas as I crossed toward my horse that stood with my equisio nearby.

The young hero who had come from almost nothing to be one of my most trusted men cleared his throat.

'Volusianus awaits you in your aula regia. He wishes to discuss the defence of the city and the preparations.'

I could see the frustration emanating from Zenas at having been used as little more than a messenger by my Praetorian Prefect. 'I shall go there now. I have updates on my thoughts regarding the walls. We can discuss all else as we ride.'

I mounted, watching the others around me. Had I not felt so dismal and tense it might have been funny. Zenas leapt astride his horse like a racer, swiping the reins from his man who had held them. Pansa, short, misshapen and ugly with that stray eye, was hauled and pushed up into the saddle by two men, along with a great deal of foul language and grunting and farting. Meno could not ride. He was an administrator in the palace. He climbed into his litter and then had to lean oddly to the side, almost overbalancing it, so that he could both see and talk out of the window as we moved. We must have looked a peculiar bunch, even surrounded by Praetorians.

'Speak,' I said to Pansa now that we were moving.

'Our intelligence says that Constantine is moving across the Apenninus now, driven away from the coast by our fleet. He walks directly into your traps along the way. His unpreparedness tells me that whoever was responsible for removing Ruricius' support at Taurinorum, and leaking information, is not moving with them. If he were, I doubt Constantine would have suffered as he did.'

'And what of Valeria?' I murmured quietly. I had voiced my worries about the potential use of my seal by my wife to both Pansa and Zenas before now, and for a moment Meno was out of earshot as he struggled with his bearers.

'I cannot say, Domine. I cannot believe it is the case, for the empress is as staunch a supporter of your cause now as any, but she was present in the north at the time of the seal's use, with access to it, and now she is in Rome where she cannot possibly contact him and he blunders into our snares. But then, the same could be said for half the court and the army staff, so that is far from a condemnation. The fact is that the investigation remains ongoing.'

I nodded as we passed beneath the grand Claudian arch of the Aqua Virgo. I hated to think it might be her, and it eased my heart somewhat to think that my master of the frumentarii, Pansa, shared my doubt. As we ambled on, I heard the clattering of hooves on the cobbles and blinked as Meno's secretary came careering around the corner and hauled on his reins.

'Diotimus?' Meno said, leaning precariously out of his litter window. 'Some disaster from the palace? We have run out of shrimp perhaps?'

It was a light-hearted comment but had been cast into a huge dark well of gloom and disappeared without trace as the secretary turned away from his master and addressed me directly, though with respectfully downcast eyes. 'It is Aurelius Caesar, Domine.'

My heart was suddenly gripped in a fist of ice. My son. 'And?'

'He is in decline, Domine.'

'He has been in decline for months.'

'The speed of his fading has increased, Domine. The medicus would not leave his side to tell you and would not trust such tidings to a slave who might be waylaid. He believes Aurelius has a month left. Two at most. In a rather callous manner he told me that he would buy me a horse if your son made it to Saturnalia. It is imperative that you spend time with him. The medicus' words, of course, Domine.'

I nodded sadly and gestured at Zenas and Pansa. 'Ride ahead. Tell Volusianus I am on the way, but I must visit my son first.'

They looked unhappy but went nonetheless. I gestured at Meno's litter bearers. 'A diversion. Follow.' With my lictors leading the way and Praetorians all about we turned and began to make our way up the slope of the Quirinal. I was further disheartened by the looks on the faces of Rome as we passed. Six years ago they had borne expressions of love and hope. Now it was hate and resentment. I *had* to win this back, else what had it all been for?

A few moments later we were at the Temple of Salus. It seemed ridiculous to beseech the healing god Aesculapius for Aurelius – there was no real healing to be had, for he had no wounds – but the age-old divine maiden of health seemed appropriate.

The temple emptied before we arrived, my lictors doing their job admirably. Only a duty priest who would rather be anywhere else right then mooched about inside. My eyes adjusted to the gloom. I could see the goddess herself, larger than life, seated on her basalt throne, legs crossed in the ancient fashion, left hand clutching a snake-wound staff just like that of the god of healing, right proffering a shallow bowl at which another stone snake lunged.

I peered into the bowl, noting the stains and marks of many offerings. With a start I realised I had nothing on me. No purse or pouch. What had I to offer? Feeling strangely sheepish, I beckoned my entire escort and demanded of them anything they had. No man had more than a few coins.

'Try this, Domine,' said one of the Praetorian centurions. He held up a scrap of parchment and I stared at him as though a hunting hound had suddenly grown out of the side of his head. He smiled. 'It is more impressive than it appears. It is a fragment of one of the Sibylline books that was burned in ancient times, and it is doubly sacred, for it was somehow preserved in the water and made it upstream to Rome where it was gathered up: a fragment of prophecy found in odd circumstances.'

'A soggy piece of parchment that may once have held inscrutable prophecy but has since been dunked in a river full of corpses and dung. This you feel to be a suitable sacrifice to a goddess of health and wellbeing?'

The soldier gave me an odd look as though he could not comprehend what I had said. 'It is sacred beyond sacred, Domine, rarer than a tree fart, more valuable than all the gold in Dacia, and baptised in the waters of Father Tiber. What could be greater?'

I lifted one eyebrow. Half the things I had on my dresser for a start. This piece of worthless hokum had cost a soldier half a year's pay from some pedlar in the forum. I knew too what sect in my empire considered 'baptism' important. What value a Christian who so prized pagan artefacts? Still, the value of an object is defined by those who want it, and this man had paid the world in coin to own it, yet offered it to me freely. I took it solemnly, reverentially, and placed it in the bowl in the hand of Salus. I felt like a fraud. I hoped giving the gods Tiber water and the fake words of the Sibyl would not come back to haunt me, fool that I was, and made my prayers.

The salutations complete, we made once more for the Palatine. At the grand door I dismounted and dismissed the men, granting an on-the-spot promotion to the man who had given me his most prized possession. I transferred him from ordinary Praetorian guardsman to the tribunate among the Second Parthica Stationarii.

I hurried through the corridors of the palace. It was not cold, being September in Rome, but I shivered nonetheless. I reached the suite of my boy and his nurse swiftly, the cubicularius still at my heel. I dismissed him at the door and knocked only once before entering.

How old was Euna now? She never seemed to age despite her advanced years. Yet today, for the first time, she looked her age; worried and old all of a sudden.

I peered at Aurelius in his bed. He was still curved and twisted, my darling second boy. The only remaining child of our line. He was so pale I might have thought him already dead had he not heaved in a shuddering breath. I felt a single tear leap to the corner of my eye. All that remained of my legacy lay here.

'He has not long,' said a quiet voice behind me. I did not turn, and a moment later, Valeria laid her hands across my shoulders.

'Is this how it is for emperors?' she said. 'No hope. Watching the dynasty fail.'

I shook my head, though I could not find words to argue with her.

SIMON TURNEY & GORDON DOHERTY

'Once I thought you my enemy,' Valeria murmured. 'My father foisted me off on you like chattel. I resented you for what Father did to me. I should have stayed in his court, but was given to what appeared to be a weak boy with no imperial ambition. It took death and loss and disaster for me to recognise in you a strength that surpasses common understanding. You are a weak man by nature and I do not begrudge you that. Most men are weak and play strong and most women do precisely the opposite. But despite a weakness in your soul, you have girded yourself and made yourself strive and fight. Such a man is worth a vast amount more than a born warrior who fails to live up to his potential. Do you understand?'

I gave her a weary look. 'I am weak but I strive not to be, which is better than being strong and indolent, yes?'

'It was meant to be a compliment. It took time to turn my head to the truth. It took the death of my father and your simple strength and understanding in how you dealt with it to make me realise. When we lost Romulus I was already partially there. I already knew that he was more than I had ever let him be. In some way I think I continued to shun you because I was jealous that I had abandoned the closeness he offered, while you had been the perfect father. In retrospect, I missed being a mother to Romulus, and his passing left a hole in me about which I can do nothing.'

Candour was never a problem for Valeria, but she had never been candid on this subject before. I did not know how to reply, and she continued.

'I hated Aurelius. I still do, though it is now laced with pity, and it tortures me that I have a son who is dying, yet once again I repeat the mistake I made with Romulus and starve him of love.'

'He will soon be gone. Perhaps there will be time for another child? A new progeny?' I said in an odd tone.

'Perhaps, when this is over. When Constantine is rendered down to ash, I will bear you strong sons and we will build a new Rome. You will be the emperor you always should have been and I shall be Juno to your Jove. Is that good?'

I laughed. 'Oh, but for our poor boy here, those words would rank highest in my whole life, my beloved.'

Her face became serious once more. Valeria was ever a practical woman, after all. 'But a good general prepares for failure. They say Marcellus always had a sharp blade at his side, not because he would ever have to draw it on an enemy, but in case he had to take his life in failure.'

'I will not flee,' I told her resolutely. 'If I lose this war, I will die in the losing.'

'I know, and that is why I also must prepare. Victorious armies are brutal. You once passed on to me the story of what happened when Constantine and his men burst into the tent of the King of Kings, how the woman was raped. That will not happen. When you win, we will celebrate and toast your eternal reign with a bevy of strong sons. Should you lose, know that my knife will find my throat long before the enemy do, and all those about whom we care will go before the enemy can touch them.'

I found her words hauntingly calming and kissed her on the forehead, then gently planted another kiss on the cold, fevered head of my twisted son before turning.

'Volusianus wants me.'

'Be calm with him.'

I left the room with an odd smile. For the first time in many, many months I felt weirdly positive. It is astounding what the support of a loved one can do. Defeat Constantine and heal Rome. Defeat Constantine and start a new dynasty. We were still young. It was not a foolish notion.

I almost had a skip in my step when I reached my aula regia and found Volusianus poring over maps on a trestle table.

'Ah, good. There is a critical decision to be made.'

I ignored the lack of reverence and honorific in his tone. Volusianus would never change and I had to simply accept that and make use of him. 'What?'

'Where do we fight your friend?'

I frowned. 'You mean if he does not fall in the mountains or at the walls of some redoubt on the Via Flaminia? Then here. We have spent years preparing Rome. There is not a more secure city in the empire and we have a good supply source. If he reaches the Tiber, we cut the Milvian Bridge and make him besiege us. He will starve long before us, and he can never take these walls.'

'Would that such was the case, Domine,' he replied, finally remembering an honorific. 'How many cities have fallen in the past to a door opened by a disgruntled soldier or a desperate citizen?'

I shook my head, though my imagination was suddenly stocked with images of those Illyrian cities who had betrayed their Pompeian garrisons and declared for Caesar, throwing open the gates to the enemy. Worse still, the cities of the north who had welcomed Constantine to their bosom. 'Do you think it likely?'

'The people are at best restive,' he replied. 'At worst borderline rebellious.'

'We have vast forces. They cannot hope to open the gate to Constantine if we man them strongly enough.'

'But every siege-bound force also relies on the citizens. They have to provide and ferry food and munitions. They support the defending army. How likely do you think it is that a populace will rush to help the army of an emperor who ordered the butchering of their citizens.'

I railed, angrily. '*You* gave that order.'

A flash of discontent passed across Volusianus again. For all his faults he continued to serve me well despite my recent denigration of him. '*You* implicitly gave me the authority to do so. The people see it as you. Can we trust the populace?'

I shrugged. 'What is the alternative?'

'Meet them across the Tiber in open ground. Defeat them in straight battle.'

I stared. 'Are you mad?'

He pursed his lips. 'Caesar won Rome at Pharsalus. Augustus at Actium. Rome does not have to be the battleground. Indeed, if you win away from these walls and save the people the agony and worry of a siege, it will repair much of your reputation. And our forces already outnumber his by three to one even before he has fought his way through every redoubt along the Via Flaminia, where the veterans of the Second Parthica are stationed.'

I felt a moment of guilt at having sent 'parchment boy' to join them as a tribune, but quickly I pulled myself back to the present. 'No. Rome has walls for this very situation. We can starve him, even in the open. We will still control Ostia, Portus and Puteoli. We have supplies and he will not, for the Adriatic Fleet will harry his lines. Soon he will run back north with his tail between his legs as did Severus and Galerius before him, but we will not let him run as we did the others. I will have him before he can flee.'

Volusianus was giving me an odd look and I could not quite work out what it meant.

'That is not the most sensible option, Domine. There is still the chance that the journey across our road of knives will cost Constantine so much that he is forced to retreat, and if not, then the force he brings here will be further diminished, easy prey in the field for our vastly superior force.'

'It is my decision, Volusianus. Yes, Constantine may yet falter and fail before he even reaches the walls, but unless the gods themselves tell me otherwise, if he comes, we will hold him at the walls of Rome until he starves.'

Gods love a joke, don't they?

23

CONSTANTINE

The Via Flaminia, early October 312 AD

The *shush* of mail and thunder of boots and hooves echoed across the deserted green meadows and low hills of Umbria as my army rolled westwards along the Via Flaminia, the road across Italia's interior, the route onto which Maxentius' cruel boats had driven us. The air was still warm and streaked with dust that stung the eyes and parched the throat. I rode at the head of the cavalry now – taking over poor Vitalianus' command. Up ahead, Krocus and his Regii forged like a spearhead, their eyes flicking back and forth, as they plunged deeper into this land that most of them had only ever heard about. I stroked the mane of my white mare as we went, often fondly thinking of Celeritas. The old stallion had deserved a burial at least, but had been left for the wolves back on the coast road. I remembered then a moment back in Nicomedia, when Maxentius, young Romulus and I had taken the faithful steed to the circus on a day when the great arena was empty. We took turns at riding with Maxentius' lad on Celeritas' back. Together we had brushed and fed the stallion, Romulus giggling as the mount snorted and licked his face. Together…

And now Maxentius' hurled rocks and bolts had torn the old steed down like an unwanted dog. The same storm of missiles had cut down thousands of my men. I gripped the reins until my knuckles grew white and my hands shook. At the same time, my throat thickened with emotion, my heart achingly sad for the lost past, when things had been so different.

Following the coastal slaughter, we had spent fourteen nights in the brush, my camp like a massive valetudinarium, dotted with medical staff, strewn with red-soaked wounded, crying out, blinded by pain. After we had tended to the stricken – most slipping away into death – we had left behind the outline of a great camp, and a blackened field of spent pyres. More than sixteen hundred men, gone.

The fate of one soul, still living, troubled me like no other. I gave command to the draconarius riding by my side, and slowed my mount, falling back along the column until I rode level with the medicus wagons. 'How is he?' I asked for the dozenth time that day.

Fausta, tending to him, looked up, her face sullen. The medicus kneeling over old Lactantius turned to me too, and the look on his face was answer enough. 'His body is weak with age, Domine. The fever has become something deeper, darker. He neither speaks nor opens his eyes now, and his limbs hang loose. His breaths grow shallow too.'

I pinched my eyes closed and tensed my whole body, fending off images of Father's last moments – similar to this. 'What caused it? He was fine in Ravenna.'

'Fevers such as this strike like vipers,' said Fausta sadly.

'As I say, Domine, he is a great age,' the medicus said.

I noticed a younger medicus in the back of the wagon, frowning, his lips pursed like one wary of contradicting a more senior colleague.

'What do you think, lad?' I prompted him.

He blanched for a moment, then gulped, glancing at his senior, before speaking: 'I have seen this type of malady before, Domine. So sudden, so grave. The fever then the coma. It happened when I was stationed in Antioch to stand watch over a local grain magnate who had received threats to his life. One night, he visited a business rival to share a meal and discuss opportunities.' He shook his head. 'I remember escorting him home. He muttered all the way about the frivolity and pointlessness of the meeting. Nothing had been agreed. Nothing of use had been discussed. Soon after, he fell ill just like this. We only found out after he died – more than a month later – that the business rival had been spotted talking with a local poisoner.'

'Poison,' I said, hurt and confused. I looked across my marching column. 'How? We have had no enemy in our midst.'

My head began to reel… and then I remembered: the stranger who had been shot while escaping our Ravenna camp. It must have been him. No, something wasn't right. 'How long after the meal did you say this magnate fell ill?'

'Hours, Domine,' the lad replied.

My eyes twitched this way and that. Over a month had passed between the wretched spy dying on the end of my sentries' arrows and poor Lactantius' illness. A horrid, cold bile rose within me as I realised what this meant. After fears there might be other spies in our camp, I'd had a census taken: every man had to be vouched for by another. The results? There were no strangers in the camp. Fine news then. Now? Now it meant that someone apparently loyal to me had done this. I glared around the many faces of the marching men, and at the backs of those ahead. Who… *who* would do this to the old goat? And what chance had I of weeding out the culprit from so many thousands?

'Domine!' the draconarius called from my horse wing.

Sucking in a cold breath, I demanded of the medicus pair: 'Give him everything he needs. Never leave him alone.' Then I clicked my fingers at a pair of Lancearii. 'You two, guard this wagon with your lives. Nobody is to tend to my old tutor apart from Lady Fausta and these healers.'

With that, I heeled my mare back to the front of the column. I could see why the *decurion* had called me, for we had reached the rocky wall of the Apenninus Mountains: sultry late afternoon sunlight glared around the outline of the range, a thickly-wooded sierra – the slopes a canopy of green, gold and brown. The men eyed these heights suspiciously as the road bent around the southern scarp of the massif. Just how many warriors could such a colossal forest hide? My lips quirked as I realised that dozens of legions could be in those trees... but only if they had a commander sharp enough to have spotted the ambush opportunity. Maxentius' use of the Ravenna Fleet had been shrewd, as had his snare at Taurinorum, but I could see that the earth around the treeline was undisturbed. More, there were no signs of agitated bird flocks rising from the trees. My scouts soon confirmed my suspicions; the way and the woods were clear. He had missed his chance here.

On we went, following the old road. A tributary to the River Metaurus quarrelled away on our left, fast-flowing, dappled with white-knot rapids. When we came to the next of the mountain ranges, it was like a rampart built by giants – no woods, just a pale, stony hand thrown up in our faces, stretching for miles either side. This was the Petra massif. There were old, broken tracks leading south and north – routes that would take us around this daunting sierra, though not quickly. A scout thundered in from the northern track as if he had heard my thoughts. He shook his head once, his face pinched as if he had just tasted a spoonful of bad stew. 'The track is in ruins, and a large stretch of it is swamped with mud.' A runner came in from the south too. 'The old way has become entangled with gorse and wild trees, Domine,' he panted. 'For miles and miles. It will take many days to clear the road.'

I let a sigh slip from my lips, then quickly disguised it with a cough. The low routes were not to be – not without the woe of scores of broken cartwheels and sumpter mules becoming trapped in morasses. Such trivial hindrances quickly sapped morale and would be seized upon by the more suspicious soldiers as bleak omens, as if the gods themselves had been responsible for the natural obstacles.

So my gaze rolled directly ahead, to the continuing Via Flaminia, the ancient flagstones slicing into and through the Petra Mountains, a canyon route known as the Intercisa Pass.

Why, you may ask, had I even halted here, if there was a direct route through – a paved road no less? Why all the deliberation about inferior and diversionary tracks? Well the main route through the mountains was laid with fine flagstones, yes, and it was direct and quick too. Yet even the sight of it sent shudders through me, and I saw my men eyeing it askance also. It was as if the same giants who had built that high, stony range of mountains had taken up an axe and brought it swishing down upon their creation. The resultant canyon was painfully narrow, the gurgling tributary hugging the left side of the paved road like a vein all the way through that thin corridor. The Intercisa Pass was a route that made much sense in times of peace – when swiftness to and from Rome was the key to profitable trade, and the high pass sides would be patrolled by imperial watchmen to chase off bandits. But on a march of war, it was a mighty olive press, the most perfect choke point.

'We have to forge on,' Batius whispered. 'If we hesitate here the men's suspicions will fester and grow horns.'

I glanced around the skies, distrustful first of the coming night. More, any day now the early frosts might appear, then talk of the winter would soon follow, and the usual murmurings of despair that always arose from soldiers asked to live in hibernal camp, far from home. Saving even a day's march was important, I realised.

I slid my head forward once in grudging assent. 'Very well. But I will lead.'

Batius eyed me sideways. 'Be wary, Domine. You can polish tales of heroics once this war is done, but for now, pragmatism is key. You are their champion. If you were to be hurt or to fall, then this campaign would fall with you.'

'Then see that I go unscathed,' I replied.

I raised and flicked a finger. The cavalry draconarius read the signal and lifted the bronze dragon-head standard. A trumpeter sounded for the advance and in some small way at least, the growing clamour of doubtful whispers quietened a little. Yet still I saw the looks of doubt on their faces.

As we approached the axe-wound of the Intercisa Pass, it seemed to triple in height, the stony walls either side like pillars. Before I entered the ravine, I called over a knot of bare-footed scouts. As they edged their way through my ranks towards me, I finalised the plan in my mind and balanced orders on my tongue: for them to scale the pass sides and scout the heights.

As soon as we entered the pass, the world changed.

The air was stale, like the breath of shades, and the echo of our march was maddening, reverberating and ringing in strange ways that made our sixteen thousand men and fifteen hundred cavalry – walking just three abreast, for that was all the narrow section of road would allow – sound like an earthquake. On our right, the sheer stony side of the ravine towered, and on our left the river thrashed and spat, wetting our path, and the base of the ravine's opposite wall. Worse, the sun was dipping in the west, and the ravine was beginning to fill with the shade of dusk. I began to doubt my promptness in coming in here instead of making camp back at the ravine entrance and waiting for morning. Then, we rounded a slight bend and saw a dead end of rock... and the rock-cut tunnel cut there. The tunnel burrowed through the mountains themselves, and I could see a small arch-shape of light at the far end. That was befuddling enough, but then the most drawling drone rose from behind me. The four bishops led a Christian chorus, a dirge of chants that filled the pass. 'Great and marvellous are thy works, Lord God Almighty; just and true are thy ways, thou King of saints...' It was sung in bullish, aggressive tones. I knew what was coming next.

'Shut up, you wailing fools!' cried a centurion of the Seventh Gemina.

'Sing of the ancient gods, or shut the fuck up!' roared another.

'Besmirch the chosen four at your peril, benighted dog!' a Lancearius howled back.

My eyes slid shut.

The clatter of men barging at one another, of shouting and cursing, shoving, punches being thrown rose to drown out the Christian song.

'Order!' I heard Batius scream.

'Calm down, you mutts!' Krocus roared.

The din was awful. A pair of the fighting ones even toppled into the waters. Still they fought, more interested in braining one another than not drowning. This was the province of old Lactantius. His walks along the column-side and a few wry words and observations were usually all it took for him to calm this type of unrest. Yet he lay unconscious in a medicus wagon. The yammering and clattering grew so noisy it took me a while to hear the one voice right next to me, repeating over and over: 'Domine... Domine? What would you have us do?'

I blinked and looked down. There, by my steed's side, stood the barefoot climber scout and his cadre. Down here. Down *here*. In the chaos of the religious squabbling, I had neglected to actually give the order to those climbers. I glanced up at the pass sides. A flash of steel. *No!*

A wall of iron-garbed Maxentians rose into view on the leftmost heights above the ravine. I recognised their standard too: the Second Parthica Legion. They grinned, yelled and spat down at us, a rank of them stepping to the very edge and pointing nocked bows down into the ravine.

The clamour of unrest among my column suddenly exploded into a yammer of alarm and hoisting their shields to face up at the left cliff-edge like ants staring up at eagles. My spirit was anchored to the ground, and so I could not even rouse myself to lift my shield. Instead I stared up at the Parthica officer leaping around behind the archers, bleating about how a piece of parchment from the pages of the sacred Sibylline books had guaranteed them victory today. It was he who gave the order. 'Loose!'

The arrows and spears rained down in their hundreds. I felt

the wind of the hail, heard the panicked whinny of my mare and the screams of my men, run through or splashing into the river, screaming as they were carried away. A horseman next to me shuddered and sighed, then slumped forward in the saddle, an arrow jutting from the vertex of his skull, black blood pumping out around the point where the shaft was embedded. 'No… not again,' I groaned, seeing the mind's-eye image of the coast road slaughter again. I set my gaze upon the dark tunnel ahead. Shelter, just a few hundred paces away. 'Make for the tunnel,' I bawled, heeling my steed round, swishing my hand towards that burrow. As my mount's forelegs clacked down again and I heeled her on, I heard the panicked cries of my army, forging towards that only hope of shelter. That was when the hidden iron portcullis at the tunnel's near end slammed down, like teeth gnashing into that sad arch of hope. My mount reared up, nearly throwing me. Other riders bunched up behind me, some falling from the saddles. Legionaries pressed against those horsemen, blinded by those in front of them, not understanding that the tunnel had been closed to us.

'The tunnel is blocked. Get back!' Batius roared at them, realising what was happening. 'In a crush, no man will be able to raise his shield. Spread out along the road, backs to the rock face, hold your shields up to the attackers.'

The advice was barely heeded as more spears and arrows hurtled down. Bodies pirouetted from the roadside and into the river, now running red and bobbing with corpses. Men slid and slipped in their state of terror into the rapids where their armour became their tombstone, anchoring them to the deep riverbed.

'They are pinned. Bring the artillery!' the Parthican officer squealed. 'There he is,' the man exclaimed, falling into a crouch like a vulture, pointing a finger right at me. 'The Emperor wants him dead. His corpse will make some prize! Now, whose prize will it be? Which is my most skilful catapult crew?'

Now arrows ricocheted and battered down all around me. I slid from my mare and threw my shield up to take shelter at last, pulling on my battle helm in that precious trice of respite. A spear shredded a section of my shield, a dozen arrows whacked into it and I heard the rumble of catapults and bolt throwers being dragged up to the cliff top to do quickly and for certain what these missiles might take some time to achieve. There were dozens of them: ballistae, scorpions, onagers, and hundreds of crewmen, all bearing hefty balls of rock, dumping them down on the cliff edge and ferrying more there. Maxentius had commissioned another massacre, I realised. It should not have been a surprise – for all now knew this was his forte: soldier or citizen – it mattered little, so long as Maxentius got his way and the earth turned red.

The stone and bolt throwers creaked and groaned. The Parthican officer raised a hand... and then it happened.

With a mighty, thunderous *boom*, a jagged black line struck across the leftmost ravine-side, just a short way below the high edge, shooting like lightning along its length. The rumbling weight of all those men, all those devices, all the polished catapult stones, I realised. There was the briefest hiatus, when the cliff edge shuddered and the Parthican officer's eyes met mine. His face changed from a look of unbridled glee to one of pale, drawn, horror.

The cliff-side sloughed away, as if the giant axe that had made this place had returned to cleave it free. Masses of rock plummeted into the river, taking with it the artillery and more Maxentians than I dared count. The noise was terrifying, and I thought for a moment that my head might explode. The momentous rockfall crashed into the river. I saw groups of my men too being snatched away by stray boulders bouncing over to this side. Water leapt up, thick dust filled the ravine, and I was blinded and deafened for an age. When the chaos began to settle, I saw my army – the shapes of men veiled in dust, blinking, agape, cowering along our narrow road below the rightmost cliff. Then I saw the Parthican leader again – trapped at the waist between two giant shards of rock that now lay lodged in the river, jutting free of the surface. His hips were crushed, and he vomited blood with every breath. His precious piece of parchment had guaranteed nothing. His body fell still and remained there, arms bobbing like strands of weed in the river's current. Around him, hundreds of his Parthicans – or should I say segments of their crushed bodies – floated downstream.

I shared a look with Ruga, Batius, Hisarnis and Scaurus – the nearest of my officers. They stared at me with looks of pale-faced relief. But my soldiers glanced around, confused by what had just happened. It was the four bishops who seized upon the moment.

'The Lord has shown the way to those whom he favours!' cried Ossius.

'It was our deep song that cracked the rock and smote the enemy!' added Marinus.

As quickly as that, the fighting and shouting returned. My men, coated in dust, scraped and bloodied, piled into one another yet again. An ambush, a victory – granted by the Christian God, or Fortuna maybe, or perhaps by pure chance – and then chaos again. My army was eating itself from within.

My teeth became a cage, and I bellowed at my most trusted, nearby, swinging a finger at the blocked tunnel. 'Get that portcullis open. Get us out of this cursed place!'

24

MAXENTIUS

Rome, early October 312 AD

I was furious. I was as angry as I had ever been. I had been betrayed before now, had my family murdered, been stabbed in the back by my closest friend, and yet, perhaps in an unwarranted manner, and perhaps because I had already been in a foul mood, this had really dragged me to mountainous ire.

I flung open the doors with such force that they ricocheted from the marble, cracking the tiles, sending fragments and dust into the air and startling the Praetorians beside them. Volusianus and Pansa stood at a table, poring over a huge campaign map dotted with small wooden markers. Zenas stood in the corner like a child being punished, and his face suggested that he was almost as angry as I was. It might perhaps have endeared him to me, but I was my father's son, and the anger was too strong. It just made him look weak.

'What is the fucking meaning of this?' I bellowed.

My two top military minds, one a master of the battlefield and the other a clever tactician, turned in surprise, perhaps half expecting me to be holding a severed head, such was my language and tone.

'Domine?' Pansa said, his stray eye examining some tile of Numidian marble close to my left elbow. I had long since ceased to find such details humorous.

'Ostia?' I prompted.

'Securing Rome's safe harbour is paramount,' Volusianus said, as though speaking to a child. My anger actually increased, which I had not thought possible.

'When we left Verona,' I snapped violently, waving arms and stomping through the room, 'we had in excess of a hundred thousand men to guard the city against attack. We spent half a year stripping them from other regions, gathering them ready to save Rome, and Constantine had, what, twenty thousand? It was our secured victory. Five to one is a victory, no matter what the quality of the men, especially since we had all the advantage of defending territory and secure supply lines. If these reports are to be believed, we have now perhaps seventy thousand troops here at the most, having shipped legion after legion out to Ostia. Now answer me, what is the meaning of this?'

It was true. We'd had, on parchment at least, enough men to swamp Constantine and halt his army. That was the whole point of rallying at Rome, after all. Suddenly, the numbers looked a lot more even than I liked.

'It is necessary, Domine,' Volusianus retorted, his eyebrow crooked. 'If we are to survive, we must secure everything for Rome's continuation. Our grain fleets need manpower, lest Daia suddenly decide our opposition looks more favourable.'

I snapped my glance to Zenas, who had brokered the deal with that eastern dog. The source of my Christian officer's own argument had become apparent. Volusianus had no faith in Zenas' work. Again, I could have leapt to his defence, but I hated Daia so strongly that it was difficult.

'So we released troops,' Volusianus went on with spread hands of innocence. 'Fifty thousand men have been deployed away from Rome, yes, but thirty thousand of them are based along Constantine's route to slow or stop him. The other twenty secure the fleet and every port in Italia, making sure that we have a constant flow of supplies, and helping deny the same to Constantine. Having men to throw spears at him is less valuable than starving him while we have strong walls to protect us, and don't forget that Constantine controls Hispania and Gaul. Without adequate protection, our western shores and the fleet on the *Mare Internum* could be prey to his ships. Curtail your panic, Domine, for we will need to draw more men away from Rome yet. I shall not be concerned as long as our final number outweighs his, and he will lose many thousands along the Via Flaminia.'

I glowered. The logic was hard to dispute, but I was in an argumentative mood. My eyes flicked to Zenas once more.

'Daia's legions await mere days away,' I grumbled. 'If the enemy look to stand a chance of resupply, we can always call on those men and ships without weakening Rome. We need the army *here!*'

'You were quite clear, Domine, that you wanted Daia as uninvolved as possible. He was only to commit if Licinius sent men to Constantine, and that sweating arse-bag has done no such thing, so Daia waits patiently. Is that not what you wanted?'

Damn it but yes, that was it precisely.

'We will continue to bleed Rome of troops to secure the region and our supply routes. Better that than finding ourselves cut off and starving, and before you hear it from someone else, I have sent out orders to have the Milvian Bridge cut.'

I stared.

'*What?*' My voice was at least half an octave higher now. 'I said we would cut the bridge *if and when* his army arrived at Rome. To do so now, while he flounders somewhere in the mountains with my legions battering him, is previous to say the *least*. We may yet need that bridge.'

'Constantine is somewhere on the Via Flaminia,' he explained with exaggerated patience. 'We were waiting for confirmation from the Second Parthica that he had been halted, but no such news has arrived, and he must have passed the Intercisa tunnel by now. In this case, no news is bad news. He may be closing on Rome and have somehow managed to circumvent our strongest bastions. Until we hear where he is from a trusted source, he could be anywhere – even but a few miles from here.'

'You think breaking the bridge will solve this?'

Pansa took the fore now. 'With our men scattered and no known position for the enemy it is prudent to destroy the main crossing between us and them. We can, with luck, hold Constantine on the Tiber's north bank and starve him there without his ever even seeing our walls. We have cut every bridge downstream of the city of Tibur, barring the arterial Milvian. If we demolish that, he is stranded on the far side. The Misenum Fleet controls the coast with over ten thousand new marines, preventing supplies from reaching him. The Ravenna Fleet does the same in the east. If he cannot cross the river, then we control Ostia and Puteoli, and Constantine's army will slowly starve on the north bank.'

I really wanted to argue. I was angry, and they had seriously diminished the number of men defending Rome, but their reasons were all so damned rational and their conjectures plausible. Would this be yet another case of my advisors proposing things so sensible and rational that they lost me more cities and strength? In the end, I gave them both a grumpy nod and gestured for Zenas to join me. We left the room and found a cold, damp balcony nearby, where we could look out across the city to the Capitol, shrouded in cold fog. We leaned on the stonework and said nothing for a while; two men, both incensed with anger. In the end, it was Zenas who broke the silence.

'There is a decline in public support, I'm afraid, Domine,' he murmured.

Fabulous. Something else to worry about. I remained sullenly silent until he continued.

'The walls seethe with men. Soldiers are everywhere. Marines too. You can't buy bread without a soldier at the stall. Every bar is packed with them. The streets look like a military parade some days.'

'That should reassure people. My men are there to save them.'

Zenas shook his head. 'That's not how it works, Domine. I've seen it in Africa many times. The mere presence of soldiers suggests danger. So many armoured figures in Rome makes Romans think they are in peril. The continued presence of so many soldiers is a constant reminder of the danger facing everyone. Remember that victorious armies are a plague to an innocent populace. They all know that if Constantine gets through the walls, they will live or die on his word, and his reputation is far from peaceful. So no, soldiers do not reassure the people. They frighten them.'

I tried not to picture the mob in Rome rebelling.

I failed.

I had seen them tear through a Moesian cohort in the forum as though they were spring grain dolls.

'Might the people turn on me?'

'Who knows, Domine, but do not count on the two thousand men of the Urban Cohorts for defence of the city. They will have their own work controlling the frightened and fractious inhabitants. It will be down to the cohorts to keep the public from revolting and opening a gate in panic.'

'Shit.'

'Quite.'

We stared out across the Palatine for some time. Eventually, it was me that broke the silence this time.

'Can we beat him?'

I trusted Zenas. I trusted Volusianus, too, but only to do what he thought was prudent, not necessarily what was best for all. No one in their right mind trusted the frumentarii, so Pansa was out. But Zenas had served loyally as long as I'd known him. His faith denied the very nature of divinity that was at the heart of my position, yet still he served me.

Zenas nodded.

'It matters not how things look. Barring unforeseen disaster, we will win. Even if those fools strip us of more troops we will outnumber Constantine, and we have good supplies and strong walls. He has neither. His only true chance is with Licinius' aid, and we have the *other* eastern shithound's legions to ensure success if that happens.'

Despite my mood, I grinned at his description of Daia and we fell silent once more, looking out across the sea of white mist, the Capitol rising from it like an island. To my right the door opened and a figure stepped onto the balcony. Without looking, I waved at him.

'Wine, and for Zenas, too.'

But it was no slave or servant that had emerged from the palace. Wherever the bastard had come from, he ripped a sharp knife from his tunic and ran at me, shrieking. I was so surprised that I should have died there and then. Only Zenas saved me. As the blade came in a sweep for my neck, his arm was suddenly in the way. I saw the blade shear through flesh and blood, exposing the bone.

Zenas had saved my life, and he howled in pain as he clutched at the arm that poured out blood.

I had been angry, and what my ire had really needed was a viable target. My would-be assassin became that target in a heartbeat. Foiled, he withdrew and swung again, but he was just some talentless nobody, not a true killer. I might not be the most martial of men, but I had still been trained by the best. I caught the blow swiftly, grabbing his wrist with both hands. I jerked my grip and snapped a number of bones. The man shrieked and the knife fell from his grasp.

The assassin fell to his knees, unarmed, but I was far from done with him. The son of Maximian still carried his father's temper. I ducked down and grabbed the knife, rising like some Tartarean monster, then loomed over the stricken man with a gleaming blade and a feral snarl.

I was still stabbing and hacking at a lifeless corpse almost a quarter of an hour later when Zenas, his wounded arm bound tight with a strip of his cloak, dragged me off the torn bundle of flesh that looked like offcuts from a butcher's stall.

I straightened, drenched in blood, and cast away the knife, shaking as I began the inevitable slide from anger to regret. Zenas eyed me curiously.

'Perhaps we should send the whole army to Ostia and just have you stand on the bridge with a fruit knife, Domine?'

I laughed. For the first time in many days I actually laughed properly. Zenas was my antidote to anger.

'There will be no bridge to stand on,' I reminded him in bittersweet tones.

'True. We might have to send you in on a duck.'

Again, I laughed. Why were Christians generally such a dour and humourless lot? Clearly, from Zenas' example, they didn't have to be.

'Do you believe in prophecy, Zenas?'

The African shot me an odd look as we stood over the ravaged body of the would-be assassin.

'Domine?'

'I'm no Christian, as you know. I don't have anything against your lot, mind you,' I added hurriedly. 'To be entirely frank, the divinity of emperors is, for me, highly suspect at best, especially given the very idea that my father might now reside among the hallowed, but do you believe in prophecy?'

Zenas gave me the oddest smile I had ever seen. 'A central tenet of my faith, Domine, is an unshakeable belief in prophecy.'

'You know of the Sibylline books?'

He nodded.

'They are simply the most sacred prophecy in all the empire. I was reminded of them recently, and as I watch Volusianus, Pansa and the rest of us struggle and argue, trying to decide what to do for the best, I wonder whether it might not be simpler to put the entire matter in the hands of the gods,' I sighed.

'Of God,' he said with unaccustomed firmness.

'Gods,' I insisted, but I chuckled.

'Go for a bath, lie down, eat and try to forget about all this, Domine.' He smiled in a tired way. 'Constantine will not be here within the hour.'

Grateful, I nodded and left Zenas on that balcony with a

mashed corpse. I slipped past Valeria's apartments, for I had enough to worry about, and I skirted the rooms of my poor ill son, for misery was really not what I sought. Though it was awful to even consider it with Aurelius in such a condition, I had already begun to think of a new dynasty and new children with Valeria.

I spent some time in my aula regia, entirely alone, which was something of a new experience. I examined the sceptres and spear and orb of state that stood on a cunningly fashioned stand beside my throne, secure under the guard of a dozen Praetorians outside the room. The orb on the end of the gleaming sceptre was bedded in a garden of gold leaves, which reminded me rather unpleasantly of the wall decorations in that room where so long ago I had built a wooden city, and first met my friend and nemesis.

He was coming. Now. For my head. That man with whom I had rescued poor Romulus from a burning building, with whom I had damned the old emperors as vile. With whom I had raced horses and watched my son laugh with delight. How had it ever come to this?

No. Constantine would never be the emperor of Rome. He might destroy my army and might take my lands, but he would value Rome no more than the reprobates Galerius and Diocletian. These sceptres and staves had been the symbols of Roman rule for centuries. Oh, they weren't original, but these particular ones went back to at least Commodus. Without them, a man could never hope to rule Rome legitimately. So I would deny him that. Should the day come that I ride out to meet him, or he seem likely to breach the walls, I would bury them.

And I should look to the Sibylline oracles for guidance.

That night, as I prayed to all the gods for guidance, I was

brought soul-destroying tidings. The man who had managed to reach my private balcony, wielding a knife against me and almost ending my reign, was not some dreadful assassin sent against me by my enemy, but a cheesemonger from the Subura! When did tradesmen become so ambitious, and how did he ever get access to the imperial apartments? Important questions, yes, but they obscured an issue much larger:

If even the ordinary folk of Rome now sought my end, what was left to fight for?

25

CONSTANTINE

The Via Flaminia, mid-October 312 AD

After the near-disaster at the Intercisa Pass and the miracle that followed, and the near-disastrous squabble that nearly turned into a civil war within my own ranks, I split my army into two halves: the followers of the old gods and the Christians – for those broad factions seemed to be the most frictional. Of course, this meant breaking apart individual legions in some cases, separating the Christian Cornuti from the others within that regiment and separating the Bructeri men of the old tribal ways from their Christian comrades. It was an awkward dichotomy and one that flouted martial code, but we marched like that, in two separate columns, abreast: one of the old gods, one of the new, with a thin screen of trusted men between. Equally, we dug and fortified two camps each night.

It worked for a time, for we thundered across the high mountain route like two prides of lions, generals roaring, men in song. They had been on the edge of quarrel and camaraderie the whole way, but they were rarely together long enough for things to fall apart. Each of them pinned my name to their divinity as if it lent their faith credence. I was Apollo's chosen one. I was Mars' spear. I was Mithras' hand. I was a warrior of Christ – although the officer who proclaimed this was plagued by rumours that he had been sending missives right under the nose of Maxentius and to the Pope of Rome, beseeching him to declare me as the chosen emperor. They were lions, aye, but with thorns in their paws. It was down to me to lead them, keep them together as best I could, until it was done. But damn, how I missed old Lactantius.

I visited the old goat's bedside twice every day, holding his cold hand and mopping his sweat-beaded brow. 'Who did this to you?' I asked him over and over again, watching his unmoving, gummed-together lips for an answer his unconscious body could not give. The medicus and his apprentice had made sure he was given water regularly, and Fausta changed his bedding and cleaned him when nature called. Horribly, it felt as if we were merely dressing a corpse for its funeral.

On the journey through the mountains went. We climbed the Apenninus ridge in small groups, knowing that these heights – the true spine of Italia – would be guarded even more staunchly than the Petra region. The Intercisa ambush had compelled me to send my scouts ahead early, and they reported that indeed, the way forward was bolstered thoroughly with enemy positions. On those snow-capped heights, Maxentius had serried his legions behind redoubts of earth, boulder and picket that blocked the good routes. He had festooned the high parts with turrets, crammed with archers, and he had tasked his men with smashing up the Via Flaminia, so we trod upon shards of stone and shifting earth. We chased many of his forces off; captured some too. So, what of the others who would not yield?

With sharpened steel, we destroyed them.

One by one, those mountain bulwarks were overrun, the turrets swamped by my men scurrying up ladders and hauling the defenders from the platforms, tossing them to their deaths. I used the weakness of the division within my army as a weapon, tasking each half to act like a pincer. Each party stole up on one such camp – laden with enemy supplies and reinforcements – from opposite sides, and launched a firestorm of arrows into the grounds, men hurling pots of pitch into the mix too. The place lit up the night like Vulcan's forge. I watched it all, smelling the stink of burning men, hearing the screams of poor wretches rolling in the snow in a hopeless effort to douse their blazing flesh. I felt nothing.

You cursed my mother, stole my land, denounced me as a bastard, sent a cutthroat to murder me, I said, staring over the flames and into the darkness in the direction of Rome. *Then when I came to confront you like a noble general at Verona, you fled like a boy. Then you assailed my men on the coast road, striking at us from afar like cowardly gulls. You cut off our only hope of retreat! You brought us to this, Maxentius. You!*

In the morning after that blaze, we woke to a crisp autumn sky and a biting wind. A fresh snowfall had mercifully covered the dead and doused the flames of the ruined fort. We were masters of the mountains. From this high eyrie, I could see what looked like an infinite haze of plains, stretching off into the western horizon. The ancient land of Latium. The final stretch of the road to Rome. What lay in wait? More resistance, certainly. Maxentius' huge numbers... and what of Daia? The thought sent a stark chill across me. I could face an army of far greater numbers. But to face *two*? Thus, the burning dilemma remained: to face Maxentius and maybe even Daia too, my army would have to be as one. No divisions, no quarrels. I could not see the answer, and old Lactantius was not here to show me the way towards it. *Who poisoned you, old tutor?* I asked myself again and again, each time casting an angrier, more suspicious eye across my army.

In any case, I could not tarry in hope of inspiration to the matter of my fractured army nor that of Lactantius' poisoner. I had to press on, even though it felt as if I was rushing towards disaster with an ever-diminishing and fragmenting force.

We forged ahead at good speed, only to find every single damned bridge smashed down, and every field burnt black and robbed of provision. My men threw up timber crossings and raft pontoons, my two *funditores* slinger cohorts foraging wide of the dual column to bring in wild wheat, berries and game to stop our supply wagons from running too low.

Now I ask of you this: what kind of man would slaughter a fellow searching for food? A coward, a monster? Well Maxentius' auxiliaries acted on *his* orders, and murdered over two hundred of my slinger cohorts out there in the woods – when they were armed with no more than baskets and sacks. We found their bodies, buried them, then marched on with empty bellies, hearts hungry for vengeance. That united my men a little.

Within two days of this, we reached the city of Assissium, to the drone of cheering and the sound of trumpets. A great city – a marble milestone on the road to Rome, so *close* to Rome – declaring for me!

The gates groaned open and a troupe of dancers leapt out to greet me, along with wagons and chariots, upon which stood rich men, gushing honeyed words about their liberation. A garrison tribunus led the group, his martial step a stark contrast. He saluted me stiffly. 'Assissium is yours, Domine,' he boomed.

We walked – heavily guarded by my black-armoured Cornuti – through an arbour of ribbons and petals, the air reverberating with the aria of singers and the melody of a hundred lyres, drums and whistles. 'You have many friends in Rome,' the garrison tribunus shouted over the noise as we went, 'and my soldiers will march upon the city with you.'

Men drank neat wine and cried out my name. Mothers held up their children as I passed, as if I had somehow saved them by not attacking the city. In truth, I hated it all, for once the pride passed, I could not see anything in my mind's eye but the image of myself as the fat sack of shit Galerius, or the poisonous Diocletian, or even that drunken snake Maximian.

'These are his heartlands,' big Batius said. 'If a city like this is so quick to turn to you, then what of Rome? What of the cradle of the empire – whose streets he turned red with butchery? Maybe the people will throw Maxentius from his throne? Perhaps there will be no need for battle at the end of this road?' As he spoke, he clasped his Chi-Rho necklace zealously, as if calling for his god to tell him it was all true. Yet there was sadness in his weary eyes too. I had seen that look in him just once before, in Nicomedia when his beloved old hound, Ferox, had developed a weakness in its back legs. The vet had said the old dog had only a short time to live. Batius had cradled the poor beast for those last few days, whispering words of affection, talking of sweet futures where they would run together in the fields. Sweet futures. False futures. False hopes.

I deliberately billeted and confined the two halves of my men in separate areas of the city that night. Thus, each half of my army enjoyed the festivities in their respective wards, and blessedly there were no bouts of religious fighting. It had to be this way, for I had other matters to address. I thought of the slave who had come to me quietly the previous evening. He had been waiting for many days to catch me alone, to tell me when there were no keen ears nearby: *On the night of the poisoning, the fish broth old Lactantius ate was prepared, cooked and served in your consilium tent, Domine. It was one of your trusted men who poisoned the old man.*

* * *

That night the basilica of Assissium glowed orange, myriad shadows dancing on the walls. In one corner, a lute player plucked a delicate, bittersweet tune while an old man sang a stirring, baritone song of ancient glory. Wine, sweetened water, cooked game, breads, honey, nuts and yoghurt were passed around the feasting table. The chatter ebbed and flowed like the drone of bees in a meadow. I let my gaze drift around them every so often. There was the governor, his proconsul, the pontifices and the garrison commanders. My commanders too: Batius, Krocus, Ruga, Vindex...

Vindex. The man who led the Martia like the war god himself. A charismatic and resolute member of my consilium. The man who had organised the gathering of that select group on the night my tutor was poisoned. The one who had cooked the cursed fish broth. The rest of the slave's words echoed in my mind...

It was one of your trusted men who poisoned the old man. I was there. I saw not the moment the poison was added to Lactantius' broth... but I am certain that of all your officers, it was only Vindex who had the opportunity. He jealously prepared and served the broth, waving away others who offered to help.

'To our liberator,' the governor toasted me, snapping me

from my darkening thoughts. Victor, emperor, Augustus, they hailed me. All added equally spiteful words of condemnation for Maxentius. The tyrant, the one who had painted Rome's streets red in a slaughter of innocent citizens. The one who stole bread from their children's mouths to feed his overblown armies. The one who would put even Tarquin the Proud to shame. But, they said, Maxentius and his army of geese had fled these parts now the true Augustus was here. Their words had been intended to ridicule him and flatter me, but all they served to do was remind me that for every one of Maxentius' retreats, his forces would be stacking closer, more densely together. Such vast numbers of legions he had. Geese? I thought, imagining his forces amassed. The sacred birds of Juno... the chosen ones of Rome. Doubt sat with me for some time after that.

I listened to their ongoing sentiments, offering no more than gentle waves of my hand or even a slow blink of the eyes to acknowledge. Through it all Fausta sat, so delicate, so restrained, while insults rained upon her brother from every direction. She was the antithesis of the braggarts and drunken men feasting here, a swan among a murder of crows.

After a time, my belly full and my blood warmed, I left the table, ascending the stairs to the mezzanine of the basilica. A clutch of them tried to follow... including Vindex. Crossed spears from two of my Cornuti put an end to that. Up there, blissfully alone, I stepped from the sconce-lit basilica's interior and out onto a stony balcony, overlooking the moonlight shadows and the peaceful wards of Assissium. The only movement was from the bubbles of torchlight that flickered here and there, and the slow-moving trains of wagons that were coming in from the nearby towns – wagons of tribute, even now, in the darkest part of night. I had planned to despatch envoys or even legions to secure those towns, but there was no need. They sent grain, grain that would have been going to Maxentius' armies, to me instead. Fragments of garrisons too – centuries of red-caped auxiliary archers, silver-helmed legionaries, knowledgeable officers and skilled engineers. Too few to really ease my concerns over my diminishing numbers, but welcome nonetheless.

As I gazed beyond the thin trains of tribute and into the grey-black haze of the western horizon, I shivered in the chill of the autumn night, but not from the freshness of the air. I could sense it. He was near. Rome was but a few days' march from here. There, I would find neither find his ambushing generals, nor an open-gated city. There, an army dwarfing mine awaited and would offer battle. We would put steel against steel. My balled fist slammed against the balcony edge. *You lit this fire, Maxentius, I seethed inwardly, with your slurs, your killers and your descent into madness.* I tried to imagine once again my old friend standing in Rome's famous avenues, his cloak billowing in the wind yet weighted at the hems with the blood of his citizens. Thousands, they said, he had ordered to death. His face: in my mind's eye it was even stranger now – bent in malice, black with blood and shadow.

I swung away from the balcony and back into the basilica. Treading round the mezzanine, gazing down on the celebrations below, I came to a small tablinum on the other side of that upper floor. It was deserted and had been for many moons, I realised, seeing the thick coating of dust on the floor. So it was with horror that I noticed something from the corner of my eye: lit by a finger of pale moonlight falling from an oculus above, lurked the shape of a man.

I started, instantly fearing that some killer had followed me up here, mind flashing with thoughts of Vindex' treachery. My hand slapped down to my swordbelt, then fell slack. It was merely a coat of armour that had tricked my mind: a moulded breastplate, resting upon a man-high frame, leather pteruges hanging from the waist, bronze whorls on the shoulders. Above it on the tip of a pole stood a silver helm and a red plume. Old parade armour, I realised – and an inscription below explained that it had once belonged to Maximian, the father of my adversary. The body was absent from within because I had ordered his death. The old bastard had deserved it, I knew then and still knew now... but the loneliness, the coldness of this suit of armour troubled me. A man – a father, a son and now a shade, dead and gone... purely because of me. Was there any difference in what had happened to Baudio, to so many others? Dead because of my ventures? I reached out and stroked a finger across the surface of the helm, just above the brow. A thick layer of dust slid away and I saw in the thin stripe of clean metal my face, gazing back at me, as if my spirit had donned Maximian's armour. Now I saw in my mind's eye Maxentius, bloodstained and spiteful, and myself, standing across from him, warlike and bullish. What had we become? I wept inside.

I heard a noise: Vindex' laughter, sharp and louder than that of any other. I swung away from the sad old armour and to the mezzanine balcony, looking down over the banquet below, my face uplit by torchlight. My eyes sought him out and found him quickly.

Batius, seated near him, saw me. He did at that moment what I had asked him to, letting the wine carry his words a little too readily as he spoke to Tribunus Ruga – just enough so that those seated immediately nearby could hear. I watched my trusted man's lips move, already knowing the words.

We will move from here two hours before dawn, to steal a march upon our enemy's next ambuscade...

My eyes shifted to Vindex. His laughter had stopped, his eyes were staring into space but seeing nothing. His ears were taking in everything Batius said. Every. False. Word.

I watched him for some time. Like all skilful traitors, he was subtle and patient. He waited for a while – eating and drinking long after Batius had divulged this 'secret'. Eventually, he rose and slipped from the basilica quietly and swiftly.

Your death will be slow and painful, I seethed. Batius had arranged for Krocus and a pair of his Regii, dressed as civilians, to follow him when he left the hall, wait for him to pass on word to whomever his contact was, then arrest them both.

I stormed back to the balcony and I was lost in rage for a time. I did not even hear the shadow behind me approaching. I only realised I was not alone when a hand rested on the balcony edge, next to mine. I swear my soul turned to ice at that moment. I swung to face the stranger, knowing that if it was an assassin then I was dead already.

'Domine,' Vindex said.

I baulked, eyes rolling to the mezzanine edge, thinking of the lower-floor basilica doorway through which I had watched him slip. 'How did you...'

'I wanted to avert suspicion,' he said quietly.

I glanced at his hands. Empty. No weapon.

'This must be hard for you to hear, Domine, but I think you should know. You have been looking for a traitor, haven't you? Someone poisoned old Lactantius – someone who knew how important he was to the integrity of your army. I have no wish to label any of my fellow officers as a traitor but... but...'

'Out with it,' I demanded.

He sighed. 'Tribunus Batius has been acting strangely tonight. Especially when I asked how the old goat was faring.' He gazed at me. Like a boy, almost, grudgingly speaking ill of a friend. 'The thing is, it couldn't have been him.'

'So you think it might have been Batius even though you know it wasn't?' I scoffed.

He shrugged. 'It couldn't have been. You know how particular I am when I cook. I don't like others meddling. Batius came nowhere near the pot. In fact, neither did any of the officers... I think.'

I nodded, slowly. 'Thank you, Vindex. That will be all.'

He slunk away as silently as he had come. I stared into space, lost, robbed of the order I had cobbled together from the murky events. If not Vindex, then who?

At this moment, when Maxentius and I were drawing ever closer, I needed certainty, I needed confidence. Yet now it felt like there was a vein of chaos within my camp... and an invisible threat hovering at my side.

★ ★ ★

We set off again in the morning, accompanied by one thousand fresh men drawn from the Assissium garrison.

Two more days brought us to Spoletium, a pale-walled metropolis lodged at the head of a green valley. New sounds of tribute and veneration rose in the air even before we saw the delegations pour forth. *Another* key Maxentian city, falling into my palm. It was a second sweet mercy, and a sense of invincibility began to swell within my men. In truth I soared on a wave of hubris too, but somewhere deep inside, a voice wailed in lament, knowing the moment was now so close. The moment when I would have to face him... to end this.

That night I retired to the quarters offered to me by Spoletium's city prefect, a white-haired old fellow with a kindly manner. After a visit to old Lactantius' bedside where I helped wash his skin with the sombre Fausta, I moved to the rooftop of my quarters and sat back to observe the goings-on in the city.

The night lit up with the glow of tavern hearths and open festivities in the forum, where every splash of wine in the province was consumed, going by the hoarse singing that went on and on well after midnight. I watched it all. Nobles staggered around the gardens below, slaves too, laughing and shrieking in their games. There was a small white *tholus* shrine – a circle of pillars supporting a roof – down there, dedicated to Venus. The city prefect sat on a bench within, glugging on wine, raising his cup to the passing revellers. Krocus was out on the streets, attempting to woo a local woman by opening his robe and showing her something, urging her to touch 'it'. She did, with a Herculean kick. Then there was Tribunus Hisarnis, arguing with a wall, and losing. Big Batius was a lion, still, refusing the chance to pickle his brain and instead leading a Cornuti watch on the walls. A strong watch too – two centuries of them. The public of Spoletium might have welcomed me here, but who was to say what might be lurking out in the countryside, beyond the walls of the valley?

More, the big man and I had talked over a tentative reunion between two legions – one each from the divided halves of the army – to see if the hotness of their dispute had cooled at all during their time apart. It was a wise and safe time to try such a thing. We had to find *some* way of mending the wounds before we reached Rome. Thus, I posted a century of the Gemina and one from the Eighth Augusta around the edges of the gardens.

I watched them for a time. All was quiet. Some chatting, others playing dice, some standing like stiff posts, eyes watchful.

I chewed on a scrap of bread topped with bacon fat, then drained a cup of heated berry juice. I felt my eyelids grow heavy. Like it or not, I was now of an age where the promise of a warm, comfortable bed was just as appealing as wine or women. *Age*, I sighed, *that creeping tendril*. A wistful image of myself and Maxentius as boys and as young men... as friends, breezed across my mind. I chased it away, choked the deep sadness back.

Tomorrow, we would set off early once more. Four more days, I realised, glancing down at the map on the old table beside me. Four more days and we would be in sight of Rome. The end of the war was coming. At least the experiment with the two centuries appeared to be worki—

The thought went unfinished. A fist flew, a dice bounced across the gardens. Sentries nearby rushed over and the pair of grappling soldiers – one from each legion – became several pairs. They kicked lumps out of one another. How a game of dice can lead to a battle of faiths, I do not know, but those men managed it somehow.

I sighed, then sighed again. That festering sore of a problem was as raw as ever. Rome loomed, and my army was riven.

As I turned from the balcony and towards my bed, I halted, something snagging my senses. It was a strange thing – like a breath of wind in a sealed room, or a shadow on a cloudless day. In the corner of my eye, I saw the blackness of night outside ripple.

Movement. Down in the villa gardens... where there should have been no movement.

A stark chill rolled through me, right to my marrow. At

once I recalled the hired blade Maxentius had sent to murder me. Was this another? I grabbed the balcony edge again and stared down. Had it been an assassin, I would have been afraid, but sure of myself too. Yet what I saw ripped the heart from me, and convinced me I had but moments to live. So *many* of them.

Men, pouring from the hatch in the floor of that Shrine of Venus. Two, four, twelve... scores of them. Ironclad soldiers. Not mine. *Maxentians!* Soldiers who had been waiting in the catacombs for this moment – for the veil of hubris and inebriation to fall over my men, and then for those patrolling the garden's edge to begin quarrelling. The danger lay not out in the hills which Batius watched, but right here under my feet.

One of them looked up: his soil-blackened face was baleful, his eyes white like chalk as they met mine. It was the look of a killer. *There he is*, his mouth moved. His hushed words directed the rest. They sped around and into the villa like ants attacking a dropped honeycomb.

'Guards!' I roared.

Nothing.

I felt my body shamble into action, pulled on my helm and grabbed my spatha. A forlorn last stand, I knew. I heard the rap of boots inside, on the bottom floor, then the echoing clatter of them rising like wicked applause. The first of the intruders bobbed into view atop the marble stairs. I stamped my foot once to drive off fear, and readied to meet my death fighting.

I barely understood what happened next. A black shape burst from the chambers nearest mine. Baudio, the Italica Prefect and my golden-torqued Protector, leapt in front of me to shoulder the foremost Maxentian, and six of Baudio's legionaries spilled out after him. They rushed to the top of the stairs and lashed their swords like fiends, battering the rising Maxentians back with their shields. I stumbled over to join them, running one Maxentian through, nearly losing my arm in the process. One of Baudio's men screamed, ripped from shoulder to thigh, black blood pumping across the steps as he pitched over the stair balustrade and fell with a wet crunch onto the tessellated floor below.

Another of Baudio's men yelled out from the window of their chamber, raising the alarm. We would succumb in moments. I thrust my sword hilt into one man's face, breaking his jaw, then kicked him back. He flailed down the steps in a ball, knocking over a handful of his own men. Another of Baudio's soldiers fell, chest ruptured, and then the head of a third spun through the air, vanishing over the balustrade. The Maxentians poured up now, swarming around me eagerly like wolves. Baudio lost another man and another, until it was but the two of us, back to back, blocking, parrying, backstepping towards my chambers. Inside, we bumped against the wall. Nowhere else to go. Swords slashed at me, tearing at my skin, one nicking my neck. I heard the din of reinforcements entering the villa now, but it was too late. As I blocked the strike of one Maxentian brute, a second roared and lunged, sword tip streaking towards my exposed armpit.

I have never forgotten Prefect Baudio. He taught me the true meaning of courage and selflessness. When he leapt once more and this time in front of the blade, I froze, hearing his breaking ribs as if they were my own. When he shuddered, so did I. When he slid from the killer's blade, I caught him, oblivious to the marauding Maxentians who would take my head.

Yet they did not. Like a gale, my reinforcements plunged into the room, and butchered Maxentius' soldiers. Their blood sprayed across me as I knelt, cradling Baudio. His lips moved almost soundlessly, the blood soaking his chin and chest. *Look after my boy, Vario*, he whispered, *tell him I am with God now.*

He died with a look of certainty in his eyes. I set his body down. All around me I heard the panting and swearing of my men, nothing else. It was over.

Batius and Krocus were there, streaked in red. So too were the ashen-faced centuries who had failed to spot the hidden men because they were too busy fighting one another.

'Clever bastard,' Krocus growled, looking over the dead Maxentians then out from the balcony to see the hatch in the shrine floor. He barked at one of his men: 'Send a twenty down there just in case there are any more rats hiding.'

I saw Ruga, Scaurus, Hisarnis there too. All of my surviving officers in one place, all wearing looks of great concern. For a moment my mind flickered with suspicion and anger. *One of you wears a mask. Who poisoned my old tutor?*

The thought faded when I realised the true culprit. The man who had sent the spy into my camp to instigate the poisoning. *Maxentius*, I mouthed, shaking.

Batius knelt beside me, his big, evil face for once lost, like a boy's. My thoughts returned to poor Baudio.

'He asked me to look out for his son,' I whispered. Another impossible oath.

'Vario, of the Italica's First Cohort?' Batius whispered. 'That's a promise no general can keep... as I know only too well.'

We stayed an extra day at Spoletium, giving young Vario time to commission a gravestone for his father and to perform the burial under a sullen grey sky. Vario led the Christian incantations by the grave: 'Sleep, child of Christ. Like a seed sown in this age, you will rise anew in another, when the Lord calls...' The low reverberating funereal chants reminded me of my youth, of the Christian gatherings Mother took me to. I thought of home, of Mother, far away in the north. *Let this be over*, I thought. In truth, I knew there was only one way it could end, my gaze rising from brave Baudio's tomb to the night horizon in the west... towards Rome.

Terse words shook me back to the present. The First Martia and the Fourth Jovia watched on from afar, and it was some of those men who were cursing, deriding the Christian rites. If ever I needed clarity on just how deeply the religious divide was among my army, it was not at that moment. But clarity I had. A deep rupture in my band of veterans. Such animus to fight alongside me, but such hatred for one another. A perfect, unsolvable problem... and one that might just destroy everything.

I promoted Vario to prefect – leader of the Second Italica – that night. He was already a well-respected optio, and the men wanted the son to lead them. More, as an officer, he would have a better chance of surviving... what was to come. When we left Spoletium, it was so very different to the manner in which we had entered. The populace was quiet – ashamed almost. I didn't doubt that most of them were innocent or at least oblivious to the ruse of the hidden soldiers. There was one who clearly knew what was supposed to have happened to me that night of our arrival. I glanced up at the city walls, and at the white-haired old bastard hanging from them by his ankles. Crows and vultures hovered nearby and perched on the crenels, taking turns to swoop down at the city prefect and peck at his face. The stonework under him was already stained with his blood, urine and watery faeces. A drawn-out creak and groan of sinew echoed across the valley as my army filtered past him. Then a *snap*, as one of the vultures flew away with an eyeball. His screams echoed across the land.

That evening we reached Tyrrhenia, and they too declared for me – in a way I knew was sincere. Regardless, I had Hisarnis and Ruga comb the city streets and search the cellars. At night, I had a decoy sleep in my quarters and instead made my bed in one of the Cornuti tents. We marched on past Narnia, and weathered a devious cavalry assault at Ocriculum, where thousands of Maxentian Moorish riders cantered infuriatingly alongside my dual column, raining arrows and javelins upon us. Every time we tried to break out our own horsemen, the nimble Moors would speed away like doves evading a prowling cat, only to return from some unseen supply base with freshly restocked quivers and the whole pattern would repeat itself, their gaunt, bloodshot-eyed prefect howling the darkest insults at us as his bowmen worked. They slowed us down dreadfully, and we lost hundreds of men to them. More, when they drew away my riders, concealed Maxentian saboteurs burst from the nearby brush, running over to smash the wheels of our supply wagons and hurl flaming pots into the heaped grain sacks there. We lost a grievous amount of provisions, and more men fell than I could keep track of. All along the Via Flaminia, we erected grave markers.

Fausta's words back at Ravenna echoed through my head: *I will advise the surgeons to sharpen their saws and wind many sutures, and the gravediggers to bring good spades...*

It caused me to think of her brother, holed up in Rome.

You send blades to kill me in the night. You arranged for my old tutor to be poisoned. You force me to build this road of graves, I seethed, staring at the western horizon. *Does that make you swell with pride? Why don't you come and face me, you bastard?*

On the fourth day, the Moors were curiously absent. I had by then learned to mistrust fortune acutely. I despatched three cohorts from the First Minervia, tasking them with scouting ahead. They moved fast, carrying no shields or spears, just helms and swords. Soon, they vanished from sight. Come night, they had neither returned nor sent back a messenger. I felt my guts twist like an old rope.

But on we had to go. Late afternoon on the fifth day after leaving Spoletium, we came to the banks of the Tiber. The men fell silent as they realised just how close we were. Now they were beginning to twitch with fear and awe too as they scoured the south-western horizon for sight of the great city.

Instead, they spotted a range of red hills – rocky warts rising from the autumnal landscape. This was Saxa Rubra: a bottleneck, forcing the Via Flaminia between the red cliffs and the Tiber. Even from here, they could see the flashes of silver positioned on those heights, and the troops guarding the stockade of earth and palisades that had been erected across the road. Their doubts rose in a terse chatter. As we drew closer, their murmurs turned into wails of dismay as we saw what had become of the missing First Minervia men: the Maxentians up on the red rocks swished and swirled poles, bearing the heads of the dead men. They jeered, sang and whistled.

I almost felt the great animus of my army drain there and then. I even heard that cursed yammer of religious strife rise among them, each blaming the other for this turn of events.

With a jerk of the reins, I swung my mare round to face them, halting them. 'How many of you have been to Rome?' I called to them, my voice echoing around the river land.

Nobody answered. A few sheepishly raised a hand, but almost all stared back at me blankly.

'The navel of the empire,' I said, then swept a hand towards the Tiber. 'And these are her sweet waters. Think of all the times we have fought together, in this campaign and in the years before. Of the expeditions you took part in with my father, and with the true emperors of the past. What was it for, I ask you… if not for the empire? And is Rome not the jewel at the heart of the empire? The heart of it all?'

They rumbled in hubris.

'Yet a rogue languishes in Rome. A man who has done nothing but fester in Italia, fighting off those who come to prise him from his lair.' I threw a finger back at the grotesque head-standards. '*That* is the measure of the man we face. He knows nothing of the hardships you have endured in the name of empire. Nothing! Yet he plots to keep this ancient land as his own. Is he deserving?'

'No,' they rumbled.

'You have shed your own blood to keep this place safe. He seeks to deny you even a sight of the city. Are you not more worthy than he?'

'Aye,' they boomed.

'Will a wretched stockade and a hill of murderous thugs deny you this?'

'No!' they thundered, rattling their spears and swords on their shields.

I turned to Batius and Krocus. 'Bring the men into two broad fronts. Send the Christian legions into the hills.

Construct and array the artillery… and blow that redoubt apart.'

The buccinae wailed, and my legions fanned out like a pair of great talons, set to tear this last line of defence apart, like an eagle ripping a worm from the earth.

26

Rome, 26th October 312 AD

I t was supposed to be a grand event; an unpicking of the evils of recent days. It was supposed to be a celebration. Of me. Of Rome. Of what we meant to each other. The problem was that Rome to me had always meant the heart of civilisation, but now it meant little more than a constant headache. To Rome I had always meant Romanitas and salvation, but now, despite everything, I meant disaster.

It was the games to mark the anniversary of my succession. I tried to please everyone, really I did. It had long since become apparent to me that a sizeable portion my population were Christians, so I avoided the old-fashioned punishments and even kept the games in the arena to the more professional gladiators and beast hunts rather than the bloodthirsty executions that had always sickened me, but which the public so adored. I sponsored pro-Roman plays. The readings in the odeon were from the Aeneid. Everything was designed to promote the very idea of being Roman and my place as its champion, now ascendant after six years bearing the purple. But I was not ascendant. I was fighting for a fingerhold on my own empire, and everyone knew it.

I spent time with the administrators of the festival, various faceless lackeys. I made it clear to them that we needed to make Rome feel secure and proud. Half of any successful siege is confidence, after all, and if Constantine was where they said he was, then a siege looked inevitable. I had my people persuading the populace that they would prevail. Rome had strong walls and our army was still superior, with all supply lines open and Daia's reserves on call.

Oddly, though this was absolutely true, and there really was no need for the people to worry, *I* did. I felt certain that things were not as simple as they seemed.

I could hear the roar of the circus from my chambers. The races were to start soon. In fact, the chariots were already doing their laps, showing the quality of riders and horses to the crowd, lithe girls and acrobatic men from exotic locations cartwheeling and pirouetting around them, dwarves, musicians and entertainers in the line.

I stood silent in my chamber for some time. I was alone, and that was so unusual. Aurelius was suffering and being attended as well as Euna and the physicians could. Valeria was already out in the circus being the face of Roman matronhood. Volusianus was working with the military somewhere, as were Zenas and Pansa. I was alone. I tried to picture a Rome that had fallen to my old friend. That had fought for me and yet lay beneath his feet.

How could it have come to this? Constantine and I had spent our whole lives watching the wayward wickedness of men like our fathers, of Galerius, of Licinius and others. We both knew what was best for Rome. How, then, had we managed to tear her in two? We should be able to share the world. We should be able to have our lives and our dreams and keep them going. Was it too late? Constantine and his army were on my doorstep now but the end was far from written. He had to be dreading what might happen as much as I. Surely in his march south he had woken, sweating, from sleep, fearful of the imminent clash. Was it too late? Constantine was in alliance with Licinius, and I knew my old friend hated that dog more than most living men, certainly more than he hated me. I, similarly, was in alliance with Daia, and I loathed the man with a passion. Two old friends colluding with people they hated in order to kill one another? Was there still time to form some kind of pact with him and face our true enemies? After all, all it would really require was for one of us to accept the other as our superior. One Augustus of the West and one Caesar... But to accept Constantine as my superior not only denied our relative claims to accession, for my father had been superior to his, but also would condemn me as a failure among the people I ruled. I might be able to look up to Constantine, but Rome could not, as long as I bore the purple.

My memory threw bitter images at me. My father strangled on a cellar floor as my old friend laughed over the corpse. My mother weeping at the defamation heaped upon her name by that same friend. My garrisons in the Alpes overrun, in the *winter* of all times, by my old friend's troops.

No. I was deluding myself to consider peace. The twisted animal that had once been my friend would never now consider a treaty with me. All hope for peace was gone.

I recalled a strange conversation with Valeria a few nights earlier:

'*What will you do with him?*' *she had asked suddenly.*

'*Who?*'

'*Constantine. When you have him roped and begging for mercy.*'

I felt somewhat blindsided by the question. 'If we win...'

'Yes?'

'If we win, and he dies, he will be allowed the burial rites appropriate to an emperor of Rome. His ashes will be interred in the oldest of mausolea – that of Augustus. His father's ashes will be brought from wherever they lie and interred there too.'

'You have clearly thought this through. What if he lives?'

'If he surrenders or is captured I.... I don't know. What should I do?'

'You should put a blade through his windpipe in an instant, and then bless him and do everything you just said.'

'What?' I stared at her.

'How many times did your own father have to be put down before he stopped coming back from nowhere and trying to claim the purple? Only the cold embrace of death stopped him trying to usurp you. What makes you think Constantine would be any different?'

'I don't know. He just would. He is my friend.'

'Oh wake up, husband. Any closeness or connection you ever had is gone. Constantine sees you only as an obstacle now. You must sever all emotional connections.'

'But I am Romanitas. I must offer clemency. I will be Julius Caesar.'

'You will be Caesar for little more than half an hour with such idiotic romantic notions. If you take him alive, he must die. Preferably swiftly and without commotion.'

And that was it. I stared into that imperfect bronze mirror, and instead of my own features all I could see was the flat-faced Constantine, laughing at me.

Bastard.

Why was I letting such things get to me so on a day that was supposed to be all *about* me? I scurried back through the imperial apartments, aware that my guard would be tapping their feet impatiently. As I swept through the corridors, picking up irritating slaves like a lodestone passing metal fragments, I hurried past a door where I heard my son Aurelius cry out, only to be soothed by the voice of faithful Euna.

My sons. One among the gods and one preparing his way for that same journey. It was almost too much to bear, and some days I managed to subdue the pain beneath the idea that Valeria and I might yet give issue to a whole new dynasty.

But it only took the rumble of a chariot or the laugh of a boy to drag me back through the torture I had endured for so long, and often still did in my sleep.

Thus it was that I was not in the best of moods when I arrived at the Circus Maximus.

I was still in time for the first race. The eight chariots running were each named for me. Imperator Caesar Marcus Aurelius Valerius Maxentius Augustus Pius Felix. By rights Felix should always win, but you'd be surprised how often something is named that and yet loses. As I entered the *pulvinar* a call held the door behind me and to a mix of relief and irritation, Volusianus pushed his way in. He strolled over with a curt bow of the head and only just waited for me to sit beside Valeria before sinking into one of the other seats.

'How are things?' I asked.

'Constantine is an idiot. His army is strong, but seems to be riven by some internal dispute from what little information we can secure. Still, he cannot hope to take Rome. He will besiege us for a month or two, but when the season turns to true winter and the forage runs dry he will be forced to retreat to his own lands. Then we will have him.'

'I wasn't after a grand strategy,' I said, thinking back on

those men Valeria had sent and wondering just how much of this internal dispute might have been their work. 'Just the state of the defences.'

'And that's what you got, Domine. The defences are impregnable.'

'I wish they had your confidence,' I murmured and gestured with a sweep of my hand at the crowd. There was a low susurration of dissent rippling around the seating and while I could not make out any individual words, it was clearly triggered by my arrival. It was not a positive sound.

'They do sound unhappy, don't they? What have you said to them?'

I flashed him a sour glance. 'I just arrived. This is what Rome is like now.'

'Do something.'

'Do what precisely?'

Volusianus spread his hands. 'Speak to them. Soothe the crowd.'

I nodded. I had no idea what to say, but Volusianus was right. They needed some kind of reassurance. I rose, and silence descended as people realised the emperor was about to address them. A bird shat on the stonework in front of me, and I couldn't decide whether it was an omen, a warning or an insult. Probably all three. I cleared my throat.

'People of Rome, I thank you.'

Silence. Was it reverential or insolent? So hard to tell.

'Six years ago I assumed the robe of office and vowed to make the glory and preservation of Rome my one and only concern. Through hunger and poverty, danger and schism, we have prevailed, and we continue to do so.'

The silence was now beginning to make me very edgy, and I stumbled over the next words.

'Galerius, the ape of the east, came for us and we sent him home in chagrin. Severus the rasping fool tried to fell us and died for his efforts. Rome prevails.'

Still silent. How could I make them realise what they had weathered?

'Now our various faiths live in peace with one another. Grain is plentiful, and the taxes are steady.' A slightly dubious one there. They simply had not been increased yet again. They were steadily high.

'Constantine comes,' a voice bellowed from the crowd. My gaze snapped towards it but it was hopeless. I could never hope to identify the speaker.

'Constantine comes, as the fellow over there so rightly says,' I replied to the whole crowd. 'But he will meet high walls, strong troops and defiant Romans. Do not forget that half his forces are little more than Germanic barbarians.'

'Constantine can't be beat,' called out another wag, and this drew my attention. I tried to spot the man, and was irritated that the speaker was lost in the crowd once more.

'Constantine has God with him,' called another, and my gaze moved to a new area of crowd, only to fail to spot that speaker too. Shit. This was going from bad to worse. The Christians of the city were already blaming the old ways for the impending danger, thanks to a ridiculous rumour that their god had singled him out in some shrine in Gaul. No matter what Miltiades said, the rumour persisted. Though I knew very well just how fractious Constantine's army was thanks to Valeria's agents, I found that Christians generally become very single minded and inflexible where their faith is concerned.

'Constantine might have *a* god with him, but we have many.'

I had thought it quite clever, but that was hubris in action. Unwittingly, I opened up yet another nightmare with the crowd. Immediately small fights broke out as Christians and old-fashioned Romans began to argue over the importance of their deities' concerns. I stared. The whole damn place was starting to shout now. The racers waited impatiently, embarrassed, unable to set off with not one pair of eyes watching them. I heard the same sentiments time and again in the crowd, never with a face to put to the voice.

Constantine cannot be beaten.

Yes, he fucking could. I cleared my throat and bellowed: 'Fellow Romans.' No one heard. The din was immense. I turned and shouted up to my musicians above the pulvinar to blow a fanfare, but even *they* could not hear me. I was being ignored by people who were starting to blame me for Constantine having some ridiculous divine favour, just because of that rumour.

I was exasperated.

'Do something,' Volusianus said again.

'What?'

'I don't know. You're the orator and politician, but this sort of thing can mean disaster. If it turns to a riot you know what I'll have to do, and if it doesn't, then that sort of attitude opens gates in the night and infects defending armies. This has to stop, Domine.'

I stared at him. Valeria was shouting at me now, too. And half a dozen other luminaries. And many thousands of Roman citizens. A din. A cacophony of fear, distrust and imploring, and all aimed at me. I experienced the oddest thing: a moment of utter calm amidst the chaos. All I could see in my mind's eye now was Romulus. My wonderful, glowing boy. The only person in my whole life who had always had confidence in me. Looked up to me. Believed in me. Never once had his faith in me wavered, and yet he had been torn from me.

I turned my back on the dissenting voice of Rome. I turned my back on my worried wife. I turned my back on Volusianus. I turned my back on it all, and simply left. I know I cried, for somewhere outside, on my way back to the palace, I stopped and wiped away the tears with a fold of my toga.

Volusianus followed me. I was aware of his ranting in the way a recently awakened person is aware of the morning birdsong. Somewhere along the way, I managed to pick up Zenas, too. The pair harangued me as I stalked away, angry at Rome, at Constantine, at the gods who would take my sons from me.

Volusianus was telling me that I needed to sort things out or I might still lose. Zenas was telling me that I had the larger army, still, only to be countered by the Praetorian Prefect telling him that numbers counted for nothing without spirit.

I remembered a man with spirit. A centurion of the guard who had given me his most treasured possession – a fragment of the Sibylline books – to offer for my son's health. A man probably now dead on the Via Flaminia, with Constantine's footprint on his face. I came to a sudden halt and spun. My anger must have been clearly visible, for both men recoiled.

'You think spirit will make the difference, do you? Spirit will win us the war and restore Rome? Very well, then, let's go and find some spirit.'

I was off again. The two men hurried after me, throwing out apologies that were at best half-meant, and using them as overtures to their ongoing concerns and harangues. It was odd how easy it was to gather a retinue. I wasn't even trying, but on my way through the palace I picked up my lictors, half a dozen Praetorians, a couple of old senators who'd been hanging around in the hopes of achieving an unexpected audience, two scribes, a personal slave and even an acrobat. I have no idea where he came from, but he cavorted along the corridors in my wake like a madman. I emerged from the heart of the palace through a side door and made for the ancient Temple of Apollo Palatinus, considered one of the most sacred places in the empire, where even emperors might submit to a binding oath in the presence of the progenitor god.

I stopped when we reached the temple, my ever-growing retinue tired and sweating. Volusianus and Zenas clung to my shadow and now, from some unknown source, even the Christian pope Miltiades had managed to slip into the entourage.

'What are you doing, Domine?'

'Finding spirit. Heart. Strength. Remember that centurion who had a fragment of the Sibyl's books? He's given me a notion. The books are our most ancient, most sacred prophecies. If they are filled with the same doom and gloom as the people, then perhaps they are right, but if not, then you can rouse the people with the knowledge that our most sacred texts prophesy our victory. The priests will announce it, and they will be believed.'

'What will you do if they tell you we are going to lose?' Volusianus sniped.

'You keep telling me that can't happen. Come on.'

While Zenas bore that typical mistrustful sneer I have seen on the face of the majority of Christians whenever they encounter solid Roman tradition, his fellow in that cult, Miltiades, looked utterly sick at the notion of what I proposed.

'Do not put your trust in such pagan magicks, Domine,'

SIMON TURNEY & GORDON DOHERTY

the man said imploringly, his hands clawing at the air. 'The Lord will provide.'

'Your *Lord* seems to be concentrating on providing for Constantine at the moment,' I retorted somewhat sharply, and he fell silent, though he remained distinctly unhappy and radiated that emotion as he followed.

I am not sure even now fully why I decided to consult the books. Perhaps it was angry impulse. Perhaps I was driven to it by having all the strength and sureness torn from me. Perhaps I truly felt that the end was closing in on me and I was seeking some sort of comfort or confirmation that I was doing the right thing. I could hear Miltiades, Zenas and Volusianus muttering quietly among themselves behind me, but I blocked out their tattle and concentrated on the great structure ahead of me.

The priests and attendants of the temple were largely absent as I threw open the great gold-and-ivory doors, allowing a trapezium of light to fall across the shadowed floor. It was a great festival day, and they would be busy. Besides, only I and those who had a place on the Palatine ever had real access to the temple, and the majority of those would be out somewhere celebrating.

Only an old man with jug-handle ears and a young lad with a twig broom occupied the place. I fixed on them. 'Where are the *Quindecemviri Sacris Faciundis*?' I demanded of the old man.

You see, the Sibylline books have a long and complex history. From their original acquisition when a Roman king had been short-sighted enough to refuse to pay an exorbitant price for nine books and ended up desperately clutching at three for the same price, they had changed and moved. Originally kept on the Capitol and looked after by ten men dedicated to the task, they had unfortunately succumbed to fire centuries ago. They had been replaced with part copies, fragments and even oracular prophecy from other sources. Despite the replacement, they remained Rome's most sacred text. A forward-thinking emperor had moved them from the Capitol to the Palatine. Now they were kept here and administered by the Quindecemviri – a group of fifteen ex-luminaries who were devoted to their care and interpretation.

It was those men I needed to see. No other mortal, even an emperor, would or could touch the books. It was the province only of those fifteen men. In the event I stood waiting, somewhat impatiently, while the old man bowed and scraped and then ran off to find someone of that illustrious group. It was almost a quarter of an hour later when he returned and I was close to ordering his execution, so bored was I of the ongoing muttering among my entourage while we waited.

In the wake of the old man was a priest who, from the interesting protuberance in his robe, had been hauled off some wanton harlot in order to service his emperor instead. Along with him came a young man with a serious face and a nose like a beak.

'Domine,' the priest said, bowing deeply. 'You required my presence?'

'I do. Consult the books. I want to know the outcome of battle if I face Constantine.'

A panicked look flooded across the man's face. 'Majesty, that is not truly how the books work. They are more a guide for Rome and her worship. Anything specific must be interpreted from the vaguest source words.'

'And that, I believe, is your job. Your *only* job, in fact. Answer my question. The future of Rome may hang in the balance, man.'

The priest still dithered, looking torn and uncomfortable. Even Volusianus' drawing his sword a fraction from the scabbard didn't daunt him, but the moment Miltiades, openly bedecked with his Christian symbols, moved toward him, he shrank away as though contact with a Christian would burn his skin. Reluctantly, he produced three keys on a chain and ring from his waist and hurried over to the great statue of Apollo that had been the focus of the worship of perhaps fifty emperors. Below the statue, in the solid yet decorative base, there was a sealed iron door with three locks. He hurriedly opened them, fumbling with the keys more than once. Finally, he was in and hunched over the alcove as though he could protect the contents from the world. When he finally rose, he had selected one tome of vellum, and he carried it reverently over to the altar, making sure to close and lock the repository first. He stood at the altar and opened the book.

The ways of gods and priests have always baffled me. The man simply allowed the book to open at whatever page chance dictated, then set his Greek-speaking young friend to reading the ancient text. The younger man muttered to his master, inaudible to me. Finally the priest rose and turned. He looked me square in the eye – a thing few were willing to do.

'Tell me,' I said, my own tension and excitement building. The others with me were crowding far closer than was proper with their emperor. Everyone wanted to know the answer to this.

He cleared his throat somewhat nervously.

'It will end two days hence, Domine. Constantine will face you, and brothers will become killers.'

I shivered. Only I clung to the mental fiction that my old

friend and I were as brothers. No one else should think like that. It was as though the man lifted the knowledge from my own consciousness. If ever I needed proof that the old ways were true and the Christians strayed from the truth, I was seeing it that day in the temple.

'Tell me,' I breathed, and the others closed in even further. A tremor of excitement fluttered through me. I had come here in anger, largely to mollify the mob, to provide them with an external confirmation of the notion that we would prevail. I had not felt it myself, no matter how much I tried to convince others of it, but oddly, the strange ancient magic of that place was working on me. I started to feel the confidence I had been lacking. The translator of the books had somehow known Constantine and I were connected as brothers, despite everything, and he said we would face and kill. In two days. Oddly specific for a notoriously vague set of prophecies. The hairs stood proud on the back of my neck and my flesh puckered into goosebumps.

I stared at the man, willing him to give me good news. I had felt so unsure, but this was trust. This was certainty. By the time he cleared his throat and began to speak I was almost ready to reach out and grab him.

'You will meet Constantine on the field of battle,' he confirmed, then went into brief consultation with his interpreter again as I twitched impatiently. I had all but forgotten the others were with me now. When the priest looked up, he wore a relieved smile. 'A man will die a miserable death on that day, but it shall all be as it should, for he shall be a man who only portends harm to the Roman people. The saviour of Rome shall prevail.'

A flood of relief. Of joyous vindication. I smiled in return and spun to the others. 'You heard.'

'Yes,' Volusianus muttered. 'I heard vague and inconclusive ramblings.'

'The saviour of Rome shall prevail,' I repeated, 'That is me. It is all I have ever striven to be, and you know that. The man who will bring harm to Rome will die. Two days hence we meet Constantine in battle, and he will lose.'

I felt a sudden chill. I didn't really want him to die a miserable death. I didn't really want him to die at all, but if one of us had to go, it would damn well be him, not me. The oracles had spoken. I was the champion of Rome. Constantine came to besiege the city. Our roles in the words were clear, but I did not need to endure a siege. The books had spoken of me meeting Constantine on the field of battle and it being swiftly resolved. They had not suggested a siege of months. No, I was wrong to hide behind my high walls, whatever Constantine had said all those years ago.

'Volusianus, you took down the Milvian Bridge.'

'I did, as any sensible commander would.'

'But when he arrives, we shall face him in the field and defeat him there, saving the people of Rome from a siege, as the books suggest.'

'It all sounds like drivel to me,' Volusianus grunted, and for once the two Christians beside him nodded their agreement.

'I want you to replace the bridge so we can cross to meet Constantine.'

'There's no time to build a bridge, Domine. You know that.'

'Then make a pontoon bridge. Gods, man, but Caligula strung a bridge across the Bay of Baia in days. Caesar bridged the Rhenus. Trajan the Danubius. Are you telling me you cannot pull together enough boats and craftsmen to bridge the Tiber?'

'No,' sighed Volusianus.

'Good. Do it, then. Two days hence we will resoundingly defeat our adversary within sight of the Milvian Bridge.'

Ah, fate, you bitches...

27

CONSTANTINE

*The Fifth Milestone north of Rome,
27th October 312* AD

I trekked up into the pale-yellow tufa hills to the song of thrushes, the chirping of cicadas and the low croak of toads. It was a scene of rustic idyll: the late morning sky cornflower blue, streaked with a solitary fishbone of cloud, and the golden sunlight bathing the stands of dark green pine on my left and red-leafed oaks to the right. I came to a small natural terrace and the remains of the ancient villa of Ovid. The tumbledown ruins were ringed by wild fruit gardens and I inhaled deeply, enjoying the scent of pine, lemons and herbs. My forty years peeled away and for a few moments I was a boy again out in the countryside of Naissus, exploring, carefree. Back then, every forest or hill track seemed destined to lead me to some forgotten cave or a tumbledown shrine where I could explore, barefoot, and let my imagination run riot. Every horizon seemed pregnant with adventure, calling out to me like a siren. I glanced down, seeing not those skinny boy's legs or bare feet, but muscular, well-scarred limbs and worn soldier boots. My arms and hands too – chapped and knotted with veins and the marks of old wounds. I looked uphill again at the small outcrop to which I was headed and almost laughed: for when I was a boy, I would have sprinted up there, free of the grinding pain in my hip and heedless of my thirst. I was almost smiling... until I approached the outcrop and the horizon fell away to reveal not Naissus, not a ruin I could use as a den or an old quarry in which I could play... but a hazy vista of Latium, of the heart of the empire. Here I was, on the edge of eternity.

A sea of activity stretched out immediately below the hills. Goatskin tents, legionaries on parade or being drilled by their commanders, craftsmen and smiths working feverishly to forge new weapons and repair damaged ones, horses whinnying and being led around the dusty expanse near the Tiber's banks. Trumpets sputtered and men darted to and fro, practising full battle manoeuvres. Archers and slingers loosed relentlessly near a ruined brick stable just north of our camp. One camp, one army. United? I crouched there, toying with my lower lip, watching... watching.

For a moment, it all seemed suspiciously ordered... and then I heard the raised voices near the western edge of the camp. I could see men there shoving and gesticulating. A low grumble sounded behind my closed lips. All last night I had heard them squabbling and cursing one another, each insisting their favoured god would be the one to carry them to victory when we met Maxentius' army, to overturn the reportedly huge advantage in numbers the enemy commanded. I'd even had to rise from my bed and despatch a century of Batius' men to separate the most boisterous of them.

Every time... every damned time we halted anywhere, dissent swelled like a boil. It was only when faced with a charging enemy that they stopped kicking the shit out of one another. I thought of the near-disaster at the Intercisa Pass, and of the close thing with Maxentius' hidden men at Spoletium. Twice, the friction between my forces had almost destroyed the campaign. Yet here, now, so close to the end, I needed them to be united.

My eyes combed the scene, time and again, then slowly slid southwards like the Tiber current, past the pickets at that edge of my camp, on past the ancient tombs lining the edges of the Via Flaminia, towards the smashed Milvian Bridge around a mile away. The countryside changed on the far banks, warts of stone and marble rising in gradually greater density as far as the eye could see: waystations, workhouses, storage silos, the buildings like tiny creatures hoping to shelter in the shadow of the giantess, further south. Everything melted into the hazy distance, except her. I could see the shape of her even from here.

Rome.

Five miles. After a journey that had begun forty years ago, only five miles remained. I stared at the ancient city, then back at my army, here to claim her.

In my youth, I had often imagined myself leading bands of soldiers and heroes, and even barked out commands to them as I played. Sunset would see them vanish and my games end. But this was no game, and this sunset promised to be a terrible shade of red. A great sadness crept across me like a shadow, and I felt a thickening in my throat.

The light rumble of an empty belly broke my chain of thought. I turned to see the two Cornuti who had shadowed me up here – they had read my pensive mood well and remained watchful but discreet. I spotted the two caped, felt-capped *exploratores* too: like hawks, one perched on a tree branch and another on his haunches in the long grass, scouring the hills for any sign of a threat. There were no Maxentians up here, were there?

I noticed one explorator's head rise, and heard the light scuffing of a sandal. My eyes narrowed with a cold acuity and the four watchmen went for their weapons. I saw the approaching boy before they did – clambering up the hill like a spider. The guards relaxed. My heart melted.

Crispus, all gangly limbs and brown curls. It was as if he had leapt from the visions of my own youth. He had grown much in the many months we had been parted. I had not expected to see him again until the campaign was over. Part of me wondered if that meant I might never see him again. Regardless, he had taken matters into his own hands, 'borrowing' the seal of Treverorum's Urban Prefect and writing a false letter which endorsed his journey here. He had travelled south with the latest grain convoy and a reinforcement trio of auxiliary cohorts, arriving the day before last. I watched him climb, holding roots and clambering up rocks, coming for this outcrop the hard way. I smiled fondly, seeing myself in him... and seeing Minervina in him too. Fausta had been sharp-tongued with him for disobeying her demands that he remain safe and far away in Treverorum. She even tried to have him taken back to Assissium, distant from the clash that was to come, but he refused, showing a streak of stubbornness that he surely gained from me. Most upsetting of all, she stopped him from coming to me, confining him to the northern edge of the camp. Yet it seemed like he had other ideas.

When he reached the lip of the outcrop, I crouched and offered him a hand. He took fright, only now realising that his approach had not been as furtive as he probably hoped. I clasped his forearm and hauled him up to stand before me.

He took a moment to catch his breath, and when he did,

he seemed to suddenly shrink as if weighed down by a cloak of shyness. He was nine now, and perhaps it was only normal for him to have shed his boyish exuberance and lack of self-awareness, but I knew there was more to his awkwardness than that. For years now, Fausta had lectured him on my flaws and vices, poisoning him against me – a cut deeper than could be made by any sword. And here, when I had the weight – and the fate – of the world on my back, she seemed intent on making that burden all the greater. For hours that morning she had hovered near me as I spoke with my retinue; all the time she did nothing but glare at me, her eyes like icy augurs.

I scoured my camp, far below, until I found the large tent I had organised for her. I could not see her down there amidst the masses, but I sensed her staring up here even now.

'Father,' Crispus said. 'I climbed all the way up.'

The words snapped me from my spiralling thoughts. When I turned to him, he grinned and quickly looked at his sandals.

I ruffled my lad's hair. 'Your mother knows you are here with me?' I asked, knowing the answer.

He shook his head.

'Your journey from the north was comfortable?' I queried instead.

'The ride was long, but the soldiers regaled me with stories of your success. I even play-fought with some of them just south of Ravenna – one showed me how to hold a wooden sword,' he said with an excited grin.

I felt a sudden shame, realising that at the same age I had been trained well in the use of the sword. Yet I had spent so little time with my boy in these last years. 'Perhaps, once this is over, we can spend days in the training fields as I once did with big Batius. I can teach you to handle a bow too and—'

'Mother has already arranged for an archer to teach me

how to shoot,' he said, then bit his lower lip as if realising how much this stung me.

'Still, there is much I have to show you,' I said, sitting near the outcrop edge, the sun-warmed rock pleasant against the backs of my legs. I patted the spot next to me and he sat too. 'So much time we should have had together and I have instead been absent,' I sighed, sliding a leather bag from my shoulder, bringing out and breaking a cake of soldier-bread and offering him half. Such a pathetic and inadequate gesture, I cursed myself inwardly.

We ate in silence, both of us peering across the countryside. I uncorked a drinking skin and gulped, then offered him some. He shook his head. We sat there for a time, our shadows gradually shifting with the afternoon sun. We exchanged simple talk, threaded by long bouts of silence. So many times before I should have spent time with him like this, so many opportunities missed.

'I went to the stables to see Celeritas,' he said after one spell of quiet, 'I took a brush and a bag of hay to feed him with but the decurion there seemed confused when I asked where he was.'

I felt my throat swell again. 'The road here was long and dangerous. Celeritas was... brave. He...' I could not even finish the sentence.

Crispus understood, his eyes welling and a deep sob spilling from his lips.

I put an arm around his shoulder and pulled him close. 'I will never forget him. He carried me to my every victory.' I said, feeling the lad shake with weak sobs. Celeritas had been like a pet to him. I had led the stallion into a storm of arrows and flying bolts. This war had blinded me to so many of my failings.

We sat like that for a time, saying nothing, but close, together. After a time, a trumpet call from the camp sounded: the Bructeri filed out onto the broad plain in the north, motivated by Hisarnis' hectoring cries, each of them casting short shadows as the sun began to descend into late afternoon.

'We should return to camp,' I said, the spell of familial comfort evaporating, unease creeping across my shoulders as I imagined what the hazy shape of Rome might at any moment be about to spit forth. Already, I noticed, there were men – not soldiers but surely Maxentians nonetheless – buzzing around on the southern banks near the broken Milvian Bridge. A few dozen boats had gathered there too, I noticed, and a team of engineers were busy erecting a palisade near the far bridgehead. Defensive works were underway there, it seemed.

As I rose to take a better look, Crispus grabbed my hand. 'The soldiers say you are here to kill Uncle Maxentius,' he said quietly, squinting up at me. 'Just as you... killed Grandpapa.'

That almost knocked me from my feet. Almost, and still I sank to one knee to be level in the eye with him.

'Had your grandfather lived, then he would have had me killed... and Maxentius too, likely.' I could see the dead end into which I was wandering only once it was too late. 'But I did not come here to kill Maxentius, or any one man. You are young, but not so young. You remember all the years of war we have endured. War is a ravenous beast, and once she has risen, few can tame her. She cast us – all of us – into this moment.'

He hugged his knees to his chest and picked at a stalk of wild wheat. 'Yet when we were in Britannia and in Gaul, we had a good life, did we not? I remember entire years when there were no wars across the empire... when you were with us every day. Why did you choose to leave our home and come here to make a war when there was none?'

My mind sped with a thousand answers – acerbic ripostes I might spit back at my senators, or maxims that would invigorate my generals, old lessons from Lactantius, Father... Galerius even. *War sleeps with one eye open! In times of peace, prepare for war!* But for my son, I knew none of these would suffice.

'I once asked your grandmother what brought men to choose their god, what drove men to make war. She could not explain to me, other than to say that one day I would know the answer for myself. Here I am,' I sighed, waving a hand across the scene below and around us.

'So you know the answer now?'

I stared into his eyes, wishing it were so.

'Domine!' one of the exploratores hissed, his tone clipped and desperate.

My head snapped round. He was perched on the outcrop near us having sneaked up like an asp. At first I looked south, in the direction of Rome. Then I saw that the explorator's wide, alarmed eyes were staring down into my camp. 'Trouble.'

I followed his gaze and saw the swell of men there. They swayed in great packs, like a tavern brawl on a grand scale. The Ubii and the Fourth Jovia at odds, and others from nearby legions piling in. Plates and cups flew, tents collapsed. When I heard a piercing scream and saw a puff of red, I shot to my feet. With a snap of my fingers, my four watchmen and my son followed me down the tufa hill track. We sped into the camp and shoved our way through the growing fray. It was a terrible tangle of flashing steel and thrashing limbs.

Tables and stools being used as cudgels, troughs being booted over and horses whinnying in panic.

'Christian scum!' one man seethed, slamming his fist into the face of another, breaking his nose.

'You backwards, barbarian pigs!' howled one of the Second Italica men, brandishing his legion's standard like a spear, sweeping it to and fro. Around him, a dozen men of his unit had drawn their swords and gathered beside him as if to make a last stand.

A group of Krocus' Regii had already waded in to part the troublemakers, but there were so many of them, tumbling across tents, punching, kicking. More screams. One man staggered past me, clutching a ripped belly. Worse, the four bishops stood among it all, denouncing the ones who fought against the Christian legions, orchestrating the 'followers of Christ' with swishes of their hands. Batius led a fully armed and armoured cohort of Cornuti into the swell, roaring at the brawlers on both sides, driving them apart, although some of them took to shouting over the words of the bishops: 'This is not the true way of Christ. Their words are false!' which only fuelled the flames.

Incensed, the bishops howled even louder, waving more Eighth Augusta soldiers to the scene like reinforcements. Suddenly, the whole camp seemed to be at war with itself. A timber watchtower suddenly erupted in flames, set alight by a kicked-over campfire. The watchmen up there screamed as they realised they were trapped. Dreadful memories of the burning silo in Nicomedia came blazing back into my mind's eye. A pair of brawlers staggered between me and Crispus. One held a stake like a club and swung it back to strike at his opponent. Had I not snatched Crispus out of his way, the cudgel would have inadvertently struck him on the temple.

I pulled him close to me and heard a great, thunderous roar spill from my lips and across the camp.

'Enough,' I boomed. '*Enough!*'

But my cry was lost in the terrible din.

It was only when the watchtower came crashing down with a fiery *whoosh*, exploding as it crushed a row of supply tents and unfortunate baggage train handlers and mules, that the fighting slowed. All heads gradually turned to the scene: puffs of dark smoke, flying embers, the men from the tower top lying broken and burnt alongside the crushed handlers and animals, a gaping hole in the camp perimeter where the tower had been and a blaze that threatened to sweep across all of our tents.

Panting men slowed and backed away from their opponents. Some of Krocus' men ran to aid the injured ones around the fallen tower and Batius and his Cornuti threw water troughs over the blaze. More rushed to help them. As the fire was tamed, I stomped up on the ash mound where the tower had been and looked around: the bishops had scuttled away – I knew then they had most likely kindled this latest mess. My army clustered around me in their thousands. I met the eyes of so many. 'We have come so far together. Now we stand on the edge of a knife: greatness on one side and calamity on the other. You cannot even make camp together without pushing with all your might towards calamity. What must I say for you to make this madness stop?' I cried to them.

'Tell us, Domine. Which of us is right?' one asked.

'Which god is the *true* god?' said another.

'Under whose banner and protection do we march?'

I felt invisible hands wrap around my throat, choking away my confidence. Constantine the Great, some would remember me as. Never short of a homily or a show of might. Here I was, dumbstruck. I stared skywards, lost.

I prayed then. I knew not to whom. That was when it happened.

The fishbone of cloud was gone, the sky unmarked, so all those within my ranks – the quarrellers and the many others – saw it just as clearly as I did: a bright, radiant halo that seemed to explode from and stretch around the sun; a burst of light that briefly illuminated the late afternoon as if it were noonday once more. I shielded my eyes to the glare, heard my legions gasp, the thud of their knees hitting the ground, the cantillating songs of many faiths rising in awe. Within a few heartbeats it was gone, the sky a darkening shade of blue, the sun a tired amber as it continued its slow descent towards the western horizon. In the wake of the incredible light, the songs of wonder faded, and a fearful babble rose. Officers, baggage handlers, slaves – every soul in my army, confused, stricken with fear and awe, looking at the sky and then to me as if certain it was my doing. 'God shines upon you, Domine,' one man shouted.

'But *which* god,' called another. 'It is Mithras, surely?'

'It is the light of Apollo's chariot!' cut in another angrily.

'We must have an answer, Domine,' begged one man. 'Before we march to battle against the tyrant.'

I saw tears on his cheeks. I saw blind hope on the faces of others as many more pled the case of their god. How could I answer, without cleaving my army apart? So when I did speak, it was to the person who mattered most of all.

'Go to your mother,' I said, kissing Crispus' head.

As he scampered away, I regarded my massed forces. 'I will have my answer for you soon,' I said, screaming inside, for I knew it was an unanswerable question.

With that, I stepped down from the ash mound and retreated to my command tent, yanking the leather flap shut. Behind me, the voices rose into dispute once again, and continued after darkness fell. The torches and campfires cast up tall, angry and restless shadows of the rowing men, outlined in the orange glow, against the four goatskin walls of my fragile sanctuary.

Slumping down on a stool, I poured myself a cup of wine from an urn on the table and took a deep draught. I had planned to spend the afternoon in here drawing up a plan of action for tomorrow – if, how and when I would move my army. Yet the map pinned on the table was still unmarked and the wooden pieces representing my legions still in their felt-lined box. I took another gulp of wine, tried to block out the noise from outside and set my mind to the matter. First, I would have my artillery prepared and order them to smash whatever resistance he was building at the Milvian Bridge remains. Then I would throw a timber walkway across the Tiber, cross the river and soldier towards Rome's walls and gates. A memory scampered across my thoughts again: of an adolescent me advising young Maxentius to appreciate the value of strong walls. I jolted once in dry, horrible humour.

I had pieced together no more than a mental picture of what my siege strategy might be when the first of my generals arrived: Prefect Vindex. He stumbled inside, like a man loping in from a blizzard. He cast a sour look back at the squabbling masses outside and swept what looked like a spray of spittle from his shoulder and his gold-finned helm – held underarm.

'You need to address the legions, Domine,' he said, resting his palms on the other side of the map table. 'They are again turning into an angry mob out there.'

I rolled my eyes up to meet his in a tacit rebuff. 'We have more important work to do. Pull up a stool.'

'They will not sleep tonight if you do not give them an answer, Domine. Some are even beginning to talk of the sign in the sky as an omen of ill fortune – foretelling our defeat.'

'Defeat – why?' He had my full attention now. 'Each of them has been with me all the way here. We have suffered every step of the way, lost many comrades.... but have we ever tasted defeat? Not once!'

'Because you cannot assure them which god spoke to you from the sky, they begin to fear that it must have been a message not for you, but for Maxentius.'

My jaw slackened in disbelief.

Scaurus of the Petulantes came in now, the rugged tribunus shooting an equally bemused look back at the squall he had just escaped. 'They're working themselves into a fever, Domine, and those bloody bishops are prowling about again.'

They entered like this, one by one. Batius, Krocus, Ruga, Hisarnis. Prefect Vario of the Second Italica too. 'The legions need to hear your answer, Domine,' said the young leader.

I pushed back from the table with a sigh and rubbed at my temples. 'They want me to name a god? Any answer I give will alienate half of my army.'

'Yet if you don't answer,' Batius said sadly, 'then you will approach Rome leading a disintegrating rabble, at war with itself.'

That hurt, but I knew the big man was only speaking the painful truth.

Then things got even worse: the four bishops entered the tent and began warbling about how the sign in the sky had clearly been the Christian God's light, a sign one thousand times stronger than the one at the Shrine of Apollo back in Gaul. Ossius of Colonia Patricia 'kindly' offered to speak to the legions in my place. 'I will placate the soldiers, Domine. I will explain to those from the... other... faiths how wrong they are.'

I stared at him, unblinking, until his confidence crumbled. 'Get out,' I said in a low growl.

Few heard. Ossius did not even move.

'Get... *out!*' I roared, shooting to my feet and upending the map table.

The many voices within the tent dropped to nothing. Ossius staggered backwards gracelessly.

I met Batius' eyes among the others. The big man read my mood well and shepherded the rest outside. I slumped into a chair in the corner with a deep, rattling sigh, pouring myself another cup of wine and raking my fingers through my hair.

When the tent flap whooshed open again, I was quite set on beating the unwelcome visitor to death with my bare fists, but there was something odd about this one. Not a soldier, a medicus. Smiling, joyous.

'Domine, you must come,' he whispered.

I sat proud, a thrill rising through me. I didn't want my hopes to swell, but this could only mean one thing. I threw on a dark cloak, pulling up the hood, then slipped outside with him. The shouting, quarrelling soldiers didn't pay any attention to me in my hooded guise as I followed the man to the valetudinarium tents. He pulled back the flap of the main tent, and my heart almost burst with relief when I looked inside.

'Old tutor?' I croaked.

Lactantius, sitting up in his bed, sipping on some root brew, smacked his lips together and grinned. 'I can smell smoke, hear swearing and angry voices... things are going well?'

I laughed and tears stole down my cheeks at the same time as I strode inside and embraced him. He had never been one for shows of affection like this but at that moment he didn't have any choice.

'It was most unexpected, Domine,' the medicus explained. 'He was in the deepest of comas still, even this morning. Then, after Lady Fausta had bathed him, I came in to give him water and I found him rousing, as if waking from a long sleep.'

Lactantius patted my back awkwardly as we parted, and I sat on the stool by his bedside. 'You look terrible,' I said.

'Ever the charmer,' Lactantius replied with a wry smile.

'But you looked worse during the time you were unconscious. I thought you were... I thought we had lost yo—'

'I will never be lost,' he cut me off, lifting his Chi-Rho necklace and kissing it. 'Though my head feels as if it has been subject to a stampede.'

I noticed his eyes drift to his scrolls, on his bedside table.

'I have seen men lying unconscious before. I often wondered if it was a world of blackness they knew. Weightless, senseless, nothing.'

'It was not?' I surmised.

His eyes lifted to meet mine, and they seemed to age several years in those few moments. 'I saw things that assured me of the Christian God, more so than ever before... and things that turned my soul to stone.'

'Tutor?' I asked.

'Now I know how to finish my script,' he said quietly, a

fleeting, haunted madness in his eyes. 'Now I know what becomes of the wicked.'

An invisible breath of ice crept up and over me, so unnerved was I by the old man's words.

From outside, the sound of a smashing pot rang out and the shouting rose, jolting me back to reality.

I glanced over my shoulder in the direction of the noise, then slowly looked back to Lactantius. 'I have missed your company first as a friend, but also as a guide. Through all the battles since you fell ill, I have led and led well. Yet in the gaps between, the army has peeled apart. I have even had to field them in two halves. Now, they threaten to crumble into a million tiny fragments. Even the Mithraists have started to argue with one another – one sect certain that the gathering before the tauroctony should happen at midnight, the other saying it should be pre-dawn. They and the mobs of the bishops nearly burnt the camp down this afternoon.'

'Nearly?' Lactantius said. 'So you put a halt to it?'

I paused as I felt a shiver pass up through me, remembering the moment: 'When I climbed up onto the smouldering hump that remained of the fire to address them, the sun blazed in a strange show of light over the camp. It shut them up for a moment – seeing the sun "speaking" to their emperor like that. Yet as soon as it was gone they began to demand of me an answer: to tell them *which* god had sent the sign.'

'Ah, yes, the medicus told me about the halo of light,' Lactantius said. 'Trust me to sleep through the main event!'

I smiled. 'Guide me, old tutor. What should I tell the legions?'

'I am no longer your teacher, Constantine. *You* are the teacher, and you have many pupils.'

333

'Then one last time, Tutor, guide me,' I begged him.

Lactantius took a moment to choose his words, stroking his Chi-Rho in thought. 'Who is the highest god?'

'Ah, answering a question with a question,' I chuckled dryly. 'No doubt you too think it was a sign of Christ? His guarantee of conquest? But then Sol Invictus is the highest god, is he not – the divine, guiding light? Or Mars, or Mithras... Apollo!' I threw my hands in the air as if casting petals, then slapped them down in frustration onto my knees.

Lactantius merely arched an eyebrow. 'Do you remember the storm in Naissus, when you were a boy. The one you used to tell me about? The legionary who stayed on the walls when the others fled for shelter.'

I frowned. 'How could I forget? It was the first moment I felt truly alive. In the eye of danger too!'

'It has been a long journey since then, has it not? Just as your mother told you it would be.'

'What are you trying to say, old tutor? I love your lessons, apart from the ones that meander into some vague mist. Tell me: what do I say to the thousands of men outside who demand answers from me. That Christ is the true God? Or should I champion one of the old gods? Either way, I will estrange many, and break the spirit that has propelled us here. Your lessons are fused in my mind.' I wagged a finger, aping his teaching style. 'Xenophon once said "When one side goes against the enemy with the gods' gift of a stronger morale, then their adversaries, as a rule, cannot withstand them." Well my men are beating the morale out of one other. But *damn*, who is our god?'

Lactantius smoothed at his blanket. 'If a hungry man sees a fig tree and knows he can eat its fruit, and a weary traveller sees that same tree and knows he can take shelter from the rain under its canopy… does it matter that one calls it a source of food and the other refuge? Is it not more important that both men are content? It matters not *how* you find Him… it only matters that you *do* find Him, in whichever guise that may be.'

'Emperors past have tried to hammer and fuse beliefs old and new. It is impossible,' I sighed.

'Is it? Think about it, Constantine.' He gazed through me and off into his own memories. 'Once I was a pupil and I learned much. But it was not until my beard turned white that I learned the greatest lesson of all: men cannot be *told* what to believe. However, they can be guided towards the truth. The key is to find your fig tree – that blessed thing that makes the hearts of different men content, the beacon that leads all to the truth.'

His words swirled like a Socratic mist – all theory and no form. I felt like a boy again, leaning in towards him, hanging on his every word. 'Where will I find my beacon?'

Lactantius' old face creased with a gentle smile. 'It has already found you. It shone upon you today.'

With a stark thrill, I understood. Lessons he had long ago seeded in my mind suddenly grew shoots, growing, rising. *Now I understood!*

I took his old hand and kissed it. Standing, I turned to the tent flap. Just before I stepped outside, I let my cloak slip to the ground, then walked out and into the storm of voices, armour glittering. Instantly, they spotted me. Within a moment, they surrounded me, howling, demanding I tell them my answer. I climbed back to the top of that ash mound, and I spoke at last.

'A god spoke to me today,' I began.

They were rapt.

'He told me we would be victorious, that we would take Rome.'

A swell of cheering rose from all factions. 'But which god was it, Domine?' one shouted.

I picked out the man in the crowd. 'You saw the blazing lights in the sky today? The sun came alive, did it not?'

'Aye,' many rumbled.

'The sun: is it not Apollo's chariot, charging across the sky every day?'

The Apollonian legions rose in a triumphant cheer.

Before the others could complain, I added: 'Does it not also represent Christ's death and resurrection?'

The many Christians cried out joyously at this. The bishops' jaws flapped, thunder stolen.

'Is Mithras not the god of the light?' I boomed now, pointing a finger skywards. 'Does Mars Neton not wear a glowing crown of sunlight?' On and on different sections rose in triumphant roars. 'Is Sol Invictus not the sun incarnate?' I found myself listing their many gods, showing them why it must have been each and every one of those deities who had spoken to me through the glowing lights of the sun that afternoon, why their gods were not enemies, but allies. Solar brothers. *One*, as Lactantius would insist. Bless the old man and his fig tree.

'When we march on Rome,' I finished, 'it will be with *all* the gods on our side, in our hearts... and with their sign upon our shields!'

* * *

With the reinforcements from the north and the Maxentian regiments who had declared for me, my camp housed nearly twenty thousand soldiers. I walked among them as they worked in the hours of darkness, silent again, the great question answered. The unrest was over, and all thanks to a simple address and one order formed in my now clear and sharp mind. Bellies full, they sat around their campfires, quietly passing around pots of paint and brushes. As I passed each group, they would look up, their eyes bright. 'Domine,' the greeting came in a gentle swell of voices everywhere I went.

'We march to battle tomorrow, and Mithras will walk with us,' said one young lad in the Cornuti. I eyed the thick lashings of bright red paint as he applied them. Bit by bit, the ancient amber design of serpents disappeared. I glanced to the soldier next to him – his shield already coated in red, the man now carefully painting a golden sun on top of it, six spiked 'rays' projecting from it. 'Mithras, God of the Light, will shield you,' I assured them, '*and* your brother legions who march under his sign.'

They rumbled in approval. I moved on, coming to the Second Italica area. Vario encouraged his men to paint with care. He had been a fine appointment, his only desire to live up to his father's proud name. They painted their shields with the same crimson and dazzling golden suns. I noticed how they added their own touch – a loop at the tip of the sun's topmost 'ray'. It transformed the solar emblem into a Chi-Rho of sorts. The Italica men sang low songs of Christian lore as they worked, but the nearby Martia men now did not complain or protest, for they too were painting the solar crown of Mars on their shields. On through the ranks I went. Each of my legions decorated their shields and banners like this. Germanic wolves, Minerva's owl, leaping hounds – all became blazing suns of one sort or another. Each of my regiments, united by the one common symbol that linked their preferred gods. Maxentius might have nearly twice my number, but nobody was speaking about that now. The animus of my legions – the shared experience of this campaign – was one thing, but this binding of faiths was another. Something never before seen.

I stopped near the edge of camp, gazing into the night and the dark stretch leading towards the broken Milvian Bridge. I knew then that some in future years would denounce me as a cold, ambitious monster, choosing to affront all the gods, to deceive my own men in order to achieve my own goals. But there was no deceit, no affront. In my heart I knew who my god was. My journey was coming to an end. I had simply allowed my men to make their way too, and to at last set the glue that would bind us together as an invincible army for the one last battle that remained. When my army lined up tomorrow to march on Rome, they would do so with a shield-shell of bright red and blazing gold suns. One invincible force. One god... *every* god on our side. Every man charged with pride and divine authority. My heart began to soar.

... and then I heard something. From the south. From the Tiber. From the broken Milvian Bridge. The distant splash of oars.

My army, distracted, hearts set on battle – but not until tomorrow – looked up in shock. The thick watch around my camp's southern edge rose like hares detecting a nearby predator. I gazed across the night, eyes locked on the distant darkness of that ancient river. A lone, white-sailed galley emerged from the blackness like Charon's ferry. Gently coming towards the banks. The torches on board uplit a few purple standards and a ceremonial spear topped with white feathers. An embassy. At this great distance I could not identify the crew or this delegation. Yet in my blood… to my marrow, I knew that *he* was on board.

Maxentius? I mouthed.

PART 4

Omnes una manet nox
(One night awaits everyone)
– *Horace*

28

MAXENTIUS

It was probably foolish. I know that most of my officers and advisors would rather we had stayed in the city and planned for the coming day, but something had driven me to this.

'Do you really think you can end this with words?' Valeria had said as I pinned my cloak resolutely in place over the burnished bronze cuirass.

'No,' I'd admitted. 'Though I wish beyond reason I could, and if there is still the faintest possibility that I can, I owe it to myself, and to Rome, to try.'

'He might have you killed.'

'I doubt he could, and if he did, such an act would erode his honour so thoroughly that he would lose everything he has built. No, even if he hates me now, he will not have me killed like a criminal.'

'*You* could have *him* killed,' Volusianus added from where he stroked the edge of his sword with a whetstone, ominously.

'And that would do precisely the same to me. Any emperor who must rely on murder for his authority cannot remain in the purple for long before murder in turn finds him. No.

343

This will end properly, on the field of battle as two powerful Roman emperors vie for primacy.'

Whatever my old friend might think, there could still be men in his army who were reticent, or who could be won over, and consequently I had made careful adjustments to my party. I had trimmed my hair down and shaved my beard close. I looked more like a bristly Trajan now than the man Constantine had last seen, and I wore a panoply of the oldest style, complete with a knotted belt announcing my imperium, a gorgon's head embossed on my chest to attract good fortune, and breeches of ancient design rather than the long trousers we so often wore. I looked like an ancient emperor, from the glory days of Rome.

Moreover, I had Volusianus and my Praetorians with me, in their gleaming archaic uniforms with the scorpion-design shields – a reminder of traditional Roman power. I had legionaries, too, in old-fashioned crimson. We were Romanitas incarnate, but still we were more. For along with the *fetial* priest with his white robe and covered head, whose duties centred on both diplomacy and war and its proper prosecution, I had brought other priests. The fetial stood side by side with Miltiades, the head of the Christian church. Neither looked particularly comfortable with their enforced proximity, but they were putting on a good show of unity for me, as we all knew what might be at stake. Two robes, representing the old and the new, working together for a strong Rome.

Strength and faith on display, tradition and a sweeping acceptance. That was the Rome I wanted Constantine's army to see. I wanted his Christians to think of the fact that they were being asked to take a blade's edge to their fellow worshippers. I wanted his army, who had to be made up of all faiths, old and new, to see that Rome was now a place for both of them, and that their master's designs threatened that.

It was a tissue of lies, of course. A thin façade concealing the truth: a city that was beleaguered and tearing itself apart. But if I wanted the time to heal all this, I needed to win here, or at least not to lose, and so we would show the enemy that they were wrong.

We reached the river soon enough and had to wait there. The pontoon bridge was not yet complete, though it was almost ready, the span reaching out to the north bank and closing on it, even as the tethered line of boats bent downstream with the current. The boats were being filled with ballast as they were manoeuvred into position and roped into place. Then the heavy, solid boards were nailed down to create the bridge surface. I had been assured that it would be finished by sunset. It was almost sunset, and there still seemed so much to do. Yet I was now being assured that it would be in place by midnight.

The delay as we waited to cross gave me more opportunity than I really wanted to examine the enemy on the far bank.

I had been told time and again that we outnumbered Constantine's force, and the numbers I had seen on parchment had certainly borne that out, but the simple fact is that comparing odds becomes impossible once the numbers reach a certain height. Looking at the camp of the northern veterans facing us, I couldn't tell at all whether there were more or fewer of them than mine on this side of the river. All I knew was that the immense golden glow of a thousand camp fires that rose from behind a seemingly endless palisade spoke of a *vast* force, and that any general – even the great Caesar himself – would have blanched at the prospect of meeting them in the field. I felt confidence drain from me once more, and it worried me that sitting here and looking at them, the same would be happening for every man under my command.

Gods, but this was hard.

Not soon enough the largest of the vessels present – one that was in use by the engineers rather than a mere piece in the bridge works – was brought over, two smaller boats behind it, and we were ushered on board for the crossing.

Since the day my beloved boy disappeared beneath the surface of the Tiber and was torn from me, I had harboured a private hatred of rivers. I had stopped paying my respects to the statues of Father Tiber, for he had dragged away my Romulus. I hated *all* rivers, but I reserved the core and iron-melting fire of my anger for the Tiber. I felt fear crossing it. I felt fear, and loathing, and anger and panic and, most of all, hollow loss. I was so close to where Romulus had drowned right now. The cold rhythmic lapping of the oars seemed to call his name in a whispering tone over and over. I had to hold myself rigid, staring at the far bank, for every instinct in my body was to dive over the edge and into the cold blackness of the water, seeking the pale, reaching hand of my drowning son.

Foolish, for that hand had long since been rendered to ash with the rest of him and interred in that grand mausoleum at the villa. Yet I could almost see him there, struggling in the water as he sank.

Damn my vivid imagination.

I almost yelped in shock as the boat touched the far bank and near threw me from my feet. I stepped up onto the grass with a little help, for near the Milvian Bridge the banks are neither low nor shallow. There I waited with my companions as our horses were brought up. It seemed that at least I had been correct about not being butchered out of hand. Even the men building the pontoon bridge could so easily have been peppered with arrows or battered with artillery from Constantine's position, but they were being left in peace. Odd, that. Volusianus had had stretches of palisade erected on the southern bank, along with watchtowers and encampments of artillery and missile troops to defend the work on the bridge and they sat untouched, unheeded. Was Constantine so sure of himself that he did not even see the need to strive for control of the water?

Once we were all gathered and mounted once more, I gave the signal and we moved. The blackness of night was pushed back to the north by the immense glow of the camp, and above and around the serrated teeth of his palisade I could see soldiers of many sorts. The world seemed to be full to the brim with Constantine's men. There were strange, fur-clad, mail-wearing bearded barbarians from the fringe of the civilised world alongside Hispanic legionaries clad in gleaming steel. It was an odd conglomeration, and it seemed to me that they were so different and utterly unlike one another that the only thing that tied them together was that they were all, uniformly, here to kill me.

As we approached that huge camp and its forbidding palisade, something struck me as odd. I had spent so long listening to the fractious arguments of my city as its people denounced their neighbour's faith as profane that it seemed the normal sound of humanity. Its absence was suddenly extremely unsettling, especially when I had expected much the opposite of Constantine's camp. They had been torn apart by division even far back in the north, before Valeria's agents had begun their insidious work. How, then, had such a peaceful concord settled upon this camp? What could have caused such a thing?

It was in that moment that I knew this visit was futile. Valeria had been right. This could no longer be resolved with words, just as it could not be avoided by deception. Somehow that did not make me angry or resolute or anything it probably should have. It just made me a little sad.

'This will be a bloodbath,' Volusianus said quietly.

I frowned at him and he swept his hand from the right to the left, indicating the terrain before Constantine's camp, upon which I now planned to lead my forces in the morning.

'Riverbank to the right,' he said. 'Steep and troublesome. Any figure in armour who gets pushed over there is a dead man. Cliffs over there to the left. Not astoundingly high, but high enough to be worse than any wall in battle. Behind us, the plain narrows as it approaches the site of our demolished bridge, and again it narrows behind Constantine's force to the north. If we fight here more men will die than in any battle in Roman history. It is a killing ground and nothing more. No tactics will make the slightest difference.'

I shivered. He made it sound so much worse than I already thought it.

From my far side, Zenas cleared his throat. 'That could be to our advantage. Constantine's tricks and plots have won him every battle so far, but here he is stripped of that option. There will be no ruses or surprises. Just men facing men. Our forces are every bit the veterans of his army, and we have more of them. As long as our men's morale holds then it is down to a simple matter of courage and numbers. If that is the case then for the first time in this war, we can truly say we have the advantage.'

Volusianus seemed less certain. He simply grunted in reply, his gaze straying across the scene before us. I felt my nerves tingling, the hairs on my neck standing proud. This was where we would fight and where men would die, and there was no stopping that now, but the Sibylline books had spoken. I, the champion of Rome, would rise from this slaughter to be the sole emperor in the West, and with the end of this bloody war, I would be able to rebuild. With the resources Gaul, Britannia and Hispania would bring, I could return everything to normal. Put things right. And the man who would do harm to Rome, who sat awaiting me amidst that throng, would die. I still wished that were not the case, but I continued in the determination that if it were to be one of us butchered on the cold ground, it would not be me.

We approached a gateway in the strong palisade, no gates barring our path, its guards drawn to the side, inviting if cold. Beyond, the massed ranks of Constantine's army parted like a sea and a wide thoroughfare was thus created for our party to pass into the heart of their camp. It felt peculiar. I had faced armies before, and not only Constantine's. Severus'. Galerius'. I had endured that tense moment when the two forces first view one another and size up their chances. This was not like that. There was no cheering, no jeering, no threats or entreaties. There was only utter silence. The enemy remained so still and quiet that I could hear the wind hissing through the leaves and the dull thuds of our hooves on the turf. It was eerie, to say the least.

As we moved into the very centre of their camp, another sound began to appear in the quiet evening, a rhythmic scraping, and it was only as my searching eyes picked out pockets of men to either side that I realised what it was. Men were busy repainting their shields. Their ancient symbols of wolves and lightning bolts, of eagles and winged horses were being submerged beneath a new design of bright red, overlaid with a golden sunburst. A uniform design that seemed to be omnipresent. I shivered suddenly, looking around me. That design was everywhere, on Hispanic legionaries and Germanic auxiliaries, on Batavians and Britons, on Gauls and Raetians, those with a Chi-Rho dangling from their neck, and those with the owl of Minerva tattooed on their arms. Uniformity. Combined with the silence of concord that lay across the camp it was suddenly clear that in everything Valeria's agents had sought to achieve, they had failed. Constantine's army was no rabble of opposed forces, but a single armoured fist.

I felt a chill run through me.

Then, while I was still reeling over what I had seen, we were there. I could see Constantine's *principia*. His principia was no ostentatious show of power like those of Galerius or Severus, or even my own father in his day. Constantine's headquarters was a square of tents, each the abode of a soldier rather than a golden prince, albeit larger than most and surrounded by the planted standards of his army. His personal guards stood in shining strength nearby. There was no sign of my old friend. He remained in the largest of the tents, no doubt. I wondered then just how long it had been since we had set eyes upon one another. Verona, I thought, though that had been but brief and distant.

We reined in amidst the standards of the enemy, and dismounted. I left the bulk of my Praetorians in the saddle, though. A big man emerged from one tent's doorway and it took me some time to realise that it was Batius, Constantine's old friend, and the bodyguard who had served his father. He looked old, to me, and weary. But then weren't we all?

The big man stepped aside and gestured at the tent.

'Only you, Imperator,' he said. Volusianus made to object, angry noises rising in his throat, and old Batius pointed at my second. 'The emperor sits alone in his tent. This is not a time for you, but for your master.'

My Praetorian Prefect – a consul of Rome, no less – looked extremely unhappy as I nodded to Batius and held up a restraining hand to Volusianus. I suspect it was less that he worried about my safety than that he wanted personal involvement. Either way, he would stay outside.

I walked forward, arranging my cloak so that it did not entangle with my sword. I half expected the big man to demand my weapon, but he did not. I nodded at him and passed through the tent entrance inside. As my eyesight adjusted and my flesh felt the sooty warmth of the braziers that lit and heated the great tent, I heard Batius closing the flap behind me and securing it. Whatever happened here was just for us.

As promised, Constantine was alone. He sat at a table with one hand drumming a staccato rhythm on the surface and the other resting on his knee – just two hand-widths from a sword leaning against the table leg.

Gods but he looked different. He had hardened in the vast gulf of time since we had last met. His face was still broad and flat, but now it looked somehow stony and powerful, his brow heavy and lined, his eyes dark and troubled. His jaw was strong and bristling with a growth of hair that would undoubtedly be shaved off in the morning. He was dressed not to impress nor for comfort. He was dressed as a soldier.

In that strange moment I saw all the Constantines I had known superimposed in that seat. The most wonderful straw-haired young man who had saved me from a brutal beating in Treverorum. The glorious golden soldier who had come back from the east with tales of victory over the King of Kings. The great friend who had helped Romulus learn to ride in the stables of Nicomedia. The glowing father who had helped me save my boy from the burning granary. The burgeoning emperor who had defied the tetrarchy. The brutal master who had murdered my father. The dark ruler who had met me at Galerius' deathbed where the very last cords that bound us together had been severed in the heat of stupid words, and now the weary-looking general who had come to contest with me for the future of Rome.

I wondered what he saw in me, and almost laughed aloud when he said: 'You've changed, Maxentius. You might be dressed in glory, but you seem somehow darker. Tired. Old.'

'War inflicts that on all of us, Constantine.'

'Truly. Will you sit?'

I did so with the requisite difficulty of a man in a breastplate with a sword at his side. When I was finally settled and marginally comfortable, he offered me wine. I did not really feel like it, but I accepted anyway, largely to avoid appearing churlish. Odd, really, given how we had last parted. This seemed strangely civilised. The reason became clear as Constantine poured and watered the wine.

'This is just a formality, of course,' he noted.

'Nothing can be stopped now, can it?'

He shook his head as he passed me the cup and poured one for himself. 'This has to be finished, and I am determined now to do it without Licinius. You know the old dog would bite my hand off for the chance?'

I nodded. 'And if you'd brought him, I'd have had to deploy Daia's legions. Then this would no longer be about us, and those animals would have a part in the future of the world. Better that we face this without them.'

Constantine sighed. 'We have come past the point at which

we could turn back, I think, and some time ago at that. I cannot leave now without adding Rome to my empire, for without it, I will never truly be emperor, and you will not simply concede, else you would have done it before now.'

'I cannot deny that there have been times when I have considered it. But in my darkest hour I turned to the gods and they promised me victory. How can I turn back or surrender now?'

'Beware such prophecies, Maxentius. The old gods do not have the power they once held, and priests lie and are mistaken.'

I felt a wrinkle of indignation now. 'Your Christian god claims all the power now, does he?'

'If only you knew the trouble I had been through on that very question. Still, let us not debate religion now. That is not why we are here. In fact, other than the mere protocol of war, I'm not sure why we *are* here.'

'I came because I wanted to see if there was anything left of my old friend. To see whether I was fighting the Constantine who had once been so close to me, or whether this Constantine is the hard, territorial monster of which my advisors paint an image.'

'And?'

'And I fear the answer lies somewhere in between. You are right. This cannot be avoided. Tomorrow will be a bloodbath, and you and I will try to kill one another, and when it is over, the West will have only one emperor. I know you will not surrender, and I do not want you to die, old friend. I pray that somehow in the press you are captured and the war can be won without your death. I tell you here and now that if you still live when I am victorious, then you will be spared. Rome will always need good men.'

I realised even as I spoke that I was lying. I would have loved it to be true, but Valeria was right. Constantine would become another Maximian. He would always be a threat, capable of rising up. If he lived through the fight, he would still have to die, but I would do it quickly, and would afford him every honour. Still I clung to the lie and said nothing more, despite the sadness enclosing my heart like an icy fist.

'And I will bend every effort to making sure that while you lose, you still live,' Constantine replied in kind, and there was something there again in his eyes that I could not quite grasp, but it was unsettling. Perhaps he too was lying. Was *I* another Maximian to *him*? An echo of my father?

'All friendships end,' Constantine said stoically. 'Even unwillingly. At the very end, death at least will sever any bond. Let us understand here that ours has ended. We cannot consider each other a friend in the morning.'

I nodded. 'To the victor belong the spoils.'

My gaze strayed across the tent for a moment as I shuffled uncomfortably, and fell upon a comb that looked oddly out of place. Most definitely a woman's comb. That could have only one source.

'How is Fausta?'

A strange look crossed my old friend's face, at once both hard and unyielding, yet sad and worried. 'She is fine,' he said, making the lie so easy, 'she has had a hand in the campaign: ever by my side; ever by old Lactantius' bedside too.' He looked up, his eyes bleary. 'You remember my old tutor?'

I nodded, heart thumping a little harder.

'Someone within my ranks poisoned him,' he said. 'Perhaps you have heard this rumour?'

I shook my head wearily. 'Speak your mind, Constantine.

You think I was behind the old man's poisoning? No, it was Valeria who organised and despatched spies into your camp, but they were sent to divide your forces and cause dissent, not to murder civilians. Besides, you cut them all down, long before the old man fell ill.' As I spoke, I realised it was a weak argument, for Valeria's men *had* done their job, passing their mission on to dissenters within the enemy ranks before they were caught and killed. Lactantius' poisoning might not have been my doing, but I was far from devoid of culpability. I glanced away from him, angry, and found my gaze falling once more upon the comb. The gods rolled their dice, and something fell into place in my understanding. Fausta...

A flintiness entered Constantine's gaze. 'The spies were sent to sow dissent and not to murder civilians?' he said in a slow, dry burr. 'What of the citizens of Rome you massacred? Where were your morals that day?'

I felt irritation building, and fought it down. Now was not the time for snarled recriminations. Once, beside Galerius' deathbed, we'd had an opportunity to seek peace, and instead heated words had swept that chance away forever. I leaned forward.

'The bloodsoaked event to which you refer was the regrettable culmination of a series of awful events, and was the snap decision of my Praetorian Prefect, over which he and I have argued time and again. Do not be so quick to judge over things you do not understand, Constantine.'

He glared at me now. 'You cannot paint yourself the peacemaker now, Maxentius.'

'And you cannot paint away the warmonger you have become,' I snapped back. I glanced at the comb and then back to him. That was when I said it. Once again that old fiery anger that simmered within me, the gift from my father, rose up and brought to my lips words that could never be taken back.

'It was Fausta, you fool!'

He just stared at me now, and I could have stopped there, probably should have, with the damage already done, but the bile was pouring from me now. How dare he accuse me of butchering my people; he who had carved a bloody path the length of Italia to oust me from my throne. I rose, accusing finger out now.

'You brought Lactantius' poisoning on yourself. I figured it, even if you continue to delude yourself. It was not my doing, nor Valeria's, so it had to come from within your own camp, but who among those with access to the old man might want to see your campaign fail? She is your wife, but she is my *sister*. The two closest people to her in the world were facing one another with their swords bared, and you had already murdered our father, so she knows exactly what you have planned for me, though we shall not be hidden away in a torturer's cellar this time. What choice did you leave her? Just be grateful it was the old man and not you she chose. She must still have a flicker of love for you, else it would have been you waiting to see your god's face with Lactantius by your bedside and not the other way around. *Your* murderous ways brought you to this.'

I stood, almost panting from angry exertion. For a moment I worried for Fausta. In my anger I had forged her into a weapon and stabbed him with it. What would it cost her?

Constantine sat, stony-faced and pale through the tirade. Now he straightened. When he spoke, it was in a low, leaden tone. 'Once again we discover how distance clouds the vision. Perhaps the thousand shades of dead in Rome do not owe you, but before you condemn me for your father's death and for marching south with my army, remember both what your father was, and that I too hold imperium.'

'I should not have come,' I said coldly, and threw down my wine, slapping the cup back to the table. 'It might have been better than reopening wounds. And while Volusianus would have me hold back all as a surprise, I would rather things be clear between us. I shall not cower behind the city walls and wait for you. The Milvian Bridge rises once more upon pontoon hulls, and with first light I shall march out and meet you in the field, the way an emperor should.'

There was a strange silence, as though Constantine were trying to weigh up the truth of my words, and finally he nodded. I felt that dangerous anger draining away once more, to be replaced with the familiar cold discontent that came whenever I considered what had brought us to this place. I could see in Constantine's eyes a similar calming as we both moved to considering what was to come.

Had we just passed another of those moments when we could change things, but once more blazed through it instead in anger? No. I would not delude myself. Any chance at peace had long since gone. Now we would try to kill one another.

'In the coming days, whether I conquer Rome or die in the attempt,' Constantine replied earnestly, 'I will try to tell myself that you were still you, and not the barbarous creature some say you have become.'

I nodded. 'You have changed, but part of you is still the Constantine of old, I think, somewhere inside.'

I rose and paused, wondering whether we would shake hands. We did not. He remained in his chair and I turned and walked to the tent door. I turned at the last and regarded my old friend. He was pouring himself a second wine and this one, I noted, was barely watered at all. I gave him a sad smile but said nothing. There was nothing more to say.

All the way back through the enemy camp and down to the river, I could feel Volusianus almost vibrating with the need to speak. Finally, as we dismounted and waited to board, watching the last pontoon vessels being brought up to make the bridge, I turned to him.

'What?'

'Tell me what was said, Domine.'

'No. Because nothing of import was said.'

'He offered no hints? You read nothing in his words of what he intends on the morrow?'

'We did not talk of our plans.'

I could feel the man's frustration. He would have used that time to sound out everything he could. I had used it to end a friendship with bittersweet sorrow while I could, before the blade's edge did it for me.

Volusianus was unhappy all the way back to the city. In truth he had been unhappy with me ever since I passed over his command and left him in Rome while I rode north to war, but now, once again, he was at the fore in a place of command, and the resentment seemed to have subsided. We rode in silence. At the Palatine I met the slaves who had been tasked with a particularly important duty. They reverentially handed me their burden and I took it as though it were a babe, swaddled in linen. Valeria joined me then, and Miltiades, as I had instructed earlier. Volusianus and Zenas left to go about their military business. Not I. I had other matters of import to which to attend. Accompanied by appropriate guards, the pope, the empress and I descended the Palatine hill towards the forum and the Temple of Venus and Rome. I turned right, passed the arch commemorating the great victories of Titus over the Jews, and closed on the house that had belonged to my friend and colleague Anullinus before his brutal demise.

The house was mine now. I had taken it following his death and had not had the heart to reuse it or sell it. For me it still held the spirit of my first Praetorian Prefect – the man who had first raised me to the purple – and I feared it always would. What better place for these, then?

'This is lunacy,' Valeria said, though quietly as we entered. 'You will need them when you are victorious.'

I nodded. 'And then I shall know where they are. But just in case, they will go into hiding.'

I looked for the hole that had been made in accordance with my instructions. I found it in the room where Anullinus had died, beneath the very spot where his rent and bloodied body had been discovered. A marble tile had been lifted, the concrete chiselled and removed, and a hole left, the spoil to one side ready to replace. Before I stooped, I unwrapped the bundle one last time and looked upon the sceptres and rods of office, the accoutrements of an emperor. Tomorrow I would wield only a sword, and if for some reason I did not come back, then there would forever be a small portion of the old Rome beneath the place where my friend had died. Moreover, the man who tried to rule Rome without them would undoubtedly fail to do so for long. In my own way, I was laying a curse on any man who might follow me.

I covered the orb once more and lowered the sacred bundle into the hole, where slaves would then bury them. I would retrieve them when Rome was secure, but in the meantime, just to be sure, I turned to Miltiades, the Bishop of Rome and a man who had saved my soul in a time of desperate blackness. I held out to him the other thing I had kept: documents of ownership. He took them and examined them for a moment, frowning.

'Are you sure, Domine?'

'I am. The house is yours. Look after it, for there is no one else I could ever give it to. If the oracles were lying and tomorrow goes ill for me, then know that at least Constantine is a friend to the Christian, and you and the house will be safe.'

Miltiades nodded and tactfully withdrew. I stepped past the hole that held the very symbols of rule in Rome and reached out to embrace Valeria. She did not resist, though I could still see her disapproval and the calculation going on in her mind. She thought I was being defeatist in burying the sceptres. Perhaps she thought I feared a loss. I did. Even though the Sibylline books had promised me victory, a small part of me feared defeat. I shook it off. It was undoubtedly the influence of Miltiades and Zenas and their distrust of the pagan prophecies. I hugged Valeria to my chest and held her tight. We said nothing. No farewell. I could not, for she was all I had left, and she *would* not, for she would not countenance the possibility that I might lose.

We stood for some time, and when finally she left, I asked the shade of Anullinus to wish me luck, and departed the building, nodding to the slave who hurried inside to bury the sceptres. For myself, I think sleep was never very likely, and I would far rather have been at the villa on the Via Appia close to my boy's tomb than here on the Palatine. Still, I looked in rather sadly on little Aurelius, who was suffering more now every day, and then went to the place where I felt I could be alone: the balcony that overlooked the Circus Maximus. On the way, I passed slaves whom I told to bring me wine, and along a hall that had been a favourite of mine over the years, where the busts of Rome's most remembered emperors lined the walls beneath the windows, implacable and cold in their appraisal of whoever passed.

I stopped there, somewhere between Hadrian and Galerius, two benevolent-looking bearded men who looked neither down on their people nor up to the heavens, but straight at me.

'Have I done all I can do?' I asked the assembled luminaries. Even in their cold marble stares I found no answer, though I swear I saw the edge of ghosts gathering around me: Galerius and Severus, Diocletian and Constantius, Anullinus and Romulus...

I marched on to the balcony, where I could stand and savour the chilly night and drink my wine in contemplation of what the morning would bring without the glares of dead emperors upon me.

29

CONSTANTINE

The Milvian Bridge, 28th October 312 AD

Deep into the night I remained at my table, nursing wine. I could hear nothing but a sharp ringing sound in my ears. Deafening, disorienting. What had Maxentius said? I barely remembered the last few words we had shared. It was the tombstone-like revelation he had dropped before me that resonated over and over.

It was Fausta, you fool!

Every so often, my heart raced like a stallion's hooves, then slowed to a hard, steady *thump!* Waves of half-formed thoughts came and went uselessly. Here, on the eve of a clash that would shake this ancient land to its core, it had reduced me to a mess.

And then I acted. It all happened in a blur. Maybe it was partly fuelled by all the wine I had thrown down. I remember only the rough scrape of the tent flap on my face as I barged outside, the fast thud of my boots on the earth and the surprised murmurs of my sentries as they saw me striding to my wife's pavilion. I swept inside, teeth grinding like stones, blood pounding in my ears.

She was awake. Sitting on piled cushions by the orange

bubble of light from a lamp, writing on a wax tablet. She looked up at me, surprised, then with a flare of disgust, before turning back to her writing. 'You've taken a wrong turn – the wine tent is by the stables,' she rumbled.

'Is it true?' I barked.

'What?' she scoffed. 'Go and sleep off your stupor.'

'Maxentius was here. We talked about what happened… to Lactantius.'

Now her gaze slowly peeled away from the tablet and up to me, her face paling and slackening.

'Is. It. True?' I drawled.

There was a moment between us. Me realising that I did not want to know the answer, and she understanding the magnitude of my anger.

'Do not lie to me,' I seethed. 'I will find out. You know I will. Just tell me the truth.'

With a sigh, she gently closed over her wax tablet and set it down, resting the stylus on top. 'You remember that night when he was poisoned?' she spoke at last. 'I entered your tent and watched you sleeping. I wondered for a time whether I should wake you and tell you what I had done.'

My heart began to crumble.

'But what would have been the point?' she continued. 'The poison had been administered, and it would mean nothing were I to confess. So I said nothing. You went on to cast your suspicions across your officers as I knew you would. For what was I that night it happened, but a quiet, dutiful wife? A mere attendant, helping Vindex by passing around the broth bowls. Then, after it happened I was simply a carer, standing vigil by Lactantius' sick bed… feeding him weak doses of the poison every day to keep him in the abyss of unconsciousness. During my youth in Syria I saw many die thanks to that mixture. I learned how to make it for myself back then.'

My eyes closed over, recalling the junior medicus' tale of the grain magnate in Antioch, his sudden illness and eventual death. So blank her face had remained as the young healer had spoken of the theory. So blind had I been. Something deep in my chest snapped then, and I almost sobbed. 'Why?'

'I learned the recipe not as a weapon, but as a shield. For I always felt – given the bleak history of imperial families – that a time would come when I would need it.' Her eyes became moist as she spoke. 'Valeria's spy was in your camp for some time – ever since you first arrived at Ravenna. He caused minor disputes among the legions, but nothing more. Frustrated, he came to me, asked if I could help him. And indeed I could, for there were opportunities only I could see. Lactantius was the only one capable of keeping your legions from erupting against one another.' Her lips quirked in a tight gulp, badly disguising sadness. That was something, at least. 'I saw an opportunity to spare the world another campaign of graves and blood, to prevent this finale from ever happening. I hoped your army might disintegrate on the road south, that you might be forced to retreat... that you and my brother might yet find a future without war.'

'So it was for peace that you poisoned our old friend?' I let a horrible laugh slide from my lips. 'You drape a pretty veil over an ugly bride, Fausta.'

'He is alive, isn't he?' she hissed back at me, standing, her fists balled at her sides. 'When it became clear that my plan was not going to prevent you from reaching Rome, I stopped feeding him the weakened poison and instead administered a remedy. That is why he is well again.'

I batted my chest. 'I nearly died in the Apenninus passes, so distracted were we by the religious unrest. In Spoletium too.'

She sighed hotly. 'There are many widows and weeping mothers and fatherless children who wish you had. For then the war would have ended. One death that could have spared so many others. You are a hero, Constantine.' She spat the word like a fatty lump. 'Isn't that what heroes do – put the lives of others before themselves?'

I felt a great rage build within me, almost as great as the sadness in there – for those words of hers could never be taken back.

She strode towards me then, her arms open, and for an absurd moment I thought she meant to take me in an embrace. But then she jolted suddenly, snatching my dagger from my belt, turning the tip upon her belly and pressing the hilt into my palm then holding it there. She stared up into my tear-blurred eyes and I into hers, glassy. I felt the blood pound in her veins and in mine. A mocking harmony.

I tried to pull my hand from the weapon. 'So shy?' she hissed, gripping my wrist with her nails to keep it there, drawing blood. 'You have trekked halfway across the empire, dragging thousands of souls with you, to hunt down and destroy my brother. You have turned Italia into a land of graves. All because of your pride, because of twisted words you supposedly threw at each other.'

'He tried to have me killed!' I shouted over her.

'So did I,' she blared back with an iron confidence. 'Remember the night I sat astride you with steel at your throat?' Though her words dripped with derision, she was shaking with nerves.

'That was different!' I snapped.

'Maybe. But perhaps I should have gone through with it

and then this war would never have begun. But begun it has, and the coming battle will end it. Throughout all of this, I never cared about who might win. Only the consequence mattered to me: that for one to triumph, the other must die. You told me at Verona it need not be like that. But do not dare tell me that is still the case. In the coming clash, you or my brother will perish. If it is you who falls, I will not weep, for it will mean that the world will be spared your future ambitions,' she rasped, pulling the dagger closer until the tip was pressing through her robe.

'And Crispus?' I seethed. 'You would wish him robbed of his father?'

She blanched at that, then shook her head as if to get rid of a persistent wasp. 'Why do you pursue my brother to this bloody end, when you are too cowardly to do the same with me? Now you know that it was me who tried to sabotage all your efforts to come here to Rome. Am I to be forgiven for that too?' she said, pulling the tip of the dagger even closer. I could feel the wetness of new blood. Her blood, running along one of my fingers. And then the splash of a tear on my wrist – mine or hers, I could not tell. 'Now I have told you that I hope you lose tomorrow, am I still to be spared? Am I? I am to live while my brother must feel the wrath of your armies?' She pulled the dagger sharply towards her. 'Kill me!'

In a surge of fright, I threw her off. The dagger clattered across the tent, red at the tip. Her robes were blotted with blood at the waist. It was only a small cut, but it shook me more than some of the grievous battle wounds I have seen in my time. I backed away from her. 'I am already locked in one nightmare, doomed to fight to the death with your brother, a man I once loved. Do not cast me into another.'

'Doomed? I think not. These were all choices of yours, Constantine.' She laughed without humour. 'Too afraid to kill me. Too prideful to spare my brother, to admit this war should never have happened.'

I backed towards the tent flap. She paced towards me as I went, pointing her bloody fingernails at me. 'I know you better than anyone, Constantine. I know that you will never turn around, never stop making war. The seed of love I spoke of at Verona is now dead, crushed by the things I have seen on this "glorious" campaign of yours. In its place rises a dark and ugly weed – a weed you sowed... and that one day you will reap.'

With a rush of goatskin I backed through the tent flap and outside. I stood there, panting in the night air like a man who had just woken from a deep nightmare. Sentries nearby tried desperately to look anywhere but at me. The nearest of them – who had clearly heard everything – pretended to be counting the hairs on his forearm.

I heard something then: a jaunty voice from the medicus tents. It was old Lactantius singing – terribly – to cover up the sound of our angry words. It was a ditty about a green goose from Gythion, and Crispus giggled at every silly line. What were those two doing up at this hour? Had we woken them too? A deep groan slid from my lips. I wondered if the old man had heard Fausta's confession. I hoped not, but suspected he had.

In a stupor, I trudged back to my tent. All the way, I saw flashes of the campaign – the butchery in the north, the massacre at the coast road, the bloody streets of the cities all the way here. I thought of Maxentius. What had we created, if not a horrible parody of the persecutions we both hated? And one thing Fausta had said rang in my ears, over and over: *The seed of love is now dead. In its place rises a dark and ugly weed – a weed you sowed… and that one day you will reap.*

I did not understand what she meant by that. But by all the gods I would, just as she swore.

★ ★ ★

It is always an intense thing, waking on the morning of battle and contemplating what lies ahead. Yet when the fiery wings of dawn spread across my camp, I was still staring at the same spot on the ceiling of my tent that I had been gazing at all throughout the night. Instead of rested and ready, I felt tired and anxious. Part of me wondered if this was how condemned men feel as they wake on their final day. Ahead lay the chance to win the greatest prize in the world… but at what cost?

The sound of crunching boots swept past my tent: the buccinators, rising in preparation to issue their dawn trumpet call. Familiar, almost comforting sounds for any soldier well-used to life on the march. Yet this time, these heralds of the new day felt like a cold hand twisting my guts. For there could be no doubting it now: we had come to it, after all these years. No more fiery insults, posturing, ploys or deliberation. The soil of Latium would be sown with bones and doused with blood today. That was what it had come to, after all this time. This time, there was nowhere left for Maxentius to run.

The trumpets sounded and I rose, annoyed by the slight tremor in my limbs from last night's wine and lack of sleep. So I placed forefinger and thumb together as Lactantius had taught me many years ago and I breathed, deeply and slowly, until my mind drained of the storm of thoughts in there. A soldier who goes into battle distracted is fighting two enemies, after all.

I washed briskly using a small basin of water on a table, then dressed in my boots and tunic. A slave entered with a jug of fruit water and a spiced, baked carp on a silver plate – gifted to me by the Governor of Assissium. I stared at this rich man's meal as if it was cursed. 'Today, I am a soldier. I will eat soldier-bread,' I said, sending him away with the fare and lifting hard tack from a leather bag on the floor. While officers shouted and the clatter of men equipping themselves filled the air outside, I ate alone. I thought again of the imaginary condemned man at his final meal as I chewed the tasteless hard tack, but not for long. My eyes drifted to the spot upon which Maxentius had been last night. Perhaps we *were* fools – no better than Diocletian, Galerius and Severus – for letting it to come to this but what matter either of those things? Neither would change the present and the shared destiny that hovered in both of our near futures like an angry crow demanding one of our bodies as carrion.

I set the hard tack down and took a good gulp of cold water, then rose and approached the chest and stand holding my armour. An attentive body servant entered and helped me buckle on my bronze scale jacket, and I drew on my swordbelt. The man used a bronze cloak pin fashioned in the shape of a small crossbow to fasten my bear cloak across my shoulders. The smell of oil and steel, of leather and wool, evoked a thousand memories of battles past. I cupped my jewelled battle helm underarm, my fingertips tracing the scrapes and scars of war that could not be polished out. I closed my eyes and took three slow, deep breaths then stepped outside into the sunshine and the mild morning.

The two Cornuti standing guard there shifted aside, beat

fists on their chests and threw their hands up in salute. 'Imperator!'

All at once I saw the goings-on in the camp: flashes of steel, of bright pennants being prepared and musclebound war horses nickering and trotting to and fro. Men silhouetted by the sun in one direction and shining like silver in the other. Songs rose from the various units but – blessedly – there was harmony. *Concordia!* The symbol of the sun had solved the impossible riddle.

Snorting and a padding of hooves sounded just behind me. 'Domine.' A stable hand saluted and gave me the reins of the black stallion bedecked in a silver scale apron and bronze-plated mask. Just as I was about to mount, a light padding of feet sounded behind me.

'Father!' Crispus cried. He hugged me. Damn my armour, for I could not hug him back. Instead, I fondly brushed his cheek with my thumb. I could feel her gaze on me the whole time. Fausta stood back, arms folded, face pale. When she called on Crispus, the lad went running to her. Somehow I knew it would always be the way.

I climbed into the saddle, resting my helm on one of the four leather horns that held me in place. I gazed back at my wife and lad for a short time then realised there were no words that would suffice, so I heeled the beast around and walked him towards the assembling legions.

'The emperor is ready to lead us to battle,' a herald called from somewhere behind me.

The shout was like the spark that lit a forest fire. All across the sea of tents and campfires, men rose, turned to see I had emerged and thrust their hands and spears into the air in salute, my generals too, amidst some tactical conversation. Priests of all kinds, servants, slaves too.

'Imperator!' The cry reverberated around the sky of Latium like a thunderclap. I walked solemnly through them all and towards the camp's southern palisade, for the last leg of my great journey. A draconarius fell in behind me, a low moan of wind passing through the fearsome standard. Batius, Krocus, Hisarnis and Ruga shouted and screamed orders then joined me. Soon I felt the ground shake as the regiments rose and moved with me. I led them through the camp's southern gate and we spilled onto the plain: many banners – reds, greens, blues, golds, all fluttering in the gentle autumn wind; infantry and horse bedizened in steel, all holding the fresh crimson and gold sun shields they had decorated together last night – each resembling the strange light in the sky we had all seen, the moment we had all shared. Free of the camp's confines, the legions began to form up in a broad column, the cavalry their screening wings.

As they fell into place, I gazed into the southern haze, spotting the pontoon bridge Maxentius' engineers had completed during the hours of darkness, just a short way west from the smashed stumps of the Milvian Bridge. The roped-together galleys had been stripped of their masts and rigging, and were anchored side by side, facing upriver.

A horrible thrill raced across my skin when the morning haze beyond the bridge of boats began to flicker. Sunlight on iron. A huge glittering mass, endless, roiling. An army approaching from Rome. The great army of Maxentius.

With a clatter of distant hooves and boots, they reached and poured across the pontoon bridge, over the Tiber and onto the northern banks like quicksilver. On and on the Maxentians crossed, spreading out along that far end of the plain. I had no way of counting the masses from this distance but even from here I could see we were significantly outnumbered. Rumours of his advantage had not been exaggerated. No wonder he had chosen to march out and face me!

The foremost waves of his sea of men moved forward a short way and halted, a river kink shielding their right flank, with the southern stretches of the tufa range anchoring their left. On and on more poured across the bridge, filling the space behind the front ranks. It took nearly an hour before slowly, steadily, they settled, like a calm, sparkling sea. No sign of Daia's standards, thankfully, but even if that eastern cur had been there, he would have struggled to find room on this plain for his lot.

From across the meadows that would be today's killing ground, a distant echo of some homily rose and fell on the gentle wind, punctuated by booming cheers from the Maxentians.

'How do you see it, Domine?' Batius asked, his big craggy face regarding the colossal force arrayed before us. 'I see at least two of them for every one of us.'

'We could anchor here,' suggested Krocus, 'use the camp to shield our backs and have our riders protect the flanks.'

'No,' I said quietly. 'I did not come here to cower. The men's spirits are high. They all believe in me and in the cause. All the way here we have struck hard and fast... and won. It would quash their morale to suddenly, at the last, become defenders.' I stroked my chin, evaluating the Maxentian lines carefully. Different regiments stood out here and there. Threats, opportunities. 'Spread the legions out to match the Maxentian front,' I said quietly. After a din of boots, trumpet calls and hectoring cries, my legions fell quiet again, rearranged. Next, I called over my shoulder to the draconarius. 'Bring the cavalry to the left.'

'Are you sure? We cannot strike their flanks, Domine,' the

cavalry officer tried to complain. 'They are protected by the terrain.' I heard a fair few among the ranks begin to voice their doubts too. So I heeled my battle stallion around to face them, trotting along their front, meeting the eyes of as many as I could.

'Do you see the glow of our enemy in the south?' I said as I went. 'Do you hear the distant chatter of their steel?'

I saw them bristle with anticipation, rise with awe at my words, the doubtful murmuring chased away.

'What do you think they see here?' I said, extending my arms as if to pose the question to every one of them. 'I see heroes who have marched from distant Gaul, Britannia and Hispania! I hear the beating hearts of lions!' I rapped a fist against my breastbone, my scale vest clanking. 'Have we not toppled the cities and routed the armies of our enemy at every turn so far? And now at this last mile, are we not stronger than ever? The sun glows over us. It speaks to me still, tells me of its strength'—I pointed my spear first at the sky, then at one end of my line, before I swept it across the front of sun-emblem shields—'of yours! I look at you and I *know* this day will be ours. So lift your weapons. Charge your lungs with sweet breath and march with me... to battle... to victory!'

There was a moment of utter silence and a sea of wide eyes... and then they exploded, as one, in the most thunderous cry I have ever heard. Tears streaked craggy and scarred faces, mouths stretched wide, fists beat chests, spears rapped on shields and steeds reared up and whinnied. I swear the Maxentian army in the south fell silent. I lifted my helm from the saddle horn and pulled it on, the brow band casting my eyes in shade, the sun-warmed metal cheek guards and aventail firmly caressing my skull.

'Now bring the cavalry to the left,' I repeated to the draconarius in a drawl. This time he did not question my order. As the riders rumbled over, I took my place with them. I raised my spear and the eyes of the many standard bearers and musicians watched, breaths held. When I chopped the spear-hand down, hundreds of banners rose, the trumpets blared, and we walked to war.

We moved across the plain in a fast, drumming march. Batius led the Cornuti in the centre, Krocus the Regii on the right. I rode at the head of the cataphracti on the left – a three-hundred-strong wedge like a silvery spearhead with the thousand equites serried behind in a stout column. Moments after we set off, the Maxentian masses rippled into life too, edging north to meet our advance, careful to keep the river kink and the bluffs at their flanks.

We drew to within half a mile and I could hear, see – even smell – the Maxentians clearly. There were scale-clad Praetorians – his steely centre. Thousands of them. Ancient legions arranged in thick iron blocks filled out the centre alongside the Praetorians. The most notable were the Herculia – one-time guardsmen of Galerius, now Maxentius' men, wrapped in bronze cuirasses, draped in black and blood-red cloaks, a soaring eagle on each shield. Moorish horsemen too, waiting in packs of many thousands on the Maxentian right. I even saw the gaunt, bloodshot-eyed Moorish prefect who had taunted me with the heads of my men on the approach to Saxa Rubra. A barked order rang out from within the Maxentian lines and for a moment, I thought thunder had pealed some way distant. But no, it was the almighty boom of many thousands of shields and spears clacking into place as his front line braced, advancing more slowly. An impenetrable wall of steel. No way through and no room to flank as my officers had protested. They rose in a low, baritone song of war, some in the rear ranks, nearer the Tiber banks, banging on drums and rattling their spear hafts on the ground. I felt my heart throb in my throat, heard the blood crashing in my ears, felt the moisture drain from my mouth and an invisible hand squeeze on my bladder as I beheld these colossal steely jaws waiting to grind me to pieces.

Fear not, Fausta, I thought – stricken with doubt, once again the condemned man, this time on his final steps – *for your brother will come to no harm today – unless he pulls a muscle when he and his armies are carrying my corpse from the field!*

A soldier scampered across our advancing front, from the centre. 'A message, Domine, from Tribunus Batius. He says you should drop behind the first infantry line, for safety and morale.'

I looked over to our centre, caught the big man's eye. Doubts began attacking me from every angle. So once again I placed forefinger and thumb together, inhaled deeply, and fixed my gaze on what lay ahead. 'I led you all here, and so I will lead you today. Keep the legions well-spaced – match our front to his to preserve our flanks,' I insisted as tight cries and final commands rose from both forces.

Another barking command rang out from the Maxentian lines as we drew to within three hundred paces. An enemy archer regiment shuffled to attention. Several thousand bows were cocked skywards and the judder of stretching bowstrings followed. 'Hooold…' the archer commander blared, one hand raised, his head dipped and his eyes trained on me.

'Domine, drop back!' Batius roared at me from our centre.

'I will weather the storm with my soldiers,' I burred back at him.

'Loose!' a Maxentian commander bellowed. At once, the sky dulled as many thousands of arrows leapt into the air. My stomach felt like a writhing sack of snakes as the hail reached its high point, then turned and plunged down towards us. I dipped my head just in time. *Clang*, a shaft ricocheted from my helm. All around me rose a din of iron tips on mail and scale, threaded by the wet, unctuous sound of missiles plunging into gaps in armour and unprotected flesh. From the edges of my eyes I saw men in my lines halt, spasm and sink to their knees. Seven of my precious cataphracti fell, one horse struck in the leg, another taking an arrow on the iron plate mask, near the eye – enough to panic the creature and cause it to throw its rider. 'Hold the line!' Batius screamed, my legions and my cavalry continuing to advance in time.

One hundred paces. Ninety, eighty... as the archers nocked and drew again, I scoured the wide and deep Maxentian front, searching for the missing scale in the armour, the merest hint of weakness. *Every suit of armour has a weakness*, my father hissed from the vaults of memory. The central legions and Praetorians were a shell of shields, pricked with deadly lances. No horse would charge a spear line. The guard cavalry on the right, opposite my cataphracti, seemed impossibly numerous. Those damned Moorish horsemen between the guard cavalry and the infantry centre were equally closely packed. Deadly, swift and... it was like a flash of divine light, as I realised *they* were the weak spot. They were skirmishers, and here there was no space for them to use their advantage of lightness and speed as they had done with their endless harrying attacks on the road to Rome.

'Cataphracti,' I cried as I watched the next volley of deadly hail rising, '...with me!'

With a shrill, sputtering song of a cavalry trumpet – like the heartbeat of a walking man suddenly compelled to sprint – we burst from a walk into a gallop, riding hard in a wedge, arrowing for the Moors. At this sudden jolt of urgency, whistles, drums and trumpets spat and sputtered from both sides. I saw the gaunt Moorish prefect's face twist and contort as he tried to work out what his next order should be. Only when we drew to twenty paces did he realise this was no feint or looping raid to merely throw javelins at them.

'Brace... *brace!*' he howled over our storm of hooves. At the same time, the low, confident Maxentian song faltered.

I dipped forward in my saddle, levelled my spear, the riders with me at the tip of the wedge screaming in a frenzy, plumes and banners streaming in the wind of the charge.

I trained my spear on the luckless Moorish prefect, and with a stark crack, a sharp jolt on my spear arm and a burst of blood mizzle, he was gone. We plunged deep into the enemy lines. Chaos reigned: whinnying, screaming, weapons whacking into flesh, bursting heads and limbs spinning free of bodies, horses rolling, hooves flailing, enemy riders peeling from the saddle, hacked and cleaved from shoulder to gut. Red madness all around me as I carved into their midst. Moments later the rolling thunder of shield against shield exploded over the Tiber's banks as the two infantry centres met with a shrill storm of screams. Hot blood spray hit me square in the face as I ploughed on deep into the Maxentian right, hurling my spear into the chest of a brutish Herculian as I tried to guide my crack horsemen into the flank of the enemy infantry centre at a lethally oblique angle.

I saw him then, some way back and screaming orders at his Praetorians, clad in golden armour and an emperor's cloak. Maxentius reared on his horse, his eyes fixed on me like a huntsman. The winter breath of all the shades we had created during this war crawled across my flesh. I snatched a replacement spear from a wounded Maxentian, dipped in my saddle and drove into his masses, cutting through steel and flesh towards him.

The Battle for Rome had begun.

30

MAXENTIUS

The Milvian Bridge, 28th October 312 AD

I watched, heart pulsing fear into my throat. I knew without a doubt that my forces outnumbered those of Constantine considerably but what historians and playwrights fail to comprehend is that from the view of a horseman or foot soldier in the field, a sea of men is just a sea of men, regardless of numbers. That was what we were. Around, before and behind me: a sea of men in Praetorian blue and white, the madder-red and plain linen of legionaries, the black and red of the Herculia, the dun and browns of southern auxiliaries, and everywhere the flashing bronze and steel. And across the gap in the field another sea. A horribly uniform one.

The painting of the shields the previous night now came clear in the morning light, and its reason hammered nails of fear into my heart. He had achieved Concordia in a way I had striven to manage for years, and had forged it into a blade he could wield. I had to admire the simplicity of what the clever bastard had done.

Every shield across that field was painted with a burst of light. Some maintained their tribal colours behind it, some the traditional red of the old legions, some odd barbarian designs, and most had some kind of tailored image to suit them: an owl of Minerva for the Romans of the true gods, a Chi-Rho for the Christians, some boar-like design for the Germanics. But each and every one had that bright sunburst. Every man might be of a different people with his own faith and culture, but each was bound as a brother to those beside him by that glorious flash of sunlight on every shield. I knew damn well what that sun was. It was Constantine. He was on every shield and in every heart.

So my nerves began to fray, for numbers can only carry a battle so far.

His force was so disparate and hotchpotch, yet they were a single blade with a single purpose, driven by a single will. I knew then that there would be no victory for me on that field without the total annihilation of the enemy, for a force with that sun in their heart was going to fight to the very last man.

I wished the same could be said of my massive army. No matter how hard I tried, the Christian officers in my army still regarded their traditional brethren as somehow different and less, while those who followed the gods of Rome clung to a certain mistrust of the Nazarene followers. As for the bulk of the men? They still kept to their own units and faiths, with little or no intermixing and precious few signs of unity. They deployed as ordered, but there could be no doubt that they lacked that accord I could see in my old friend's army. Indeed, the low battle hymn – a homily to Mars – that rose from our ranks was carried only on the voices of the Praetorians and the black-and-red-clad Herculia, and not even all of them, for the Christians would have no part in such pagan praise. At least they'd had the sense not to begin their own Nazarene battle songs in competition.

I sat tall in my saddle, a shining figure even among my

glittering forces. Volusianus had urged me to wear a dulled and practical panoply, largely, I think, to make me less of a target for the enemy. Zenas had urged me to wear a gaudy creation of gold and gems like some eastern potentate. I had settled on that very same armour I had worn many years ago when Severus had come to Rome with his army, intent on taking my city from me, and had been whipped across the Anio. My shining bronze Augustan cuirass of gods and mythical beasts sat atop my subarmalis of purple and white leather. A purple cloak hung draped across my back and my horse's hindquarters, and I had forgone a helmet in favour of a simple soldier's hat, proving my fearlessness and allowing my expression to give the men heart. That latter might have been a mistake as the nerves continued to get the better of me.

I peered at that mass moving towards us across the field. Like us, they were jammed into the killing area, bound on the east by the steep banks of the wide, fast Tiber and on the west by the high bluff, topped by the mausolea and monuments on the Via Flaminia. Below the bluffs, facing my veteran legions was a force of horse supported by irregular infantry. In the centre, moving on my Praetorians, were the bulk of his legions and auxilia, and above that fast-flowing torrent and its steep banks, our main cavalry forces faced one another.

The enemy closed inexorably, approaching the moment when two armies would unleash death on an unprecedented scale. I found myself praying to Mars and Minerva, to Jove and to Hercules, and once even to the Christians' Jewish god, for deliverance here.

'They are so powerful,' I breathed.

Beside me, a tribune snorted. 'They are half our number, Domine.'

I simply nodded, speculating whether it could be that easy.

I wondered when Volusianus or Zenas, or perhaps Ancharius Pansa, would give the signal to engage, for surely we would not all stand braced and wait for the inevitable? Surely we would charge them with our superior numbers? The signal came not from us, though, but from across the field among the enemy forces. The enemy pace increased, and I thought I noticed his flanking cavalry begin to move ahead slightly.

In answer, the tribune in overall command of my auxiliary archers gave the command to loose. I have never entirely understood how archers are capable of effective attacks from the rear of a force without accidentally raining death down upon their fellows in the front line in the process, but I have to give them their due, for they sent a shiver up my spine with their efficiency.

A black cloud of shafts like a murmuration of starlings hissed over our heads from the auxilia in the rear ranks of the main force. I had seen arrow clouds before, but never on this scale. *Rome* had never seen a force on this scale fielded in her countryside. For precious heartbeats the sky went black, the cold sunlight almost entirely blotted out with missiles, the advancing forces below driven into gloom. The slither of arrows was a deafening hiss that overlaid all other sounds, drowning out even the praising of Mars in the army's centre.

I saw the enemy lines falter then, and for a moment hope eclipsed the growing uneasiness in me. Men and horses fell, sprouting shafts and fountaining blood, shrieking and whinnying, bellowing and gurgling, their compatriots forced to stomp across the stricken men in the thick press of bodies. If we could keep up such momentum, perhaps their unity of spirit would break and then it would be merely a matter of numbers.

Like a man who needs to know the door is shut behind him, I turned in my saddle, looking past the rows of legionaries and the auxilia beyond them, into the distance, back south-west. I couldn't see what I was looking for. In fact, I couldn't really see past the sea of soldiers, let alone to the bridge of boats that led back across the Tiber. I certainly couldn't see my rearguard. Stationed at an important meeting of roads just to the north of the now-demolished Milvian Bridge stood a solid force of infantry, auxilia and horse, positioned carefully to prevent the possibility of Constantine's having sent some unseen force out during the night to the north to come down the Via Flaminia and fall upon our rear. It was my safeguard and, with the numbers we had fielded, the loss of manpower from the main force was negligible.

As the archers nocked for a second volley, my eyes slid back to the enemy, and I wondered whether the worry about being hit in the rear was fanciful. There was a lot more to worry about directly in front of me. Volusianus had said again and again this was a narrow, unforgiving field of battle where tactics and clever manoeuvres would count for little, where two forces would march into one another and secure the day by pure mettle and stamina.

Even as I wavered between confidence and fear the true battle began. That large cavalry force on the river side, my right flank, suddenly burst into life at a blaring horn and a bellowed command from a glittering figure, and began to pull ahead of the marching forces, pushing into a gallop.

Constantine.

It had to be him.

A figure in brilliant and gleaming armour, every bit the shining sunbeam he had become on the shields and in the hearts of his men. Typical of my old friend. The man who had become renowned for his bold charges against the Persians, who had fought the Germanics and leapt into a burning building without a thought for his safety to save a terrified boy. *My boy...*

It could only be Constantine. While I sat between the first and second blocks of my infantry along with officers, signallers, musicians and flag bearers, waiting for my commanders to issue the commands that would lead to combat, Constantine was at the forefront amidst his riders, leading the charge. Once again I had to admire the fearless bastard.

'To the right flank,' I shouted to my officers. 'The cavalry.'

'There is no danger, Domine,' a tribune responded. 'Our riders outnumber them, and it is surely a feint.'

I nodded, hoping his confidence was well-founded. The right-hand side of the infantry block behind which I sat was filled with the serried ranks of the Herculia. They would move for no man, armed and armoured heavily and trained well. Beyond them were the fierce and feral Africans – Moorish cavalry who were champing at the bit to kill Constantinian riders. And at the extreme right, packed between the Moors and the river, were my heavy cavalry. A solid force, as the tribune had noted. There was nothing to fear.

So why was I so nervous?

The answer came swiftly. No matter what the haughty officers beside me said, it was the atmosphere rising from the men that had made my skin prickle. There was a sudden sense of urgency and even fear among those swarthy Moorish riders, and the song of the legions had died away, stilled in every throat by the anticipation of something I had not spotted.

Then it happened. As the advancing Constantinian cavalry

closed at breakneck speed, they formed into a new shape. A wedge. I had the sudden image of a knife in a slab of butter.

Constantine's cavalry were cataphracti, armoured from head to toe, their horses clad in similar fashion, with strong lances. Fearsome, deadly units Rome had learned to fear among the Parthians and had adopted for her own. They were the knife and, like a knife, if they hit my heavy cavalry or my densely packed ranks of Praetorians or Herculia it would blunt. The Moorish cavalry were not so lucky. They were skirmish riders, lightly armoured. It occurred to me only now, when it was too late, that the commander who had positioned them there had either been blind or monumentally stupid. They were no match for heavily armoured cataphracti.

I watched with horror as my old friend's cavalry, forged into a deadly tip, angled directly for the Moors. The officers did what they could. The Moorish commanders braced their riders for the coming cataclysm and the heavy cavalry tried to advance to create a shield of armour in front of the Moors. They were too late.

Constantine's cavalry wedge hit the Moors and drove in deep like an arrow punching into unprotected flesh. Even from my limited viewpoint I could see the terrible effect of the charge. Men were literally thrown into the air. The Moors were hit like a stack of logs by a runaway cart. Their lines bent, buckled and gave in a heartbeat, and Constantine's cavalry were in among my men. Their angle had also brought them into contact with the Herculia, as was evidenced by the fact that the entire centre juddered for a moment, their line faltering momentarily as they met the horsemen's head-on charge. At least they stood a chance.

I swear I could see the air filling with a mist of blood spray over on that flank. I looked around me in astonishment.

No senior officer was bellowing commands. The standards remained still and the horns unblown. The attack had been so unexpected and so violent and effective that it had seemingly robbed my commanders of their wits. Where were my three stalwarts when I needed them?

The truth was that all three of them had troubles of their own. Ancharius Pansa led the Herculia somewhere in front of me, where they were now reeling from the enemy cavalry wedge, yet attempting to hold the advancing line. Volusianus was at the centre left, commanding the Praetorians as he had so often done during our time together, keeping the line steady and the spirit strong as they faced Constantine's infantry. And Zenas? He led the Equites Singulares, my mounted elite guard, who were currently in the block behind the broken Moors. Zenas would be making sure his men kept morale and formation and that the Moors didn't break through them and flee to the west.

No one with real wit could take control, and those who could do so lacked the strength for it, seemingly. In a single, glorious moment, I was Trajan, or Germanicus, or Marcus Aurelius, battle-worthy emperor of Rome, commanding the field. I felt twenty generations of emperors flowing through my veins as I rose in my saddle, sword held aloft, drawing the attention of officers and signallers around me.

'The Herculia are pressured. Open ranks, Praetorians file to the right and support. Signal the Moors to withdraw and reform in the second rank.'

Galvanised into action by a welcome commanding and authoritative voice, the signals and orders rang out. Fresh heart flooded into the men, and chanting began to rise from the central infantry blocks once more. Leaving them to it, I knew what I had to do. I could see that gleaming golden figure of my enemy amidst the crush and violence of the cavalry, and I knew he was angling for me, having spotted me. I had to meet him equal to equal. I had to lead my cavalry.

Wheeling my horse as the army reformed under enemy pressure, I thundered off at an angle towards the river, at the rear of the first block of horse. With space opening up, I spotted Zenas, his face contorted into a furious snarl, unable to reach the enemy for those very Moors who were being cleaved in droves.

'The Moors, Domine...' he began urgently, gesturing forwards with a clean, gleaming blade.

'I know. Constantine is there himself, leading their horse. The Moors are pulling back.'

And they were, in surprisingly good order. Caught between the Herculia and the heavy horse, they were stepping back slowly, allowing space to open up between them and the aggressor. There was a risk here, albeit a calculated one. If Constantine felt confident enough, he could drive on with his horse, breaking deep into our lines. He had routed the Moors and they had pulled back. Every commander of a wedge dreams of breaking through the enemy force into the unprotected and soft rear of the army.

But to do so would have spelled the end for Constantine. He might stand a small chance of causing a general rout in doing so, but if my officers and men could hold it together he would instead find himself trapped by the rear block of reserve cavalry, boxed in between them, the heavy horse on the flank, and the Herculia toward the centre. No commander wants his force surrounded on three sides.

Constantine was no fool. He had lost sight of me in the struggle and even as the Moors withdrew he remained at the front, still hacking at the Herculia and now at the heavy cavalry too, trying to make the flank crumble and collapse, and probably trying to spot me once more in the press. Well he would see me soon enough.

I couldn't see the clash as the infantry finally met from my new position at the rear of the first blocks on the flank, but gods, I could hear it. There is no sound to match the meeting of heavy infantry on equal terms. The entire valley echoed to the grate, clang and ring of metal on metal, a sound like Vulcan's hammer over and over again, and threading through the aural tapestry: the screams of men. I was just grateful I couldn't smell it. Here, between front and rear cavalry blocks all I could really smell was horses. It's a pungent enough odour, certainly, but it beats the smell of butchered men any day.

'Form to fit the ranks,' I told Zenas, somewhat unnecessarily. He had seen what I'd done and was already anticipating the next step. Where the Moors had withdrawn and were now moving back to reform, the Equites Singulares would take their place. The bodyguard were no skirmishers, being instead armed and armoured for heavy mounted warfare. These men would give Constantine and his heavy riders the opposition we needed, and even now the flank was weakening, back-stepping out of the press. We needed to bolster them.

The Equites moved forward at a horn blast, riding into that gap even as the last of the Moors pulled out of it. I slipped in among the front lines, and Zenas shook his head.

'No, Domine, you can't risk…'

'I can do whatever that fucking sun-baked Illyrian peasant can do,' I snarled. 'Forward my heroes of Rome.'

With a roar, the horse guard raced forward to meet the enemy. Despite my determination to be among them like a proper soldier-emperor, I did not complain when they manoeuvred on the ride such that I suddenly found myself in the third line of the horsemen. There is a difference between bravery and stupidity, after all.

Our flank's front lines had lost cohesion, and we could see it now as we moved in to fill the gap left by the Moors. In desperation, worrying that the enemy would drive that wedge deep into our lines, the Herculia and heavy horse had both expanded into the gap. The fighting there was fierce, Constantine's cataphracti cleaving and spearing men with such wild abandon that the ground was steadily growing into a hummock of corpses, and riders were being cautious how their mounts stepped.

Zenas had the horn blown once more, and that carnage at the front faltered for just a moment as they all turned to see me and my block of white-clad riders bearing down on them.

'Roma aeterna!' bellowed an optio, and the call was taken up by the entire unit. Eternal Rome. A fitting battle cry for my army. We might be Roman, Italian, African and Moorish, and there might be followers of Mithras or the Jewish divinity as well as our old gods, but one thing we all fought for was Rome. *The saviour of Rome shall prevail*, the Sibylline books had said, and that was the knowledge carried deep in the heart of every man in my army.

We fought for Rome.

I caught sight once more of that gleaming helm as my Equites Singulares crashed into the cataphracti and the business of true killing began.

31

CONSTANTINE

The Milvian Bridge, 28th October 312 AD

Blood, everywhere. Bronze and iron scales puffing in the air with every strike of my lance through a Maxentian chest. The whistling wind of our still-undampened charge, the screaming, whinnying steeds, commanders whistling and roaring, cracking shields and snapping bones, the keening of slingshot and thrum of arrows, the stink of ripped-open bellies and sweat, and all to the tune of my heart thudding like a runner's footsteps as my cataphracti wedge sliced into his infantry heart. Closer... closer. I hurled my spear into the chest of one Italian legionary, numb now to such grim and terse allegory, then tore my spatha free of its scabbard. Another few dozen ranks of men and then the Praetorian shell stood between me and *him*, but at that moment I felt invincible. I saw him edge his horse around, watching my approach with hunter's eyes, swishing his spatha twice like an expert fighter. Ready for the moment we both knew had to come. Two monsters wrestled within me: one with talons and horns, hungry for his blood, craving the finality of a victory libated with the enemy leader's blood; the other nimbate and glowing, the sun, the light, everything, keeping the horned one at bay with ferocious blows. I met his eye again, and for the merest moment, time slowed. Low groans stretched out impossibly around me, the frenzied spin of battle slowed as if caught in Saturn's hand for that heartbeat. Maxentius, my brother, my oldest friend. Oh, how the gods must have laughed to watch us carve out this path. My dilemma seemed foolish now: as if I would have a choice at all on this red and roiling sepulchral field. Here we were in battle, and one of us *would* fall. I screamed and I wept in one horrible noise, tears streaking across my face in the wind of my charge as I flexed my fingers around sword hilt.

And then it happened. The inevitable disaster that follows hubris like a shadow.

Blinded by the sight of my rival, I didn't notice the Moorish rider tracking me to my right. His mace crunched down on my shoulder. The scales there flew off in a glittering cloud and I roared aloud. It was only the cushioning of the bear fur that stopped the cudgel from tearing deep into my flesh and smashing bone, but the sheer power of the strike sent me listing in my saddle. Blades and arrows swished and spat as I tried to right myself. Before I could, another horseman – one of his Equites Singulares no less – came at me screaming, his lance held level and trained on my exposed midriff. I saw my life flash in front of me in those moments, before a sword hacked at the rider's waist from one side. The blow cut through his spine and near halved him. His screaming turned visceral as the top half of his body sagged to one side with a sound of tearing meat, exposing the horrific, pearlescent and pulsing mess of his innards. Blood puffed up from the awful wound, a mist of it settling on my face, stinging on my lips. The horse carrying him off past me, torso flailing like a rag from his still-saddled bottom half. I righted myself to see my saviour: a Primigenia legionary who had burst through the struggle of the two infantry fronts. He was now surrounded by Maxentians. In a breath, he was gone, hacked to pieces in a flurry of enemy swords. No sooner had he fallen than his killers were swamped by scores more Primigenians. The enemy centre had caved in, you see, right where the Primigenia had attacked – a second talon, like my cavalry wedge's first, deep in the enemy flesh. It was a tiny gap, but my legionaries were now swarming over their foes, stabbing down on men who had been pushed over in the press. All along the Tiber banks the two armies – some sixty thousand men – swayed and tussled, like two great dragons interlocked, biting and clawing in flashes of silver and red. I parried a strike from one Herculian on my left and stabbed down into the shoulder of another who was about to run a Primigenian through, and in doing so I nearly took a spear through the eye. A sharp twitch of my head to one side saved me, the lance streaking across the side of my helm instead, dislodging a few of the jewels embedded there.

I glanced over one shoulder to see my cataphracti still with me: scores had fallen or been pulled from the saddle and were being bludgeoned and torn to death, but we were still a wedge, still pointing in the direction of... 'Where is he?' I cried, head switching this way and that. Maxentius was gone.

'Domine!' Batius roared from somewhere in the fray. I swung round to find him, and caught sight of his big, panicked face, nearly black with blood. 'Domi—'

I did not hear the end of his shout. Because a cudgel or a mace of some sort hammered into my back. Sky and earth changed places as I fell from my steed, rolling over bloody mud and broken bodies. Dazed, I half sprang, half staggered to my feet, swinging in every direction in anticipation of attack, fending off blows and seeing – beyond the attackers – my men die in droves.

I saw Batius leading a Cornuti charge towards my position. I felt a surge of hope, a sense of safety just to see him coming to shield me as he always had. Then the big man jerked and spasmed, run through. I swear that part of my heart turned grey and died at that moment.

I watched his lips quirk in one final craggy smile, wet with blood, his eyes sparkling with tears, before he sank from view. I heard myself cry out towards him. More of a mentor to me than my own sire, an elder brother in these later years. Batius was gone.

I slashed the belly of another attacker. He fell to reveal a terrible scene, of the Primigenia being driven back out of the Maxentian lines with a concerted push of his Italian troops like fingers squeezing a boil. Worse, the enemy now pushed on out from their original line and into my legions, blood spraying in the air as they tore into the Ubii, beheading Tribunus Ruga and capturing the standard. I parried another attack and at last some of poor Batius' Cornuti men reached me. We formed a small defensive knot, perched upon a small mound of bodies. From here I saw the goings-on at the foot of the tufa hills: the First Minervia and the Eighth Augusta on my right flanks had surged against the Maxentian left, knocking his tightly packed infantry down like stacked boards then scrambling over the fallen masses. I saw Scaurus and the Petulantes and Hisarnis and the Bructeri screaming to their charges to join this push, then leading a great thrust that drove the Maxentian left back towards the riverbanks... only for a dull *buck* of highly stressed timber and twine, suddenly released, to sing out across the din of battle. For a trice, I was confused, before Scaurus' chest exploded and the ballista bolt hammered on through three more of his men. The groan and whistle of dozens more bolts rang out and Scaurus' men were ripped apart. When Hisarnis rallied his Bructeri to try to drive towards the well-positioned and partly concealed Maxentian bolt throwers, enemy legionaries rushed their flank. I saw Hisarnis sink to his knees with six or more foes spearing down into his shoulders. My finest generals were being mown down like wheat.

'Support our right!' Krocus screamed above it all. Trumpets howled and the bearded warrior led his Regii to the disaster on our right, but their departure from the centre let Maxentians forge into the Fourth Jovia whom the Regii had been supporting.

But we were undeterred. My Second Italica pitched into Maxentius' lines, their standard bearer, Genialis, lofted on the shoulders of his comrades so he could wave the Martia into the breach with them. He was streaked with blood and without a shield, but he cried across the awful din with all he had, doing just enough to alert the Martia before a spear took him full in the gut and turned the air red.

I was guilty of watching the battle around me and not spotting what was coming for me. With a judder, my Cornuti comrades were blown apart by an enemy shoulder charge. I sliced the hand from the Herculian brute, ducked the sword-cut of his comrade then swung on my heel to drive my sword up and under his armour. As he fell, I planted a boot on the thigh of his sighing corpse and tried to rip my sword free. Panic rose, for the blade was lodged and I could sense another attack coming from behind. Never would I have guessed what was about to happen.

It was like the moon rolling across the sun, a wing of

Praetorians cut through the fray. They barged and shoved even their own men as they encircled and separated me from the Cornuti, who battered and hacked and shouted in great alarm and dismay when they saw that I had been captured.

And captured I was. Hundreds of Praetorians forming this circle faced out into the battle like a palisade, and hundreds more faced inwards, trapping me inside it, their spears levelled at me. A deadly eye in a mighty storm. There were a dozen or so Cornuti and Primigenia lads in here with me, but with one cold, silent volley of close-range arrows, they fell. I twisted in every direction. No way out.

I was alone. It was over.

It was the strangest thing: an eye of stillness and calm amidst the fray, arrows, slingshot and spears whizzing above us. The order of battle fell to pieces as men fought men in clusters and packs, rolling through the red, wet earth, kicking, biting, bludgeoning and slashing. Some of my riders still drove on towards the Maxentian command, but they had lost their impetus. A hammer without the swing of a strong arm.

And here I stood within this curious Praetorian oculus. Panting, dripping with gore.

I barely noticed the swarthy figure approaching. He strode towards me through the maw of Praetorian spears. His black cloak, his tarnished, moulded cuirass and curled beard dripped with filth, his eyes were ravening. I saw that he was no ordinary Praetorian, for the ancient guards of Rome were obeying him. Their leader, I realised. I knew then there was only one man this could be: Volusianus, Maxentius' Praetorian Prefect and Consul. Throughout all of this, I had only ever heard of him and, as one does, I had formed an image of him in my head: a black raven with a beak of steel. Why was I not already dead?

'This battle sways like a fleet in a storm,' Volusianus said. He walked around me, holding his sword up like an accusing finger, the tip hovering past several points on my torso where a short, swift jab would have been fatal. 'One wave to overturn the flagship, and it will all be over.'

A shiver streaked through me: my body was beginning to cool after the frantic charge, the sweat and blood on my skin now felt like icy raindrops. 'Then make it swift,' I said, dropping my spatha and extending my arms to the sides. 'End this.'

'Oh, I will...' he said. 'One way or another.'

I stared at him, confused by the lustful smile on his lips – like a predator enjoying the taste of living blood before he bites through a major organ.

'You see, my current master is myopic to my talents. Did you know that I won Africa for him? Africa – that great and life-giving land. Without it, he would have fallen to the mob of Rome long before now, and when I led the cull of those very same ingrates on Rome's streets, all he could do was bemoan my actions. Perhaps, had I let the mob have their way, it would be me leading this army against you today instead?'

'You stand here in the Maxentian ranks, holding a sword to my gut. Is there a difference?' I spat.

He laughed. In the midst of this terrible slaughter, he found the power to laugh. 'The difference is that today I serve when I should reign.'

'Who are you to make such a bold claim?'

'Didn't people say the same about you once?' He shot back instantly with a smirk.

I bristled, but he was quick to jab the sword point closer to my torso in warning.

'The great Constantine. Always so fiery!' he chuckled. 'Perhaps, for once, you should listen. I have an offer for you,' he said.

My eyes narrowed. 'I do not negotiate with snakes.'

'Really? You were once the lackey of Galerius. You have made pacts with the likes of Licinius. Always, Constantine, you have done what needs to be done to get what you want.'

'Only a fool would presume to know a man so well at their first meeting.' I rumbled.

He smiled tightly. 'Enough of the barbed words, for time is short.' He leaned a little closer. 'With one tacit order... I can turn the Praetorians – the hardened core of this army – against Maxentius. But only at a price: that when you become Augustus... *I* will be your Caesar. I will bend my knee to you but I will be recognised as emperor of Italia and Africa.'

You are no Caesar. You will never wear the purple, I thought. I watched his top lip twitch like a hound's, angry at my hesitation. His sword hand rose as if ready to give an order to his encircling men. The archers among them nocked and drew their bows. Flashes of a thousand futures crossed my mind then, and in that instant, I heard the cries of hundreds of dying men – my own and those of Maxentius beyond this ring of steel. If I rejected his offer then I would be executed here and now, and no doubt soon after Maxentius would be cut down so this dog could take Rome for himself. At the end of this bleak day there could only be one victor: Maxentius or me... no other. I knew what I had to do. This cur and his ambitions could be dealt with afterwards. 'Do what must be done,' I growled.

His sword hand fell slowly, and his lips peeled apart in a fresh grin, ill-fitting of battle. 'It will be so.'

He turned away, black cloak swishing, calling out for his

ring of Praetorians to break up and re-join the battle in full. I felt as if I had stolen life from the clutches of Pluto.

Then a possibility struck me like a hammer striking a bell. A way for this day to end in a way neither me nor my one-time friend had imagined. 'I demand one condition: bring Maxentius to me alive. You hear? *Alive!*'

Volusianus swung round on his heel, one eyebrow raised. 'How noble,' he said, before turning away again to join the scrum of his men.

All around me, the cataphracti and legionaries clamouring to save me swarmed in and surrounded me, erupting in a great cheer of relief and triumph. Yet one look across the swaying, crimson fray and I knew it was far from over – regardless of what Volusianus chose to do.

32

MAXENTIUS

The Milvian Bridge, 28th October 312 AD

The tides of men surged around the field of battle, crashing against one another, lapping the bluff to the left and the riverbank to the right, eddying here and there as individual small skirmishes inevitably broke out amidst the grand press. The din was almost ear-splitting, and I probably had a pounding headache by that time, although it was impossible to tell through the chaos and thundering emotions in my skull. The stench was horrible, of course, but most of what I could smell was a mixture of my own fear-riddled perspiration and the damp warm wool smell from my sweat-sodden hat.

We were breaking the dangerous cavalry charge of Constantine's riders. My own horsemen were winning ground now, sealing the gap the bastard had caused with his cavalry wedge. I had even taken part to some small extent. I had bloodied my sword three times in that push and taken a narrow red line of honour across my shin for my troubles. It bothered me not. Men were suffering far worse on that day and yet still fighting.

Now that the initial danger was past and the battle had settled into this stormy swell, I drew back from the fighting a little and rose as high as I could manage in the saddle, trying to gain some semblance of understanding of how things were going on the grand scale.

It took me precious time, but I gradually came to see how things were going, and the sight was more pleasing than I had expected, given what had just happened.

We were winning.

I was no great military strategist – I knew my stuff to an extent, but not like an Arrian or a Caesar – and yet even I could see that we were winning. The numbers had been in our favour from the beginning. We had all known that the only real hope Constantine had was to somehow trick us or break our morale. I thought his new shields and the unity of his army might do it, but it seemed not. Then his surprising and well-placed cavalry charge had nearly done it again, but now that had been countered, with no small thanks to my own efforts. But he was running out of tricks, and now it was coming down to numbers at last. Even my artillery were better and more numerous than his, and they were now coming into play.

We were going to win.

The far flank, beneath that bluff, was heaved back and forth, but it was holding. The near flank we had saved and were now securing. The centre should never be in doubt, commanded by Volusianus and manned primarily with veteran legions and the gleaming Praetorian ranks. Even as I watched, things were changing there.

My heart swelled with relief as I saw the Praetorians break the enemy ranks. Suddenly they were among Constantine's men and the killing impossibly increased pace. And there, in the very midst of it, I could see Constantine himself, in his gleaming, bejewelled helm, swaddled in blood like some child of Tartarus. I watched, almost stunned, as he was unhorsed, and the Praetorians cut my old friend off from the bulk of his men. Encircled in the heart of the battle, we had him. Slowly, his men were flayed from his side, and my great enemy was gradually stripped of defence.

The emotions came thick and fast.

Joy. Constantine was captured, or even killed. The threat to my throne was over. For the first time in so many years I could return to the city in victory, finally bringing pax to Rome.

Sadness, even fear. My old friend had failed and was going to die, and for all the trouble he had brought me, I could not imagine a world in which my first and oldest friend, the man who had saved both my son and me, was dead.

Jealousy. Because it should have been me that dealt with him, and Volusianus and his Praetorians had robbed me of a meeting I had been both anticipating and dreading.

Relief. It was over...

... panic?

That was unexpected, but even as I watched, I saw something different happening. Volusianus had stopped beside Constantine in the wide ring of Praetorian steel. One might think he was an executioner, gloating. Threatening. Jeering. But I knew Volusianus. He was not that kind of man. Had he the chance to put the tip of his sword to Constantine's neck, I knew he would not hesitate for a single moment. He knew the man's death had to come and he knew it had to be swift. So why was he delaying? What was he doing?

The dreadful, horrifying, earth-shaking answer came in but a moment as the circle of men shifted and Constantine, far from falling at the end of the consul's sword, was suddenly free, moving back amidst his men. I knew what it meant instantly, but I simply couldn't wrap my thoughts around the concept. My mind wouldn't permit me to comprehend the truth.

Even as the Praetorians turned and began to move against the veterans of the Second Parthica – against *my* men – I couldn't bring myself to say it. I simply stared as the man who had been my sword arm and my strategist for all the years of this long war took Constantine's coin and betrayed me, taking my veteran guard with him. Betrayal. I had missed the signs. Oh, I'd seen his sullen resentment since the day I passed over his command and relegated him to the role of camp prefect. I'd seen the way he looked at me. The way he looked at the purple robe I wore. The signs had been there and I'd seen them, but I had not recognised them for what they were. And now my anger and my short-sightedness in not listening to him had come back to defeat me. He had warned me about Constantine and I had not listened. He had advised me about the north and I had turned away. He had demanded that I do something and I had. I had betrayed him. All the years he had served and advised and when it mattered most I had turned on him and removed from him all his power. Now he had gone to seek that power elsewhere and I would become a victim of his ambition.

I was so stunned, in fact, that I missed the first two warning shouts.

The third finally caught my attention and my head snapped round urgently, my mind still numbed with the realisation of what had happened, and what it would mean. It took precious, critical moments to spot the source of the calls, but finally my gaze fell upon Zenas. The young Christian officer, who had become as critical to my consilium as Volusianus, was pushing his way through the throng, horse forging a path like the prow of a trireme through the glassy waters of the Mare Internum. Primed with the treachery of Volusianus, my heart froze. What now? Was Zenas to betray me too?

No, he was not. Not that even my knowledge of his strict Christian ethics made me so certain. What made me sure he remained loyal was the fact that he was clearly warning me of something, and not of Volusianus, for he was shouting and gesturing, pointing to the other side, behind me, toward the rear of our lines.

I turned.

His warning saved my life, for what that was worth. I caught the blade descending towards me before I even saw the figure wielding it. Had I not heard the warning, it would have plunged into my spine above the neckline of my cuirass, unchecked. As it was, I had no time to bring my own weapon to bear, and all I could do was to throw up my arm in a desperate attempt to ward off the blow.

The pain as I took the blow on my forearm would at any other time and in any other place have been all-consuming, for it was no mere scratch. But the cancer of betrayal was eating into my heart. The realisation that a Praetorian cohort's betrayal might cause a reverse on the battlefield filled me with unassuageable fear, and the further discovery that someone meant to take my life by treachery even here amidst the heat of battle, was far too brutal to care about mere pain.

I howled, more anger than agony. The sword had torn through leather and linen and deep into the flesh, carving its own Intercisa Pass in my arm. The blow had wounded me, both physically and mentally, and continued on down, deflected from its intended target. A blow that should have killed an emperor had failed. My eyes rose from the spray of blood from my arm and beyond the swinging sword to its holder.

The squat, hideous figure of Ancharius Pansa.

My spymaster.

Another of my most trusted men.

Even in the press of battle, in that single, horrible moment so many things fell into place. I had been betrayed in the north. Ruricius had died because his officer corps had been withdrawn using the imperial seal. I had blamed Valeria in my head, for I could not see how anyone else could have used my seal. Pansa himself had personally vouched that no one else had touched the seal, but I had never realised that this meant Pansa himself, of course, had always had access. He had guarded my apartment. He had guarded the seal, by extension. Pansa had betrayed me in the north.

It could only be a conspiracy. Pansa and Volusianus, and gods knew how many of the Praetorian officers and men. Pansa attacked me the very moment Volusianus sold me out to Constantine. Two men who had been at the heart of my war, who had advised and controlled, and whom I had trusted implicitly. They must have been working together for at least a year to bring this about. I could understand Volusianus. I hated it, but I could understand it. Ambition and bitterness had mixed in the crucible of war to become betrayal and revenge. But I had never done anything to Pansa. I had held him high throughout, a senior officer and one of my familia. Yet I had said as much before: Pansa was frumentarii and their very nature meant duplicity and murder. I had even said to myself, as I organised the defence of Rome, that I could never put my full trust in him. So Volusianus had claimed the spymaster for his plot, and Pansa had gone along with it.

Volusianus had used Pansa because I had forced him out

of the light to languish in Rome, and Pansa, who could have killed me a hundred times then, had presumably been playing both sides to keep himself safe until now when, at the end, the tide had turned against me.

I felt hollow. My faithful familia had turned out to be worse enemies than my bitterest foe.

I was so stunned in fact that I almost died once more as Pansa lashed out again, this time with the knife in his other hand. I twisted out of the way with some difficulty, and the knife carved a line through the air a hair's breadth from my chest. I roared and raised my sword, but somehow there was now a Praetorian riding at me, sword levelled. I could not fight them both, and I was forced to face the guardsman now. My sword clanged against his and then shrieked and grated all along the blade as we separated, horses dancing in the little space we had. It took all my skill with the sword to find an opening on our third pass and deliver a powerful enough blow to put him down.

Pansa should have had the opportunity to take my life before I managed to turn to face him again, of course. The reason he hadn't became apparent as I spun to find him engaged in a vicious duel with Zenas, the pair of them hacking and stabbing and punching and slicing like madmen. I watched with fascinated horror as the two men battered at one another, and for a moment, I was forced to turn and face another treacherous Praetorian, though the man was felled by a blow from one of my faithful legionaries in an instant, and I could turn back to the collision of titans behind me.

I saw Pansa's last moment now, as Zenas' sword carved a deep cleft in his neck, severing the cord that holds the head up. Pansa screamed and his head snapped to the far side, as though glued to his shoulder, where it rolled back and forth as he moved.

He was done for, and the fight went out of him instantly.

Zenas turned to me and yelled another timely warning, which saved me once again. The Praetorian blade that had almost transfixed me instead severed the upper strap of my cuirass, carved a deep gouge in my side and became wedged in the bronze armour. The weapon's jamming was his end, for it was easy work then for me to slam my own sword into him. The blow was a small victory in the midst of a great failure.

It was hopeless.

The Praetorians were coming for me, and even Zenas and the few loyal legionaries nearby could do nothing about it. Logic told me that it was only a core of treason in the guard, for the numbers here were too few. Had the entire Praetorian force turned to the enemy they would have swamped us easily. Less than a cohort had come against mine, I figured, but it was enough. There were plenty of men around to kill us two defiant leaders – Zenas and myself – and with the Praetorian numbers withdrawn from my centre, our lines were failing. Soon the centre would crumble and Constantine's army would carve a path into our heart.

I knew in that moment that the battle was over.

My teeth bared into a snarl. I had been charged by Constantine's cataphracti and had survived. He had galvanised his army while mine remained fractious, yet I had survived. My closest and dearest had betrayed me, and I had survived. I would yet survive.

The battle was lost. Not the war.

A cohort or so of Praetorians had turned to the enemy, along with my senior officers, but the vast majority of the army remained loyal, and we still outnumbered Constantine. I had lost the field on the Milvian Bridge, but there was an image now in the back of my mind.

A young Constantine swung an arm through my wooden block city. He told me that I had not built my walls high enough.

But I *had*. I had built walls that could keep out the world from my city. Why in the name of the counsellor gods had I left them to fight my enemy on this evil field, where tactics and intelligence meant nothing? Why had I ignored everything I had ever learned? But another lesson had been taught to me, albeit for a high cost. I still had my walls and we could still withstand a siege.

Rome. We had to retreat to the walls. Constantine could not maintain a siege over the winter, and if my alliance held, the loathsome Daia would come to my aid. I could still win this, and should never have begun this stupid battle.

Why had I done this?

I fought down the memory of what the interpreter of the Sibylline Oracle had told me.

I denied absolute truth.

Instead, I returned my consciousness to the present and found that Zenas and I were fighting a last defence against the renegade Praetorians, with just a few loyal legionaries alongside. The army was caving in. The flanks were in panic and the centre already shouting and in partial retreat.

The battle was lost. I had to survive to take this back to Rome.

A voice cut through the din and as I parried a blow from a man who had taken an oath to protect me, I risked a momentary glance back. My heart lifted. The Equites Singulares were coming up behind, roaring their loyalty.

My horse guard, trained and, until recently, commanded by Ruricius.

The Equites hit the perfidious Praetorians like a wall of death, carving their oath into the traitors, and I found myself turned and hauled, despite all impropriety. The officers of the Equites, along with Zenas, were guiding me from the field, calling for a return to the city.

The treacherous Praetorian cohort were fighting their last now. The traitors had been undone – all but Volusianus, who was out there somewhere. My army was being ground to dust against the high bluffs and pressed against the river, where men were falling into the dark torrent, where their armour would drag them to their doom. We ran. We headed for the pontoon bridge across the Tiber, which would carry us back to Rome and the safety of her high walls.

Calls were blaring across the field now, though they were conflicting with the roar of human voices. Oddly, everything was driving the army the same way now. The din of cries and screams accompanied my men as they turned in panic and fled the field, running for safety, while the blare of horns and whistles and the shouts of officers commanded their men to do just that, but in good order, pulling back to the city.

We were in retreat, but things teetered. It was yet undecided as to whether it was a withdrawal or a rout.

As we rode for the bridge amidst the torrent of men now heading the same way, I was already putting plans in place. We would concentrate men and artillery on every gate from the Porta Flaminia to the Porta Tiburtina. We would draw lines from the Tiburtina to the river, trying to limit the enemy's access. We would prepare every bridge across the Tiber, ready to cede the Transtiberim region to the enemy should the most remote section of walls fall. I would...

We reached the bridge far sooner than I expected. It appeared all of a sudden in the press of men. Once upon a time, emperors were given space, protected by guardsmen and the awe of their position. Once upon a time, they were preceded by lictors and horns. Once upon a time, any man who came too close to an emperor risked losing his head.

As we closed on the end of the causeway bridge, I was jostled from all sides by all manner of soldiers, some of rank, some of none, some who were elite Praetorians, some legionaries from the provinces, some even African non-citizens, the slings hanging from their belts more often used for lions than men.

No one cared about propriety. No one less than me, in fact. In that press, I found that the oddest thing happened. I still wanted to get to the city and man the walls to drive away Constantine, but that had now taken second place. What was of prime concern was the desire to live. Valeria remained in the city, as did my poor second son. There might still be a future. There might still be a dynasty, but only beyond those walls, away from Constantine, and from traitors in my own court.

Next to me, Zenas gestured.

'Stay close to the centre. The timbers are wet. When we get back, I will take control of the nearest gate. Move on and secure the city.'

I barked my agreement, and we guided the nervous horses with difficulty onto the long, damp timber walkway, strung along the top of the tethered ships. All around me fleeing legionaries clumped and scraped with hobnails on timber, horses clattering and whinnying. Shields knocked and metal clinked. It was the oddest thing, for I heard all the minutiae of rout because the fleeing army was so silent in defeat. The entire bridge bowed with the current, and we had the strangest sensation of beginning to walk our horses downstream with the curve.

I didn't see or hear it happen. All I knew was that suddenly the bridge lurched sideways, downriver. People cried out in panic and my horse, already nervous and twitchy, nickered and reared twice before I could calm it enough to walk on. Instantly I regretted being mounted. Men on foot were running without having to worry about soothing a beast. And that was what was happening. Suddenly, men were running for their lives. The bridge became the setting for the worst kind of flight. Men were hurtling, climbing over one another, pushing compatriots and brothers out of the way as the natural instinct for survival kicked in. The horses danced dangerously again.

The reason was simple, and came to me in mere moments. The bridge could only be moving if one end had come disconnected. Given the way we were drifting it had to be the northern end, towards Constantine's army.

I glanced back. Whether it had been a purposeful act or sheer accident, the bridge had come free of the northern shore. Most of my army was now trapped back there on the bank beyond the river. I realised with a plummeting spirit that my chances of defending Rome against Constantine had just declined to almost nothing. I had only a fragment of my panicked army, and the rest would be cut down in short order.

There was no time to contemplate the leaden consequences of this, though. The churning, swaying bridge was moving, and with every jerk, bits of it broke free. Men were fleeing to the south bank and freedom, but those of us on the northern half of the bridge could see our haven becoming ever more remote.

There was suddenly the most horrendous cracking noise. Before I could wonder what it was, Zenas, next to me, grabbed my elbow. 'Get to the city, Domine. Rally the—'

His last words died in his throat as an arrow punched into his neck. He stared at me, but I could not look at his face, only the bloody point jutting from his throat apple. He gurgled something and lolled in his saddle.

My last friend on the field died before my eyes.

I stared.

The reason for the cracking noise I had heard became clear, then, as the entire bridge bucked and jerked. My horse reared again and I fought hard to control her. The southern edge had broken free too, now. We were mid-stream on a makeshift barge formed of ships filled with ballast, tied together.

Those ties were not to last long.

The pounding feet and hooves of the panicked men atop it broke ropes and loosened pegs and with every heartbeat a ship broke free and planks fell away into the water. The bridge was disintegrating beneath our feet. Men were desperately dropping their weapons and throwing off their helmets and heavy chain shirts, aware of what they would mean should the water claim them.

I had no idea what to do. My advisors were all gone, turned to the enemy or dead, or both. Moments later my horse was rearing again, this time beyond my ability to control. I fought merely to stay in the saddle, my eyes wide as the animal tried to unseat me right in the middle of the river. She rose up above the entire crowd, screeching, amidst the panicked men.

Oddly, I still had my sword in my hand and it was accidentally thrust into the air as though in some odd signal for a charge.

I knew it was happening. I cannot say whether I fought it or not. The latter I think. I had now lost everything, and there really was no hope. I had no allies. No officers. No army. My horse jerked and bucked once more, and I felt myself fall. I probably cried out.

It felt like forever that I was suspended in that cold air in the bitter autumn sunlight of the winter of my reign, before Father Tiber enfolded me in his arms.

Despite everything, despite knowing that it was over, nature kicked in and made me fight. As the cold, dark waters of the river claimed me, I thrashed and swam, trying to pull myself to safety. Momentarily I managed. I grasped timber and pulled, and my face broke the surface, heaving in breaths. Wild eyes took in the death of my army. I swear I could see the enemy now on the northern bank. Perhaps I even saw Constantine, for I was sure I caught the flash of gold and jewels. Then my fingers were slipping, I lost my grip and fought some more, grasping another handhold only to have hobnails drive down into my knuckles as someone stood on my hand.

I fell again, and the river swallowed me once more.

My eyes were wide open in horror and I watched as trails of tiny bubbles marked the passage of arrows through the water, some of them leaving an inky trail of blood in the deep. I saw the panicked face of a legionary plummeting past me, eyes wide and white, mouth opening and closing as though there were air to find.

Everywhere I turned as I thrashed and fought now, I saw men, horses, missiles, pieces of armour. It was the aftermath of a battle, floating slowly downwards before my eyes.

Momentarily, and don't ask me how, I broke the surface again. There were cries of victory in the air, and they had to be my old friend's. Then I was down in the black water once more, sinking, unable to rise again.

I closed my eyes.

I could feel it.

All was not lost, for there was something calling me now...

With a sad smile, I surrendered myself to the river.

33

CONSTANTINE

Rome, 29th October 312 AD

*C*ornua keened and blared in rising paeans from the towering gatehouse of Rome's Porta Flaminia as I led the *Adventus* procession in a chariot drawn by four white stallions. The ancient wards were thronged with citizens, all here to see this, my first entry into Rome: they were on the rooftops, packing out the Gardens of Lucullus and the terraced slopes of the Quirinal Hill, on ledges around the Tomb of Augustus, climbing columns and standing on the edges of ancient travertine fountains for a better view. Timpani rumbled and lutes blared, their cheering rose and fell like the swell of an ocean. Sweet incense smoke wafted across my path mixing with the smell of roasting meats and rich wine. A trio of Vestals and a knot of priests led songs of acclaim and threw bucketloads of bright petals down upon us from the roof of the Temple of the Nymphs, the vivid rain floating and mixing with my entourage's majestic bright standards and fluttering ribbons. My skin was scrubbed clean of yesterday's gore and my hair washed, anointed with sweet oils and swept back neatly. While the train of cavalry behind me was armoured, polished and glittering in the bright midday light, someone had dressed me in a crisp white *pallium* edged with purple and gold. At the same time, another attendant had slid a laurel wreath on my head. I had barely noticed. I found myself standing upright in the chariot cabin like a soldier as I had always been trained to, by Father… by Batius. The mere thought of the big man nearly choked me. I hid it all behind stern, imperious looks, cast across the masses. It was what they expected from their new master, or liberator, as some shouted.

'The war is over!' one boy yelled again and again, his gaunt face streaked with tears of joy. 'The tyrant has fallen!' boomed an older man bearing recent scars on his bare shoulders.

Yet all I could see was something beyond those myriad wide and joyous faces. Back through time itself. Back to the moment when the bridge had collapsed. Back to the last instant – the final trice – in which he and I had breathed the same air of life. My heart crumbled. I thought of the long-gone years when we had been brothers, and longed to be there again, to have found another way.

Near my right, Volusianus walked, basking in the adulation as if it were aimed at him. The pontoon bridge had broken under the weight of the mass retreat, he had protested. He had explained the sequence of events convincingly, but then all the best liars did. These torrid years had taught me many harsh lessons, and one was how to spot a rogue. All through the evening following the battle, while the survivors of both sides had walked the cadaver-field to gather bodies of fellow Romans for burial before they were stripped of flesh by the vultures and stinking mass of flies, Volusianus had been crowing about his plans: to erect a giant statue of me in the Forum of Trajan; to deface a great arch near the heart of Rome and rework and dedicate it to me instead. I would have to be careful around this one, and to gather the evidence I needed. When I had it, I would throw him from the top of his damned arch.

I saw something then: men clambering up a marble statue in front of the Theatre of Balbus. Splinters of stone and dust puffed up and the sound of chisels rang out. I saw the statue's forlorn, infinite gaze then. Maxentius. A few strikes of iron and the face was gone. Nearby another cheer rose up and a great groan as another Maxentian monument was brought crashing down. Someone fell under the collapsing stone and died, but their shriek was drowned out by the booming cheers and drunken songs.

We marched through the gilded remains of the Porta Triumphalis, the ancient ceremonial gate that had once been part of the city's original and much smaller curtain walls – long before Maxentius had raised his mighty defences – then we skirted the great Circus Flaminius. We went on past the foot of the Capitoline Hill, and here the frenzied celebrations ebbed for a moment. Since the beginning of Rome's history, all new emperors were expected to climb the slopes and enter the great Temple of Capitoline Jove to give dedication and make sacrifice. But not me. I remembered all too well the 'Test of Sacrifice' Diocletian and Galerius had demanded of their citizens. Jove and the Tetrarchic Gods had overseen the beginnings of this wretched tug of war. I would not bow to them. Foolish? Perhaps... but I knew a stronger force was with me. I was at last beginning to understand Mother's words from my childhood... and to see the final stretches of my journey.

What brings a man to war? What brings a man to choose his god?

That is for each of us to find out, Constantine. Our choices in this life define us. That is the journey we each must make.

I heard it then, echoing in the vaults of memory: the drilling rain from the storm on that night, long ago in my childhood. The lone legionary atop Naissus' city walls, soaked by the deluge. I thought of his clenched fist, and the thing he held, the source of his strength.

As I bypassed the ancient temple and looped round the Capitoline's southern slopes, I let my iron glower sear across the crowds, daring any or all of them to challenge me. None did. With that one action, the world began to shift. The old ways were already fading, and I would see that the worst of them were vanquished entirely.

I crossed the packed forum, the crowds parting before me with the help of my persuasive soldiers. The chariot slowed as it approached the foot of the Palatine Hill. I stared up that ancient rising cluster of terraced marble, realising that this had been Maxentius' home during the days he chose to stay in this city. Such a sad thing, to look upon the empty rooms or forgotten things of someone who has passed. The chariot halted at the base of a set of broad and beautiful marble stairs that led all the way up to the palace. I disembarked and began to ascend. I felt every one of my forty summers, my back, knees and hips aching from the recent stresses of battle. Part of me longed to believe the shouts and songs rising up around me – that the last war had been fought, that unbroken peace and harmony lay ahead. The rest of me laughed inwardly like a drunken chieftain at the idea, images of the loathsome Licinius and his swollen eastern army skittering across my mind's eye. As for Daia? I needed no such imagining – the wretch was right here, on a nearby balcony, grinning at me obsequiously. Apparently, had Maxentius called upon him, he would never have rallied against me.

I reached a porphyry terrace where two copper sconces crackled and flickered with burning cedar, and turned here to face the crowds: endless masses covering every flagstone of the forum, leaning from windowsills and balconies and on rooftops, filling the marble valleys of this ancient city. The endless clamour of adulation shook me to my bones.

Cornua players stationed on the temple roofs blared a long, rising note that brought the masses to silence. I addressed them then, telling them that the war was over, that taxes would be lowered, that games and bread would be plentiful for a time. I declared that men unjustly imprisoned during Maxentius' reign would be freed – all the while offending great Socrates by neglecting to give a definition of 'justice'. I decreed that there would be freedom of worship, to which my soldiers cried out, holding up their sun-blazoned shields. Few of the citizens understood the journey we had been through and what those suns meant, and least of all the Bishop of Rome – a seemingly humble man who echoed my words then added his own, declaring that 'Christians would be free at last, and find a home in the empire's heart.' I did not try to correct him, for he was right – in part at least; the Christians *would* be free to do as they pleased, within reason, but so too would followers of all and any gods. Over the days, months and years to come, I knew the full message had to spread: that the religious strife had to end, that men could worship freely the empire over.

That was not to say that I would be a meek leader. You know me better than any other and thus you know that is not my way. Obstacles would be pushed over and opponents would be beaten to their knees. My eyes drifted to the looming, dark eyrie of the Praetorian Fortress perched on the Esquiline Hill. That stony wart would be razed to dust and the venal, treacherous corps who lived within – or what was left of them – would be cast to the corners of the empire to serve in the harshest places. Those who resisted… I let my train of thought fade, exhausted by the rising idea of violence so soon after yesterday.

I called forth the most distinguished of the soldiers who had fought so valiantly for me yesterday. Officers, riders, recent recruits, stable hands even who had joined the fight. I placed a golden torque on each man's neck, all the while longing to see the fallen ones appear at the end of the queue as if risen again.

As I addressed each officer, I felt my voice rise and swell, filling the air over Rome, my prize. I saw my loved ones in the crowd too. Lactantius, his eyes distant, as if gazing into that strange future he had for so long been struggling to see. Beside him, Fausta and young Crispus. I had not seen or spoken to my wife since the moments before battle yesterday. Her brother, apparently, now lay dead in the depths of the Tiber. I was only too aware then of the bronze statue of the Capitoline Wolf, dark and staring from a high temple roof. Over one thousand years she had suckled the twins, Romulus and Remus, only for the former to murder his sibling. Today, the Seven Hills were once again wet with the blood of brothers.

Fausta glared at me as if I had personally run him through. Yet it was not I who slew him. In fact I did what I could to save him – not for her but for me. All throughout our great struggle I had many moments where I would have wrung his neck with my own hands, yet at the last, when we brought our steely ranks to battle, I did not injure my brother. Yet fate – or perhaps something more corporeal, I thought with another sideways look at Volusianus – had taken his life. I would honour him. Once the fervour to scratch his name and likeness from the city had cooled. I would do what was right – even some private ceremony or dedication. Perhaps at his boy's tomb.

It was then that I saw it coming. Like a nightmare walking. The crowds at the north end of the forum shuffled and swore as one tall man moved through them. No, not a man...

I stared at the horrific vision, aghast and shaking. Maxentius, taller than all others, bobbing and weaving through the crowd towards me like a shark's fin cutting through calm waters. It took me a few moments of breathless astonishment to see what it really was. My brother's grey, bloated head, affixed atop a spear. His lips were blue, his lolling tongue black and distended.

'We found him, Domine! We dragged him from the river and hacked off his head for you,' cried the well-meaning Italian legionary – a man who had yesterday lined up with Maxentius to fight me. Behind him, the four bishops who had accompanied me on my campaign like a lingering gut-wind rode on a wagon, waving their hands upwards as if to conjure a storm. The storm came, in the form of a rising, thunderous roar of joy from the crowd.

'He was an illegitimate son of Maximian,' Bishop Ossius crowed, pointing accusingly at the sorry severed head. 'Small and weak. The wretched tyrant and his cruel, ungodly ways are at an end. You will no longer starve, you need no longer tremble under his sinful yoke.'

'The tyrant has fallen!' the people of Rome screamed over and over.

'Today begins the reign of Constantine. Unconquered... and unconquerable!'

The crescendo of cries, drums, trumpets and spears beating on shields shook Rome to its ancient core. I stared into the grey, unseeing eyes of my childhood friend... my brother.

Then another group of Italian legionaries, keen to show me their fealty, dragged two strange shapes out from the portico behind me. One was the body of a woman, wet with blood... a recent corpse. Valeria... Galerius' daughter who had once been offered to me. Rags of flesh hung from the terrible sword wounds on her back. The other shape was small and twisted, black with blood, the face mutilated and the limbs broken. Unidentifiable. Yet I knew at once that I was looking upon Maxentius' last son, Aurelius.

'We caught them hiding in the palace. They were just about to open their wrist veins,' one soldier grinned. 'We sliced open their bodies instead.'

As the soldiers tossed the two corpses down the marble steps, staining them red, the great cheer of the crowds disguised my weak sob. A voice deep inside me hissed, congratulating me for being so noble as to grieve for my opponent, while at the same time mocking me – for his every misfortune had been my doing.

The bodies of Maxentius' wife and boy rolled to a halt near the feet of the Italian legionary bearing the spear and the head. Amidst the blur of people around the hoisted spear, I spotted my loved ones again: Lactantius, face sagging in woe as he stared up at Maxentius' head; Crispus, bawling in horror at sight of the butchered family; Fausta, not a tear in her eyes, staring not at the cadavers or the head of her brother, but at me, unblinking.

Her terse oath echoed in my head like a viper's hiss: *The seed of love is now dead. In its place rises a dark and ugly weed – a weed you sowed... and that one day you will reap.*

A nearby attendant offered me a cup of wine as if to toast the executions. I took a deep gulp of it as if it would help me in this awful moment. In truth it tasted like decay on my tongue. I had won it all... I had lost it all. Fausta and Crispus would never love me again. Batius was gone along with legions of military comrades. And my brother, my oldest friend... I stared up into the noon sun, and closed my eyes, thinking of our childhood laughter in the halls of Treverorum.

They said I was unconquerable like the sun. They said I was the will of the gods. They hailed me as their true emperor. They called me Constantine the Great. Some would later say I inspired my army at the Milvian Bridge with the Word of Christ. There were groups who crooned about my lifelong devotion to the Christian way, and others who denounced me as a creature of ambition. But they were not there. You were, and you witnessed how I had my men of *all* faiths gather behind the common symbol of the sun.

Still, even as I entered Rome and rode through its ancient streets, I knew not who was *my* god. It was only at that moment on the steps overlooking the forum that I began to see the truth: the lone legionary in that childhood rainstorm, the moment he opened his clenched fist... the sparkling Chi-Rho in his palm. It was at that moment that I knew my journey was complete.

Yes, I won a great victory at the Milvian Bridge. But at the sight of my old friend's terrible fate, something inside me broke. Neither bone nor flesh, but it hurt more than any such wound. Since boyhood, I had been taught that the Christ God healed broken souls, and at that moment more than ever, on the steps of the Palatine Hill of Rome, I wanted it to be true. I did not turn to Christ in order to win Rome. I turned to Christ because of *how* Rome was won.

What brings a man to choose his god? Well, now you know.

Epilogue

MAXENTIUS

The water became increasingly dark with every foot of descent. Somehow, though, while it should have been terrifying, and clearly was from the bubbled thrashing of so many armoured men around me, I found it oddly peaceful.

Indeed, the further I sank, the fewer signs of panicked strife there were, until finally, in the almost absolute darkness I was finally alone. Was I dead? If not then it was only a matter of moments. The tightly held breath that had been in there so long it burned in my chest like a thousand suns. Then the surrender. The inability to hold it any longer. No matter what the mind chooses, the body reacts. I might be dying for want of air, but the innards do not realise when there is none. The mounting urgency, the jerking, thrashing, as conscious mind tries to stop the inevitable. Then the failure. The single breath that sends dark, cold water into every tiny part of one's being.

No, it had already happened. I remembered it now. I was thrashing my last as I sank, still conscious, yet with only moments to go.

Peace. It is an odd thing.

I have found peace.

My struggles are over – with my father, with the empire, with opponents and with Rome, with family and with grief, with the absence of one son and the ruin of another, with an old friend who became my greatest enemy...

At least Rome will not suffer, and had that not been what I had promised? A strong emperor for Rome. Constantine will not persecute and proscribe. He has endured that living Tartarus alongside me, and he would never be a man to do such a thing. So Rome will go on, and he will not revenge himself on my family and close ones, for he was also once my family. We are all one family, even now. Look after him, dear sister. He may have won the day, but he will feel the price in the days to come.

No, I am at peace, and I can rest now.

I jerk once more with the shock and pain. It's a dull thing, though. Already removed from me by several degrees. Death enfolds me now. Did I put that coin beneath my tongue as I sank? I cannot remember, but then there is no need for a boatman here. I almost smile in the murky depths at the thought.

But something shines through the darkness below now.

I can see it. A hand. Pale, and blue, almost translucent, reaching up for me. I see the face, the waving hair, the pale, excitable eyes.

Romulus.

My beloved son, the piece of my heart gone for so many years. Who better to welcome me to the next world. And I am happy to go. To go with my son, whose smile is as infectious as ever.

I jerk one last time.
I stop.
I drift.
But I have a smile on my face.

Historical Note

Part 1 – The Civil War of 312 AD

The first two volumes in this trilogy have been somewhat grand in scale, with book one taking us from the deserts of the Middle East to the cold north of England and book two from the distant Danube to the grain fields of Africa. This third book, however, takes place over less than a year, and all in a relatively small theatre of war and is by its very nature more focused and military. In the last months of 311 AD, the Roman Empire was gridlocked. Interregional travel ground to a halt as the four huge armies of the Tetrarchy gathered near their borders. War was an inevitability.

It was Constantine who made the opening moves, sweeping down across the Cottian Alps in late winter. He mustered some forty thousand men for his campaign – amounting to roughly a quarter of his available forces, with the rest required to maintain order around his vast territory of Britannia, Hispania, Gaul and the ever-troublesome Rhine frontier.

Maxentius, stationed in Rome, was caught unawares. It seems that he had positioned the majority of his northern defenders at Italy's north-eastern shoulder, fearing a Licinian invasion. But the element of surprise did not hamper Maxentius for long, and when he did react, he reportedly had more than one hundred and twenty thousand legionaries at his disposal to throw at the invader.

Often, a work of military historical fiction pivots around one or two battles, but throughout spring, summer and autumn of 312 there were scores of them as Constantine's subsequent advance along the Po Valley and then southwards through Italy was achieved in rapid, devastating bursts. We have Edward Gibbon's attestations of the siege at Susa where Constantine first offered the city the chance to surrender. When the defending force declined, his legions fired the gates and scaled the walls, slaying the garrison but sparing the population.

Then there was heavy fighting at Turin: Maxentius' elite cavalry ambush was thwarted by Constantine's forfex (forceps) and mace tactic, and the surviving Maxentians then had the city gates shut on them as they tried to flee inside for shelter. There is no record of treachery within Maxentius' army or the drawing away of his best officers. The scene we created at Taurinorum is our own interpretation. The trilogy is a work of historical fiction, after all. In our planning, there were several places where the historical record leaves unanswered questions and where simple logic tells us that other forces were at work. There can be little doubt that treachery and espionage occurred among both forces, at some level.

Next came Milan, whose inhabitants threw open the gates, and here Constantine rested for a spell. Some scholars think he may have paused here from spring until summer, but we've shortened his stay somewhat to keep the narrative continuous and compelling. Brescia came next. Here, Ruricius

Pompeanius delaying tactics and stout defences were blown aside, leaving the way open to Verona... where Maxentius waited.

The city of Verona was the keystone of the north. It was surrounded on three sides by the River Adige and garrisoned heavily. Constantine found himself faced with a costly siege. Ruricius, bruised by his previous encounters with Constantine, led the defence. The assault on the city walls would have been fierce and involved one or many night battles. Gibbon tells us, in fact: *'this engagement began towards the close of the day, and was contested with great obstinacy during the whole night'*.

Ruricius, close to defeat during one sally, escaped capture and slipped through Constantine's siege lines to rendezvous and return with a huge reinforcement army which almost succeeded in pounding Constantine's force against Verona's defences. Instead, the sheer nous of Constantine and the animus of his army came to the fore: he left all but a skeleton force facing Verona to maintain the siege while ordering the rest to turn and face Ruricius' reinforcements. Outnumbered, surprised, Constantine's army should not have prevailed, but they did, responding to their emperor-general's demands to collapse their triple lines into one single, wider front that would match the enemy advance, then attacking ferociously. Ruricius fell during the fighting and the rest of his reinforcement regiments scattered in flight. Reports suggest that the captured were bound with manacles made from their own swords.

Most historical texts assume that Maxentius spent this opening period of the war in Rome, with Ruricius Pompeianus doing the actual commanding. No evidence exists to confirm this one way or the other, and given John Curran's statement (*Pagan City and Christian Capital* 2000) that Maxentius was in Verona with his army and retired to Rome when the city was lost, we decided to take that approach, which allows a first-hand view of that critical battle.

Soon after Verona's fall, Constantine found himself residing at Ravenna as master of the north, contemplating the road south to Rome. Frustrated by an unsuccessful attempt to blockade the Italian ports, he was forced to set off along the Via Flaminia without naval support.

All the while Maxentius, now certainly in Rome, was ever-involved in his own little world as he watched the enemy close on him. There is no evidence that Maxentius set up an attack at Furlo Pass (Intercisa), but the rock-cut tunnel through this painfully tight spot would have been a perfect and deadly pinch point. We can be sure that, all the way to Rome, Constantine met fierce resistance from Maxentian forces. This can be inferred from the plethora of Constantinian gravestones that line the route, including Florius Baudio, Prefect of the Second Italica Divitensis, honoured as a protector of the emperor for acts of heroism in battle. He was indeed buried by his son Vario outside Spoletium (modern Spoleto).

The religious schism we portrayed within Constantine's camp is an invention, though a plausible one, especially given the recent memories of the Persecutions and the variety of faiths and backgrounds within his campaign force – comprised of tribal legions and more ancient regiments from far and wide, worshipping a wide range of gods.

Fausta's part in fanning these flames of faith is speculative, but her relationship with Constantine must have been strained to say the least: he'd had her father killed and was on his way to tackle her brother. Of course, the darkest part of hers and Constantine's relationship would not arrive until long after the Milvian Bridge. When young Crispus reached adulthood, he and Fausta became lovers, and Constantine had both of them executed. This is what we were hinting at with her threat about the *'dark and ugly weed you sowed... and that one day you will reap'*. Anyway, putting future tragedy aside, Constantine finally came within sight of Rome, and Maxentius.

The Battle of the Milvian Bridge – despite being better recorded than the other battles of the war – still leaves many grey areas, and we have attempted to fill in the blanks. The very nature of the bridge itself that stood during the battle and how it collapsed is still debated, though the course of events we have used is both widely accepted and logical. History tells us that Maxentius was in the perfect situation in October 312. He had the greater army, some of the best city walls in the world to defend, and plenty of resources, while Constantine had fewer men, a potential troublesome siege, and the usual supply difficulties an army in the field faces.

Why then did Maxentius lose? Quite simply, as seems to have been Maxentius' eternal problem, a series of bad decisions – that provided the foundations of failure. Lactantius, in his 'On the Deaths of the Persecutors' tells us:

In the meantime a sedition arose at Rome, and Maxentius was reviled as one who had abandoned all concern for the safety of the commonwealth; and suddenly, while he exhibited the Circensian games on the anniversary of his reign, the people cried with one voice, 'Constantine cannot be overcome!' Dismayed at this, Maxentius burst from the assembly, and having called some senators together, ordered the Sibylline books to be searched. In them it was found that: 'On the same day the enemy of

433

the Romans should perish.' Led by this response to the hopes of victory, he went to the field.

We have portrayed a version of these events that fits more snugly with the political situation, with the characters, and with the plot as it stands, for Lactantius' version is heavily biased by his Christian dislike of Maxentius. So Maxentius, pushed by civic and political pressures, paints himself into a corner, where prophecy forces him to take the field against Constantine, ignoring the safety of his walls and seeking battle in a place where his superior numbers would make little difference. There can be no doubt that throughout this tale, Maxentius has been plagued by bad luck and worse advice, and this is but the culmination of that run.

There is a moment in the Battle of the Milvian Bridge when despite everything being uncertain (for at almost any time either side might well have won that engagement) suddenly the balance tips and everything goes wrong for Maxentius. We know *what* happened to alter the course of the battle, but from the ancient sources we are left to guess precisely *why* it happened.

Lactantius, in his usual zealous fashion, tells us only:

The bridge in his rear was broken down. At sight of that the battle grew hotter. The hand of the Lord prevailed, and the forces of Maxentius were routed.

Zosimus gives us:

As long as the cavalry kept their ground, Maxentius retained some hopes, but when they gave way, he fled with the rest over the bridge into the city.

We shall omit Eusebius' account, which more or less rants in a TV Evangelist style about how God drew Maxentius onto the field so that he could drown him as the pharaoh had drowned after Moses crossed the Red Sea.

But what forced Maxentius back to the bridge? We decided upon treachery from within. Maxentius' position as emperor was becoming ever less tenuous now. Had he won this battle, he could probably have consolidated and initiated a new dynasty in Rome, but there is a history of an emperor's closest men abandoning him when all looks bleak.

Despite the murkiness of how the battle for Rome was won, we know for certain that Constantine was the victor. He made his triumphal entry into the ancient capital the day after the battle. Unlike his predecessors, he neglected to make the trip to the Capitoline Hill and perform customary sacrifices at the Temple of Jove. Perhaps this was because – as we have portrayed – of Jove's Tetrarchic connotations. He then proceeded to issue decrees returning property that was lost under Maxentius, recalled political exiles, and released Maxentius' imprisoned opponents. In *Constantine, The Emperor*, David Potter debates whether this was a Christian act, or simply a show of humanity.

Despite such magnanimity, the violence was not over. Rome's Praetorian camp was razed. Valeria and Aurelius, Maxentius' family, were slain. Maxentius' body was fished from the Tiber and his head brought through the city on the end of a spear, before it was sent off to Africa to do the rounds in those provinces. The city of Rome was given a rapid facelift as well, with every memory and mention of Maxentius erased in a frenzied *damnatio memoriae*. Statues of him were defaced, inscriptions chiselled away and monuments re-dedicated instead to Constantine. The most famous of these is the 'Arch of Constantine' near the Colosseum, which depicts Constantine's military feats. In fact, this is almost certainly a repurposed 'Arch of Maxentius' (and even contains images taken from older arches as far back as Domitian). Perhaps our villain, Volusianus, played a part in this? We know that he did find favour in Constantine's court for a time, even being made Urban Prefect and securing the consulate, before being turned upon and disgraced. This somewhat hints at a treacherous act, for until October 312 he had been one of the top men controlling the army Constantine was fighting.

With Maxentius' fall, whether you consider Constantine a hero or not, the world changes. Rome shifts distinctly in both attitude and physicality. In many ways, the ancient Rome disappears with Maxentius, for after him no emperor will ever sit on the throne in the Palatine again. Constantine inaugurates his 'New Rome' of Constantinople and alters the very focus of the empire. Within his lifetime, Christianity shifts from being a troublesome and overlooked sect to being one of the main threads of religion in the empire.

A monumental episode in the history of the Roman Empire, I'm sure you'll agree. With that in mind, let's look a little closer at the lives of the two men behind this tale...

Part 2 – Simon Turney on Maxentius

While it was traditional in the Roman world to campaign from spring to autumn and go into winter quarters in between, given the tensions of the year 312 no alert and proactive ruler in Rome would be content that the north was safe throughout the winter. Painting Maxentius as a reactive rather than a proactive character made his unpreparedness more understandable. Moreover, his fear of a Licinian advance from the east also made sense, and there is some evidence to support this.

Thus, despite what history tells us, we have spent three books making Constantine and Maxentius simply men rather than 'heroes' and 'villains'. We have tried to portray both with their own value and both all-too human, and in the end it is the ousted and volatile Volusianus who turns out to be the villain after all.

Why consider Volusianus here when we are speaking of Maxentius? Simply, given the enormous impact the man has on Maxentius' life and fate (especially in this trilogy), it seems pertinent to consider him alongside the man he has helped destroy. We put together a fairly exhaustive history of each involved character during our planning of the entire trilogy, and Volusianus' run of power under first one emperor and then his opponent seems a little convenient.

Volusianus served as governor of Africa and then as Maxentius' Praetorian Prefect. Whatever else he was during the years 306 to 312, including consul, the fact was that he was integral to the emperor's reign and his war effort. As such it seems fascinating that while the majority of those who even peripherally supported Maxentius fell after his death, and the Praetorian Guard were disbanded for good, Volusianus went from strength to strength, even being called 'companion to the emperor Constantine'. This was clearly a man happy to serve whomever was beneficial at the time, and so from Volusianus the selfish, the notion of Volusianus the traitor was born. It really wasn't much of a reach.

Maxentius' journey through this trilogy has been a tragic one, filled with loss and betrayal, and it is hard not to sympathise with the man. We simply do not truly know the relationship he had with his wife, but it seems unlikely to have been warm and homely, especially when he was at war with her father. In that there is something of a parallel with Constantine and Fausta. What we can be sure of is how the loss of his son hit him, for where some emperors were able to cast aside the memory of lost children and focus on the future there is plenty of evidence of the heartbroken father. Having portrayed Maxentius thus throughout two books, it would have been oddly jarring to produce Maxentius the warrior in this third volume which is, quite clearly, a war story. So how does a relatively peaceful man fit into a war?

Well, there the recipe for Maxentius came from the *Mos Maiorum*, that innate sense of Roman ancestral custom. Romans are supposed to be practical and family-oriented. They are supposed to devote their time to agriculture and to politics. But every Roman must always be prepared to pick up the sword to defend that very Romanness. This, then, is Maxentius explained. I have throughout tried to portray Maxentius as an old-fashioned Roman in a world where that was becoming a rarity and where everything was changing. And how better could Maxentius prove his Romanitas than setting aside everything and marching to defend Rome as the Mos Maiorum demands.

He begins the tale unprepared and reactive, but despite everything, when he reacts he does so strongly. It is not for want of trying that Maxentius fails. He is simply destined to fail. Falling back to Rome he watches his world contract more and more until all there is for him is the city and his army.

It would be too easy to end this great saga on a tremendous negative moment. For fans of Constantine, the battle's victory should be glorious, and for Maxentius' adherents horrifying. But these are men we have given you, and not heroes and monsters. Constantine's victory is tempered by the horrors he sees in it, while Maxentius' cold, black fate is somehow alleviated by the knowledge that he will be reunited with his beloved Romulus.

Now my decision in book two to have Romulus die by tipping his chariot into the Tiber close to the Milvian Bridge will make sense. In the very end I have reunited father and son.

As we've noted, with Maxentius' fall the world changes. In the last throes of my tale, Maxentius can almost see that coming. He takes the regalia of the ancient world, the sceptres, orbs and other symbols of imperium, and he has them buried in the house of his old friend Anullinus. In truth, who owned the late Roman house that sits between the Palatine and the Temple of Venus and Roma remains unknown, but it has now been under excavation for many years. In 2005, archaeologists there uncovered a box hidden beneath a staircase, and within it they discovered a unique and wonderful thing: the sceptres of a Roman emperor. It is widely accepted that they are those of Maxentius, hidden before, or just in the aftermath of, the Battle of the Milvian Bridge. They are now on display in the Palazzo Massimo in Rome, and are a must-visit for anyone interested in the era. They are totally unique, the only Roman sceptres ever found.

Thus has Maxentius in his last moments bequeathed to us his legacy. And a visit to Rome should also include a journey along the Via Appia, where you can even now see the great circus Maxentius built for his villa, and the tomb of his son Romulus beside it, now once more open to visitors after years of restoration. Work on the villa itself is ongoing.

While in Rome itself, a visitor might also want to visit the other few reminders the doomed pagan emperor left us. On the Palatine, above the Severan Arcades, stands the bath suite Maxentius had built there. In the forum stands the basilica that still carries his name. The Aurelian Walls around the city still sport the massive additions Maxentius instituted from his accession to 312 – those walls of wooden blocks that once tied him and Constantine together as friends. And finally, on the Capitoline Hill, in the courtyard of the museum, stand the remaining fragments of the famous 'colossus' of Constantine: a statue that would have stood immensely tall, towering over the populace. There is good reason to believe that this was once a likeness of Maxentius, reworked to resemble his enemy after his death.

Maxentius reigned but briefly, and yet has left much to mark his time in the world. Now he can rest in the afterlife with his beloved son, and we thank you for taking the time to read his story.

Simon Turney, October 2019

Part 3 – Gordon Doherty on Constantine

There is little doubt that Constantine was a first-rate general: strong-willed and domineering, yet also approachable, enjoying a close rapport with his soldiers. However, opinions of Constantine the man tend to be polarised: either he is the first great Christian emperor, devout and carried to victory by God, or he is a cynical, manipulative politician who used Christianity to seize victory and ultimate power. Which is right? Frankly, during the process of examining the available evidence, I have found that neither view really stacks up. As with Maxentius (tyrant or hero?), the answer appears to lie in the nuanced territory in between. Here's how I see it:

Religious conversion is never a momentary phenomenon; it is, as I have portrayed through the lips of Constantine's mother Helena, 'a journey'. Constantine's journey began well before the Milvian Bridge and ended long after. So let us first look at his early life, beginning with his relationship with his parents – a lens that often sheds a telling light on the psyche of any child.

Constantine's childhood was rocked when his father walked out on the family, leaving him plagued with temper and feelings of shame and illegitimacy. This seems to have redoubled his utter devotion to his mother. Given the depths of love for Helena, and his apparent respect for her piety, could he have been capable of exploiting her faith in exchange for power? Perhaps. Yet he and Helena remained the doting mother and son for the rest of their time together on earth, so if Constantine's Christian affinity was a mask, then it was worn impeccably.

His father, Constantius, was devoted to Mars, the Roman God of War. Yet he was also tolerant of Christianity. He never allowed the Persecutions to take hold in the West during his reign there. When Constantine succeeded his father (some years after the family break-up), he too forbade persecution of Christians throughout his lands, even when Tetrarchic colleagues pursued adherents of the faith most fiercely. It seems that, despite the damaged paternal relationship, Constantine respected his father's principles.

Parents aside, some of the most influential figures in our lives are our teachers. Constantine was tutored by Lactantius (about as devout a Christian as you'll get), so it seems safe to assume that he would have imparted upon Constantine a full understanding of the faith. This of course does not prove that Constantine 'believed' in Christ, but it does suggest that when he eventually patronised Christianity, it was a considered and educated decision.

But the most guiding piece of evidence regarding Constantine's character – and indeed his ethics – comes from one of his familial choices. Long before the events of 312 AD, he was offered the hand of Valeria, the daughter of Galerius (at that time Tetrarchic Caesar of the East) and eventual wife of Maxentius. Accepting her as his bride would have placed him comfortably by Galerius' side and surely in the line of succession. Given Constantine's illegitimacy complex, the 'political-monster' theorists would probably imagine that he would jump at such a chance of power. However, Constantine refused the offer and instead chose to wed Minervina, a relatively low-born Syrian Christian. By doing so, he not only rejected the chance of a huge step-up in station, but also risked the wrath of Galerius and Diocletian – the Great Christian Persecutors. This surely proves that while he may well have been ambitious, he clearly had principles too.

Constantine is sometimes criticised for embracing Christianity and ruining the harmony of the pagan empire, but it must be said that there was little 'harmony' in the officially pagan empire of the fourth century AD. Constantine would have witnessed first-hand the harrowing effects of the Edict of Persecution, with the Christian faith burgeoning among the people, and emperors trying to beat it back with fire and steel. Thus, it seems only rational that, following his winning of Rome, he adopted a stance of religious tolerance (it is a common misconception that Constantine made Christianity the official religion of the Roman Empire. In fact, that only happened some seventy years after our tale, when Theodosius I issued such a decree – the ruling stoking riots as ancient pagan shrines and universities were closed and demolished).

Some argue that Constantine chose not to be baptised until he lay on his death bed, some twenty-five years after his victory at the Milvian Bridge: this, surely, proves he only wore a mask of Christianity until beset by the fear of death? Not quite. Modern baptism is performed on the young, but in the early to mid-fourth century, it was the opposite. For a normal catechumen – one who wished to become a member of the Christian Church – the sacrament of baptism was the culmination of a course of instruction lasting up to three years and was often not carried out until nearer the end of a person's life.

Regarding Constantine's 'vision' prior to the Battle of the Milvian Bridge: we cannot be certain what happened here. While I went with the popular cross or Chi-Rho in the sky theory commonly depicted by later chroniclers, there is actually no documented evidence to confirm this. In fact, Lactantius – in his 'On the Deaths of the Persecutors' – attests that the divine direction in fact came to Constantine in his sleep:

Constantine was directed in a dream to cause the heavenly sign to be delineated on the shields of his soldiers, and so to proceed to battle.

The notion of a pre-battle dream was quite normal in late antiquity. Stirring dreams were commonly described by generals and emperors in an effort to inspire their troops and convince them they were destined to be victorious.

Whatever the source of the message was – dream, lights or outright fabrication – it seems to have forged Constantine's forces together on the eve of battle. They painted their shields – previously of many colours and designs – in one common pattern. But what was that 'heavenly sign'? It certainly wasn't a cross. Lactantius later insists that each man daubed a Christian Chi-Rho on their shield. But that could mean nothing more than Christos or Chrestos (good luck). More puzzling, carvings on Rome's Constantinian arch depict soldiers bearing shields decorated with nothing but traditional emblems. None show the Chi-Rho – though this may be due to the earlier origins of the repurposed monument.

There is another school of thought: that he had his men paint a solar image on his shields – for in the age of our story, the sun was a common symbol underpinning Christ, Mithras, Mars, Apollo, Sol Invictus and more. It is easy to see how such a symbol could be adapted and tweaked to suit the imagery of each deity as needs be, pleasing all of his multi-faith regiments. This theory seemed most rational to me: the identification of a 'Supreme God' or Summus Deus behind which all of his soldiers could rally. Indeed, Constantine later espoused a carefully worded pre-battle prayer dedicated to an intriguingly ambiguous 'one true god'.

Perhaps Constantine is destined to remain something of an enigma, unquantifiable in any objective sense. Both fragile and invincible; kind and brutal; patient and rash; loving but vengeful; pious and pragmatic. I can only hope that his portrayal in this tale has been illuminating and enjoyable, that it has allowed you to fathom his hopes, fears and motivations for yourself, and has helped you to understand him and his world that little bit better. Thank you for travelling with me on this most famous of journeys!

Gordon Doherty, October 2019

CONSTANTINE

MAXENTIUS

Glossary of Latin Terms

Ab admissionibus – Official who controlled access to an emperor.

Adventus – Ceremony in which an emperor was formally welcomed into a city after a military campaign.

Ala – A cavalry wing.

Apenninus – The Apennine mountain range, the backbone of Italy.

Apodyterium – Changing room in a Roman bathhouse.

Aquilifer – Senior standard bearer of a Roman legion and carrier of the legionary eagle.

Aula Regia – Reception hall of the imperial palace.

Barritus – A Roman battle cry which Tacitus tells us it began as a "harsh, intermittent roar." By holding their shields to their mouth, the reverberating sound of the legionaries' cries would swell into a deafening crescendo, like waves smashing into the rocky shore.

Buccina – Curved horn used by the military for signalling and issuing of commands.

Caldarium – The room in a Roman bath complex containing a hot plunge pool.

Cardo Maximus – The main north-south street in a Roman city.

Castrum – A defensive Roman military structure. Could be

446

used to describe a permanent fort, a marching camp, a palisade on a natural choke point of terrain or a fortified bridgehead.

Cataphracti – A class of cavalry with a well-armoured rider.

Chi-Rho – The Chi-Rho is one of the earliest forms of Christogram, and was used by the early Christian Roman Empire. It is formed by superimposing the first two letters in the Greek spelling of the word Christ, chi = ch and rho = r, in such a way to produce the following monogram:

Clavica – Decorative vertical stripes that ran over the shoulder on the front and back of a Late Roman tunic.

Clibanarii – A class of cavalry where horse and rider are heavily and almost completely armoured with iron. Derived from the term clibanus, meaning oven.

Collis Hortorum – The 'Hill of Gardens' in the northeast of Rome.

Comitatus – A 'companion' army or retinue, quartered near and moving with the emperor. A separate entity to the border garrison legions. This wing of the army was composed of the crack troops and grew steadily larger over the course of the fourth century AD (up to thirty thousand men strong).

Comites Alani – Cavalry regiment drawn from the tribe of the Alani, serving the emperor.

Consilium – The emperor's close council of advisors.

Cornua – Roman horn.

Cubicularius – An imperial chamberlain.

Cursus Publicus – The empire's state-run system of couriers and transportation.

Decurion – Leader of a cavalry unit.

Dominus/Domine – 'Master'.

Domus – A house.

Draco – A 'dragon' style standard adopted by some later Roman units. Famed for the eerie moan it makes when hoisted to catch the wind.

Draconarius – Cavalry standard bearer.

Duplex Acies – A double-line infantry formation.

Dux Militum – The commander of the military.

Equisio – Individual assigned to the care, supply and grooming of horses.

Equites Promoti – elite cavalry units detached from the legions.

Equites Singulares – The emperor's horse guard.

Explorator (pl. Exploratores) – Swift, skilled scout cavalry, tasked with ranging far ahead of marching armies and into enemy territory to confirm the marching route was clear.

Familia - a Roman household, comprising blood relatives and those connected closely to the family.

Fanum – A Celtic/Gallo-Roman rural religious sanctuary.

Fetial – A priest of Jupiter whose worldly duties included the concluding of treaties and of declarations of war.

Forfex – A battle formation in the shape of a forceps, intended to draw, then envelop and trap the enemy.

Frumentarii – 'Grain men'. Imperial agents who move from unit to unit on clandestine business.

Funditores – Roman slingers.

Horreum (pl. Horrea) - The Roman granary and storehouse for other consumables such as wine and olive oil.

Imperator – Emperor.

Laconicum – The dry sweating chamber of a Roman bath house.

Liburnian – Small galley used for patrols or light commerce.

Lictor – Civil servant who accompanied Roman officials in public.

Lilia – Spike pits.

Lupus – a defensive crushing device set inside city or fort gatehouses

Mare Adriaticum – the Adriatic Sea

Mare Internum – Roman name for the Mediterranean Sea.

Medicus – Legionary medic.

Mithras – A pagan deity particularly loved by the legions – probably something to do with the belief that Mithras was born with a sword in his hand. The cult of Mithras is thought to have evolved from the Persian Mithra, the God of Light and Wisdom. Also, although Mithras is often described as 'Deus Sol Invictus Mithras', he is not to be confused with the Sol Invictus (the god of the official imperial cult established by emperor Aurelian) whose birthday was celebrated on 25th December.

Optio – Second-in-command of a Roman century. Hand-chosen by the centurion.

Ordo – A provincial Roman town council.

Pallium – A rich man's robe in the times of the later empire. Equivalent to the older toga.

Pilentum – A luxurious carriage used often to convey noblewomen.

Pomerium – The outermost road in a Roman city, running just inside its walls. The word originated from the sacred boundary of the city of Rome.

Praepositus – A commander of a military detachment (infantry and/or cavalry).

Primicerius (pl. Primicerii) – Junior administrative officer in the Roman army.

Primus Pilus – The chief centurion of a legion. So called, as his own century would line up in the first file (primus) of the first cohort (pilus – a term harking back to the manipular legions).

Principia – Situated in the centre of a Roman fort or marching camp, the principia served as the headquarters. In a standing fort, the principia would be laid out as a square, with three wings enclosing a parade area. The legionary standards, wage chest and religious shrines were housed inside the wings along with various administrative offices.

Protector (pl. protectores) – An elite bodyguard dedicated to the emperor's personal protection.

Pteruges – leather strops attached to a garment worn under armour, protecting the upper arms and thighs.

Pulvinar – Latin term for the imperial box at an entertainment venue. Cf. kathisma.

Quadriga – Chariot drawn by a team of four horses.

Romanitas – Romanism, the Roman way or manner.

Sagittarius (pl. Sagittarii) - Roman foot archer. Typically equipped with a bronze helm and nose-guard, mail vest, composite bow and quiver.

Sestertius – Roman coin made of silver and, later, brass.

Shahanshah – The Persian ruler (literally 'King of Kings'.)

Simplex Acies – A single-line infantry formation.

Spatha – Roman sword.

Spiculum – Roman javelin.

Stigma – Cultural identifying mark, sometimes in the form of a tattoo.

Subligaculum – Roman undergarment similar to a loincloth.

Tablinum – Room set aside in a Roman residence as the master's office, where all work is carried out.

Testudo – Formation where infantry place shields around all sides and overhead of their unit, thus providing protection from missiles from all directions.

Tholus – A circular building with a conical or vaulted roof, peristyle and surrounding colonnade.

Tribunus – By this period in history, the term 'prefect' was used to denote a legionary commander, but 'Tribunus' was still the title given to the commanders of an auxilium regiment (e.g. Hisarnis, Tribunus of the Bructeri).

Triclinium – The dining room of a Roman household.

Turma – Roman cavalry unit of 30 men, the subunit of an ala of 120 riders.

Valetudinarium – Medical building in a Roman camp or fort.

About the authors

SIMON TURNEY is from Yorkshire
and, having spent much of his childhood visiting historic
sites, he fell in love with the Roman heritage of the
region. His fascination with the ancient world snowballed
from there with great interest in Rome, Egypt, Greece and
Byzantium. His works include
the Marius' Mules and Praetorian series, as
well as the Tales of the Empire series and
The Damned Emperor series.

www.simonturney.com   @SJATurney

GORDON DOHERTY is a Scottish author,
addicted to reading and writing historical fiction. Inspired
by visits to the misty Roman ruins of Britain and the
sun-baked antiquities of Turkey and Greece, Gordon
has written tales of the later Roman Empire, Byzantium,
Classical Greece and the Bronze Age.
His works include the Legionary, Strategos
and Empires of Bronze series, and the
Assassin's Creed tie-in novel *Odyssey*.

www.gordondoherty.co.uk   @GordonDoherty

Y047929